HEART'S INSANITY

Book 1, Angel Fire Rock Romance series

ELLIE MASTERS

JEM Publishing

Image/art disclaimer: Licensed material is being used for illustrative purposes only. Any person depicted in the licensed material is a model. Interior chapter heading base images provided by Elias Raven.

Editor: Jovana Shirley, Unforeseen Editing, www.unforeseenediting.com

Cover Artist: Ellie Masters

Interior Design/Formatting: Ellie Masters

Published in the United States of America

JEM Publishing

This is a work of fiction. While reference might be made to actual historical events or existing locations, the names, characters, businesses, places, and incidents are either the product of the author's imagination or are used fictitiously, and any resemblance to actual persons, living or dead, business establishments, events, or locales is entirely coincidental.

ISBN: 978-0-9978450-0-6

 Created with Vellum

Dedication

This book is dedicated to my one and only—my amazing and wonderful husband.

Thank you, my dearest love, my heart and soul, for putting up with me, for believing in me, and for loving me.

You pushed me when I needed to be pushed. You supported me when I felt discouraged. You believed in me when I didn't believe in myself.

If it weren't for you, this book never would have come to life.

Books by Ellie Masters

The LIGHTER SIDE

Ellie Masters is the lighter side of the Jet & Ellie Masters writing duo! You will find Contemporary Romance, Military Romance, Romantic Suspense, Billionaire Romance, and Rock Star Romance in Ellie's Works.

YOU CAN FIND ELLIE'S BOOKS HERE:

ELLIEMASTERS.COM/BOOKS

Military Romance

Guardian Hostage Rescue Specialists

Rescuing Melissa

(Get a FREE copy of Rescuing Melissa

when you join Ellie's Newsletter)

Alpha Team

Rescuing Zoe

Rescuing Moira

Rescuing Eve

Rescuing Lily

Rescuing Jinx

Rescuing Maria

Bravo Team

Rescuing Angie

Military Romance

Guardian Personal Protection Specialists

Sybil's Protector

The One I Want Series
(Small Town, Military Heroes)
By Jet & Ellie Masters

EACH BOOK IN THIS SERIES CAN BE READ AS A STANDALONE AND IS ABOUT A DIFFERENT COUPLE WITH AN HEA.

Saving Ariel

Saving Brie

Saving Cate

Saving Dani

Saving Jen

Saving Abby

Rockstar Romance

The Angel Fire Rock Romance Series

EACH BOOK IN THIS SERIES CAN BE READ AS A STANDALONE AND IS ABOUT A DIFFERENT COUPLE WITH AN HEA. IT IS RECOMMENDED THEY ARE READ IN ORDER.

Ashes to New (prequel)

Heart's Insanity (book 1)

Heart's Desire (book 2)

Heart's Collide (book 3)

Hearts Divided (book 4)

Hearts Entwined (book5)

Forest's FALL (book 6)

Hearts The Last Beat (book7)

Contemporary Romance

Firestorm

(KRISTY BROMBERG'S EVERYDAY HEROES WORLD)

Billionaire Romance

Billionaire Boys Club

Hawke

Richard

Brody

Contemporary Romance

Cocky Captain

(VI KEELAND & PENELOPE WARD'S COCKY HERO WORLD)

Romantic Suspense

EACH BOOK IS A STANDALONE NOVEL.

The Starling

~AND~

Science Fiction

Ellie Masters writing as L.A. Warren

Vendel Rising: a Science Fiction Serialized Novel

Contents

Grab the First Book in The Guardian Hostage
Rescue Specialists Series for Free   1

Chapter 1   3

Chapter 2   7

Chapter 3   15

Chapter 4   25

Chapter 5   39

Chapter 6   49

Chapter 7   55

Chapter 8   75

Chapter 9   85

Chapter 10   97

Chapter 11   107

Chapter 12   117

Chapter 13   137

Chapter 14   151

Chapter 15   167

Chapter 16   183

Chapter 17   195

Chapter 18   205

Chapter 19   223

Chapter 20   235

Chapter 21   255

Chapter 22   265

Chapter 23   275

Chapter 24   285

Chapter 25   301

Chapter 26   311

Chapter 27   321

28. Sample Chapter: HEART'S DESIRE   337

29. Get a FREE Copy of Ashes to New, Prequel to the
Angel Fire Series   349

First Chapters: ASHES TO NEW   351

Please consider leaving a review   357

ELLZ BELLZ   359

Also by Ellie Masters   361
Books by Jet Masters   365

About the Author   367
Connect with Ellie Masters   369
Final Thoughts   371
The End   375

Grab the First Book in The Guardian Hostage Rescue Specialists Series for Free

https://elliemasters.com/RescuingMelissa

Chapter One

THE COOL DECEMBER WIND WHIPPED THROUGH THE AIR, piercing the thin cotton of Skye Summers's scrubs. Spencer McAdams's Queen Anne townhouse stood before her as she twisted the diamond ring he had placed on her finger last night.

Funny, how she found herself here. Her complicated life could have headed in any number of directions, but the broken foster girl of her past was finally seeing all her dreams come true. Skye was *almost* normal.

With her stomach fluttering, she searched for her key. The day Spencer had given it to her, she'd nearly toppled over, but she rarely came here without him. Within a year, it would be *their* key.

Today, she planned on surprising him.

His favorite music played through the surround sound speakers, drowning out her grand entrance. A smile ghosted her lips. She would greet him with a kiss and finish with something more.

His shoes littered the marble entryway, and she placed her backpack beside the mess. Spencer had perfected the disorganized clutter of the quintessential bachelor. The tie he had worn last night dangled over the back of a chair, and his dress shirt was draped over the couch. It lay precisely where she'd tossed it last night after ripping it off his body. His tailored pants were still sprawled across the hall, exactly where he'd kicked them off in his rush to get her to bed. The man was such a gorgeous mess.

She snuck down the hall and twisted her ankle as she stumbled over something. *A red stiletto?* Her stride faltered, and her gaze cut to a silk blouse lying in a crumpled heap. She grabbed the wall for support and stepped over a lacy bra. Another scrap of fabric was bunched on the floor not two feet away. It was a flimsy thong she would never wear.

She fisted her hand against her belly, her palm slick with sweat. With her heart banging against the cage of her chest, beating so feverishly she thought it would explode, she tiptoed. Discordant notes blared through the house, covering the sound of her footsteps. With each step forward, she feared what she would find, but she had to see for herself.

The cries of a woman spilled out of Spencer's master suite. She peeked inside. Spencer had his back to the door, his naked ass gyrating in a primal rhythm as he plunged into the woman sprawled on the bed. Skye's nails bit into the flesh of her palms as she curled her fingers into impotent fists.

He panted while the woman's staccato cries rose in counterpoint to his guttural moans. Long, slender legs were wrapped around Spencer's waist, and the woman writhed in orgasmic ecstasy.

Skye wanted to claw the bitch's eyes out. She wanted to scream, kick Spencer in the ass, stomp on his nuts, or cut off his dick. But she did nothing, not until Spencer looked over his shoulder. Only then did she gasp, mortified that she'd been caught spying.

He didn't stop fucking, but he did slow his pace. "What are you doing here?" His voice was filled with accusation, as if she had no right to be in his home.

She should have picked up one of those stilettos. Then she could have thrown one at his head. Instead she backed away.

"Don't you dare leave!" Spencer called out.

He had his dick buried in another woman, the cheating ass, and he wanted her to stay?

The trail of discarded clothing mocked her as she staggered through a veil of blurred tears toward the front door. She grabbed her backpack and slung it over her shoulder, desperate to escape. Her hands shook so hard that she could barely open the front door, but she made it outside where she stopped cold. Her emotions billowed in a turbulent flow. A normal person would have been filled with rage, but humiliation and resignation were much more familiar emotions. She embraced those.

As she stood on Spencer's front stoop, she pulled the diamond ring off her finger. She had half a mind to leave it inside, but she wasn't setting foot back in that house. *Maybe she should toss it in the bushes?*

The ring wasn't hers. Not anymore.

For now, she placed it in the deepest pocket of her scrub pants. She'd give it back later.

Wasn't it enough that Spencer had shredded her heart? Now, the biting cold was also stealing her warmth. Icy tendrils pierced her flesh and delved deep to brush against her heart. She adjusted her backpack and snuggled deep into her heavy winter coat. The frigid wind clawed at her and then moved on in search of other victims. She was too numb to care, but she was determined to make it through the day, albeit mechanically and in an emotional fog.

To survive her upcoming twelve-hour shift in the emergency department, Skye made a list of things she needed to do. It was a coping mechanism she'd mastered years ago.

Hot cocoa.

Ride Metro.

Work.

Finish her shift.

Home.

Collapse with a movie and a gallon of coffee ice cream.

Pack for trip.

Shit. Spencer was supposed to join her on her mini vacation. Now, she'd have to go alone, and she hated traveling by herself. Like the ring, she'd deal with that later, too.

First, she had to make it to the coffee shop.

She slipped her hand into her pocket and clutched two carats of broken dreams. A symbol of love and trust, the ring was now nothing more than a shattered promise.

Recessed in the corner of her mind, a lingering doubt remained. Maybe Spencer had been right. Was it possible she was too damaged for love?

Enough!

Up ahead, the coffee house beckoned. Skye quickened her steps. Her breath coalesced in the frigid air and drifted away in the swirl of a passing breeze, disintegrating, like her relationship and the future it had promised.

The small coffee shop had been her refuge during a grueling residency and still was today. It was a place where she had gathered with a small group of fellow residents who were coffee lovers. Leading up to their board exams, they'd crammed everything they needed to know about medicine while indulging in their favorite addiction—caffeine. With her residency finished, she still stopped in every day to get her favorite piping hot beverage.

Of course, she'd met Spencer there, too.

Maybe she needed new dreams and a new future?

Chapter Two

As Skye approached the coffee shop, two black Hummers pulled up alongside the curb. The drivers jumped out and rushed around their respective vehicles to open the passenger doors. Five men spilled out, two from the lead vehicle and three from the rear, laughing and joking, shoving one another toward the entrance. Despite the frigid temperature, they wore nothing but T-shirts and beat-up blue jeans.

Two ladies with snow-white hair approached the shop as well. Unlike the men, the women were hunched in their heavy jackets with scarves wrapped tightly around their necks as they shivered against the cold. The men scampered around the women, yanked on the door, and filed inside. The last man, tall and slender, kept the door from slamming shut while the women ducked under his arm.

Skye hurried to catch the door and snagged her toe on the uneven sidewalk. The man steadied her, gripping her arm. He stared down, his eyes a piercing forest green.

"Well, hello, beautiful." A cocksure smile brought a mischievous twinkle to those eyes.

Skye shrugged herself free. Spencer's betrayal was too fresh, and her emotions were too raw for her to engage in any sort of flirtation.

With an unfriendly glare, she said, "Thank you."

Skye gripped her backpack and moved quickly over the threshold to the back of the line. The invigorating aroma of brewed coffee washed over her, and she breathed deep. The welcoming warmth dispelled her chill, and she shrugged off her backpack, unzipped her heavy coat, and draped it over her arm.

The men from the Hummers had taken over her favorite corner by the fire, filling the plush leather couches with their large frames as well as the one chair she generally claimed as her own. They sprawled out, like they owned the entire store, taking up more room than they needed, despite the morning rush.

The place was packed with a standing-room-only crowd. Couples and singles buried their noses in their cell phones and tablets. A few people worked on laptops. And, sprinkled here and there, the rare newspaper or book found itself clutched in the hands of a reader engrossed in the magic of the printed word.

Skye basked in the normalcy of the pleasant atmosphere and let her shoulders drop as she exhaled in a desperate effort to keep herself together.

She glanced at the clock hanging behind the barista station. If she got her cocoa and left immediately, she could take the early train. Her boss would appreciate her relieving him a few minutes early.

Boisterous laughter exploded from the corner by the fire. By their casual postures and open expressions the men were more than simply good friends. They teased one another in a nonstop barrage of verbal put-downs and animated conversation, acting like frat boys but appearing a few years older than the standard college crowd. The decibel level of that part of the room rose at least ten points.

They sported a variety of hairstyles from a close-cut buzz to rocker-style long hair. One with curly dark hair caught her staring and winked. She couldn't see the one who had held the door.

The elderly women moved to the front of the line, and Skye shuffled behind them.

One of the women spoke, and her jowls wobbled with her shaky enunciation. "Frieda, can you see the menu? I don't want any of that fancy stuff."

Her friend obliged and read the drink choices out loud.

Skye waited for the women to navigate the menu, and her thoughts turned to Spencer's clenching ass while he pumped into the unknown woman sprawled on his bed, the same bed where he'd made love to Skye the night before. An upwelling of indignation surged forth, seeking an outlet, but she found none.

The barista called out a name, something Skye didn't catch, and placed a cup on the counter. The man who'd held the door claimed the steaming beverage and returned to his friends as the two older women completed their order. They settled the bill after arguing over whose turn it was to pay.

Skye took a step forward as they moved off, still twittering about the bill.

The barista called out, "Bent, Bash, Spike, and Noodles," and placed four cups on the counter.

Odd names. Maybe they were in a fraternity?

Skye ordered and paid for her cocoa with the remaining balance left on a gift card Spencer had given her six months ago on her birthday. She wasn't sad to see the card go. She was eager to rid herself of all things Spencer. She stepped back to wait.

While the men lounged, the elderly women wobbled, bracing themselves against a counter behind one of the couches. The men propped their legs on the coffee tables, laughing and joking. Not one of them offered their seats.

Maybe it was the rock sitting in her pocket or the men's rude behavior, but an acute hatred of all things male burst forth, finally finding that outlet. Skye rolled her shoulders and stiffened her spine. She marched to the corner, dropped her backpack on the floor, and slapped the closest asshole on the back of his head.

"Get up," she said with more fury than intended. "Since when was it okay to run over old ladies and make them stand while you sit? Give up your damn seat!"

"What the fuck?" The tall one who'd held the door for her glanced up.

Skye jutted her chin forward and met the intensity of his gaze. Emerald green sparked and then shifted to follow her finger pointing toward the women. Frieda struggled to sip her coffee, fine tremors shaking her hand. Liquid sloshed over the rim, covering her hand and spilling onto the counter.

Skye poked his shoulder, a growl growing in her throat. "Get your sorry ass off the couch, and let them sit."

The buff one with curly hair, who'd winked at her, gave an indignant snort. "Pretty girl, do you have any idea who you're talking to?"

She put fists to her hips and lifted her chin. "Five men without a brain between them. Does it matter?" His mouth opened, but before he could speak, she held up a hand. "Seems to me you think being somebody is more important than good manners."

She turned her attention back to the one who'd held the door. The tattoo on his neck, a web with a dragon, distracted her. She shook her head and refocused her anger. "Do you even realize your friends practically knocked down those poor ladies in their rush to get inside?"

A beefy man with piercings in his brows, nose, and lips shifted on the couch. "It's fucking cold outside."

"And you think those ladies were warm and toasty?" She lifted her jacket. "Newfangled invention, wiseass. It's called a jacket. You'll be surprised at the amazing warming properties it has."

The green-eyed hunk snorted a laugh.

She pointed at each of the men in turn. "Did your mothers fail to teach you common courtesy? How would you feel if someone made your grandmother stand? Were you assholes raised by wolves?"

Green eyes huffed another laugh. He unfolded a lean body full of muscle to tower over her diminutive frame. He had the trim body of a swimmer with broad shoulders tapering to a narrow waist. He stood entirely too close for her comfort, but she held her ground, which forced her to look up into his handsome and somehow familiar face. Her pulse jumped, but she refused to be intimidated by his size.

"Wolves? Not exactly. My mother did, however, teach me that a true lady never swore." He laughed, filling the air with a soft, velvety thrum.

Damn, what a voice. Male, deep. Nice. Really nice and layered with tonal qualities she'd never experienced before.

Her broken heart stirred in the strangest way, probably latching on to the wrong thing.

Her cheeks burned with the insult, and she readied herself to give him another piece of her mind. But, first, she had to meet the power of his impossibly green eyes. They barely looked real, but she'd peeled enough cosmetic contacts out of other people's eyes to know a natural green when she saw it.

And, now, she was staring. She lowered her gaze to the tattoo covering the entirety of his neck—a spiderweb with a dragon perched in the center, clutching a blackbird in its claw.

She endured the full force of his intoxicating scent—woodsy spice mingled with the aroma of coffee—and paused to admire him. The man was a potent combination of sight, smell, and sound.

A smirk tilted the corner of his lips, and a twinkle danced in his eyes. The cocky bastard knew the effect he was having on her. His stance broadened, and he puffed out his chest. She took a step back and regrouped, clearing her throat, before pointing again to the women.

He lifted his chin at his friend with all the piercings. "Get up, Spike."

"Damn it, Ash." Spike sipped from his cup. "Just when I was getting cozy, too." But the big man rose and stepped over to the opposite couch. He took a seat on the armrest.

Spike's hard gaze latched on to Skye. She shifted her attention back to Ash and his stunning eyes.

Ash called out to Frieda and her friend, gesturing to the vacated seats, "Ladies, it has come to my attention that we have been exceedingly rude. Please, have a seat." His mouth twitched into a smile as he glanced at Skye. Taking the women's cups, he stepped out of the way while they settled themselves.

The barista called out Skye's name and set her hot cocoa on the counter. What a perfect opportunity to make an exit. Skye collected her drink and left the coffee shop in a daze. Although trained in defense, she hated altercations, yet she'd faced down five strangers because Spencer had stirred her anger.

An icy gust beat at her as she headed to the Metro. A few blocks later, stairs led down into the subway and welcomed the morning commuters. She clutched her drink as she hurried down the steps to merge into the crowd.

Something felt off, but she couldn't put her finger on it. She patted her scrubs and felt the diamond safe in her pocket. Her lanyard with her badge swung around her neck. She tucked it back inside her heavy coat, but she sensed she had forgotten something. It was probably just her nerves.

Someone behind her called out, "Miss!"

Skye pivoted, surprised to see Ash jogging in her direction. His white T-shirt was pulled taut across the muscles of his chest.

What was he doing? Whatever it was, she wasn't in the mood to engage in a conversation with the arrogant bastard.

Turning back, she ignored him and followed the flow of the crowd.

"Hey!" His voice resonated down the escalator.

She glanced over her shoulder and saw he'd quickened his stride.

"What the fuck?" Annoyance salted the deep timbre of his voice, so like an arrogant prick.

Very much like Spencer.

"Come back here," he called out.

His feet pounded atop the concrete floor, and Skye did what she always did when a man confronted her.

She ran.

Chapter Three

SKYE PUSHED PAST THE MORNING METRO COMMUTERS AND FUMBLED for the lanyard at her neck, not interested in dealing with Ash.

Along with the bundled travelers, the frigid wind spilled down the long escalators heading into the DC Metro. A true feat of engineering, the warren of Metro lines and the cavernous design of the platforms kept the busy subway system of the nation's capital one of the cleanest among large metropolitan cities.

Why was he chasing her? The last thing she needed was some cocksure asshole trying to pick her up.

"Goddamn it. Stop!" Ash yelled.

She ignored him and fished out her Metro pass, but then his hand fell on her shoulder, yanking her to a stop.

With a yelp, she reached for his wrist—or tried to. She'd forgotten about her drink. The top popped off, and hot cocoa spewed directly toward his chest. The steaming liquid splattered across his taut white cotton shirt. Many of those passing by gawked, but as a whole, the crowd parted around them.

"Oh my God!" The empty paper cup tumbled to the floor, more hot cocoa flying, and Skye shook out her hand.

Droplets splattered his jeans and the tops of his Converse sneakers. The tail end of the dark chocolaty goodness coated his hand as well as his shirt.

"Fuck." He pulled the fabric away from his chest.

Only then did she notice her backpack slung over his shoulder. Her attention shifted from the brown stain on his shirt to the hot cocoa dripping off his hand and back to her bag.

"I'm so sorry." She prayed the liquid had cooled enough not to scald him.

His nose scrunched. "What the fuck is this?" He leveled the full intensity of his gaze on her. Then, he sniffed his shirt. "That's not coffee."

The wet T-shirt outlined a six-pack beneath the fabric, and she couldn't help but stare.

"It's cocoa."

"Isn't that a kiddie drink?"

"I like it," she said with a huff.

"Whatever." He thrust her bag forward. "You left this."

She tried to take her bag, but his grip stayed firm.

Ash closed the distance between them. "Why did you run?"

The combination of cocoa and his scent did strange things to her insides. There was no rational answer for why she'd run, so she shook her head and tugged on her bag, but he didn't let go. Instead, the tip of his finger lifted her chin, and forced her to meet the most amazing eyes.

Emerald irises flecked with gold pulsed with a magnetism that drew her in. Dark hair curled over his forehead and swept to the side. His hair framed a strong jaw and square chin peppered with a day's growth of beard. Her mouth dropped as her attention dipped downward to the expanse of hot cocoa drenching his shirt.

"Give me my bag."

"What? No, *thank-you*?" Ash's eyes sparked with mischief. "And, here I thought I was the one who was raised by wolves and lacked all manners. You know, I didn't have to brave the cold to chase you down. I could have left your bag there for you to find later, but I figured you might need it." His brow arched. "Call it my good deed for the day."

Her eyes flicked to the passersby bundled in wool jackets, scarves, and mittens while he wore nothing but a shirt and jeans. There went that burning in her cheeks again—part thank-you, part guilty shame, part *hello, good-looking*. Now that her drink saturated his shirt —well, wet T-shirts weren't just for men to admire.

"I appreciate it. More than you know."

He rubbed his neck. "You know, it's been a really long time since anyone's had the balls to call me out on anything, let alone call me an ass. And I can't remember the last time a woman ran away from me."

"Yeah, well, about that…" She couldn't believe she'd done it either. If it weren't for all those volatile feelings regarding Spencer, she never would've lashed out. Conflict avoidance had been branded into her from a very young age. It was the best way to survive.

He brushed aside her hair and gave a fractional shake of his head. "Don't."

Skye jerked back, not comfortable with such an intimate gesture. "Don't what?"

"Don't apologize."

"Who said I was going to apologize?"

He scrunched his forehead. "Well, you should. You were rude."

There was a quality about him she couldn't ignore. When Ash smiled, he lifted her up inside.

"You just told me not to. Besides, you deserved it." Then, she laughed, playfully punching him on the chest, violating his personal space the same way he had hers.

Holy shit, had she just done that?

"You and your friends were acting like asses, and I was just calling you out on it."

His hand flew to his chest, as if her words had wounded him. "Point taken. I guess we've just kind of gotten used to..." His words trailed off as he released her bag, giving her an opportunity to step back and place distance between them.

She needed that. His proximity was disarming. His smile truly was a thing of beauty. With his good looks and killer smile, he probably got away with a lot, but she wasn't going to let him use his charm against her.

He breathed out a long sigh and glanced at the escalators and then back down at his shirt. "Sorry about your coffee—um, kiddie drink."

"It's not a kiddie drink. It's hot cocoa. I don't like coffee."

"Will you let me buy you another? I feel like I owe you one."

"Owe me? I ruined your shirt. Let me pay to get it cleaned." She unzipped the leather pouch hanging from the lanyard and dug out a twenty.

He pushed her hand away. "I've got plenty of shirts."

"But no jackets? You know, it's below freezing. Most people wear more than a T-shirt in DC during the wintertime."

"We were stopping for a cup of coffee, not planning on taking a stroll—thus the whole running into the store before freezing our asses off." He gave another wink and rubbed his hands on his jeans.

"Sure I can't buy you a drink?"

"I have to get to work."

He seemed to consider the situation and then nodded. "It's definitely warmer in here than out there." He looked at the ticket machines. "Maybe I can ride with you and buy you one at the other end? How do these things work?"

"Seriously? You've never bought a pass before?"

His lips curved at the corners. "Nope."

"Come on, I'll show you how this works."

He followed her to the banks of ticket machines and fished out change from his pockets for the fare to her stop.

"There's a place that sells coffee at my stop, and I can buy you a shirt there, too."

"No worries." He waved off her offer.

She placed a hand on a firm bicep and paused to take a breath. "I insist. I pay for what I break."

He laughed. "Shirt's not broken, babe. Just smells like chocolate."

She rolled her eyes. "Nevertheless, I'm buying you a shirt. It's the least I can do."

"And I'm buying your damn kiddie drink."

When Skye protested, he put an arm around her waist and drew her in. He pressed his lips to the top of her head. The gesture may have been sweet and innocent, but her head spun with the intimacy of that kiss. She held her breath until he let her go.

Ash's Metro pass popped out of the machine, and he bent to retrieve it, releasing her in the process. She stared at the way the denim of his jeans hung low on his ass and then averted her gaze before he caught her staring again.

She led him toward the turnstile. *What the hell was she doing?*

With a wave of her commuter pass over the scanner, the red circle turned to a green arrow, letting her through. He followed, whistling a hauntingly familiar tune.

She had no idea what she was doing, but she didn't really want to think about it.

He certainly was attentive as they moved through the crowds. He stood beside her on the escalator and even placed a hand on the small of her back when they boarded the train. She didn't know what she had done to deserve such kindness, but perhaps the universe was trying to even out its karmic balance for the crap it had thrown her way with Spencer. And she didn't feel guilty about being with another man, needing a distraction from the image of skinny female legs wrapped around Spencer's hips.

Ash leaned over and whispered into her ear, "Where's this coffee shop?"

People moved around them, exiting the Metro and dispersing into the underground shopping area. She glanced at her cell phone. Still twenty minutes until her shift.

"We should get you a clean shirt first." She led him to a shop selling tourist shirts and rock-band tees.

As she fished through a pile of shirts, he studied the crowd. Several young girls openly stared, but she could understand that. The guy was drop-dead gorgeous.

His lips twitched into a frown, and he grabbed a ball cap from a rack. He put it on as she pulled out a black T-shirt and held it up.

"What do you think of this one?"

He laughed. "Seriously? The Bangles? An eighties girl band? Is this some form of punishment? Or did you pick that one in honor of today being 'Manic Monday'?" He picked up a pair of sunglasses with mirrored lenses and put them on.

She turned the shirt around and scanned the front. Heat rose to her cheeks. "Sorry. I wasn't looking at the band's name." She glanced up and snorted. "You're worried about wearing a Bangles T-shirt with those glasses?"

He took the offending shirt from her hands. With a flip and tuck, he had it folded and placed back in the stack. "What's wrong with the glasses? Besides, I want a souvenir."

He wasn't local. The tension in her spine eased, and her shoulders loosened. She relaxed enough to smile and was willing to flirt a little, knowing he wouldn't be around for long.

He pointed to a shirt in the window. "How about that one?"

She glanced at the T-shirt emblazoned with the words *Angel Fire* and the band's iconic logo. "You want that one?"

"I was wondering what you thought of it."

"The shirt or the band?"

Angel Fire definitely wasn't an eighties girl band. They were hard rock to the core. And the shirt would look good on him. It was black with the outline of a guitar sporting angel wings on fire, an iconic picture from one of the most popular rock bands in recent history.

She pulled out an extra-large shirt and held it up to his chest to check the size. His eyes widened.

"Do you want it or not?" She lowered the shirt. "What's the matter? You picked it out."

"You're serious, aren't you?" He shook his head, a dark furrow etched between heavy brows. His eyes were hidden to her, buried behind the stupid mirrored lenses.

"Yes. I ruined your shirt. Honestly though, I need to get going." She pulled out her cell phone and checked the screen. "My shift starts in ten minutes." She lifted the shirt. "Yes or no? Bangles or Angel Fire?" She found another one. "Or what about Metallica?"

He laughed. "I'm definitely an Angel Fire man. Although Metallica rocks."

"Good." She took the Angel Fire shirt to the cashier and pulled out her credit card from the lanyard at her neck.

"You're not like most girls," he said.

"What do you mean?"

Ash pointed at the lanyard. "That's a pretty odd-looking purse."

"Well, when you work in a hospital, purses don't work. You learn to keep what you need close at hand."

He grabbed the lanyard, and his fingers brushed against her breast. It was a quick motion, but was it intentional?

He took a closer look at her ID while the cashier rung up the sale. "Skye. Pretty name." He looked over the top of the glasses. "You're a nurse?"

Typical. "Really? I'm female, so that's what you assume?" She pointed to the two letters after her name. "MD. That means doctor. I hate stereotypes." She waited for his apology.

The cashier finished her sale and rung up Ash's ball cap and ugly glasses. He paid cash and wore them out of the shop after pulling off the tags. "I'm full of charm today, aren't I?"

She couldn't help but laugh at the expression on his face, but her laughter died in her throat when he pulled off the soiled shirt and tossed it in the trash. *Holy hell, six-pack anyone?* A woman walking past stared as well. The unfortunate woman was so focused on Ash's bare chest that she plowed into the trash can in front of her. Skye smothered a laugh.

Ash took the bag from her hand and fished out the Angel Fire T-shirt. In the blink of an eye, all that glorious flesh was covered by black cotton and a guitar with flaming wings.

"Now, tell me where this coffee shop is, and I'll buy you that drink."

"Sorry. Time's up. Gotta go."

It was a shame they didn't have more time.

"Can't you be a few minutes late?"

"I don't like being late. Besides, after a twelve-hour shift, you're pretty beat. It's nice when your relief shows up early."

"Well, at least let me walk you there."

Skye nodded because she really wasn't ready to see him go.

He led her through the underground mall and up to street level, and then he pulled up short as Forest Skye Memorial Hospital dominated the landscape.

She had to tug him forward. "Come on. I work in the emergency department."

"Damn, that place is huge." The behemoth structure of metal and glass glittered in the early morning light.

"It opened less than four years ago. Took seven years to build. I was in the first group of residents who trained here, and now, I'm on the staff."

Ash pulled at her lanyard and checked her badge. His gaze darted to the glowing hospital signage and dipped back to her name. "Forest Skye Memorial Hospital. Any relation?"

Skye blurted one mild, "Ha!" and tossed her head back. Her cheeks flushed, and she pulled him along the sidewalk, unwilling to answer that question. "Come on. It's freezing."

She enjoyed the way his hand enveloped hers but frowned as a gust of chilled air swirled around them. The hairs on his arms stood on end although he didn't seem otherwise affected by the cold.

"I should have bought you a sweatshirt."

He tugged her close. "You can keep me warm."

"You don't have to walk me to work." But if she were honest with herself, she wasn't ready to let him go. A few more minutes of his captivating smile would make the rest of her day so much better.

"I know, but I want to."

Normally, she would have pulled away. Ash was a stranger, but there was an easiness between them, a familiarity she hadn't experienced in a long time. And it was cold, the perfect excuse to snuggle into the warmth of his body.

He brought her to the doors of the emergency department and pulled up short, giving a low whistle. "Big place."

Empty ambulances filled two of the five loading bays. She pulled him over to the staff entrance, an awning sheltering them from the cold. With a practiced flick of her badge, she activated the exterior security lock that opened the outer set of doors. She gestured for him to follow her inside to the small antechamber.

For a moment, the world narrowed down to the two of them. One set of doors led to the frigid world outside. The other set would take her into the chaos of one of the country's busiest trauma centers. But, for now, they were alone. Sadly, their time was almost at an end. She tried to memorize the planes of his face and the hard angle of his jaw.

He pressed the pad of his thumb against her lower lip. "I feel bad about your drink."

Her knees nearly bucked, weakened under the press of that thumb. He had found a way inside her private bubble, and the way he took her in with those mesmerizing eyes made her world tilt and tremble.

When he cupped her jaw, her stomach tumbled. Pressing her palm to her belly did nothing to calm the riot going on in there.

And then it happened. His eyes shifted between her mouth and her eyes, and he leaned in for a kiss.

Chapter Four

SKYE TOOK A STEP BACK, CLOSING HERSELF OFF TO ASH'S IMMINENT kiss. This was where she worked, and while no one could see them, someone could walk into the small entrance at any moment.

What was she doing anyhow? Getting back at Spencer? And, while she was angry, hurt, and devastated, wouldn't she be guilty of a similar sin, letting this stranger have his kiss?

Why was she thinking of Spencer at all?

Reckless was a word that didn't belong in her rigid existence. Every step in her life had occurred after intense deliberation. It was the only way she'd survived her childhood. She had taken a broken little girl and transformed her into a successful physician, precisely because she'd measured and weighed every risk, knowing what she was willing to lose.

Things with Spencer hadn't been perfect. Perhaps some of it had been her fault. The lingering scars from her past caused issues. Maybe she shouldn't have been surprised that he'd looked outside their relationship for sex. Despite their difficulties though, a future with Spencer had had merit.

And maybe that highlighted the problem. Maybe she didn't need safe anymore. Maybe it was time to do the unthinkable.

Ash traced the seam of her lips with his thumb, his eyes focused on where he pressed. A stillness enveloped her as his head lowered, and his lips closed the distance.

Screw Spencer.

She owed no loyalty to him.

And rational thought? Time to toss it out the window.

This was going to happen—even if her coworkers were just beyond those double doors.

Carpe diem.

She'd spent too much time being careful. In the end, by choosing Spencer, she'd still gotten hurt. Maybe it was time not to worry and to simply live in the moment without all her usual ponderous rationalization.

When Ash's lips touched hers, he gave a cautious caress, nothing like Spencer's rough and insistent demands. A smoldering heat replaced the chill from the outside air. His breath released, and she shuddered. Her eyes closed, and she leaned into him, returning his touch with a more hesitant glide of her lips against his.

His fingers swept down her jawline, trailed down her neck, and cupped the back of her head, tangling in the lengths of her hair. He supported her head and opened her lips with his warmth, letting her taste spiced coffee on his tongue. When he wrapped an arm around her waist, pulling her close, she placed a hand against his stomach, tracing the toned muscles underneath. His fingers massaged through the layers of her clothing, strong and confident, and she luxuriated in his exploration, sure but not rushed like Spencer. Then, Ash disentangled his other hand from her hair and pulled back from the kiss.

For a moment, they were separated.

They stared at each other, their faces a breath apart. She had never experienced a more intimate moment, and she couldn't help but compare this with the thousands of kisses she had shared with Spencer, so cold when contrasted with the desire this man stirred.

His expression softened, as if asking, *Is this okay?*

With her heart fluttering, she gave the briefest nod.

He walked the fingers of both hands down her back to settle above the rise of her ass. Then, he pulled her close again, kissing her deeply. His tongue tangled with hers, as if he were desperate to devour her. Masculine deep breaths surged from within him, punctuated by rumbling moans of desire in his throat.

She savored his ardor, his willingness to reveal his passion.

Ash transformed the kiss into an act of worship, more of a giving than a taking, whereas Spencer robbed the donation tray. She slid her hands around to Ash's back and melted into the strength of his embrace. He didn't hide his growing arousal, but neither did he force it. It was merely there, a potent presence of male virility, a symbol of what was happening between them.

And something most certainly was happening—not only with her, but with him as well. The long, hard length of him pressed against her belly, and an awakening pulsed between her legs.

His lips laid a blistering trail along her jawline, his stubble scratching the sensitive skin of her face. She giggled at the unfamiliar sensation.

Ash gripped her nape, angling her head, and intensified the kiss as he found her lips again. His mastery of the art of kissing sent an electrifying tingle running through her body. He released her then, his hooded eyes staring down, mesmerizing her with their incredible depths.

Was it possible that he'd enjoyed that half as much as she had?

"Wow." She shook her head to clear her thoughts. "You've done that a lot, haven't you?"

His grin confirmed her suspicions. "Don't hold my past against me, Skye. I've certainly never enjoyed it as much as just now."

Holy shit, was this guy for real?

And she loved how the harsh, sometimes jolting sound of her name tumbled from his lips. Ash caressed her name with the tonal qualities of his deep voice, sounding out each letter until her name danced from his lips.

He adjusted his erection without any sense of shame. Spencer would never have been so obvious about such a thing.

Ash winked and looked toward the double doors leading into the staff area of the emergency department. "Shame we're not somewhere more private, but I've never let that stop me before."

With a chuckle, he lifted her, and she instinctively wrapped her legs around his hips. She yelped as he pressed her against the wall. Her head whipped left and right. One set of doors led into the building. The other set led to the ambulance bay. She looked for anyone who might be watching, terrified she'd find someone.

"If we were some place else," he said, "I'd have you stripped by now."

Now, that was a little too forward, but damn if he didn't stir a rebellious streak within her mind. Some primal part of her brain was responding to his blatant proposition. But this was her workplace, and she refused to lose her job over a kiss gone wild. Besides, she would never let a man she'd just met fuck her. Skye Summers wasn't a one-night-stand kind of gal.

"Ash, let me down." Her gaze flicked to the doors. She was still worried about getting caught.

He kissed the warmth of her mouth and stopped her thoughts cold as she sank into the sensation.

When he let her up for air, he continued, "I want to be buried deep inside you until you can't think."

She could barely hold together a coherent thought as it was. Kissing him was such a bad idea. She pushed against his chest, more forceful this time. "Put me down."

Only she didn't want him to stop. She wanted him to pound her against that wall like he'd said. She wanted to feel that degree of passion at least once in her life. She wanted what every other woman had seemed to experience and enjoy. Skye wanted to fly free in the arms of a man.

His erection pressed against her inner thigh and ignited something deep within her core, driving her to a frenzy she had never felt before. Sex had always been a physical act to endure. She'd never enjoyed it, but he had her body reacting in new and different ways. Instead of her body shutting down, Ash was awakening something silent and slumbering deep inside of her.

Unlike Spencer, Ash listened when she said to stop. He set her down, steadying her on her feet, but he captured her lips with his again—kissing, licking, sucking, and leaving her breathless. Her cheeks flushed, burning with the implications of Ash's desire to fuck her against the wall. This wasn't who she was. It wasn't how she responded to a man, but she wanted exactly what he'd described.

And, as she'd feared, the outside doors swished open. Mortified at being caught, she broke off the kiss and peeked over Ash's shoulder. From there, she tumbled straight into Spencer's hard glare.

Oh, shit.

Fury filled Spencer's eyes, and anger reddened his face. Her stomach dropped, and she pushed Ash away.

"Spencer." Her voice cracked. She lifted a hand to her lips, finding them slightly swollen.

"Skye? What is this?" The restrained control in Spencer's voice stopped her heart because she knew what would come next.

Her hand flew to her pocket, her fingers feeling for his ring. "What are you doing here?"

The scowl on Spencer's face deepened, his eyes narrowing with dark intent. "I told you not to leave. We need to discuss what you saw."

Ash stepped in front of her, shielding her against Spencer. "Who are you?"

She tried to push Ash away, desperate to defuse Spencer's notorious temper, but Ash wouldn't budge.

Spencer's muscles bunched under his expensive suit. His fingers curled into fists, the veins on the backs of his hands as well as those on his forehead sticking out.

"Who am I? I'm her fiancé, asshole. Who are you, and why are you kissing my girl?"

"Your girl?" Ash crossed his arms, letting his muscles flex in a classic male pose.

Spencer's brows pinched together, casting his eyes in shadow. "Skye, tell me what's going on." He grabbed her wrist and jerked her out from behind Ash.

She yelped as pain shot to her shoulder.

"Whoa, what the fuck, man?" Ash took a step forward. "Let her go."

Spencer snapped her to his side.

"Stop! You're hurting me," she said.

But he never stopped, not when he got like this. His grip tightened.

He pulled her toward the door. "When I tell you to do something, I expect you to do it. Now, why did you leave?" He said the words without a hint of remorse, like he'd expected her to wait while he finished fucking that girl.

She fought his hold, trying to shove him away, but he was too strong. She should tell him off, but the words died on her lips as dark coal eyes bored into her with a fury reminiscent of another man who had once held great power over her life.

"Let her go." Ash pinched Spencer's wrist, pressing, until Spencer yelped and released her arm.

She stepped away, terrified.

Her attention snapped to Ash. He was stepping into a shitstorm.

Spencer's derisive snort made her flinch. "You have no idea who you're dealing with."

She should call security, but she couldn't walk away.

Ash grabbed the lapels of Spencer's expensive suit. "I don't care who you think you are. You're threatening a woman, and that's not going to fly."

The two men locked gazes as the rising testosterone level clotted the air.

"She's mine," Spencer said.

While Spencer matched Ash in height, years of law practice had softened his physique. Ash clearly worked out, and she feared what would happen if things escalated.

Ash's voice came out as a growl. "I said…don't. Touch. The. Girl."

Spencer swung, moving in a blur. His fist connected with Ash's jaw. A resounding smack echoed in the small antechamber.

Skye screamed, "Spencer, no!"

Ash gave a slow, measured smile and then launched a fist toward Spencer's face. His punch connected with Spencer's nose, producing a crunch and a red plume that flew in an arc. Ash followed with a jab to Spencer's gut, and Spencer doubled over.

Fabric ripped. Blood streaked through the air.

Her screams drew security but not before both men got in several more shots. They were all arms and legs and fists connecting with flesh. Spencer's nose was definitely broken, dripping blood. He also bled from deep cuts in his temple, jaw, and cheekbone. Ash sported a split lip and a cut under one eye, and a purplish lump was slowly forming over a cheekbone.

Two security guards separated the men. Ash grinned as he bounced on his heels, relaxed and moving back at the insistence of one of the guards. Spencer breathed heavily and surged against the second guard, who held him in an armlock.

Spencer pointed at Ash. Frothy pink spittle flew from his mouth. "You'll be hearing from my lawyers."

Oh no, his law firm would pulverize someone like Ash. She'd need to call her foster brother, Forest, and explain what happened, so she could somehow help Ash before Spencer destroyed him in court.

Ash spit out congealing blood, laughing. "Go ahead, buddy, but remember who threw the first punch." He rolled his shoulders, shaking out his arms and hands.

She rushed to Ash. "Are you okay?"

The security guard looked hard at Ash. "Hey, aren't you—"

Ash held his hands up and out, and with a quick jerk, he shook his head. "Not now, please."

Spencer struggled in the grip of the security guard. Freeing himself, he lunged forward, clocking Ash on the side of his head. Ash spun, his fist lifted, but the guard grabbed Spencer, dragging him into the emergency department.

Ash rubbed his head, the corner of his mouth quirked up.

He was enjoying this.

The guard who remained asked, "You want to press charges?"

Ash shook his head. "It's over, as far as I'm concerned."

The tiny antechamber felt entirely too crowded as coworkers rushed to check out the commotion.

Skye wrung her hands, her eyes darting around at the questions etched on the faces of colleagues who had no business knowing anything about her personal life.

Ash draped an arm over her shoulder. "Only wish I'd kicked his ass more. Are you really engaged to that asshole?"

She shook her head. "Not anymore."

He pulled her close. "Good." Then, in a whisper, he asked, "Are you okay?"

Her eyes widened as she looked at him. *He was asking her?* She should have been asking him.

Her boss, Bob Manley, walked into the chaos. "What's going on?" His keen eyes took in the scene.

She spoke to her longtime mentor, "There was a misunderstanding."

Bob knew her as the quiet one. God only knew what was going through his mind now.

"Okay." He scanned Ash's injuries with clinical efficiency. "You want me to take him, so you can take care of your boyfriend?"

"Uh...best that I don't."

Ash arched an eyebrow.

She turned back to Bob. "Can you see to Spencer?"

Bob's attention shifted from Ash to the door leading inside the emergency department. He gave a quick nod and disappeared without another word. The questions would come later.

She placed her hands on her hips and shook her head as she surveyed Ash's injuries. "You're a mess."

The grin on his face was even sexier with a swollen lip, but he was going to need stitches for the cut under his eye. The skin was swelling already.

"Tell me about your asshat fiancé." Instead of disappointment, his voice held a hint of a challenge.

She huffed out a breath. "Ex-fiancé."

His eyebrow lifted. "Well, that's good, but it didn't look like he believed he was an ex."

"It's complicated."

"Doesn't sound too complicated." He leaned forward. "And, with the way you were kissing me, I'm assuming something changed recently?" His green eyes implored her for an answer.

Spencer had his faults, but giving him up would be like amputating a part of her life. Although it was the right thing to do, it didn't make it hurt any less. Next to her foster brother, Spencer was the only family she had in the world. No matter how toxic he could be, Spencer had redeeming qualities. Even if they sometimes vanished beneath a jealous rage, they were still there.

She reached into the pocket of her scrubs and pulled out the diamond ring.

"Damn," Ash said as she held it up. "Big rock."

"He proposed last night, and this morning, I found him in bed with another woman."

Ash's eyes rounded with surprise, and he vented a low whistle. The softness of his fingers pressed against the corner of her jaw. "That's low. I'm telling you, Asshat is a douchebag."

Desperate to change the direction of the conversation, she touched his face. "You need stitches. I'll get you patched up."

He shook his head. "I need to leave."

"You're not leaving."

"I don't think he and I should be in the same building together. I don't like the way he treats you, and I've made enough of a scene." He ran his fingers against the cut beneath his eye, wincing. "Besides, it's not that bad."

She didn't want to think about the conversation she and Spencer would have. Spencer was a master at twisting words, and somehow, she always wound up at fault. She needed to hand the ring back and walk away—away from Spencer and the home and family he had come to represent. She needed to leave that dream behind. Giving Spencer up would drop the bottom out of her world, but if she were being honest, it wasn't Spencer she would be saying good-bye to. It was the idea of the family she'd never had.

A finger lifted her chin, and she met Ash's emerald stare.

"Hey, babe. You okay?"

A tear trickled down her cheek, and she wiped it away. "I'm good."

He laughed. It surprised her and brought a smile to her face, lifting her heart in the process.

He wiped his mouth with the back of his hand. "Damn bastard split my lip."

"It's not your lip I'm worried about." She touched his cheek, careful to avoid the blood seeping out of the cut. Too many years as a doctor made her cautious about other people's blood and body fluids. "You need stitches."

His fingers touched the cut under his eye, probing. "Yeah, probably." He reached for her hands. "Listen, I want to see you again. Can I meet you after work? Buy you that drink?" His eyes glittered with hope for more, but his next words confirmed it. "How about dinner?"

"You want to see me after all this?" She waved vaguely around. "I thought you'd be running for the hills."

"Maybe I like the excitement," he said. "Say yes!"

"Only if you let me stitch up your cut."

He shook his head. "I promise to have it taken care of, but I gotta go."

What was the rush? It didn't make sense when they were at an emergency room. A couple of stitches, and he'd be as good as new.

Unless he didn't have medical insurance?

Knowing the cost of a visit to the emergency room, she understood the financial liabilities associated with what seemed like a simple visit. Looking at his beat-up jeans, she assumed he might be strapped for cash. It didn't explain the Hummers, but he didn't act like he had a lot of money.

She should force him to stay, but she didn't want to embarrass him. His skin would heal, but the scar would be ugly. She bit her lower lip, deciding between practicality and impulse.

Inside, she had a difficult conversation to get through with Spencer, and with his foul mood, she didn't see it going well. It would be nice to have something positive to look forward to at the end of the day.

"I'll do dinner, but we'll split the check," she said, coming to her decision.

Ash tucked his chin. An argument was brewing in his eyes.

"After everything we've gone through about manners," he said, "a date is a date. I'm taking you out, and you're not paying."

She laughed. "I always pay my way. It makes things less complicated."

The corners of his lips twisted up. "I suppose you could use a little less complicated right now?"

"It would help."

He dropped his hands. "Fair enough. When do you get off?"

"My shift is over at eight. I'm usually done with sign-out by eight thirty."

"Sign-out?"

"Checking out the patients to my relief."

He brushed her cheek with a kiss. The swell of his split lip pressed unevenly against her skin. "Until then, babe." His eyes narrowed with purpose. "I don't envy your talk with the ex. Give that rock back. Better yet, shove it down his throat."

"I had planned on giving the ring back to him tonight. Now, I get to do it sooner."

Ash cupped her cheek. "If he ever lays a hand on you…"

She leaned in to his touch. "Don't worry about Spencer."

Spencer was her problem. Ash had done enough.

But getting rid of Spencer might take work. The man was tenacious as hell when he wanted something, and there was no doubt in her mind that he wanted her. That begged the question, *Why had he been screwing another woman?*

"I'll see you tonight." She lifted onto her tiptoes and kissed Ash on the cheek.

She took a deep breath, trying to dispel whatever madness Ash had put in her head. Skye Summers didn't kiss strangers, and she certainly didn't go out on dinner dates with them, but somehow, Ash had her breaking all the rules and taking chances.

He waved good-bye, and she entered the world of Forest Skye Memorial's trauma ED.

She had two checkboxes now.

Give back the ring.

Dinner with a stranger.

And who knew? It might turn into something more.

Chapter Five

SKYE DREADED HAVING A CONVERSATION WITH SPENCER AND decided to deal with him later. She'd mail back his ring and deny him the opportunity to twist what had happened and what he'd done. He'd try to turn the entire situation against her. She'd fallen for his manipulations for too long.

She searched for Bob, hoping he had finished taking care of Spencer's injuries. Luck was on her side. Bob stood by the nurses' station typing his note into the computer. He rubbed his temples, and then pulled out a medicine bottle from his pocket. A long time migraine sufferer, he tapped one of his migraine pills into the palm of his hand.

"Long shift?" she asked. "I didn't realize you had worked last night, too."

"Well, Jenna went into labor early, so I took her shift." He popped the pill and chased it with a long pull of his coffee. "I'm getting too old for this."

Unkempt gray hair curled around his balding head. He'd probably tried to finger-comb it into submission, but it refused to be tamed.

His haggard appearance had her worried. He'd been pulling too many extra shifts. And the gray scruff of his beard aged him, making him look more mature than his sixty-one years.

An avid sailor, he'd insisted, "Every sea dog worth his salt keeps a respectable beard."

Her cell phone buzzed. She pulled it out of her pocket and glanced at the screen. *Forest!* "Give me a second." She stepped away for privacy.

Her foster brother always knew when she needed to talk. Their bond had been forged in pain, made strong by their shared weakness, and tempered into resiliency, allowing them to survive their shared trauma.

"Hey, my summer Skye. You need a hug?"

"How'd you know, Beanpole?"

"The universe spoke to me."

Their psychic bond was the single constant in her life.

She grinned. "What are you smoking this week?"

Praying only weed held sway over him had her holding her breath. He'd smoked, ingested, and injected every form of mind-altering substance at one time or another. As far as she knew, he'd weaned himself off the more harmful stuff.

"Hey! I stopped." He hated when she got on him about his drug use.

Like her, Forest had a long, complicated history, but they medicated themselves differently to forget the past. He'd use drugs. She'd bury herself in work.

"Stopped? When?"

"My sixty-day mark is coming up."

Her stomach dropped, fluttering with excitement. He'd never made it half that long before. *Could this be it?*

She allowed a moment of hope that he'd finally be free of the drugs. "How?"

"Just decided it was time. I get my coin in ten more days."

He'd relapsed so many times in the past. She had little faith, but a never-ending well of hope remained.

"I'm going to make it," he said, proving their thoughts traveled the same airwaves.

She wished she'd had the same confidence in him as he had in himself.

"Don't worry, my summer Skye. I'm on a yacht in the middle of the Pacific. No drugs on board. I'll make it."

She breathed. Maybe he would, but what would happen when the boat docked and all the temptations were back in front of him? "Be safe, Beanpole. You with anyone?"

Knowing Forest, he wasn't floating out in the Pacific alone.

"New guy. Cute. Fucks like a bull."

Forest would dump lovers like they were last season's style. It wasn't worth asking for a name because Jack would become Mike in two weeks' time.

"Send me a pic, but keep it clean."

He'd sent too many X-rated photos in the past. Forest had difficulty with understanding the need for boundaries, not when there had been a time when there'd been none.

"Did you buy the yacht, Bean?"

He was a Frivolous Frank with money where she was a Frugal Fanny.

"Nope!" His snicker had her smiling. "This time, I caught the shark. He's taking care of me."

"Be careful!"

Forest would take too many risks with drugs, alcohol, and unprotected sex.

"Talk later. Lover's getting frisky." He cut the line without a good-bye.

Whoever this new lover was, the man had Forest distracted because, while he'd sensed her distress, he never asked why. It was unusual for him not to dig for details.

She wouldn't hear from him again until he surfaced from his newest love. Drugs and sex defined Forest's life. They filled his emptiness the same way she filled hers with extra shifts. She'd rather be busy than stare at empty walls.

"Dr. Summers," a nurse cried out, "we have a multi vehicle accident coming in. Paramedics are coding the driver—pregnant, twenty-nine weeks. Male passenger—head injury, vital signs unstable. Two-year-old in a car seat—stable."

Skye swept into the trauma bay as the paramedics wheeled in the pregnant driver while another straddled her performing chest compressions. Her gut dropped, as it always did, in that sliver of time before she ran a code. She didn't rush, pausing instead for a moment to evaluate the scene.

Bob had taught her that trick when she had been a resident. "First order of business, Skye. Don't do anything. Stand there. Think. Process. Only then do you act."

She lived that mantra and saved lives.

The paramedic shook her head. The pregnant woman was losing her fight to live.

Another ambulance crew rolled in the woman's husband, placing him in the adjoining trauma bay.

With her thoughts gathered, Skye pushed up her sleeves and barked out orders, "Call OB and Peds. We're going to save that baby. Call the surgeons, STAT." She rattled off the labs and X-rays she would need. "Hand me an ET tube."

Her hands were steady as she placed the tube down the woman's throat, securing her airway.

As the respiratory tech taped the tube in place, Skye glanced at the head nurse. "Where's OB?"

"On their way." Nancy Grier, a trauma veteran of thirty years, had a surgical tray prepped and ready.

"Stop compressions." Her command was a measured, even tone, providing an island of calm within the chaos.

The flat line on the monitor told her everything she needed to know, but she went through the motions, feeling for a pulse.

There was none.

"Resume compressions." There was still one life to save. "Let's do this."

"What about OB?" Nancy's brows lifted—not in challenge, but as a question.

Skye shook her head. "We don't have time."

Nancy gave a jerk of her chin. "Right. I'll help."

Skye cut, and less than thirty seconds later, she pulled a limp premature baby out of the incision. The room cheered when the tiny human gave a feeble gasp.

"I need a bag and mask," she called out.

"Peds team is here," someone announced from the back of the room.

Skye tried to look over the press of bodies; it was the curse of being short. When the on-call pediatric resident pushed through the crowd, she placed the premature baby into his hands.

"Got it, Dr. Summers." The pediatric resident clutched the baby to his chest.

Nancy pulled the young doctor out of the room toward a warmer.

Skye moved on to the father, hoping to save him. That baby had already lost its mother. No way was it going to lose its father, too. She knew all too well what happened to orphaned children. But a baby would have a better chance of staying out of foster care than a six-year-old girl. People wanted to adopt babies, not traumatized children.

Skye had the father stabilized by the time neurosurgery arrived, and she transferred care to their team. Then, she went to check on the least critical patient—the two-year-old. He was bruised and crying, which was a good sign. He was lucky. His car seat had minimized his injuries. She sent the child to the pediatric ward for observation.

Not every day started with a bang.

By the time she finished with the trauma, Spencer had been seen and discharged. She breathed a sigh of relief and went to find Bob. She needed to make sure he went home.

When she found him in the break room, he was rubbing his temples, fatigue pulling at the corners of his eyes.

"Looks like you've got the busy shift," he said. "Mine was steady but quiet in comparison."

"Lucky you."

"Your fiancé is all patched up. I think he left." Bob gave a significant look, but she averted her eyes.

That scene with Ash and Spencer was beyond embarrassing. The last thing she wanted was to become the object of emergency department gossip.

Bob put a hand on her shoulder. "None of my business, Skye, but if you need to talk, you know I'm here."

Her throat constricted at the unexpected tenderness. "Thank you, but I'm fine."

Bob was many things—boss, mentor, and teacher. With his paternal concern, he was also the father she wished she'd had growing up.

His shoulders stiffened. Her tone must've been too sharp. She had never been good at interpersonal…stuff.

The corners of his mouth curled up into a smile. "You know why I wanted you to work here?"

The sudden change in conversation caught her off guard.

Because she was the best. But it would be impolite to admit it. There was prestige for the hospital to hire the best of the best. *If not for her test scores, then why?*

"You always work your ass off. No one could match you on your exam scores. For that alone, I hired you." His eyes softened. "But that's not why I *wanted* you. You care, especially for the patients who have nothing—the homeless, the street kids, the druggies, the ones who were raped and abused." He pointed to the trauma bay. "You didn't hesitate. You knew what needed to be done, and you did it to save that baby."

There was a reason behind her passion, and someday, she would repay her debt to society. Everyone deserved a chance, and not everyone got one. She never had. And, while she and Forest had crawled out of their desperation together, not everyone was lucky enough to find the strength they had.

"If marrying Spencer McAdams is going to make you happy, then I wish you the best of luck. But, if you're having any second thoughts, don't do it."

Spencer must have said something about their engagement.

"How did you—"

Bob held her at arm's length. "I saw who you ran to after the fight was over. It wasn't your fiancé."

"He's no one. Just a stranger…"

Bob's eyes narrowed. "Well, sometimes, nobodies can become somebodies. I'm just saying, being in the wrong relationship can hurt more than you know."

Her eyes widened at his message. "Bob—"

Nancy ducked her head into the break room. "Go home, Dr. Manley." She gestured to Skye. "Three stabbing victims in the lobby. They're bleeding all over the linoleum. Come on." She ran off.

Skye nudged Bob toward the door. "She's right. Go home, and get some sleep. You're my relief from all this craziness, and I have a feeling, I'm going to be happy to see you on the other end."

He shook his head as he walked away from the chaos she was now running toward.

As she treated the three bleeding gang members, it occurred to her that, while talking to Forest, she had forgotten to mention Spencer's proposal or the kiss with the more interesting man. Forest was going to love that story.

She hummed the melody to "Manic Monday" while laying down a line of stitches, thinking about Ash in his T-shirt and jeans that hung low in all the right places and his promise of dinner.

After dealing with a lobby full of patients with their flu symptoms, vomiting illnesses, broken bones, and other minor catastrophes, her shift ended on a down note. A two-year-old entered the emergency room with a fever. A simple thing really until his blood work came back. She admitted him to the cancer service amid the tears of his parents.

When she finished her patient's note, the wise eyes of Bob Manley stared back at her. "Rough shift?"

"I've had worse."

His brows drew together with concern. "Someone's waiting for you outside. I guess you have a lot to think about over the next three days."

Yes! She had a string of days free from the craziness of the emergency department. Bob had offered up his cabin in the Blue Ridge Mountains, and she'd graciously accepted. She'd had plans with Spencer, a celebration of their engagement, but now, she'd be heading there alone.

First, she looked forward to getting to know Ash better over dinner.

Skye took Bob to the patient board, taking time for a thorough checkout with those marked as critical. Then, she ran outside, eager to see more of Ash.

Chapter Six

SKYE SMOOTHED THE WRINKLES FROM HER SCRUBS. ASH HAD INVITED her to dinner, and she hoped he realized she had nothing else to wear. Stopping by a small mirror on the way out, she pulled her hair out of the messy ponytail and finger-combed her long waves into submission. She wished she'd carried makeup in her bag. A bit of eyeliner or mascara would help make her appear less ragged for her date.

She exited the staff entrance, nervous but hopeful. Beneath the shelter of the covered driveway, nurses and respiratory therapists gathered, planning their off-shift rituals, while EMTs cleaned out the ambulance rigs.

Despite his promise, the sexy man with the gorgeous green eyes and toe-curling kisses was nowhere to be found.

She shifted the weight of her backpack over her shoulder. With a sigh, she headed toward the metro but pulled up short.

Someone was waiting, but it wasn't Ash.

Spencer opened the door to his car and climbed out. He walked over, his long legs devouring the distance between them in determined strides. He greeted her with a chaste kiss, taking her bag from her shoulder, as he'd done hundreds of times before.

"We need to talk." The stern, clipped tone pointed to his anger, but a vulnerability had settled in the clench of his jaw. The way he kept his chin tucked had her expecting one of his rare apologies.

She placed her hand inside her pocket and curled her index finger around the platinum band. The words that would end their relationship died in her throat while she took in his injuries. A white bandage bridged his nose and a black eye darkened his expression. He sported a swollen and cut lip, and a bruise discolored the angle of his jaw.

She stretched out to cup his cheek. "How do you feel?"

He gripped her wrist, pulling her toward the car, dominating her with his size.

"You embarrassed me in front of your coworkers." His terse words told her no apology would be forthcoming.

"I'm sorry." She couldn't help the words from tumbling past her lips even though she had no reason to apologize.

A shadow crossed his face, and he looked around, but the few people present weren't within earshot.

"We'll talk more at home where we can have the privacy we need. I understand why you did what you did, why you felt the need to get back at me, and I want you to know, I forgive you." Dark eyes implored her to accept his brand of forgiveness.

She gulped at the raw edge to his voice and placed her hand on his forearm.

"You accepted my ring. You belong to me. Yet you let another man kiss you, Skye. I'm very disappointed."

Spencer never kissed her with the passion Ash had shown. Ash's unrestrained urgency had stirred her heart. He'd made her feel like she couldn't breathe, whereas Spencer merely filled the aching loneliness eating at her life.

She looked around, searching for Ash. Maybe, just maybe, he would actually appear.

Spencer's grip tightened, and his jaw worked from side to side. "I've had all day to think about what happened. If we're to be husband and wife, you must adhere to certain standards, and there are consequences for when you fail. We must be more diligent."

She swallowed against the lump in her throat. Her eyes went to his belt and the way he stroked the leather. Run was what she should do, but a lifetime of avoiding conflict told her not to resist. They'd talk when they got home, and she'd make him understand.

With a weak smile, she lowered herself into Spencer's car. He had his flaws, but he still wanted her as his wife. Why he had been with another woman was a question she needed answered, but there were worse things than infidelity within a relationship. Her gaze dipped back to his belt, apprehension brewing in her gut.

Where was Forest? He always knew when the light grew dim.

The door to the car slammed, shutting her inside. She trembled with the feeling of being trapped.

He was disappointed, not angry. They would talk this through, like any other couple.

They'd been together for three years. Did she really want to give up their history and their future for a man she'd just met? A man who had stood her up?

Spencer was many things, but compared to the monsters of her past, he was but a flea. She didn't doubt he cared for her. She only wished it hadn't hurt so much.

He climbed into the car and laid a hand on her knee and squeezed. "You know I love you."

She gave a fragile smile but couldn't bring herself to repeat the words.

"Where's my ring?" He stared at her left ring finger.

"You know I can't wear it at work."

"I'll get a necklace for you to put it on when you're at work." He reached behind his seat and pulled out a manila envelope. "Speaking of…I need you to sign this."

"What is it?"

He guided the car through the parking lot and merged into traffic. "It's our prenup."

"Our what?"

Heat flared in her cheeks. Why did she care if he'd had a prenuptial drawn up when she'd planned to return his ring? But she did. She hated everything about a prenup. Marriage was the complete binding of two people's lives, not a contractual division of assets.

The traffic thickened.

"This can't come as a surprise."

A prenup admitted failure before the vows were even spoken, and she wasn't after Spencer's money. She didn't need it. He came from old money and a distinguished family, but she wasn't destitute.

Her finger itched to text Forest and tell him. He would have a good laugh about Spencer's money concerns, but she did nothing.

Staring at the envelope, she found her resolve. "I'm not signing this."

Spencer sucked in a breath and slowly blew it out. "Listen, we come from different backgrounds. You grew up in foster care, and while you pulled yourself out of that, you carry the debt of medical school while I have a trust fund."

"I'm not marrying you for your money." She wasn't going to marry him at all although he seemed determined to continue with their engagement. "I thought you understood that."

"I'm more than willing to shoulder the burden of whatever student loans you might have, but I owe it to my family to protect their assets."

She fished the ring out of her pocket and placed it on the dash. "I'm not marrying you."

Spencer's fingers squeezed the steering wheel, and his jaw clamped down. "You're being unreasonable."

The diamond sparkled with the light from oncoming headlights. She stared at the glittering light. "Pull over."

His grip tightened on the steering wheel, and his foot pressed on the gas. "Don't be melodramatic, Skye. I'm not pulling over."

"I'm not marrying a man who cheats on me the day after he proposed."

His jaw clenched, and he shot her a glare. "You should thank me, to be honest."

Damn, he could cut deep.

"Thank you? For cheating?"

His thumbs tapped the steering wheel. "This is a useless argument. And I don't blame you. I know what happened when you were younger, and I accept you as you are, but I have needs. I could have had some sordid affair, but I spared you that embarrassment. I keep things discreet."

Had he really shifted the blame for his infidelity to her?

His expression softened. "I haven't given up on you. We'll get help. Find a therapist who deals with sexual trauma. We'll work through this together—as man and wife. Until then, I'll manage my needs as I see fit."

"So, you'll sleep around, and I'm supposed to be grateful?" He was a true bastard. How had she been so blind?

He breathed out. "Those women are professionals, and what I do is behind closed doors, unlike your little display. You're my fiancée, and you kissed a man in front of everyone at your work. Imagine how that makes me look. The bastard broke my nose." He pointed to the envelope. "Sign the prenup, Skye." He grabbed the diamond ring off the dash and thrust it at her. "And put this back on your finger. I intend to marry you. This is nothing more than a tiny disagreement."

Tiny? Was he delusional?

They pulled off the main road onto a side street. In another few turns, they'd be at his place.

Darkness cloaked the streets and shrouded her heart as he pulled into his driveway. She sat quietly as he turned off the ignition and got out of the car.

Spencer insisted on opening her door. She lifted her hand for him to help her out.

He drew her into a hug, and she stiffened. Images of that woman's legs wrapped around his hips assaulted her mind, and she wanted to throw up. She didn't have the strength to argue though. Besides, she was afraid of what would happen when he really got mad.

Chapter Seven

THE NEXT MORNING, SKYE WOKE TO A TANGLE OF COVERS IN Spencer's bed.

He'd talked. She'd listened and come to a conclusion about life. To have a family, she didn't need the perfect man. What she wanted was a happily ever after, and Spencer offered the possibility. It was as close as she was going to get. But that kiss she'd shared with Ash had been beyond wonderful. *Maybe all she needed was good for now.*

In the end, did it really matter? Life was messy and full of compromise. Spencer wasn't perfect, but neither was she. He had her mind spinning and her heart in free fall.

She rolled over to find his side of the bed empty, and there was a note on his pillow. Sometime while she'd been sleeping, he'd slipped his ring back on her finger.

My darling Skye,

I love you more than life itself.
You make the day worth living, each breath worth taking.

You are the light to my darkness.
I forgive you.

Your truest love,
Spencer

P.S. I have to leave on business. I'll be out of the country for a week. I left the prenup papers on the breakfast table. Sign and send them to my lawyer. I'll see you next Tuesday. XOXO.

She clasped the note to her chest and stared at the ceiling. His ring twisted around her finger. *One week?* He'd told her that they'd spend the next few days away from the distractions of work and celebrating their engagement. *What was she supposed to do now? Head to the mountains alone?*

She pressed a hand to her head. The clunky ring banged against her forehead. The thing needed to be resized.

It didn't fit on so many levels.

With a groan, she climbed out of bed. Perhaps it was best that he'd been called away. A solo retreat might be exactly what she needed to decide, once and for all, if Spencer belonged in her future.

She showered and dressed, pulling on a fresh pair of scrubs from her backpack.

On her way out the door, she grabbed Spencer's prenup and set out to walk to the coffee shop. The arctic blast of yesterday had warmed to a more reasonable winter chill. Nevertheless, the crispness of the air had her cheeks burning while the wind whipped at her chapped lips. Overhead, a brilliant sun blazed, and stray wisps of clouds laced a clear deep blue sky.

A short time later, the wonderfully rich aroma of freshly brewed coffee tickled her nose. The warmth of the store enveloped her and banished the chill from her invigorating walk.

She adjusted her backpack and waited for the barista to finish the previous customer's order.

"Hiya!" Kandi's bubbly personality always brought a smile to Skye's early mornings.

"Good morning. Can I have a—"

"Hot cocoa?"

"Um, yes, please."

The girl laughed, and her ponytail swished. "You're later than usual today." She flashed a row of perfect teeth and pointed to Skye's favorite corner spot. "Cocoa's waiting on you."

"Waiting?" Knowing her favorite drink was one thing. Having it waiting was kind of creepy.

The blonde jerked her chin toward the couch. "That sexy guy has been hanging out for over an hour, hoping you'd show." She flicked her fingers in the direction of Skye's usual spot. "He's had me make a fresh cup whenever the previous one gets cold. I just walked the fifth one over. It's piping hot."

Skye twisted toward the fire, and sure enough, someone was sitting in her spot. He had on a familiar ball cap and goofy mirrored sunglasses. His head bobbed to whatever music filled his earbuds, and two cups sat on the coffee table.

She covered her mouth, surprised. "Oh my God."

The barista lowered her voice to a whisper. "It's so romantic."

"Did he pay?"

The door opened, and customers filed in line behind her.

The barista's face pinched with confusion. "He's running a tab."

Skye did a quick calculation and slapped down some cash. "Here." She couldn't let a stranger pay for such a large bill.

"I don't really think—"

"I don't care."

Spencer's ring slipped around her finger. She stared at it and all the possibilities it represented. He loved her, and despite their problems, she cared deeply about him. But, if she was going to live the rest of her life with him, she needed to know he was the right choice. She slipped the ring off and zipped it into the inner pocket of her backpack.

With a deep breath, she went to greet Ash.

He sat with an ankle kicked over the opposite knee, hands clasped and head bowed, rocking to his own beat. He wore black jeans, well-worn hiking boots, and another faded T-shirt stretched tightly over his chest. A black leather jacket was draped over the arm of the chair. With the hat and glasses, only his lips and jawline were visible. It was a shame because he had the handsomest face.

In fact, the glasses covered much of his cheekbones, and she couldn't make out the cut under his eye. *Had he taken care of it, like he'd said he would?* It would scar otherwise, and it would be a shame to mar such perfect features.

She swallowed away her nervousness, remembering how he'd held her, the way his lips had felt against her skin, the way her insides had melted, and how her body had responded to him, like it never had with Spencer.

"Hello," she said.

He didn't react, probably because he had the noise turned up too loud.

She nudged his shoulder, shaking gently.

His attention shifted from his hands to her. His entire body stilled, except for the smile sweeping across his face.

While she couldn't see his eyes, the intensity of his gaze pinned her in place. He stole all the oxygen from the room, and she could barely catch her breath.

He lowered the sunglasses, revealing the iridescent deep hue that matched the scales of the dragon tattoo wrapping up his neck. He regarded her with a look of wonder. His pupils dilated as he devoured her. Two Steri-Strips held the wound closed beneath his eye. Someone had taken care of him.

"You're here." The awe in his voice rushed over her in waves. In one fluid movement, he moved to his feet. "After you stood me up, I thought I'd never see you again. I know this is a little stalkerish, but…I just had to see you again."

"I didn't stand you up. You weren't there."

"No way in hell would I stand you up." He pulled her down onto the couch and settled beside her. He leaned forward, grabbed two cups resting on the coffee table, and handed her one. "Your drink."

She took the steaming cup, her hand a bit shaky. Hell, her entire body trembled in his presence. "The barista told me that you've been waiting."

He hung his head and chuckled softly. "Damn, that makes me look pathetic."

She put a hand on his arm. "No, it's really sweet."

She loved the way his hair hung down to his shoulders and curled around his ears. The dragon tattoo on his neck peeked out between the strands, as if it were measuring her and not the other way around.

"Where were you last night?" she asked.

"Waiting out front."

"I didn't see you."

Bob had relieved her a few minutes early. Maybe, if Spencer hadn't been waiting, she and Ash wouldn't have missed each other.

Ash's brows pulled together, and a mischievous grin curled the corners of his mouth. "We didn't get to finish that kiss." He traced a line over her thigh.

She cocked her head and suppressed the shiver running down her spine as his thumb pressed against the outer seam of her jeans. They would have more of a connection if he'd run his finger along her bare arm where there was no clothing to get in the way.

"Um, I'd say we finished just fine." That was a lie, and if he wanted another go at kissing, she was ready.

"No, we got interrupted by the Asshat. Did he steal you away from me?" He huffed a laugh. "I'm assuming that's the case because I'm not the kind of guy that girls stand up."

She took a sip of cocoa. "You're a bit cocksure, aren't you?"

Now, why wasn't that irritating, like it was with Spencer? Maybe because Ash's confidence was so sexy and stemmed from harmless egotism instead of a need to control others.

His lips curved into another smile. "Ah, but you like me, and you're dying to know how last night would've gone."

"I think you're dying to tell me how it might have gone. I hate to break it to you, but I'm not that kind of girl. A kiss is as far as you would have gotten."

Please don't be a man-whore. She desperately wanted there to be more to this man than his looks.

He reached out and toyed with a strand of her hair, curling it around his finger. "I find that oddly exciting. Now, tell me what happened last night."

He found that exciting? That she wouldn't put out? What happened to the "I want to be buried deep inside you until you can't think" comment?

Rather than ask, she answered his question, "It got complicated."

"It sounds a bit more than complicated."

They sat in silence, watching the fire in the hearth crackle and burn.

She grabbed one of his earbuds and pulled it to her ear. "What are you listening to?"

He tried to yank it back, but she held on and settled it in her ear.

"I want to know. You were really engrossed in whatever it was when I walked up."

The warbling sound of an Angel Fire song kicked in. The frenetic rhythm filled her head along with the vocals of their lead singer—"a man who could sing his ass off with blissful yet devastating melodies without losing his balls." At least, that's what her brother would say. Angel Fire was Forest's favorite band.

She tilted her head back, rocking in time with the underlying drumbeats.

The song ended, and she looked up. "I'm not familiar with that song."

He shrugged. "That band has lots of songs."

"I guess so."

"Did you like it?" His question held more than a hint of interest.

"Yeah, but they always play good stuff. They're supposed to be in town for a concert this weekend." That was as close as she would come to asking him out although getting ahold of tickets to what was probably a sold-out show would be nearly impossible.

He licked his lower lip. "Yeah, I've heard their stuff is good."

She playfully punched him in the shoulder. "What? You're not a fan?"

According to Forest, it was impossible for any male in the world not to be into Angel Fire's pounding rhythms. He'd also said every girl wanted into at least one band member's pants. She could recognize the band's signature sound, but that was where it ended for her.

Ash laughed. "Not exactly a fan. You?"

"I'm not the fangirl type." She shrugged. "Too busy with important things to follow any one band. I know what I like, but I can barely match a band with one of their songs. My brother likes Angel Fire and plays them nonstop. That's the only reason I even know who that band is."

A line formed between his brows. "Important things? Like what?"

"Well, like medical school, residency, and studying my ass off to pass the boards. I rarely listen to music, but I know what I like. That's pretty much the end of it."

Forest managed their shared music files. She'd push shuffle and let the music run, skipping over the tracks she didn't like. Otherwise, she wouldn't pay much attention. Forest, on the other hand, knew every band, every song, and the name of every musician, but then he knew just about everything.

"Oh." A frown crossed his face and then disappeared. He downed the last of his coffee and chewed his lower lip. "Look, I know your life might be a bit complex right now, but it sounds to me like you should reevaluate your priorities." He traced a circle over her kneecap.

She batted his hand away. "I don't want to talk about my fiancé."

"Asshat is back to being your fiancé?" He drew a heart shape on her upper thigh. "With the way you were kissing me, I'm surprised."

"I said it was complicated. I'm taking the next three days to figure things out." She waved her hands in the air. "My boss has a cabin, and he's letting me use it. Just me, the woods, and miles of hiking trails to sort out my head."

"What about your heart? You forgot about your heart. And where's Mr. Asshat going to be?"

"He's away on business."

Ash grew silent for a long moment. "Three days?"

She nodded.

"Alone, in a cabin, in the woods, by yourself?" He looked at her like she was crazy.

Another nod. She wished he'd stop giving her that look. She wasn't crazy.

"Interesting."

She tucked her chin and glanced at him sideways. "How is that interesting?"

More silence.

Then, he suddenly leaned forward. "Do you believe in fate?"

With her history? "No, I don't believe in fate." *What child deserved the hell she and Forest had endured?*

"I do." He stood and held out a hand. "Come."

"Excuse me?"

"I happen to have three days free."

"And?"

"I'm coming with you."

"Um…what?" Her heart dropped, pounding fast and furious with the butterflies Ash had set aflight in her stomach.

He pulled her into his arms. "It's time to uncomplicate your life. Last night, we missed each other, but now, we have a second chance. Looks like I have three days to persuade you to take a chance on someone who won't treat you like your asshat ex."

"What do you mean, like he treats me? You barely know me. I find it a bit presumptuous of you to judge me, my life, or the man I intend to marry."

He tilted his sunglasses down, looking over the rim, letting her know exactly how serious he was. Velvet green held her captive. "You're not marrying him. You and I both know this. Now, let me show you why."

"I'm sorry, but you can't invite yourself along on my trip. I don't know anything about you."

"You're right. You don't know me at all, but you want to."

The couch pressed against the backs of her calves, blocking her escape route. She put a palm against his chest to push him back. Wrong move. The hardened planes of his muscles stretched under the soft cotton of his T-shirt. His body heat radiated against her palm, and his heart thumped, slow and steady, beneath her hand. An answering resonance sounded deep in her chest.

He covered her hand, stroking it with his long fingers. "What more do you need to know? We share a connection."

She felt it all right. Every single breath, lick, and caress of it had awakened her senses. She remembered him pressing her against the wall.

"If we were somewhere more private, I'd have you stripped by now."

His bold words should have had her running for the hills.

"I want to be buried deep inside you until you can't think."

Such blatant sexuality from a man would typically have her crawling inside her shell and dissembling as past memories overtook her conscious thought. The heat of his words, however, had washed over her, and for the first time, she hadn't frozen from a man's touch.

Wanting more of that, she ran her fingers over the fabric of his shirt and thought about all the reasons to say no.

"Ash, I'm sorry, but I can't." That was a lie. And, after Spencer's betrayal, didn't she deserve a chance to find out if Ash might be right?

His hand curled around hers. "Take a chance, Skye. What do you have to lose?"

The urgency of his gaze was too much. She tried to look away. "You don't understand."

"Look at me."

He bent down until his eyes were level with hers. Golden flecks in a sea of green stared at her with confidence and need. "Give me a chance." He straightened and flashed a cocky grin. "After three nights with me, you won't even remember his name."

A shiver ran down her spine, but her practical nature overrode the reactions he'd pulled from her body. *Was that all he wanted?* Sex was the last thing she was looking for.

"Sorry, but I'm not interested in becoming another notch on your belt."

He breathed out a long sigh and tilted his head back. "I've never been stood up until you. Never been denied until—shit, this is crazy, but what if I gave my word to keep my junk in my jeans?"

She burst out laughing.

"You think that's funny?" His brows drew together as he regarded her with an intense stare. His voice lowered to a mumble. "Well, I'm serious. If that's what it takes for you to let me come with you, I'll keep my junk in my jeans."

Her hand flew to her mouth. "Oh my God, stop saying that."

His eyes narrowed. "I never tease about sex."

"You'd come with me, knowing there's no chance of sex?" *Dear God, had she just said yes?*

He lifted her hand and brushed her knuckles against his lips. "Deal, but only for three days. After that, we renegotiate."

"I have to go home and pack. Do you want to meet me back here after you get your stuff?"

He shook his head. "No, I can buy what I need on the way."

"How is it that you happen to have free time?"

He flashed a mysterious smile. "I've got the time, babe."

A worm of doubt wriggled in her belly. "Are you on vacation or something?"

"Kind of. More like, here on business, but as long as I'm back by Friday, it'll be fine." He gestured to the counter. "Look, let me pay for the drinks, and then we can go."

"Never mind. I already took care of it."

His mouth gaped. "You what?"

"I told you, I pay my own way."

"You can't do that." He ran a hand over his back pocket, searching for a wallet he wouldn't need.

"If you're coming with me, you play by my rules. We split all costs down the middle. I have a rental to pick up, but I'll pay for that and the gas."

His lips formed into a thin line. "You don't need a rental. I have a Jeep, and I'll pay for all the gas."

"We split the gas."

He crossed his arms. One corner of his lips turned up, and he arched a single brow. "Does this mean, we're negotiating?"

She laughed. "I guess so."

"I drive. We split meals and any other activities straight down the middle?"

"Yes," she said.

He held up a hand. "I'm not finished."

She rolled her eyes. "Go on."

"I'll sleep on top of the covers if I have to, but we share the bed."

She opened her mouth to protest, but he pressed a finger against her lips, silencing her retort.

"I get to hold your hand and kiss you as much as I like," he stated his terms with another smirk.

"First base only but no sex," she said. Kissing was good. *Would she respond differently to him or grow cold and shut down?*

"Well, let's not get crazy." His gaze flicked from her eyes to settle on her chest. "I mean, you have to give a guy something."

She wasn't sure if she wanted him touching her breasts, but she was willing to consider it. "Second base?"

His eyes narrowed. "Depends on your definition of second base. If you're thinking of a little tongue, we've already done that. Quite successfully, I might add. If you're talking about a little boob action, I'm all in. How about third base?"

That sounded dangerous. She didn't want his fingers anywhere near down there. "I think second is far enough. Wouldn't want to tempt you too much."

His lips twitched. "I can keep my junk stowed, especially since we'll be renegotiating on day four."

His confidence had her smiling.

"We'll see about that." She thought of another condition. "And you wear pajamas."

He frowned. "That's ridiculous. I haven't worn PJs since I was ten."

"That's the deal. Take it or leave it." Her insides flipped. *Were they really discussing sleeping attire?* What would he look like in pajamas, considering how hot a pair of jeans looked sitting on his hips?

He vented a deep sigh. "I'm going to have the bluest balls at the end of these three days."

She burst out laughing at his brutal honesty. The freedom with which he joked at his own expense was refreshing next to the rigidness of all things Spencer.

He lifted his hands, palms out. "I'm just saying." He made a classic hourglass motion with his hands. "On the seventy-third hour, we're having a talk. Now, let's blow this joint."

As they gathered their things, she wondered which one of them would be more eager for the arrival of the seventy-third hour.

She fished her phone out of her backpack and drafted a message to Forest. He needed to know about Spencer cheating on her, Ash's appearance, and whatever this three-day experiment was about. And, if Ash turned out to be some ax-wielding psychopath, Forest would need to recover her body.

Ash led her around to the parking lot out back. The lights of a beat-up black Jeep with oversized tires and a lift kit flashed.

"My baby." His chest expanded with pride. "Bought it myself when I was seventeen."

She pointed to the vehicle and then to him. Unable to keep the smile from her face, she said, "Black Jeep, black jacket, black jeans, and black shirt? Either you're crazy about the color black, or you're seriously depressed."

His lips curved. "Wiseass, get in my Jeep."

But there was a guitar case in the way. He hefted the case into the rear, freeing up the passenger seat.

"You play?"

Another of his amazing smiles brightened his face. "From time to time."

He went around to the other side. Once inside, he removed the sunglasses, folded them up, and placed them on the dash.

She leaned toward. "Let me look at that cut."

He swatted her hand away. "It's fine."

She used her authoritative doctor's voice. "Let me see it."

He turned toward her. It was not as bad as she'd feared but worse than it should have been.

Someone had slapped Steri-Strips across it and used superglue to seal the edges. Not a bad job, but she could have sutured it, so the cut would heal with hardly a scar.

"You told me you were going to have it taken care of." She traced the line of the cut. The puckered raw edges made her shake her head. "You should have let me stitch it up."

He squeezed her hand. "I know, but now, I have a battle scar from fighting over my girl." His eyes flashed in the light, sparkling with more brilliance than Spencer's diamond.

"I'm not your girl."

"Well, when I tell the story of how I won you over, it'll be priceless." He released her hand and turned on the ignition. "Now, how do I get to your place?"

She wasn't sure how she felt about the scar, but from the way Ash's chest puffed out, he seemed proud of it.

He slipped the Jeep into traffic and wove between the cars. Hard rock streamed through the speakers. As she leaned forward to reach the speaker controls so that she could turn the music down for him to hear the directions to her place, her gaze caught on the spiderweb tattoo covering his neck.

The web had been inked in black, but up close, she saw the edges had been outlined in red. Some of the strands oozed blood. In the center, the dragon she had only glimpsed before stared out at her with a defiant glare. The silk seemed to sway under the dragon's weight as its talons curled around the bloody strands. Its ruby eyes gleamed with a fiery glow, and the blackbird, which she'd originally thought was ensnared by the dragon, was instead held with a gentle grip.

Catching her out of the corner of his eye, he fractionally turned his head as he pulled up to a Stop sign. "You're staring."

A flush warmed her neck and crept up her cheeks. "Sorry, but your tattoo is amazing."

He rubbed at his neck. "Yeah, one of my many acts of teenage defiance. Totally freaked my mom out."

"How old were you when you got it?"

"Seventeen. Got it the same day I bought the Jeep, but it took a few years to finish it off."

"I thought you had to be eighteen to get a tattoo?"

"Well, I knew the artist. Mom didn't speak to me for a week. I got the web first."

"Does it mean anything?"

"Maybe. But I'm not going to spill all my secrets on the first date."

"Is that what this is? A first date?"

"Not really." He reached over and stroked her thigh. The heat of his palm radiated through the fabric of her jeans, stirring arousal elsewhere. "Technically, it's the second. No way can I forget our first kiss."

His brows quirked with mischief while her cheeks flushed again.

He focused on the traffic and curled his fingers around her hand. "You look scared to death. Don't be. I pride myself on being a man of my word."

This whole situation was crazy, their agreement was insane, but she was willing to take a chance on Ash.

Half a block later, he pulled into the driveway of her modest two-bedroom brownstone.

Forest had wanted to buy her a bigger place, but the mortgage fit within the salary she pulled from her job at the hospital. He didn't like that she'd taken out a mortgage either, but it was important to her to live within her means as a physician.

Ash put the mirrored sunglasses back on and hopped out, coming around to open her door. She wasn't sure what to think about the fact that he shared that trait with Spencer.

"Come inside."

He shook his head. "Too risky."

"What does that mean?"

"This isn't the cabin. Our three days haven't officially begun yet. Best I wait in the car." He lowered those stupid glasses and pinned her with a penetrating deep gaze. "Me and my junk will be right here. Don't take too long. Otherwise, I'll be forced to come looking for you."

"Don't be ridiculous."

He pushed the glasses up, hiding his beautiful eyes. "If I come in there, I'm going to kiss you. If I kiss you, I'm going to touch you." He took a step toward her, closing the distance, forcing her heart into a rapid flutter. His voice lowered as he spoke in her ear, "I'll peel off all your clothes and make you forget all about your maybe, maybe-not fiancé until my name is the only sound you make."

She imagined him doing exactly that and bit her lower lip.

He took a step back. "Technically, our trip hasn't started. My promise isn't in effect. As soon as I pile you into my Jeep and take you to this cabin, I'm going to regret giving you my word because I already know what it feels like to touch you. Unless that's what you want…"

She had no words.

He gave a shake of his head. "Okay then, I'll be waiting right here. I'm not fucking this up. Not that I don't want to follow you right now. Sex is great. But you should know, I'm after the bigger prize."

Holy hell in a hand basket. Did this guy have no filter?

With the sunglasses, there was no way to know if he was telling the truth or teasing.

Half of her wanted to find out if he would carry through on his threat. As threats went, that one sounded like a lot of fun.

She twisted the door handle and stepped across the threshold. "I'll be out in ten minutes. No need to come get me."

Her bags were already packed. All she needed to do was tell Forest and cancel the rental car.

Inside, the quiet of her house reminded her of the starkness of her life. The one devoid of a strange man, a three-day agreement, and scorching kisses that threatened to undo everything she'd fought to build.

She scanned Spencer's prenup into a file to send off to Forest.

Spencer promised a future she'd always dreamed of having. Could she really walk away from all the time she'd invested in achieving her most precious dream?

But she needed answers. And Ash might be the only clear signal in the confusing noise of her life right now.

A loud pounding sounded on her door after a few minutes.

"Skye," he called out, "it's been fifteen minutes. Don't make me come in there. I don't like breaking promises."

She glanced at the door, a ghost of a smile lifting the corners of her mouth. While she knew next to nothing about Ash, her gut told her that his singular comment encapsulated the truth about him.

As much fun as it would be to let him in and have him ravage her as they both wanted, deep down, she knew they needed to wait.

"I'm on my way!"

She pressed the Send button and packed up her laptop. *What would Forest think?*

With her backpack slung over her shoulder and her day bag clutched in her hand, she headed out.

Three days with a man with emerald eyes, a magnetic voice, and the ability to melt her from the inside promised so many things.

She shut the door to her brownstone and locked her practical half inside.

Chapter Eight

Skye ran right into Ash. Her stomach tightened as hope mingled with fear, but she'd made the decision to see where this thing with him would lead.

"Sorry." She took a breath. "I guess I'm ready."

He put her bags in the back, next to the guitar, and then opened the passenger door of the Jeep. He stole a peck on her cheek. "Get in."

He walked around to the driver's side. "Where's this cabin of yours?"

"It's not mine. My boss is letting me stay in it, and it's near Roanoke, up in the Blue Ridge Mountains."

He whistled. "How far is that?"

"About three or four hours, depending on which way you go. Reconsidering?"

"Hell no. I wouldn't give this trip up for the world." He leaned back and turned the key. The moment the engine cranked over, music played through the speakers. He turned the volume down and then backed out of the driveway.

"Guess I have a few hours to get to know your life story," he said.

"You don't want to know my life story."

"I do. We'll start with the easy stuff first. How about favorite food? Or music?"

"Hmm. Food is hard. Music…I like what you're playing."

His eyes widened with surprise. "Awesome! A hard-rock gal. I took you for the soft, fluffy stuff."

She made a face. "You can thank my brother for that. He buys all our music. We share playlists. Or rather, I listen to what he buys. I like Metallica, Slayer, Pantera, Seether—the list goes on."

"Most of those formed decades ago. Any newer bands?"

She shrugged. "It's hard to find a true metal band anymore. I mean, most play their asses off and crush it, but they don't have moving songs. I like bands who really blow it out of the water. When I listen, I want to feel inspired and pushed to be better at what I do. My brother is a big fan of Angel Fire, so I listen to more of their stuff than I otherwise would. I guess they'd be considered relatively new."

"You like them?"

There was something more to his question, but she couldn't figure it out.

The topic of music kept the conversation away from her life story. She struggled to remember how Forest had described music. "Like I said, I'm not a fan. Too busy with work. It's the same with television. I hardly have time to watch anything, and I rarely see movies."

The lines on his face eased.

She continued, "I recognize their sound. It's the same with Seether or Metallica. I know when I'm listening to a particular band, but that's where it stops."

"Why metal bands and not soft pop?"

She laughed. "I love the energy of metal. Soft pop is okay, but it's not inspiring. Metal bands write with heart and soul. They create a sound—something that stomps balls, makes you want to scream your head off, but doesn't make you look like an idiot while doing it. There's a melody there as well, to wrap your head around. Well-crafted songs like that are hard to come by."

His fingers tapped the steering wheel in time to the rhythm of Metallica's "Master of Puppets." His expression relaxed into a peaceful smile. "I like how you describe music."

She was repeating her brother's words almost verbatim. He was the true music fan.

Following on the tail end of the soulful notes of Metallica, the first few notes of an Angel Fire song played.

"This band is pretty good. Hard metal, but unlike other bands that yell and screech at you, you can actually sing along. I understand the words, and that voice! Oh my God, their lead singer's voice wraps around you in so many layers of sinful goodness."

He burst out laughing, which turned into a coughing fit. He glanced aside at her. "Sinful goodness?"

"Yeah. But it's a shame."

He grew quiet. "What do you mean?"

"The drugs and alcohol? In and out of rehab? They rose to the top of the charts fast and then kind of self-combusted. Drugs do that. Rips apart families, friends, and bands. I see it every day where I work—the druggies and addicts and their victims."

She'd been trying to bring Forest out of the depths of his addiction for the past decade.

Ash's voice took on a harsh edge. "Angel Fire's at the top of their game. The band's been sober for years. And they're rocking the charts."

"Oh, I guess. Like I said, I really don't follow them. I only get what my brother tells me."

His mouth twisted. "I suppose."

"There is one band I really like. The Burn is pretty amazing. If I had a favorite, it would be them. Their singer's voice is hypnotic, and his tattoo is a piece of art, steel beneath the burns." She waved at the radio. "Other than metal, who do you like?"

He stared down the road, and his fingers tapped out the beat of the song. "Believe it or not, I like listening to straight melody, letting the music capture the complexity of emotions people relate to. But I also enjoy the classics and jazz, even contemporary."

He flipped the channel to a New Age station and let the music play for a few minutes. Its penetrating sound laced the air with half-formed images.

"Music should paint a story all on its own," he explained. He gestured, drawing shapes in the air. "Like a landscape, it should form pictures and create memories, transport you to another place. When I play guitar, I try to write a sound describing another world, and if I'm really lucky, I can write the words that tap into the story's song. In the end, the words and the melody talk about the same thing."

"Wow, that's beautiful. Is that what you do? You write songs?"

He gave a quick jerk of his head. "Some days. Other days, like today"—he glanced at her and flashed his amazing smile—"I'm just a guy, hoping to impress a girl."

She rested her head against the seat. "Well, so far, you're doing just fine."

"Tell me about your family," he said. "Where did you grow up? You have a brother. What about sisters?"

"I don't want to talk about my past."

"Why not?"

She twisted in her seat. "Difficult childhood."

"I'm sorry."

"Don't be." She flipped the music back to the metal channel. When he challenged her, she held up a hand. "Sorry, but that New Age music puts me to sleep. Tell me about yours."

"My family couldn't be more stereotypical. Dad's a minister. Mom teaches elementary—fourth grade. I'm the youngest of five kids—twin older brothers and two older sisters born less than a year apart. They're practically twins themselves. I was the baby, three years younger than my sister. When the family wasn't babying me, my siblings would gang up on me."

"You were the baby? Somehow, I had you pegged for an older brother."

He certainly didn't have problems taking charge.

"Nope. I was the baby who Mom loved a little too much. The twins made straight As, played ball, went to college. The girls did the same—not football but volleyball. They're all married now and competing with one another on who can pop out the most grandbabies. Holidays are a circus, which Mom loves, but she worries about me."

"What happened with you?" She shifted in her seat. "How old are you?"

"Twenty-eight, and before you ask, I've never been married. Never found the right one. I told you about the tattoo but not about being the son of a minister. You might understand how the tat kind of threw Mom into a tizzy."

"Yeah, I can see that and on such a visible place, too. Was that on purpose?"

He nodded. "But what really set my parents off was when I dropped out senior year to pursue music."

"You're a high school dropout?"

He laughed. "Yeah. Think less of me now?"

He wasn't rich, not with his decade-old car. She loved that about him. There was a humbleness to him that made him endearing.

"I eventually got my GED to make peace with Mom, but I never went to college. I think my parents still hope I'll get a degree. College is an expectation in my house."

She considered his beat-up guitar case in the backseat. "Are you a street performer then? Or club player? Ever produce a record?" She poked him in the ribs, teasing. "Do you have any fans?"

He squeezed her hand. "Yeah, one or two." He gave a low chuckle. "My parents worried for years, but I think they've found peace because they know I'm doing what I love. And I'm not starving. That eases my mother's mind. They worry about other things now and pray for me regularly.

"But I'm more interested in you and your job. When did you know you wanted to be a doctor?"

After her foster father had sodomized Forest and left him bleeding in the basement, locked in there with her for three days while he went on a drunken spree...

But she couldn't tell Ash the truth. She didn't want his pity, and she wouldn't share her brother's secrets.

"I was twelve."

Forest was only a few weeks older, but he'd come into the home after she had. Small and innocent, something had broken inside him.

"Someone I cared about needed help. I was the only one around, and I didn't know what to do. I'd never felt so helpless."

"I'm sorry."

"Don't be. I swore, I'd learn how to help. I studied my ass off and made sure I got good grades."

The memory of Forest lying bruised and bleeding on that floor never left her mind. In between her own beatings and rapes, she'd found her motivation in Forest, discovered strength, and carved out a future.

Still, the scars remained. She could take or leave sex, except sex was an expected piece of any relationship. And a relationship would lead to her dream of having a family, everything that had been stolen when her parents died.

She'd moved past most of the bad memories, but, shame and trust issues remained. As did the triggers that would resurface during sex. She could please a man, had been trained extensively, but the thought of letting a man do the same to her would make her body shut down.

"You were a nerd then?" he asked.

Calling her a nerd would have made her younger self angry, but she'd gotten used to the term and no longer considered it derogatory. Besides, he had a smirk lifting the corners of his lips again, and he had curled his long fingers around her hand. *How could she be* upset *when he was freaking adorable?*

"Yeah, while you were busy being too cool for school with your tattoo and your music, I was busy being too school for cool."

Their foster father had had no choice but to send her to school or risk intervention by the agency. The walls of her high school had become a refuge. No one would touch her there. No one would beat her. Some of the boys had wanted to touch, but cold stares would warn them off.

But, every day, school would end, and she'd have to head home. She would have a few hours of freedom and time to study before her foster father returned home from work. Then, his evening entertainment would begin.

Pushing those memories back into the vault where they belonged, she turned away to stare out the window. Her eyes closed as she took in a breath. That man couldn't hurt her anymore. She and Forest had taken care of that.

"I can't believe you were a nerd." Ash brushed the back of her hand. "A girl with your looks? You were probably swamped by drooling boys."

Her cheeks pricked at his compliment. "I never dated. And the girls didn't like me."

"Probably afraid a pretty girl like you would steal their boyfriends."

"Nah, I was a total nerd." Long ago, she'd come to accept the label, which had once empowered her young self. Good grades had been her ticket to freedom. She'd embraced the label and worn it with pride.

"I tested out of senior year. Actually, we share something in common. I'm a GED-er, too. I found a university that fast-tracked me into their medical school under a six-year degree program. I completed my emergency residency last year, and the program director at Forest Skye hired me. Now, I'm doing what I love."

"Wow. Did you take any time to have fun?"

"No."

"How did you meet Asshat?"

"We're not talking about him."

"Okay." He grew silent for the next two songs, tapping out their beats on the steering wheel.

Then, out of the blue, he reached out and squeezed her leg. "Who in your life is involved with drugs?"

"My brother." The words escaped before she realized what she'd done. She cursed and turned away to look out the window again. That was Forest's secret to tell, and she'd violated his trust by blurting it out.

"Sorry, didn't mean to stir up bad memories."

"Bean's not a bad memory."

"Bean? That's an odd name."

"He doesn't like his real name. I'm probably the only one who uses it anymore." And only when Forest would piss her off. "Bean's short for beanpole. He used to be really small, and then he turned tall and gangly. I called him my little Beanpole. Now, everyone calls him Bean."

"Ah," he said with a nod. "And he has a drug problem?"

"Has, had." She waved a hand. "It's a process. He's been in and out of rehab so many times that I don't keep count any more. He's more of a self-medicator than an addict."

"A what?"

"Bean's...odd," she said. "He's socially awkward, practically inept, but he's brilliant. As in, he operates in a different stratosphere than the rest of us. He's a bona fide genius. He uses drugs to interact with normal people."

"And you stick with him?" Ash seemed to hear exactly what she'd said. Unlike Spencer, this man listened when she spoke.

"Yeah, and he sticks by me."

"What does he think of your maybe, maybe-not fiancé?"

She squinted. "Rule number two, we're not talking about Spencer."

"Rule number three, babe, no more rules. Let's sit back, relax, and let the next few days take us where they will." He flashed her a grin worthy of a rock star.

She grinned back. "Deal."

Chapter Nine

A CAREFREE ENERGY FLOWED BETWEEN SKYE AND ASH WHILE THE miles disappeared behind them.

Skye's heart thumped when their gazes caught. A touch sent her flying. His laughter loosened the tight grip she held on her emotions.

She offered to share the driving, but Ash refused to let her handle his baby. They split every expense right down the middle, except when they stopped at a secondhand store to buy Ash clothes for the trip.

Standing beside the Jeep, Skye stretched up on her tiptoes, gravel crunching beneath her feet, and threw her arms around his neck. Passion simmered between them with a growing desire for something more. As she pulled him down, the smile slipped from his lips, only to be replaced with a lusty smirk.

"Skye," he breathed out.

"Shut up, and kiss me," she said, letting her lips meet his.

The moment of contact short-circuited her brain. A low groan escaped him as he wrapped a hand around her waist, obliterating any free space between their bodies. His chest expanded with each pull of his breath. His hips molded against hers, his legs shifting to support their weight. His tongue skimmed along her upper lip—licking, tasting, and teasing. When she opened for him, he bit playfully at her lower lip.

He rocked his hips, pressing his erection against her. "Feel what you do to me? You're going to drive me crazy." His fingers traced the line of her jaw. "Stay here while I buy some clothes. And, while you're thinking about that kiss, I'd love if you'd think about what defines sex." He gave her a wink. "Because there are lots of definitions."

"Definitions?"

"Yeah, I want to know where the line is…so I can make sure I don't cross it." He shrugged. "I mean, we've already established kissing is on the table and this"—he traced the outline of her breast—"but we never settled on where I had to stop."

She bit her lower lip and held back a groan, unwilling to let him see how much he affected her. "Do we really have to talk about this now?"

"Better now than later."

When he cupped her breast, she turned, slapping away his hand. "Ash!"

"Was that a yes or a no?"

"Not here!"

He laughed. The sun glinted in his eyes, flashing a beautiful shade of green. "Still not sure if that's a yes or a no."

She crossed her arms under her breasts. How far was she willing to let things go?

With Spencer's jealous streak, she'd already crossed the line with the kissing, but this wasn't about Spencer—at least, not anymore. The only way to know if Spencer should remain in her life was to see if another future might be possible.

That wasn't really true though. She didn't need a backup man or someone found on the rebound. Skye needed to focus on her health, find happiness without a man, and maybe even reevaluate her life's goals.

But damn if Ash wasn't hot…

"Can we discuss this somewhere else?" she asked.

His arms crossed, mirroring hers, and his brows lifted. "I'm the one standing here with a hard-on and no sex stretching out ahead of me for days. I'm cool with that. But I want to know how much I can touch *you*."

His lip twitched when she didn't answer. Then, his eyes narrowed, making him look positively sinful.

He stepped close and whispered in her ear, "I want to know if I can kiss your breasts, lick your pussy, and finger you until you come." He took a step back and smiled down at her, looking entirely too pleased.

She wanted every bit of what he was offering—his lips on her nipples, maybe even his tongue down there. If he performed as well as he kissed, dear Lord, that spelled trouble.

Still, her body was what it was—broken and shattered. She could give him a blow job or even fuck him, and he would be happily satisfied. But for him to breach her defenses, draw pleasure from her body, that possibility had her stomach churning in knots.

He kissed her cheek. "Think about it while I go buy these pajamas you insist I wear."

Several minutes later, he exited with a gently used backpack stuffed full of clothes.

Soon, they were back on the interstate, heavy metal streaming through the radio. He tried several times to delve into her past, but she would steer him away from her childhood every time.

He showed great interest in her job, and she talked about that with enthusiasm. He spoke very little about what he did for a living, clamming up with the same tight-lipped silence she showed with her childhood. It wasn't a problem because they found plenty of other things to talk about, like what kinds of food to buy for the cabin.

They stopped at a local market and argued, once again, about splitting the bill.

Late that evening, long after dusk, they drove up the tree-lined dirt road to Bob's small cabin. The aroma of pine needles infiltrated the air, fresh and clean, filled with the promise of new beginnings. The moon peeked out between the trees. Bare trunks and branches stretched out into the night as the quiet of evening settled over them.

Ash parked and then handed her a flashlight from the glove box.

Skye found the key to the cabin under the mat and unlocked the door. The chill from outside followed her into the small one-room cabin. He placed their bags on the bed, and then went back to grab the groceries. The place had a country kitchen, a circular pine dinner table with two chairs, and a sitting nook filled with a love seat. Rustic end tables bracketed the love seat. A door led to a bathroom with a tiny shower enclosure. The cabin was cozy, quaint, and very cold.

"There must be a heater," Ash said after returning with the food. "I'll see if there's a switch."

"Bob likes to keep things rustic. The fireplace is our sole heat source, but he said there should be plenty of firewood lying about."

Compared to the photos Bob had shown her, the cabin was so much smaller in person—as was the bed she would be sharing with Ash.

Her phone buzzed with a text from Forest.

WTF, my summer Skye? UR crazy! Text me every 8 hrs, or I'm sending the cops! In the woods with a stranger? And you have a fiancé? Prenup! What? So confused. If I wasn't stuck on a boat in the GD Pacific, I'd throttle you.

Well, at least he still cared.

She texted a reply, letting him know she'd arrived.

Her attention moved to the bed. If they didn't get the heat sorted out, they could cuddle, and while kissing and a little petting was fine, she didn't want anything else. He'd realize how fucked in the head she really was, and she wasn't ready to watch him run from the mess which was her life.

Spencer claimed she was frigid. Her body worked fine. It was the memories an orgasm brought that would destroy any chance for intimacy.

If Ash touched her? If he tried to make her come?

Memories of her abuse surfaced. Pressing a hand to her mouth, she gagged as her stomach turned.

"Hey"—Ash returned with a load of wood—"I found something to burn."

She heard his words but couldn't process what he'd said, lost in the beginnings of a flashback.

The firewood clattered to the floor as Ash rushed to her side. "Are you all right?"

Ignoring him, she ran to the bathroom, barely making it before her stomach heaved.

Ash followed. "Skye?"

She slammed the door.

Images of her foster father leering over her while she was tied, spread-eagle, swam in her mind as she emptied the contents of her stomach. She curled into a ball, hugging her knees, while tears streamed down her cheeks. It'd been years since she had a meltdown. *Why now?*

Her clinical mind analyzed and dissected the problem from the viewpoint of a physician. What she needed was a psychiatrist, someone who could fix the messed up signals shooting to her brain. During medical school, residency, and now attending in the emergency department, she hadn't had time to see a shrink. Not to mention, there was the risk of what psychoanalysis might reveal or the secrets she needed to hide.

What a horrible beginning to her time with Ash and after such a wonderful drive, too.

She scrubbed tears off her cheeks. Her voice trembled as she responded to Ash, "I'll be out in a minute."

His palm dragged against the wood on the other side of the door, and it made her heart lurch. Even now, he was reaching out to comfort her.

Spencer had always tried a more direct approach, never realizing he forced her in the same way she'd been violated in the past. Not that it was entirely his fault. She'd never shared with him why her body would grow cold with his touch. She didn't want to share that with anyone. Unlike Ash, who gave her space, Spencer would have yanked the door open and pulled her into his arms, exactly the last place she needed to be.

"Please," she begged, "give me a minute. Start the fire." She leaned against the door, opposite of where she thought his hand might be, and closed her eyes. *Please, leave. Don't be like Spencer. Don't bully your way inside.*

His hand scraped against the wood. The floorboards creaked under his weight as he walked to the fireplace.

She stared at her reflection in the mirror above the sink. Speaking low enough that Ash couldn't overhear, she chastised herself, "Skye Summers, get it together."

She rinsed her mouth, and then she splashed cold water on her face. "You can do this." And, with those words of encouragement, she opened the bathroom door.

Ash turned at the sound of the hinges, a look of relief etched on his face. He started to come to her but stopped mid step, giving her the space she needed. A piece of her fell in love with him for that.

"It's late," he said. "I figured we'd turn in for the night."

He'd already changed into a pair of gray pajama bottoms and a black T-shirt. A fire blazed in the hearth, and all the lights had been turned off. He had the bed turned down. On one side, the comforter and sheets had been pulled back. On the other, he had placed a blanket over the comforter.

"I hope the sleeping arrangements are okay," he said. "I'll sleep on top. I don't trust myself to get under the covers with you. Better safe than sorry that way."

God, she loved the way he stared at her. He had an intensity that would steal her breath every time. Even better, he honored her wishes and had given her space.

"About that—"

"No worries. But if you're done in there..." He held up his toothbrush and toothpaste.

"Go ahead. I need to find mine."

He disappeared into the bathroom, leaving her alone. She flicked on a light to search her bag for her toiletry kit and noticed one item had been left in the Jeep. She went outside to get his guitar. All day, she'd been dying to hear him play, and before she went to sleep, she wanted a song.

She changed into pink sweats and turned the lights off. Sitting cross-legged on the bed, she balanced his guitar case over her lap.

When he exited the bathroom, she asked, "Will you play for me?"

In the flickering light of the fire, his expression was buried in shadows. Gently, he picked the case up and set it on the small table in the kitchen. He turned and breathed out a long, deep sigh. "Not tonight. I'm pretty beat."

The clock on the wall showed a few minutes past midnight. *Had she scared him off with that little freak-out?* Maybe he felt trapped with a crazy woman in a cabin in the woods.

She tried not to let her disappointment show, projecting as much cheer into her voice as possible. "Maybe you can play something in the morning while I make breakfast?"

His lips thinned, nearly curved at the corners, but failed to find his signature smile. "Sure, babe. That sounds great. I'm just tired from the drive, and my head hurts."

She jumped up. "Are you okay?"

Spencer had punched him, and Ash could have a concussion. Her fingers itched to shine a light in his eyes and examine his pupils, but she refrained. Like he'd said, he was probably fatigued from the drive.

Ash put a hand to his temple. "I took some Tylenol, but if you don't mind, I'd like to call it a night."

Her eyes followed each languid step of his as he moved in front of the fire. He poked the logs to the back, added a few more, and put the fire screen in place.

"That should keep us warm until morning." He moved to the bed and stretched out his long form on top of the comforter, pulling the extra blanket over, but his toes poked out at the end.

"Your feet are going to get cold." A quick search of the cabin, and she found another blanket. After laying it on top of him, she crawled under the covers. "Do you feel okay?"

His eyes pinched with pain. "It's only a headache."

He lifted up, leaned over, and pressed his lips against her brow. The velvety-soft touch skimmed across her skin, searing her with his kiss.

"Good night, babe."

She gripped his shoulder. "Good night, Ash."

Flickering firelight cast shadows over the ceiling as she clutched the blankets around her neck. All concerns over whether Ash would adhere to his promise settled within moments as he turned his back toward her and faced away. She listened to his breathing, waiting for him to fall asleep.

Thirty minutes later, the telltale glow of a cell phone lit up his side of the bed.

"Ash," she whispered, "are you awake?"

He rolled over. "Yeah, can't sleep. Sorry, did I keep you up?"

"Is it your headache?"

"No. I've got a song brewing in my head."

"Oh."

He lifted the phone. "I'm trying to get it down, so I don't forget it."

She sat up. "You won't bother me if you want to work on it. I'm not sleepy."

He glanced at her, eyes narrowing. "Earlier, when you...was it me? Did I do something?"

"What do you mean?"

"I don't know. When you were in the bathroom, it felt like I'd done something wrong."

"You're going to hate this, but it's—"

He threw his head back and laughed, interrupting her. "Let me guess. It's complicated?" His signature smile made a triumphant return.

She put a hand on his arm to reassure him. "You're getting to know me too well."

He rolled out of bed. "If you don't mind, I'd like to work this melody out. When I get a song in my head, I can get crazy if I don't write it down. Will it bother you? I'll be quiet."

"I'd love to hear you play." She'd never known a composer before. It'd be cool to listen to a song come to life.

"This isn't so much...playing. It's more messing around with what's trying to get out of my head."

Her belly churned with excitement. She pulled out her cell phone. "I'll read. You won't even know I'm here." She made a shooing motion. "Go. Create. Make music."

Ash bit at his lower lip, looking a bit uneasy, almost shy about it.

Maybe he wasn't that good, and having her watch made him self-conscious. The problem with a one-room cabin in the woods was the definite lack of privacy. Nothing she could do about that. If Ash had issues with others listening to his music, he needed to get a new career.

She turned her cell phone on and thumbed to the beginning of a new book. Out of the corner of her eye, she peeked at him pulling his guitar out of the case.

He gave a wink. "She's not as scary as she looks."

"She?"

"My baby."

"I thought your Jeep was your baby."

He held up the guitar. "This is my baby. I've had her since I was fourteen."

His fingers pressed down on the neck, and his thumb strummed out a tune. The cabin filled with a glorious full-bodied sound. His eyes closed as he picked out a series of notes.

Her jaw dropped. Ash was better than good. Damn amazing was more like it.

She forgot all about her book as he warmed up. He picked out notes and melodies and fingered chords from famous metal bands, but never played an entire song.

He merged with the guitar, the two of them becoming one unified being.

Watching him play transported her to a different world. She had never heard anything so majestic.

Ash was sex and power, all wrapped up in one glorious package, but with that guitar wrapped in his hands, he became a force of beauty. He made her head spin and other parts of her throb.

At some point, the warm-up stopped. Familiar notes and melodies of rock bands ended as new sounds emerged. A gasp escaped her lips. This was all him, and it was brilliant.

His creation developed in stages as he shaped the notes into being, each iteration morphing them into something wonderful. Notes coalesced into melodies as she listened. Chords bridged complexities, becoming a landscape of power, drawing images from her mind.

Wasn't this what he'd described during their drive?

She closed her eyes, allowing the sound to wash over her, delving into the crevices of her mind, carrying her to an alternate plane. Dancing in a different world, where anything was possible, she existed in a reality where love took root in her heart, blossomed, and transformed her into something stronger, prouder, indestructible.

It was insane.

It was creative brilliance.

He made her feel like she had the ability to take on the world, and she soared in the grip of a love so intense that nothing could touch her. Nothing could hurt her. She was safe and cherished in the arms of her chosen love.

Forever safe.

His music carried her into a dreamscape of hope and empowerment where Ash's voice lifted in song.

Chapter Ten

SKYE RUBBED AWAY THE SLEEP CRUSTING HER EYES. SHE ROLLED OVER and into the heavy weight of Ash filling the bed beside her. She must have drifted off while he played, as she had no memory of him coming to bed. He lay on his side, facing her. True to his word, he'd slept on top of the covers with the extra blankets pulled up for warmth. A moment's pause had her marveling at how the rough edges of his face softened in sleep. She slipped out of bed, trying not to wake him.

Now, what to do with him over the next few days?

Her plans had originally included a spelunking trip, hang-gliding lessons, and a helicopter flight with Spencer. Her agreement with Ash had them splitting expenses, but she worried about her plans. They were all incredibly expensive. *Maybe she should ask Ash if he wanted to go before canceling the activities?* But she didn't want to cause him any embarrassment. At least hiking in the woods was free.

She dressed quickly and put a log on the remains of the fire from last night. The coals were still warm, and it didn't take long to rekindle the blaze.

Then, she turned to the small kitchen, excited to cook, and pulled out the carton of eggs.

Several minutes later, Ash stretched in bed, groaning. "Babe, whatever you're cooking, I'm in love with it. Goddamn, that smells good."

The underlying richness of his voice rolled over her, stroking a primal core. The man had been born to seduce, and her body shuddered as she thought about just that.

"Thanks."

Eggs, bacon, sausage, nothing special, but the compliment was appreciated.

A minister's son who swore like a sailor and had an inked dragon on his neck, Ash was a clash of contradictions driving her mad.

Standing, his tall form dominated the small room, even more so when he stretched. The black T-shirt pulled tight across the muscles of his chest, and the gray pajama pants hung precariously low on his hips. The V-line of his abdomen angled down, disappearing beneath the elastic waistband, drawing her eyes to his prominent bulge.

She pressed her tongue to the roof of her mouth as her eyes followed every twist and turn of his muscular body.

"Babe, you're staring again." His eyes twinkled with mischief.

Heat bloomed in her cheeks. She turned her back to him and pushed eggs around the skillet.

He came to stand behind her, wrapping his arms around her waist. Nuzzling her neck, he whispered in her ear, "It's okay. I like looking at you, too." His palm flattened against her belly, his thumb lifting to stroke the swell of her breast. "Good morning, gorgeous."

"Good morning."

He spun her, forcing her to face him, and then cupped her ass in his hands. With a yank, he pulled their hips together. The man had no shame and didn't even try to hide his erection. His pupils dilated, swallowing flecks of gold on a field of verdant green. The anticipation of a kiss hung in the air, and she lifted her gaze to the swell of his lips. She licked hers in preparation.

His gaze lowered, watching. "First order of business…" His cocky grin made an entrance.

Someone sucked all the air out of the room because she could barely breathe—or maybe that was because Ash was nipping at her lower lip. He ran his fingers in her hair, guiding her head, while she slipped her arms around his waist. Holding on tight, she fell into the bliss of his good-morning kiss.

A hunger stirred in her belly, working its way to her heart, and traveled up to her head where her mind worked on the enigma that was this man.

How was it that her body was responding to him?

He held her tight, kissing and nibbling, sucking and biting at her lips.

Ash ignited something indescribable, both exciting and terrifying.

She parted her lips, inviting him in, and he delved inside, his tongue tangling with hers. He tasted rich, sinful, and decadent. Her insides melted with the heat he stoked in her core, warming with the rush of arousal. She moaned, needing more.

He deepened his kiss, overpowering her with his desire, and then he lifted her off her feet. As she wrapped her legs around his waist, his erection grew between them. It was impossible not to press against it. Heat blossomed between her legs, wetness dampening her panties. She wanted to feel his skin, so she pulled on the fabric of his shirt.

In his arms, she became an emotional disaster, a landslide moving toward sex, impossible to stop.

"Ash…" Her voice was uncharacteristically raw.

He effortlessly held her as he carried her across the room. Then, he tossed her down onto the bed, staring at her with labored, harsh breathing.

The fabric of his T-shirt stretched across his chest, and poking out of the elastic rim of his pajamas, the cut crown of his penis revealed itself to her eyes. Big, red, engorged, and glorious. Her mouth watered, anxious to taste him. She gazed at the object of her desire, her mouth opening, and she reached for the elastic, needing to give him a release, knowing he desired her touch.

"Ash," she said, her voice rough with desire. This, she could give.

His eyes followed her hand, and his breath caught. His hand whipped out, wrapping around her wrist, as her fingers brushed the head of his glans.

"Oh, shit. Skye…" He stumbled backward, yanking the waistband over his exposed cock. His eyes grew wide and cut to the door.

"It's okay. I want this," Skye said, reaching for him.

He moved away, his face darkening. "I can't be in here." His jaw clenched, and he tore himself away.

As he opened the door, a puff of cold air blew into the cabin, and then he stormed outside, slamming the door shut behind him.

She sat on the bed, her heart hammering, her hand still outstretched. Palpitations filled her chest as the smell of burned bacon filled the air.

"Ah, crap." She leaped off the bed and ran to the stove where she managed to salvage the eggs and sausage. The bacon was ruined.

She peered out the small window.

Ash stomped around his Jeep, kicking the tires and pounding on the hood. Every few minutes, he would start to come back inside, and then he would turn away and stalk off. His breath misted in the freezing morning air.

How long was he going to stay outside in nothing more than a T-shirt and thin pajama pants?

She placed the rescued breakfast on two plates and set them on the table. Then, she headed outside with a blanket clutched in her arms. The cold air snapped against her skin, bringing a shiver to her spine, and goose bumps lifted on her arms.

Fists clenched, he turned his back to her.

She held out the blanket. "Come inside."

He ran his fingers through the dark strands of his hair. "I didn't mean for that to get out of hand." He gestured to the cabin. "I gave my word and broke it the first chance I got."

His arm dropped, and his palm slapped against his thigh. "I want you to feel safe and trust me to keep my word." He tilted his face to the morning sun. "I don't want to ruin this." He shivered and wrapped his arms around himself, his breath puffing into the air. "Sorry I left, but I had to get out of there before I broke all the rules."

Cautiously, she took a step. "It's freezing. Come back inside, and eat breakfast before it gets cold."

He turned haunted eyes on her. "That won't happen again."

She wrapped the blanket around him. "We got carried away, and it wasn't your fault." Hell, she'd been the one reaching for his cock. With a shove, she propelled him toward the door. "We'll be more careful." Although how that was to happen, she didn't have a clue.

They managed to make it back inside, and she got him to settle at the table.

He dropped the blanket on the floor and reached across to touch her hand. "Are we okay?"

"We're okay." She pointed to his food. "Now, eat before it gets too cold."

He scraped a forkful of eggs and took a tentative bite. His eyes shut. "Fuck, this is amazing." He shoveled more into his mouth and then looked to the stove. "Is there more?"

His exuberance for her cooking eased the tension swirling between them.

Ash emptied his plate in five bites and then filled his plate with what was left in the skillet. He polished off the remaining eggs and even stole her sausage.

Although nearly ruined, breakfast was perfect, and they were laughing again by the end of the meal.

"Since you cooked, I'll clean," he offered, standing to collect their dishes.

The clatter of dishes filled the small cabin while he set to cleaning up breakfast. When he finished, he sat across from her, gathering her hands in his. His brows bunched together. "You have no idea what it's like to be around you. To be with someone who sees the real me and not Bla—well, I'm just trying to say, I'm not willing to screw this up."

His words made more sense than he knew. They were relative strangers, and in not knowing all the details of each other's lives, they had an unusual freedom to relax and let down their walls. She didn't know what the real her was like, but she found Ash entrancing.

He huffed a laugh. "It's been a long time since I've been around someone who's not judging me all the time or wanting me to give them something."

Judge? Maybe, as a struggling artist, things were difficult for him, and except for his company, she didn't need anything he might have to give.

"Maybe we could loosen the restrictions up a bit?" she said.

"Don't tempt me. Don't even go there."

She crossed her arms over her chest. "You're seriously not even going to listen to what I was going to offer?"

He shook his head. "I know exactly what you were going to say."

She scrunched her face. "No, you don't."

"Babe, you were licking your lips, staring at my cock. Trust me, I know. But I also know myself entirely too well. There are some limits, once I cross, I can't uncross. And, if your lips wrap around my cock, I'll fuck your brains out. That's the honest truth."

"That's pretty blunt."

He winked. "Was I right?"

She nodded. "Can't say I've ever known a man to turn down a blow job. That doesn't make sense."

"Because it wouldn't stop at a blow job. I'm not here to get in your pants. Not that I don't want to, but I want the bigger prize. So, how about we switch topics? Tell me what the plan is for the day."

Should she mention her plans? "What prize?"

He huffed a laugh. "Well, for one, I want to get to know you better. I connect with you in a way I never have with anyone else before. If all I wanted was sex without strings or a blow job, I could get that from any chick. It would feel great in the moment, but that's where it would end—and it would end. I don't want to ruin this." He gestured between them. "And I don't think I want this to end."

"What if I've changed my mind?"

His eyes twinkled. "We're not changing the terms of our agreement."

"Then, we probably shouldn't hang out at the cabin all day," she said. "Too much temptation."

"Before I tagged along, what did you have planned?"

"A few things." Couples activities with Spencer, which she didn't want to do with Ash. The one thing she hadn't planned were several hikes because Spencer hated walking in the woods. "How about hunting waterfalls?" She hoped he wouldn't think it was lame.

"What the hell does that mean?"

"Hiking. We go in search of waterfalls."

His brilliant eyes brightened. "I love hiking. I don't get to do much of it anymore. Sounds fucking badass."

"Good. There are some great trails."

"For us to hunt waterfalls?"

She grinned. "Yeah. Those wild, woolly, and elusive waterfalls. You have to sneak up on them, especially this time of year. If you want to see a great waterfall, we could go to Falling Springs."

"Doesn't sound like you have to hunt that one. Let's make it more interesting. Go on a search for small ones no one else has looked for?"

Sounded wonderful, and his enthusiasm was encouraging.

"Great, let me find some hikes."

As she settled into the small chair, she pulled out her phone to text Forest. Ash hummed as he poked the embers of the fire. Every now and then, he would sing a few words, and she thought she heard something about hunting waterfalls.

A peaceful haze settled over her as she dutifully checked in with Forest.

Still alive. Didn't get murdered. Going on a hike. Will keep the phone on, so you can cyberstalk me. XOXO.

"I'm going to take a shower," she announced. "You need in the bathroom?"

"Nah, I'm good. Just don't use up all the hot water. I know how you girls can be."

Rolling her eyes, she fished out what she would need from her bags while he sang about insanity. She recognized the tune from the night before.

Maybe she was insane. Locked in a cabin, in the woods, with a magnetic man who could light a dangerous fire. Was this just testing the waters, or was it the first step on the road to a psychotic break? She didn't know—not yet, at least. And the first step to finding that answer would begin with the forest trail.

Chapter Eleven

SKYE AND ASH SPENT THE DAY HIKING IN THE PINES, FOLLOWING national forest trails as they searched for Skye's elusive waterfalls. They found three—two dried up and one frozen for the winter. The frozen one sported huge icicles, which sparkled in the sunlight, creating a dazzling display. The sun climbed high, banishing the clouds, and brought warmth to the day.

A dense carpet of pine needles covered the forest floor and cushioned the ground beneath their boots. They hiked in silence with only the whisper of the wind, the scratching of squirrels scampering through the foliage, and the twittering of birds to fill the quiet.

Ash helped her scramble over the rocks, taking every opportunity to hold her hand. He hummed melodies. His mind seemed to be constantly fixated on the beauty of music. His brilliant smile lit up the gloomier parts of the trail, and the eagerness of his step pulled her forward, around the next bend, and up the steep slopes.

When they failed to find more than damp rocks during their waterfall search, he pulled her to him, fluttering light kisses all over her face. His lips banished the chill, but he broke off the kiss long before she was ready.

He scampered across the base of the last waterfall, the rocks glistening with seeping water. "I suppose it's more difficult to hunt waterfalls than I thought." He balanced on the slippery rocks, despite her insistence for him to be careful. "Who knew waterfalls could hide?"

"Sleeping maybe," she said with a smile.

"Let's do something different," he offered. "Since these fabled waterfalls seem to have been scared into hiding, let's get out of here." He winked.

"They're not hiding."

He pointed to the damp rock. "Okay, sleeping. How about we grab lunch? I remember passing a greasy spoon on our way to the cabin."

She'd packed granola bars and nuts into her backpack, intending on a light lunch on the trail, but at the mention of diner food, her stomach grumbled. "Greasy diner sounds perfect."

On the way to his Jeep, Ash would chase her on the flat parts, claiming a kiss each time she allowed him to catch her. She'd laugh while he chased, and then she'd become speechless under the press of his demanding kisses. Everything about Ash brought a smile to her face and had her heart racing.

Before long, they arrived at the trailhead, and a short drive brought them to Chuck's Bar and Grill.

Ash had on those wretched mirrored sunglasses again. His eyes were too beautiful to keep covered, and she missed the smoldering of his gaze when he looked at her.

"Can you take those glasses off?" She tried snatching the frames from his face, but he jerked out of reach.

"My headache's back, and the light is bothering my eyes."

He'd complained about a headache before.

She had pain relievers in her bag. "Do you need to take anything?"

"I'll be fine," he said with a wave of his hand. "But maybe no more hiking for the day?"

The waitress came and took their orders, placing water on the table. Skye asked for a cheeseburger with bacon, hold the fries. Ash ordered the same burger, asking for her fries to be placed on his plate.

He patted his stomach. "I'm starving from all that hunting."

The waitress gave an odd look and then left them alone.

Skye rolled her glass between her hands. "If hiking is out, what do you want to do?"

His brows lifted above his sunglasses. "I saw an ad for a helicopter tour."

She'd seen the same ad and canceled her reservations for the following day, thinking it would be too expensive for a struggling musician to manage. Her lips twisted. "I'm not so sure about that."

The waitress returned with their meals, her gazing lingering a little too long on Ash. Skye couldn't blame her. He was a hard man not to stare at.

"Oh, come on. It'll be fun." He pulled out a flyer she hadn't seen him pick up. "They have flights in the afternoon. I'm sure they're not busy this time of year. Let's call and see."

"Do you know how much that costs?" Damn, she wished she could see his eyes. It was too hard to read him with those glasses hiding his expression.

"You only live once. Come on. I'm trying to win you over here."

"But—"

"It's my treat."

"No. We're splitting everything down the middle."

"Exactly." He took a sip of his drink. "Everything but this." Tilting his head down, those magnetic eyes peeked over the rim of his glasses. "You know, I've had enough of this splitting-things-down-the-middle crap. I'm taking you out like you deserve, and I'm paying, exactly like a guy should when he takes a girl on a date. Kick and scream. Make a scene. Do what you need to, Skye, but my mind's made up."

"Your mind's made up?" She couldn't keep herself from smiling.

He looked adorable, trying to take control, and while she admitted it was sexy, he didn't know her very well. She always paid her way.

He nodded and put words to the melody he'd been humming all day, keeping his voice low. She leaned forward to catch his song.

I was confused,
Lost in nothing but my mind,
Trapped and silent within the crowd,
Until you found me.

Insanity,
It was meant to be.

My heart broken,
My soul aflame,
Until I found you.

I'm where I belong.
Light and sound,
All around.

Stuck where nothing is real,
Blackness swallowing me within the crowd,
Until you found me.

Insanity,
It was meant to be.

HER STOMACH DROPPED AS THE LIQUID TONES OF HIS VOICE DIPPED into her soul, carved out a pocket, and took root. The magic of his words transported her to another place, and she wasn't the only one affected. The other diners stopped eating and stared.

She'd never been sung to, and she didn't know how to react, not when he held her spellbound and wanting more.

"Ash," she breathed out, blinking and shaking her head, unable to form a coherent thought. "Where's that song from?"

"That's the one I was working on last night," he said with a self-satisfied grin, "for you. Did you like it?"

"Like it? It was…beyond words."

He tapped the screen of his cell phone. "I think it's going to be a hit."

Every musician hoped for a hit. *Who knew? Maybe this would be his.*

Unfolding a bill from a roll of cash, he slapped a twenty on the table.

She hadn't seen him use anything but cash. *Who didn't use plastic these days? Maybe he didn't own a credit card.*

"We're splitting the check."

The words of his song rattled around in her head, still surging in her heart, lodging deep inside and stirring up warmth.

He smirked. "Not anymore." He grabbed her wrist. "Come, let's see about that flight."

He pulled her from the booth and dragged her outside.

~

IN LESS THAN AN HOUR, SHE FOUND HERSELF STRAPPED INSIDE A helicopter, holding hands with a grinning fool who had paid way too much for the one-hour flight—except the flight they were taking was nothing like the advertisement on the brochure.

Instead of flying over the lakes of the Blue Ridge Mountains, the pilot skimmed the valleys and ravines. They found their waterfalls, tumbling sprays that no hiking paths would have ever reached. Water spilled down steep gorges and impossible canyons, casting brilliant rainbows in the fading afternoon light.

She leaned into Ash and hugged the hard muscles of his arm. She would have done more, but the seat harness only allowed so much movement.

The pilot kept flying long past the scheduled hour. After the waterfalls, their aerial guide took them down twisting canyons and over narrow waterways that stole her breath.

He dipped and soared, performing wild maneuvers that had her stomach flipping. Each new turn would bring a squeal of delight. This was all Ash; she was certain. Aerobatics were definitely not a part of the standard package.

And it worked like magic—until the sky began to darken with stormy looking clouds.

"Sir," the pilot spoke through the headsets, "a storm is coming. We have to cut it short."

Cut it short? How long had Ash booked the helicopter? The sun was almost ready to set.

Oh, a sunset.

Damn, he was a romantic.

"I understand." Ash's voice crackled through the headphones.

The pilot turned the helicopter around, and they landed as the first snowflakes drifted down. The weather report hadn't mentioned snow.

What would it be like to be snowed into a cabin with Ash? Maybe she'd get a chance to find out.

The pilot helped her out, taking her headset and hanging it on a hook over her seat. "Sorry about cutting it short."

"No problem." Her grin stretched the muscles of her cheeks. "That was spectacular."

Ash hopped out, disentangling himself from his headset and laying it on the seat.

"My buddies aren't going to believe this," the pilot said.

Ash gave a quick jerk of his head, and the pilot clamped his mouth shut.

"Thank you," she said. "But you've officially ruined roller-coaster rides for life."

The pilot puffed his chest out. "Glad you had a good time, miss."

Skye gave Ash a peck on the lips. "Thank you, too."

He wrapped his hands around her waist. "Mmm, you're welcome." His fingers brushed the top of her ass. "We should probably get back to the cabin."

"Cabin?" asked the pilot. "You're not staying in the mountains, are you?"

"Yeah," Skye said. She briefly told him where Bob's cabin was located.

The pilot shook his head. "Snow's already falling. By the time you drive up there, the road's going to be closed. You're stuck down here for the night, maybe longer."

She turned to Ash. "What are we going to do?"

Ash's lips pinched together. "This certainly complicates things."

No kidding.

"How adventurous do you feel?" He had the strangest look on his face.

"Why?"

"How about hunting the mother of all waterfalls?"

The fading light glinted in his eyes. As he stretched, the spiderweb tattoo flexed on his neck, making the dragon seem like it was about to take flight. Devastatingly handsome didn't even begin to describe this man.

"Mother of all waterfalls?"

He shrugged. "We can't go back to the cabin, but I still have two more days with you. Let's head north. I've never seen Niagara Falls."

She fisted her hands and settled them on her hips. "You want to drive to Niagara?"

He pointed to the pilot. "I want to fly."

The pilot looked to the sky. "We would have to take off within the hour."

They were crazy.

"And what about the storm?"

The pilot waved a hand. "Not a problem for the jet. I need to file a flight plan before we leave and get the jet fueled."

She tugged on Ash's coat sleeve and pulled him over to speak in private. "And how exactly are we going to pay for this?"

His smirk returned in full force. "Wooing going on, babe. You let me worry about that." His mouth dropped to her ear, and the song tumbled from his lips.

Insanity,
It was meant to be.

HE KISSED HER EAR AND THEN STRAIGHTENED. "TAKE A CHANCE. Let's hunt this waterfall. Same conditions as before. Nothing changes. What do you have to lose?"

Her sanity.

Ash shared a degree of impulsiveness with Forest. She was always the practical one. Forest took risks and did crazy things. Renting a plane would be right up his alley.

"You want to charter a plane?"

He gathered her hair and swept it to the side. "Don't worry about the money. Let's live a little. Imagine Niagara Falls in December. How cool is that?"

"Sounds pretty damn cold."

"We'll buy scarves."

She punched him. "You'll buy a hat."

"Then, it's settled." He waved to the pilot. "She said yes!"

"Great." The pilot pointed to the hangar. "There's a lounge where you can wait. I'll get the jet ready and file the flight plan." He lifted his phone. "My copilot's already on the way."

"Awesome," Ash said.

"What about our stuff? We only have your guitar and a few granola bars."

"Only thing I care about is my guitar. The rest we can buy when we get there."

She bit her lower lip. The practical decision was to say no and stay in a hotel until they could drive back to the cabin. But she'd locked that half of herself inside her brownstone. This trip was about taking risks and finding answers to her future.

What would Forest think of this change in plans?

The thing she loved most about Ash was his carefree approach to life. He flowed around decisions. He didn't ponder each step, like she did. She envied him for that freedom, and his enthusiasm was infectious. He made her feel like she could conquer anything, but she still worried.

"Why do you look so glum?" Ash spun her in a circle. "We're going to hunt the great white whale of waterfalls! Put a smile on your face." His laughter surged around her as he danced in a circle, holding her aloft.

He set her on her feet and then held her hand as he sprinted after the pilot toward the warmth of the hangar.

"Come on, our adventure awaits."

Chapter Twelve

SKYE SOARED WITH ASH SOMEWHERE ABOVE THE EASTERN SEABOARD, flying toward the northern border of the United States.

Ash reclined in the leather seat opposite her, his face scrunched in concentration, his fingers flying over the keypad of his phone. He bit at his lower lip as he typed, and when his eyes pinched together, a deep groove would appear between his brows. His attention never wavered from the screen, and hers never moved from his face.

Silence filled the cabin, wrapping around them in a comforting embrace. This easy peace was a natural thing flowing between them, but beneath the quiet, tension swirled.

"A penny for your thoughts?" His voice bathed her in its multitoned notes. He peeked up from his phone, catching her staring at him…again.

With a jerk of her chin, she indicated the closed cockpit door. "They're giving us privacy."

His smirk returned. "Yeah, maybe next time, we'll take advantage of it." Oh, the promise of sex was ever on his breath.

"What are you working on?"

"I wanted to get that song down before I forgot it." He leaned back. "It's getting late. You hungry?"

It was almost nine, and they hadn't eaten since Chuck's Bar and Grill.

"I still have those granola bars." Although that didn't sound appetizing.

He arched a brow. "They have food on these things—and alcohol. You want a drink?" At her nod, he unbuckled. "Come on. Let's raid the cupboards."

The next ten minutes netted them various fruits and cheeses, caviar, a selection of sliced meat, and a well-stocked bar of wine, beer, and scotch worthy of the rich and famous. She went for wine while he settled on soda.

Ash pulled out a tray of chocolate strawberries from somewhere, and her mouth watered.

"Where did you find those?"

"You missed the dessert fridge," he said.

She grabbed a strawberry and popped it into her mouth. "Yum."

As she enjoyed the decadence of the sweet berry chocolate at twenty-five thousand feet, his body language shifted—a subtle alteration, but there nonetheless. He chewed at his lower lip. He started to ask a question, stopped, pulled at his earlobe, and then rubbed the back of his neck. Strange gestures she hadn't noticed before.

There it was again, him nibbling at his lower lip.

"Is something wrong?"

"Something's been bugging me, and I'm not sure how to bring it up."

"Ask me anything."

He yanked on his ear. "I'm not sure I should."

"Is it about Spencer?"

She hadn't thought about Spencer all day. Ash was too much fun. *How could she ever go back to Spencer, knowing a man like Ash might be waiting for her?* Giving back the ring appealed to her more and more.

Settling—that was what she'd been doing with Spencer. *And didn't she deserve so much more?*

The past had taken her parents and destroyed her chance to grow up in a loving home. Perhaps she'd been too focused on taking back the past. It was time to give back the ring and pave a new future.

"Well, yeah, I guess we should talk about him," Ash said.

She bit her lower lip, hesitant. "But that's not what you wanted to ask, is it?"

He shook his head. "Not really."

"Then, what?"

"Do you *really* not know who I am?" He kicked his ankle across his knee and leaned his elbow on the armrest.

He'd placed particular emphasis on the word *really*, which made her neck itch. *Why would he think she should know him?*

His finger traced the cut Spencer had put under his eye. The split in his lip was almost healed. Even now, the ghost of Spencer invaded their privacy.

She gave a shrug. "Should I?"

His expression pinched, and he shook his head. "It's just…well, it's been a long time since I've met someone who didn't."

"Okay, now, you're worrying me. Are you a criminal or something?" She smiled, feeling awkward about teasing him because his brows shot up at that comment. Leaning forward, she placed a hand on his knee. Her expression softened. "Did you go to my high school or something? You're not Ash Hoorelbeck, the guy with the braces and headgear from shop class who used to shoot spit-wads at me? 'Cause, if you are, you've really changed…"   .

He laughed. "No. But I'm ready to kick that guy's ass."

She smiled. "So, are you a drug dealer?"

His eyebrows shot up again.

"Criminal? Stalker? What?" She poked her finger at him, confused. "What does it matter? You chased me. You kissed me. If you've forgotten, I was the one running from you. And you're the one who stalked me the next day, buying all those hot cocoas. Who does that?"

He shrugged. "Me, evidently."

"Well, you bullied me into bringing you on this trip," she teased.

He shook his head. "I wouldn't use *bully*, but yeah, I was persistent." His fingers unlocked his cell phone, swiped, and tapped the screen. He handed it to her. "Tell me if this looks familiar."

The sigil of a band filled the screen. It was a guitar with fiery wings, and to the side, a grouping of the band was barely discernible, their bodies cast in shadows but with spotlights hitting their faces.

Humoring him, she squinted. They did look familiar. Right—the coffee shop, laughing and lounging. Their names were scrawled at the bottom of the screen—*Blaze, Bash, Bent, Spike, and Noodles.*

Nervousness simmered in his emerald gaze, and his breath pulsed in and out.

Why did panic line the edges of his eyes?

Her finger glided over the faces of the men of Angel Fire.

Luminous green eyes stared out of the screen. Their front man, the embattled lead singer named Blaze.

Holy shit!

Her gaze skipped to the guitar stowed in the seat beside them. *His baby. His songwriting and that voice?*

A flutter tickled her stomach. Maybe she needed to pay more attention when Forest droned on about his favorite bands.

This changed everything.

"Why didn't you say something?"

His fingers pressed against his forehead. "When you picked out that T-shirt, I thought you were teasing. But then you acted so clueless about who I was. It wasn't until you paid for the shirt that I thought maybe you really didn't know. Do you know how long it's been since I've been around anyone who's treated me like a regular guy? Women don't act like that around me."

"I had no idea." She shook her head, stunned by the revelation.

Examining the screen, she compared the man sitting in front of her to the rock star named Blaze. There was no denying the truth, but the name didn't fit the man she'd come to know. She handed back the cell phone and pressed a hand to quell the queasiness brewing in her belly.

"You're Blaze then?"

He nodded. "In the flesh."

"Guess I'm one of the top ten clueless people in the world."

Forest was going to have a good laugh over this.

All the signs had been there. The sunglasses and ball cap obsession made sense. While obnoxious, Ash had been using them as a disguise. His use of cash instead of credit fit, too. Had he been avoiding leaving a trail for the paparazzi to follow? At least she understood his guitar obsession and songwriting.

And, while she couldn't believe she'd missed it, she wasn't a total idiot. Ash's voice—Blaze's voice—sounded different in person than

122 • ELLIE MASTERS

it did in the band's songs, probably because he didn't have the rest of the band backing him up. Blaze was a rock legend, which meant Ash was no starving musician.

She didn't know how these things worked. What was the proper etiquette for traveling with a rock star?

And then she laughed. If you were one clueless Skye Summers, it meant splitting all costs straight down the middle.

Frankly, she didn't care. His money meant nothing, as she had more than she had ever wanted or would ever need.

And his fame only strengthened what she'd already accepted in her heart.

There was no confusion as to their future. He was a distraction, and it seemed that she was the same for him. Eventually, real life would catch up to them. She had a career in medicine, and the music industry would demand the return of their golden child. There was only one direction for their relationship to go, even if she desired more.

It was probably for the best that she had taken sex out of the equation.

She was content to live the fantasy as it played out, only soured a little now with the knowledge that there was no future between them.

He shifted in his seat.

"So, if you're Angel Fire's front man, why were we buying clothes at a thrift store? Too cheap for Walmart? Target?"

A smile crept across his face, and his shoulders relaxed. Some of the tension in the cabin disappeared. "It was next to the gas station, and no one was in it."

"Maintaining a low profile?" She clucked her tongue. "Explains the ugly glasses. You have no idea how much I hate those things."

"You and me both." He reached over and grabbed her hands. "You really didn't know?"

"Nope." Her lips popped crisply on the P.

"When we were driving to the mountains, you kept talking about Angel Fire and the way I sing. I about lost it." His thumbs stroked the backs of her hands.

She tried to remember what she'd said exactly, something about a sinful voice. And here came the flush that would color her cheeks a deep crimson. How was she going to live this down?

"Well, to be honest, my brother's a huge fan. I was spouting off stuff he would say to keep the conversation flowing. I was nervous to be alone with you." She couldn't help the corny line spilling from her lips. "Guess I'm just not that into you."

"Bullshit!" He leaped out of his seat and knelt before her. Gently, he cupped her cheeks. "You're very much into me."

"I'm into Ash. Not sure about Blaze," she teased.

His dark hair hung down over his face, shading the verdant green of his eyes. A fire burned there. He was going to kiss her, too, and if that happened…well, her eyes flicked to the closed door between them and the cockpit.

He breathed out. "Just one kiss, babe." His infectious grin was back. He leaned his forehead to rest against hers. "Am I crazy, or do you feel this, too?"

"I don't know what to feel. I was engaged a couple of days ago." She tried to pull away, but Ash wouldn't let her go.

A breath pulsed out of her lungs and into him. His shoulders lifted as he inhaled.

"I've been on the road since I was seventeen, over a decade now. I've never had a normal girlfriend. You have no idea—"

"Oh, there's nothing remotely normal about me."

Their faces remained kissably close, their foreheads still pressed together.

"I don't want to ruin this," he said, "but, damn it, Skye. I don't want to lose you. I know you're not a believer, but fate brought us together for a reason."

His lips brushed against hers, and an answering desire stirred within her core. Once again, he incited a reaction. *But what would happen if he tried for more than a simple kiss? She was damaged beyond repair, her body's responses not hers to control. She wished things might be different with him, but didn't dare to hope.*

The captivating glide of his lips demanded a response. She felt all of him, overwhelmed by the sensations he pulled from her troublesome body. She should be terrified, but she found herself swept away.

Beneath her excitement, fear lurked, a small niggling piece of doubt. Falling for Ash would add more complexity into a life full of difficulty. Rushing into something more wasn't smart.

Ash wasn't a starving artist. He was a rock star!

Instead of thinking about all the reasons she should keep her distance, she focused on his fingers digging into her arm and those twined in her hair. The heavy rasp of his breathing mirrored her soft sighs. They connected on a level where souls melded, and while that terrified her, she couldn't stop her reckless rush toward to him.

And, as her heart rate accelerated, he deepened the kiss with a growl, pressing against her, as if he would lose her if he let her go. He licked and stroked and pushed his tongue deep, possessing her like a man on a mission.

Then, he pushed the seat back flat and crawled over her, staring down with need. She wrapped her arms around his neck and pulled him down. Her fingers dug into his scalp as he stole her very breath with another mind-bending, heart-melting kiss.

His breathing changed, and his weight shifted. He grabbed her wrists, disentangling her fingers from his hair to pin her hands above her head. "Fuck, you drive me insane."

Each time he ground his hips, a smoldering heat would flare between her legs. Adrenaline surged in her blood, pouring through her body, accelerating both her heart and the pace of her breaths.

While a flood of endorphins pumped in her veins, her body betrayed her with a familiar prickling sensation. She fought for air as the weight of childhood memories bore down with glacial surety.

Ash nibbled on the soft tissue of her neck. One hand on her wrists, holding them fast, while the other lifted the fabric of her shirt. His hand skimmed the swell of her breast as she battled with her mind.

Releasing her wrists, his hands moved down, gripping her hips. Then, his palm cupped between her legs, pressing hard and firm over the fabric of her jeans. His husky voice rasped, "I'm going to make you feel good."

Her lips and fingers prickled with the spreading numbness as the memory vault released vileness into her mind. The fire in her belly dampened. The ache between her legs disappeared, and a chill settled in her body.

She froze beneath his touch.

His hands stopped. His kisses lifted off her skin. "What's wrong?" He tilted his head back and stared into her eyes.

She couldn't turn her head fast enough.

Ash lifted away.

She rolled to her side and curled into a ball, unable to hide her body's revulsion. Images of her foster father flashed in her mind— touching, forcing...and worse.

Ash stumbled back into his seat, increasing the distance between them. "Shit, I'm sorry. I keep fucking this up, pushing you and breaking the rules." A long string of curse words followed, and then he returned to her, gathering her in his arms. "I'm not used to going slow."

She placed her hand on Ash's chest. "We need to talk."

So much about her wasn't normal. This was what had Spencer hiring professional escorts. This was why she would never have a normal relationship.

Overhead, the call light blinked.

The pilot's voice sounded. "Please buckle up and prepare for landing. You know the drill."

Ash stared at her with haunted eyes. A frantic edge lined them, but it was the hollowness in his expression that knifed deep into her heart. Her rejection had wounded him.

If she could, she would kill her foster father all over again for the pain he inflicted on those she loved. *Wasn't it enough—what he'd done to her? To Forest?* Yet the ghost of a monster continued to reach out from the grave to wreak havoc on her life.

Before she could speak about her past, she needed a moment to regroup.

Despite the pilot's orders to buckle up, Skye stood. "I need—I need to freshen up." She pushed hot tears from her cheeks and stumbled to the lavatory.

The plane pitched down, and she wondered if this was the beginning of the end for her and Ash.

Ash said nothing, but the sound of his heavy breathing followed her the entire way to the back of the plane.

He'd asked if she felt it—the thing growing between them. Yes, she felt something—an unsustainable attraction.

She pressed a hand to her stomach, sick with the mess of her past. She needed Forest. He would understand.

When she returned to her seat, Ash glanced up from his cell phone.

Was he writing another song? Who knew what rock stars did?

And it changed things, knowing who he was, but then again, he was exactly the same. Same penetrating eyes. Same quirky lift at the corner of his mouth. Same everything…except different now.

The easy way he held himself portrayed his confidence as a man who commanded the adoration of millions. The quirky humor and easy smiles he tossed her way, she now understood as snarky expressions of a rough and jaded celebrity.

The old Jeep and the beat-up guitar? *Why did he hold on to those things from his childhood? What was he clinging to? And what was she going to do with him now?*

She chewed on her lower lip, studying him.

For a rock star who surely had his share of groupies to choose from, what was he doing in a plane, twenty-five thousand feet in the air, headed to Niagara Falls, with a woman who had such a complicated life?

She wasn't supermodel hot. She wasn't tall, sexy, and lean. She was simply herself. She spoke her mind, took care of her patients, and had only ever loved one person—her foster brother, Forest, not even a romantic love. Sad, how now she realized she never truly loved Spencer.

Ash's words whispered in her head, *"Do you feel this, too?"*

Much like his song, she felt the insanity of whatever had brought them together.

The plane banked sharply to the left. She gripped her armrest, and buckled her seat belt.

Their gazes snagged with unspoken words hanging in the balance.

The pilot's voice sounded over the speaker again. "We're coming in for our final approach. It's going to be a bit bumpy."

Bumpy? He had no idea of the turbulence buffeting the passengers sitting in the back.

"Ash, I—"

He held up his cell phone. "I booked a suite. It has two rooms." He brushed the hair off his face. "We're both tired, and I think we need a good night's rest."

"We need to talk."

He nodded. "We will but not tonight."

"We can't ignore what happened."

He blew out a breath and leaned back in his chair. "I messed up. I'm sorry." He wiped his hand over his face and drew it down over his mouth. "I keep forgetting to go slow." He blinked, and his tortured eyes flashed. "Please, don't hold my past against me, but I don't know how to hold hands and kiss a girl. I've never *dated...* anyone." He gave a shrug. "I'm so used to hitting a home run that I forget about walking the bases."

The curse of a rock star, she assumed.

"As much as this sounds like a cliché," she began, "I'm going to say it anyway. It's not you. It's me."

The plane rocked as it lined up for its landing. Turbulence, her ass. This was the same pilot who'd had them swooping through the mountains in his helicopter. Bastard was probably having a blast.

Her head banged against the seat back as the wheels touched down, bounced, and hit again. The pilot nosed the front wheel down and engaged the brakes.

His voice popped through the speakers. "It'll be a few minutes while we taxi. Please remain seated until we come to a full and complete stop."

After the bumpy landing, she continued, "I'm broken and messed up ten ways till Sunday. You don't want me."

His face darkened with a scowl. "That's fucking bullshit."

She blinked. "You don't get it."

He undid the latch of his seat belt and knelt before her, clasping her hands. "We mesh"—he thumped his chest—"in here, Skye. Right the fuck in here." He brushed his lips against her knuckles. "I shouldn't have said anything."

"This has nothing to do with who you are or what you do for a living. I said, it's me, not you."

His eyes narrowed with suspicion. "I don't believe you."

She cupped his strong jaw. "I'm not sure it's fair to involve you in all my complications."

The richness of his scent enveloped her in a familiar blanket of spice and musk, a sexy fragrance that was purely Ash. He made her feel comforted and safe, an oddly unique experience.

"If it's about your ex, don't worry about him," Ash said. "I've known guys like him, and I'll make sure he doesn't hurt you anymore."

He held himself a breath apart from her. Their lips trembled but did not touch.

Oh, poor Ash. If only it were so simple…

"No, I'll take care of him." She would end the engagement once and for all even though she'd feel like the world's biggest coward doing it by phone.

Skye leaned back, breaking the connection between them, terrified they would kiss if she remained close.

"So, what's wrong then?" he asked. He settled back onto his heels, uncertainty and vulnerability framing his face. "Is it because I'm Blaze? Is the fame putting you off? You liked me well enough when you thought I was Nobody Ash." He shook his head. "Usually, it's the other way around. No one wants to know Ash, but they sure as hell are all over Blaze."

"What do you mean?"

"Only that women are predictable."

"Predictable?"

"Forget it."

Like she was going to let that comment go. "Explain what you meant."

His eyes pinched, and he tilted his head back. "Okay, this is going to sound bad, no matter how I say it, so I'm just going to say it."

"I'm listening."

He paused for a moment and then continued, "Women throw themselves at my feet, at the feet of Blaze, just to have a piece of me. And I admit, I've taken advantage of what being Blaze has done for me, but I want more. I gorged myself on sex and sin until I got sick of it. The few relationships I tried were a joke. Women take and take, like I'm some goddamn giving tree. They used me for my money or to be close to my fame, but none of them cared about who I am. I'm sick of it. I want what my father has, what my brothers have."

She listened, not saying anything, while his words cut a hole in her heart. Perhaps she wasn't the only walking cliché.

"It must be frustrating—to be used like that," she said.

It was a little odd to listen to a man complain of too much sex and to refer to himself by two different names...identities. But she understood vacuous sex; physical contact without emotional intimacy drained a person.

"It pisses me off," he continued. "So, when I ran into you, and you...well, you didn't—"

She hid a smile and finished his sentence, "Jump your bones? Or was it because I didn't know who you were?"

His smirk made a fleeting reappearance and then melted away under a frown. He scratched the side of his head. "Well, both, to be honest. You treated me like Joe Normal."

She laughed. "Technically, I treated you as Nobody Ash."

"Yeah, and it's fucking amazing. I get to be me for once and not bigger-than-life Blaze, lead singer of Angel Fire." He gestured between them. "You and I…there's something real here. Fate brought us together. Don't fuck it up and run because you're scared. I'm still the same guy even if I sing for some rock band."

The corners of her lips turned up. She couldn't help it.

And who he was or wasn't had nothing to do with her issues.

Well, that wasn't true. His fame complicated an already screwed up situation.

He rubbed his neck, his fingers stretching across the bloody strands of the tattoo, making the web twist beneath his touch. "Is it over, now that you know?" He scooted back, staring at his clasped hands.

The stupid plane rolled down the taxiway, the tires bumping over the tarmac. Slowly, they closed on their destination. Soon, they would have to climb out of the plane and face the prospect of another night together.

Another night.

Another opportunity to feel his touch.

Another chance to fuck everything up.

His simple kiss couldn't cleanse the taint staining her soul.

Her body shuddered with the remembered pain, and she wished it could be different.

Ash leaped out of his chair and captured her in a hug. "Fuck, I'm sorry. I didn't mean to make you cry."

She wiped tears from her cheeks, not really certain when they'd started to spill.

"I'm okay," she said, pushing Ash away. "But, since we're being honest, you need to know something about me, about my past…" Because it would change everything.

By the time the plane stopped, he'd probably want to turn it back around and fly far away, but she found the strength to continue and to be as honest as she dared.

Rubbing her palms on her jeans steadied her nerves. "My childhood…"

"You don't have to tell me anything you don't want to, but just because something's complicated doesn't mean it can't be fixed."

Fixed? There was no fixing.

She held up a hand. "There was a time when I was young and powerless. I was hurt in ways my body and brain couldn't deal with." She needed to explain why her body did what it did and how her shutting down wasn't his fault.

"Then, came Bean," she said, "only they hurt him worse. He was so much weaker and brittler than me. We found each other in the darkness and have been with each other ever since."

A sour expression crossed his face, like he was going to be sick or kill someone. "Skye, I'm sorry."

"Don't be. I survived, as did Bean. We came out on top." She pulled up her knees and hugged them. "The first time it happened, I was twelve." Her voice hitched at the memories. "It only got worse."

Fresh tears poured down her cheeks. She swallowed against the lump in her throat. Admitting such a private thing felt like someone was punching her in the gut all over again. She wasn't ready to discuss the training, the beatings, or the performances that had been forced upon her and Forest by the man entrusted to keep them safe.

"So, Bean's not your real brother?"

She shook her head. "No."

"And you love him?" A tone of resignation filled his voice.

"I do," she said with a vigorous nod. "I love him very much."

"I see." Ash's voice dropped to a whisper.

He pulled her into his lap, despite her protests. Strong arms enfolded her, encasing her in steel.

The plane jerked to a stop, and a few seconds later, the cockpit door popped open. "We've arrived," their pilot announced.

"I arranged a car to pick us up," Ash said to the pilot. "Can you see if it's here?"

Hydraulics whirred as the stairs unfolded and lowered to the ground.

Ash's arm cinched around her shoulders. He kissed the top of her head. "Why were you engaged to Spencer if you love Bean?" The raw edge of disappointment clouded his voice, disturbing the rich tonal notes.

A pained acceptance pronounced itself, and she realized her mistake.

She pushed off his chest to stare into his eyes. "I love Bean very much." She made certain to speak slowly, ensuring Ash understood and wouldn't miss what she was saying. "I love Bean, as my brother. He's my family. Not my—"

"Damn, you're exhausting." He laughed.

"Exhausting? You seriously didn't just say that. I spilled my guts out to you."

"Yes, you did."

"And you think it's funny?"

He'd better have a reason for the laugh, or she was going to kick his ass.

He placed her palms on his chest. "Not by a long shot. I'm going to take you out of this plane, tuck you into my bed, and sleep all night long, curled up next to you. In the morning, we're going to have breakfast in bed. Then, I'm going to show you how a man loves a woman, erasing the bad memories and replacing them with something new."

"You can't do that."

"Babe, I might be many things, but two things I know for sure."

"What is that?"

"I rock it onstage like there's no tomorrow. And I'm going to rock your world."

"It's not so easy. You can't wipe away a lifetime of abuse with a simple fuck."

He laughed. "Lucky for you, there's nothing simple about the way I fuck. Besides, I love a challenge. I'm not going anywhere, and I'm sure as shit not letting you run away."

His intensity terrified her almost as much as it exhilarated her. She didn't relish being Ash's project, but for him, she was willing to give it a try.

When the two of them collided, the world seemed to fall into place.

She pushed against his chest. "We're going to have to buy clothes before we hit the hotel."

He winked. "True, but I'm paying from here on out."

She laughed at his pathetic attempt to take control. "Oh no, Rock star. We're still splitting the bills."

His eyes rolled. "Are you fucking kidding me?"

"I won't become one of your groupies or use you as—what did you call it? A giving tree? I have my own money."

"I booked the penthouse suite, babe. You're not paying for that."

The pilot popped his head back inside the hatchway. "Sir, your limo is here."

"And the limo." A smug expression filled his face. "I'm paying for that, too."

"A limo? What happened to keeping a low profile?"

His lips twisted. "I got excited."

"You're an idiot. I'm paying for the limo and the hotel. You can't possibly have that much cash in that roll you've been using."

"I have a credit card. Seriously, don't worry about it."

When he opened his mouth to argue, she silenced him, pressing her index finger to his lips. "You already agreed to the rules. I want a quiet few days, and I don't want to be running from the paparazzi the whole time. What name did you book the room under?"

His cheeks colored. "I used an alias. This isn't my first rodeo."

"At least you're not a total idiot."

He laughed. "No, I'm not." He grabbed her hand. "Come, our shopping adventure awaits. I say, we skip the thrift stores and upscale it a bit. Your choice—Walmart or Target?"

Chapter Thirteen

ASH'S SUNGLASSES AND BASEBALL CAP DREW HARDLY A RAISED eyebrow with the midnight shopping crowd at Walmart. Skye bought the basics—an extra change of clothes, a sweater to layer, and added in a scarf and mittens to battle the harsh Upstate New York weather.

When Ash joined her with his nearly bare shopping basket, she turned him around with a shake of her head. "You're going to need something more than a pair of gloves." His leather jacket offered little protection against the freezing temperatures. "Go get a sweater and maybe a long-sleeved shirt. You're going to freeze your ass off."

Briefly, she considered sending him for a winter jacket, but she knew he'd resist. If he bought a hat, gloves, and a sweater, she'd be happy. It was important to pick the battles she knew she'd win.

His smile crinkled, and the fluorescent lights glittered in his eyes. "Bossy much?"

"No. Just realistic about the weather." She shoved him back toward the men's section, following him this time. After grabbing a long-sleeved shirt—he'd refused the turtlenecks she tried to shove in his basket—she was able to convince him to add a lightweight sweater to his collection.

They headed to the checkout counters, paying separately, and then called the limo.

After their essential shopping trip was completed—toothbrushes, shampoo, and deodorant purchased—the limo driver took them to their hotel where they checked in a little before one a.m.

The suite had a main sitting area and two separate bedrooms. While Ash deposited his shopping bags in the other room, Skye collapsed in bed, too tired and exhausted to brush her teeth. A picture window looked out into the inky-black sky. Niagara Falls roared, its awe-inspiring sound muffled by the glass.

Ash came to her a few minutes later, pulling back the covers and lying beside her. "Skye," he whispered.

"Yes?"

"You asleep?"

She rolled over. "No."

He brushed back the hair from her face and kissed her forehead. "You're keeping me awake," he teased.

Turning his back, he yanked the covers over his shoulder. When she tucked into him, he flipped over and tugged her into his arms, cuddling without demanding anything more.

She allowed her eyes to drift shut. Being held in a man's arms, without the demand for sex, was an unfamiliar but welcome sensation. And, while his breathing turned soft and measured, she was left to wonder whether to remain in his embrace or scoot away.

In the end, she stayed where she was. Ash's gentle hold made her feel safe.

With thoughts of him spinning in her head and his gentle snores whispering in her ears, Skye snuggled into his warmth.

~

WHEN SHE WOKE, HIS SIDE OF THE BED WAS EMPTY. SHE PUSHED THE hair back from her face and blinked at the strong morning light spilling in through the open curtains. Niagara's roaring thrummed in the air, and she climbed out of bed to get her first glimpse of the falls.

Ice crystals coated the edges of the windows, and the plate glass rippled with age. Beyond the frosty glass, Niagara Falls carved out its signature horseshoe shape in a spectacle of water and ice.

The bedroom door was closed. Beyond it, the gentle strumming of a guitar melded with the low vocal melodies of the sexiest voice she had ever heard. The song had matured since the last time Ash sang it.

Replaying the last few notes, Ash changed the sound, deepening it with a quality she couldn't describe. It tunneled directly into her heart. He picked up from the beginning, his voice carrying the soul of the song, painting a picture, complementing the vibrancy of the music his fingers picked out on the strings.

The song was about her. It was about him. It was about the insanity that was them. It was a song about love, but she couldn't shake a feeling that there was more.

She grabbed her shopping bag full of clothing and toiletry items and headed to the bathroom. After a quick shower, she tossed on her new clothes—a pair of jeans, a turtleneck, and a cable sweater.

With a look in the mirror, she regretted not purchasing anything from the makeup aisle, but at midnight and after the emotional roller coaster of finding out Ash's rock-star status and confessing the tiniest bit of her past, mascara and eyeliner had been the furthest things from her mind.

She dialed room service.

"Mrs. Willy, how may I help you?"

It took a moment to remember the alias Ash had used to book the room. He had called it his *Free Willy* card and had checked in under the pretense of them being newlyweds, saying it made more sense with their lack of luggage.

"I'd like to order room service."

"Yes, ma'am, but your husband has already ordered. It should be arriving within the next fifteen minutes. Is there anything you would like to add?"

Her husband? She chewed on her lower lip, uneasy with the lie. "I'm sorry, but what did he ask for?"

The operator rattled off the standard breakfast fare and then added, "He didn't request the champagne, but it comes with the honeymoon package. Would you like to add it to your order?"

"Yes, please."

Normally, she would never consider drinking first thing in the morning. But today? She deserved an alcoholic splurge.

"What else comes with the honeymoon package?"

"A tour of the falls and the city." There was a pause at the end of the line, and then the operator returned. "If you want, we can schedule your tour for later this morning?"

"That sounds perfect. Can you book us for eleven?"

Ash mentioned he'd never seen Niagara before. The tour would be a surprise she hoped he loved.

Another brief pause. "Yes, of course. We recommend rain gear for guests. You can purchase—"

"We'll purchase whatever you recommend," she cut the woman off in her eagerness to get off the phone. The music had stopped from the other side of the door. "Thank you."

"Very well. Thank you for choosing—"

Skye hung up as Ash gently knocked.

"Skye?" His voice sounded hesitant. "You awake?"

"Come in."

The door swung open. Damp hair curled around his ears and the nape of his neck. A puffy white towel was wrapped tightly around his hips. The firm six-pack begged her fingers to explore.

Skye forced her gaze upward and away from the temptation beneath his towel.

"Are you hungry?" He gave her a peck on the cheek.

"Famished."

"I called room service. Breakfast will be here soon." He rolled his shoulders and flexed his neck. The tattoo moved with him, nearly giving flight to the dragon eternally trapped on his skin. "I've been up for a couple of hours. Had to get that song out of my head and write it down."

"Did you sleep at all?" She searched for signs of fatigue on his face.

He shrugged. "I got up around five, and I've been working with Bent and Bash." His eyes widened with excitement. "They're totally stoked."

"Worked on it? How did you do that?"

His characteristic smirk perked up his face. "Modern video chat, babe. I heard the water running, so I took a shower in the other room." He glanced around. "Where the fuck did I leave my clothes?"

"You left them in the other room, remember?"

"Why the hell did I do that?" He curled his upper lip. "Ah, I remember now." His hand went to the towel. "My grand attempt to be a gentleman, but we know how that's going to end."

His fingers gripped the towel, and as he was about to reveal his nakedness, a knock sounded at the door to their suite.

"Go put your pants on, Casanova."

His smile turned upside down. "Cockblocked by room service. Now, that's a new low."

"Sounds like your next big hit. Now, go get dressed. I have a surprise."

He disappeared as she let in room service. A tall man in his late sixties wheeled in a tray covered with a silver dome. A bottle of champagne chilling in an ice bucket sat to the side. With a flourish, he revealed their morning repasts.

"Would you like me to open the champagne?"

"Yes, please."

He pulled the bottle out of the ice and used a white linen napkin to wipe off the condensation. With a twist and a pop, he had the cork free.

"Congratulations on your wedding," he said with a twinkle in his eye as he poured two glasses.

"Thank you." She handed over a generous tip.

While Ash took his time in getting dressed, she took a sip from her glass and then another. She wandered over to the expanse of windows and stared at the spectacle of Niagara. Ice pillars had formed at the extreme edges of the cascade, but nothing could contain the fury of so much water.

Ash's solid footfalls sounded behind her moments before he wrapped his arms around her waist. "It's beautiful, isn't it? Kind of takes your breath away."

He nuzzled, kissed, and licked the hollow of her throat, making her squirm and nearly drop the champagne.

"It's amazing."

But he was the one who stole her breath with a nibble to her earlobe.

She giggled and brushed him away. "Stop that."

Ash spun her around. He was dressed in a pair of denims, perched low over his hips, and a white T-shirt that strained across the muscles of his chest.

She poked him. "You're going to need more than a T-shirt. It's going to be cold at the falls."

His brows crinkled. "I have no intention of leaving this room." He reached for the edge of her shirt.

She batted his hand away and sidestepped him. "Our food is getting cold, and I booked a tour for eleven." She tilted the glass to her lips. "This champagne is amazing, compliments of our nuptials."

"Uh, yeah, sorry about that."

She waved him off. "I'm not mad. In fact, I kind of think it's funny."

"You do?"

She poured herself another glass of bubbly and sat down at the table. "Definitely."

The heavenly scent of pancakes, waffles, eggs, bacon, and sausages drifted up as she inhaled. "Oh, this smells wonderful."

She took a gulp of her second glass, her nerves suddenly flaring with the thought of staying in the penthouse suite with nothing but a long day stretching out before them.

The honeymoon suite would tempt the most practically minded individual. With thoughts of Ash ravishing her body, she poured the rest of the champagne down her throat.

Grabbing a plate, she stacked two waffles and topped them with strawberries and cream and then refilled her glass.

She gestured to the champagne sitting in front of Ash. "Grab your plate and join me. We can talk about what we want to do after the tour."

He sat and made his plate. Instead of taking the champagne, he poured a glass of orange juice.

As he dug into his food, his eyes kept darting to the bedroom, and a wistful expression filled his face. He said nothing more about staying in for the day, perhaps sensing she wasn't ready for him to fulfill the promise he'd made the night before.

The words of his song rattled in her head. The chorus had caught her and wouldn't let go.

INSANITY,

It has to be.

You belong with me.

IN A DAY AND A HALF, SHE WOULD RETURN TO HER DUTIES IN THE emergency department, and Ash's music and fans would once again consume Blaze, his rock-star persona. She would fade from his life, a tiny blip of adventure, while he'd remain forever imprinted in her heart. The inevitability of their separate futures bore down upon them.

Her fingers clenched around the champagne flute, and she downed the amber liquid with another long swallow. She cut into her waffles as he moved eggs around on his plate. Already, the alcohol surged in her blood, warming her from the inside out and numbing her to the pain of their eventual separation.

~

COLD DIDN'T EVEN BEGIN TO DESCRIBE THE NIAGARA FALLS WINTER experience. Even with her heavy coat, scarves, mittens, the cheap poncho purchased from the tourist vendor, Ash's arms wrapped firmly around her waist, and way too much alcohol floating in her veins, Skye was freezing. She couldn't feel the tip of her nose, her butt, or her thighs.

She shivered against the arctic breeze blowing over the falls, but Ash didn't seem affected. He held his phone out, snapping picture after picture, wearing his jacket and T-shirt.

"Can we go yet?" she asked for the fifth or maybe even tenth time. Although visiting the falls was her idea, she couldn't wait to get back to the heated interior of the limo.

Ash pulled her back against his chest, but the warmth of his body failed to penetrate beneath all the layers of clothing separating them. Even his breath froze on her neck.

"You wanted to hunt waterfalls, babe. We're at the mother of them all. Now, smile for another selfie."

Her teeth chattered so hard that a smile was impossible.

He kissed her cheek, leaving a cold spot.

"I never asked to fly to the frigid north."

The mists of the falls filled the air, carrying the damp and settling a chill deep into her bones, making her wonder if she had ever in her life been warm.

Ash's low chuckle weakened her knees. "I checked the weather report. Those mountains are buried under almost two feet of snow. If we'd been there, we'd be out of power, out of food, and snowed in for a week. I call this a win. Hey, come on," he said. "The group's moving on without us."

Their tour group consisted of them and an elderly couple, Ben and Edna, who were celebrating their fiftieth wedding anniversary.

The falls had frozen at the edges, forming massive ice pillars, but water still roared through the center, making it difficult to carry on a conversation. Mist coalesced into a thick fog, saturating their group in freezing rain.

"It's fucking amazing," Ash said. He hummed the first few verses of a new song, "Hunting Waterfalls."

Ben wandered over. "Do you mind taking our picture?" He held his camera out to Ash, a smile lighting his cloudy eyes.

Edna held on to Ben's arm for support. "Can you believe it?" she said. "Fifty years."

"Congratulations," Ash said. "That's a long time to be married."

Edna nodded. "We got married here."

Ben sucked in his gut and straightened his shoulders. "We eloped," he said with a twinkle in his eyes. "Her father didn't speak to us for years. Took us having a kid for him to—"

The flush that spread on Edna's face moved down to her neck. "Oh, Ben." She kissed his cheek.

Ash snapped a photo the moment Edna's lips touched Ben's cheek.

"Now, give her a kiss, Ben," Ash encouraged. Then, he proceeded to ask questions about how they'd met while getting them to pose for more pictures. "So, was it love at first sight? My father says it was like that with my mom. I didn't realize you could get married here. Isn't there a waiting period?"

"No waiting," Edna said. "That's why we came."

Ash framed the misty backdrop of the falls behind them.

Edna continued, "On the US side, you have to wait twenty-four hours, but in Canada, you can get married just like in Vegas."

"We're renewing our vows today," Ben said, puffing his chest.

Ash handed them back their camera. "That's awesome. Who's with you to celebrate?"

Ben snorted. "Ha! The kids are working, and the grandkids are in college, busy with exams. It's just the two of us."

Skye's brows pinched together. That seemed so sad.

"We were a little upset at first," Edna said. "But then we thought, what better way to celebrate our fiftieth than the way it all began?"

Ben shook his head. "Not just us. Remember that couple who was just as crazy as we were?" He turned to Ash to explain, "They acted as our witnesses, and we did the same for them."

Edna's eyes misted over, and she wiped the corner with a handkerchief. "Don't worry; it's going to be perfect."

Ash winked at Skye. "We can make your day perfect and be that couple for you. We'll re-create history. It's fate all over again."

How could she say no? And, as far as her goal went for keeping them away from the hotel room, witnessing a wedding would satisfy the bill.

She directed her comment to Edna, "If you don't mind a couple of strangers, we'd love to act as your witnesses."

Edna's eyes lit up. "Oh, Ben…"

Ben kissed his bride. Then, he stood and shook Ash's hand. "It would be my honor."

"Fine, it's settled then," Ash said. "Where's the chapel?"

Ben rubbed a finger under his nose. "No chapel. We're headed to Canada and City Hall."

"Oh, Ben"—Edna patted Ben's hand—"can we get some champagne?"

"I've got a better idea," Ash said. "Edna, have you ever ridden in a limo?"

"A limo?" Edna looked to Ben.

Skye poked Ash. "Don't you dare forget the champagne."

While joining Ben and Edna on their adventure sounded fun, her champagne buzz from breakfast was wearing off.

Ash arranged for the limo to pick them up and had the first bottle of champagne flowing before they even moved. Ben and Edna had no problem with throwing back the fizzy liquid, and Skye found herself hard-pressed to keep up with their pace.

Ash popped the cork on a second bottle before they made it to the border. He didn't drink though, digging around in the small fridge for some water.

Skye's head thickened with the alcohol. It heated her body with wicked desires, and if Ben and Edna weren't sitting in the limo with them, she would have jumped Ash, throwing their no-sex clause out the window.

His jeans needed to come off. Her fingers ached to stroke him. Her mouth watered to claim him. She needed to make his body explode with the pleasure she could not experience herself.

Instead, Ash refilled her champagne flute.

Edna's hands flapped. "Oh, we're almost there." She grabbed Skye's coat sleeve and pulled her toward the window. "See there? That's the courthouse where Ben and I eloped. I'm so excited."

Skye tilted the champagne flute to her lips and downed her drink in one swallow. Her lips still felt numb from the cold.

The limo came to a stop at the foot of the stairs, and the driver opened the door. Ash exited first and helped Skye out of the limo.

She wobbled a bit before finding her balance and wrapped her arms around Ash's neck. "I want to lick you all over."

He lifted her, steadying her on her feet. Desire burned in the depths of his voice as he cupped her ass and yanked her hips against the hard length of his arousal. "Stop teasing me, or I swear…"

Oh, how she wanted to test the limits of his restraint. "Or you'll do what?" Her words slurred.

He laughed. "You've had a bit too much to drink, babe."

Ash helped Edna out of the car.

Ben followed, camera in hand. "Do you mind taking pictures?" he asked. "I want something to show the kids and grandkids."

Ash palmed the tiny camera. "Love to."

Edna headed up the stairs. "Come on." For a woman closing on seventy years, Edna had no problem with navigating the long flight of stairs. Once inside, she made a beeline for the Department of Vital Statistics, her stride purposeful and determined.

"Don't you need an appointment?" Skye called out to Edna.

Ben eyed Skye, giving her a wary look, when she leaned on Ash to keep herself from tripping over her feet.

Edna shook her head. "Don't need one. All you need is your passport and the patience to stand in line. You fill out the paperwork and pay the fee, and then a justice of the peace makes it official. Bingo. You're married. Now, which office is it?" She separated from their little group to read the directional signs.

"Sounds painless," Ash said, tugging Skye to his side.

She wasn't sure if Ash wanted her close, or maybe he thought she might fall over. She had some concerns about that, too. The room seemed to be spinning.

Ben's cheeks colored. "I want to say thanks, in case I forget later. It's real nice of you to witness for us." His eyes turned misty, and he lowered his voice. "Edna is a bit superstitious. She wanted to re-create the day exactly like it'd happened. You have no idea how much having you here means to her."

"We're honored to be a part of making this day extra special for you both." Ash lifted the tiny camera. "And I'm going to get everything on film."

Edna returned and yanked on Ben's sleeve. "The city clerk's office is this way."

She urged their group down the hall and beyond a set of frosted glass doors. Inside, eager wedding hopefuls were queued up.

Ash tightened his grip around Skye's waist. He whistled the tune to "Insanity" and then slipped into "Hunting Waterfalls."

She jabbed him in the ribs, which seemed to be all the prompting he needed to sweep down and capture her mouth in a kiss.

"We're standing in a wedding line, Skye." His brows lifted as he tugged her close and kissed the top of her head. "Think about it." He leaned down and sucked her earlobe into his mouth. "Maybe my next song should be 'Going to the Chapel.'"

Chapter Fourteen

ASH PECKED SKYE'S CHEEK AND FLASHED A NOT-SO-INNOCENT GRIN. "You definitely need to lay off the champagne. I'm officially cutting you off."

She giggled, loving the way his lips glided against her skin. "I'm fine."

In fact, she felt fabulous—a bit tipsy certainly but happily buzzed. Ash had her forgetting about Spencer's betrayal with the long-legged bitch. And, like Ash, she was tired of the no-sex clause. When they made it back to the hotel room, she was going to peel him out of those jeans that were slung low in all the right places and show him a thing or two about payback.

A bored-looking city employee called out from behind the caged glass, "Next."

Ben and Edna shuffled to the window, and Skye and Ash trailed behind them, supportive of their newly-to-be-wed-again friends.

"May I help you?" The woman with flame-red streaks between her ebony hair barely glanced at Ben. She looked down at the paperwork on her desk, filing the requests of the previous couple. A faded smiley face decorated her name tag that proclaimed her as Marge.

Edna's voice warbled as she explained what they wanted, "We're here for a marriage certificate. Ben and I want to renew our vows." She cupped Ben's cheek, the light of her love shining in her glistening eyes.

Marge took in Ben and Edna and then blinked when she saw Ash. "Hey, you look familiar."

Ash rocked back on his heels and answered, "I have a familiar face."

"Well," Marge said with a sniff, "I need identification from the bride and groom for the marriage certificate."

Ben fumbled, pulling his wallet out of his pants pocket, while Edna had her massive purse open, digging through its contents.

Ben clasped Edna's hand and brought her knuckles to his lips. "I love you."

"I love you, too," Edna said with a tear forming in the corner of her eye.

Marge jabbed the eraser of her pencil against the glass. "Are you the witnesses?"

Marge looked to Skye and Ash. The clerk's tone turned irritated as she rolled her eyes and held out her hand. "I need IDs."

"Ours?" A confused expression crossed Ash's face.

The woman nodded with a look of incredulity. "If you're going to be a part of the ceremony, I need ID."

Marge pulled out two sets of paperwork and marked them with her pencil. Meanwhile, Skye and Ash fished out their identifications, and along with Ben and Edna, they slid their passports through the window to a grumbly Marge.

Skye whispered to Ash, "What's her problem?"

"Shh," Ash said, "be nice." He beamed a rock-star smile at Marge, who flipped through the stack of identification.

Her eyes widened when she looked at Ash's ID.

"Oh, shit," he said.

"What?"

"Didn't think this through." He discreetly nodded toward Marge and the shocked expression on her face.

"At least *she* recognized you," Skye whispered with a slur. She poked him in the ribs.

Ash stepped to the window. "Um, Marge," he said, using his ultra-sexy voice, "this is supposed to be a quiet weekend for me and my girl." He smiled at Skye, and then turned back to Marge. "You know, no fuss?"

Skye gave a dorky half-wave to Marge.

Ash laid the charm on a little thick, pressing the tips of his fingers on the glass. "Can we keep this kind of...quiet?"

Marge stared at him with starstruck eyes. She slid a piece of paper along with a ballpoint pen over to Ash. "I can't believe who's standing at my window." Her voice dropped to a whisper. "I promise not to say a word." She brought her fingers to her lips and mimed zipping them, tossing away the key. "Your secret is safe with me."

"Thank you, Marge. We're here to support Ben and Edna."

Marge moistened her lips. "Got that. Renewing vows and the wedding." She pointed to the paper. "Can you sign an autograph for me?"

"I'd love to." He graced Marge with another sparkling smile. "Now, is there any way to speed up this paperwork?"

Marge collected the forms. "Normally, I wouldn't...but considering who you..." She laughed and then waved at the four of them. With a deep breath, she paused. "I'll take care of everything. Give me a sec, and I'll have all the forms filled out. No one will know you are here."

Ben glanced at Ash. "You some kind of hotshot?"

Ash gave a sigh. "I sing a little."

Skye snorted with Marge's excited departure. "You know she's probably texting her best buddies right now."

Ash ran his fingers through his hair. "I know. That's what has me worried. She texts a few friends, and then they text a few…" He gripped her hand. "I'm sorry."

"For what?"

Ash pulled out his phone. A long expression tugged at his face as he texted. "I didn't want the crazies barging in on our time. I just wanted you."

"I want you, too." Now that she'd said it, she couldn't deny the truth even if she'd known him for only two days—three, if she counted the day they'd met. *And how could she forget that toe-curling first kiss?*

Ben wrapped his arm around Edna. "You two make a really great couple."

A flush heated Skye's face.

Marge returned with the paperwork. She slid it halfway under the counter and then collected the fee from Ben.

Her eyes devoured Ash. "You need to sign here and here."

Everyone signed the papers.

Then, Marge waved them to a set of double doors. "The justice of the peace has to make it official, but I already had the papers signed. You won't have to come back and stand in line again." She winked at Ash. "But you need the official ceremony to make it legal. The marriage certificate will be mailed in six to eight weeks."

Ben tilted Edna's chin and kissed her. Skye's stomach clenched as she watched how in love the older couple was. She was not envious of their bond but more hopeful about one day having even a slice of the magic they shared.

"The justice is waiting. I told her you wanted to keep things quiet." She put her fingers to her lips. "She thinks it's so romantic. Down that hall, second door on the left."

Ash clutched his cell phone in his hand, head bowed, while he followed Ben down the hall. He chewed at his lower lip.

"What's up?" Skye asked.

"I texted my manager, but I don't know if we can get security here fast enough."

She cocked her head. "What do you mean, security?"

"Let's just hope Marge's job keeps her too busy to keep up with her social media updates. If she lets it slip that I'm here, the paparazzi will descend on us. You have no idea what that's like."

They followed Ben and Edna into the justice of the peace's chambers, coming to a stop before the woman's mahogany desk.

"It'll be fine," Skye said softly. "We're almost done. We finish this, drop them off, go back to the hotel..."

"You don't understand. We need to leave."

Ben cleared his throat.

Skye looked up. Their conversation was holding up the festivities. "Sorry."

A woman in a business suit sat behind the massive desk. In her late forties, she had her hair swept back in an elegant and immaculate French twist. She stood and came around the desk, hand extended in greeting.

"It's a pleasure to meet you," she said to Ash. "My son is a huge fan."

Ash smiled and inclined his head. "Thank you very much, ma'am."

She looked uncertain. "I know it's unprofessional to ask, but he would kill me if he knew I'd met you and hadn't asked. Would you mind?" She held out a pad of paper.

"What's your son's name?"

"Adam. He's sixteen."

Skye was happy to see Ash taking the time to write the woman's son a lengthy note.

"Does it matter where we stand?" Skye asked.

The woman shook her head. "Not really."

Ben and Edna stood in front of the desk. Ash went to Ben's side, and Skye stood beside Edna. The justice of the peace gave them a strange look but said nothing.

"What now?" Ash asked.

She looked between the four of them. "My part is a formality. I just need to make sure the parties do indeed wish to be married. Is this so?"

Ben and Edna nodded.

Skye spoke up, "I'm sure Ben and Edna want to say their vows, right?"

Ben did more than that. He bent to one knee, adoration and the purest love radiating from his face. "Edna, I never proposed to you in the right way, so I'm fixing that now."

Skye joined Ash, nudging him to remind him to snap those photos for Ben and Edna's children and grandchildren.

Ben wobbled, and his knee popped loudly into the silence.

Edna's hand shook, and her eyes misted as he slid a diamond anniversary band over her ring finger to nestle beside her wedding ring.

She accepted his proposal with a whispered, "Yes," and a flutter of her hand over her heart.

Ash helped Ben to his feet, and then Ben and Edna exchanged vows, fifty years to the day from when they had eloped.

When they were finished, the justice of the peace turned to Skye and Ash. "Do either of you want to say anything?"

Skye glanced at Ash. "Yes. I'm really honored to be here." She wiped a tear from her cheek.

Ash gripped her hand. "Yes. Me, too."

The woman looked back to Ben and Edna. "Well then, it's official. You're married."

Edna clapped her hands. "This is so exciting."

Ash snapped a photo of Ben laying a smooch on Edna's lips.

ONCE THE CEREMONY WAS OVER, ASH HURRIED THEIR PARTY TO THE limo. Less than an hour later, they dropped the newly re-wed couple at their car parked near the Niagara Falls observation deck.

Ben shook Ash's hand and had him sign autographs for his grandchildren saying, while he had no idea what band Ash played for, he was certain his grandchildren would, and there was no way he would return home without proof. Ash indulged the couple, tossing an arm around Ben's shoulder and even gently dipping Edna to kiss her cheek.

Skye snapped several pictures before they were able to say their good-byes. Watching the easy grace with which Edna and Ben moved warmed her heart. After fifty years, love still held them deeply in its grasp.

On the ride back to the hotel, Skye's alcoholic buzz slowly wore off, and her thoughts turned to her future.

Ash put all of himself in everything he did. When they parted ways, she prayed his free spirit would have rubbed off on her. She wanted to give Ash something memorable, a tiny piece of herself, something she could offer without complications.

Sitting so close together, his woodsy scent filled her nostrils, and her thoughts turned in salacious directions. Her eyes drifted to the soft swell beneath the zipper of his pants. She wanted to feel him quiver in her hands as an orgasm ripped through his body. All she had to do was slip off her seat and free his cock.

"We need to get back to the hotel," Ash said. His leg bounced with nervous energy.

She slid forward to knock on the divider separating them from the driver.

When the smoky divider lowered, the driver met her eyes via the rearview mirror. "Yes, ma'am?"

"How much farther to the hotel?"

"About half an hour."

"Thank you."

The driver raised the screen, leaving Skye and Ash in relative privacy once again.

Ash looked at his phone. A furrow formed between his brows "I bet the hotel is swarming with paparazzi by now."

"How would your fans know which hotel?"

"You'd be surprised how resourceful fans can be."

Remembering their lack of luggage and their late-night shopping trip, Skye gave a shrug. "We don't have to go back there. We can check out by phone."

He shook his head. "My guitar is in there."

"They can mail it."

Ash's eyes rounded with an oh-hell-no expression.

"Okay," she said. "How about we have their staff meet us out front with it?"

He shook his head. "I'm not comfortable with a stranger handling my baby."

She shrugged. "Okay, then drop me off. No one is going to recognize me."

A smile curved the corners of her lips as she thought about sneaking into a hotel to retrieve a rock star's precious guitar. The fans weren't hers, and the cameras didn't care about immortalizing her face, but it was exciting to wonder what it must feel like to be so adored by strangers.

Despite his claim to fame, he was simply Ash, the guy who had chased after her to return a backpack and the one she'd poured hot cocoa on. He'd kissed her into incoherency, and as much as she felt guilty for admitting it, the sound of Ash's fist smacking Spencer's nose had been very satisfying. The cut under Ash's eye would scar, and he would carry the mark for the rest of his life. And hell if a part of her liked that a small piece of her would always be in his life.

He'd erased the sting of Spencer's betrayal. Instead of crying her eyes out, watching chick flicks, and eating ice cream to ease her broken heart, she'd found herself smiling, laughing, and looking forward to the next adventure with Ash.

And, right now, that meant retrieving a most precious guitar.

Of course, he might be blowing the whole thing out of proportion. *How many paparazzi lived in Niagara Falls?*

"How's this going to work then?" she asked. "If we pull up in this limo, we're going to draw attention." She scooted back to him, grabbed his hand, and brought it to her mouth. "Maybe we should rent a car?"

He smiled at the tender show of affection and cupped her chin. "Yeah, we could use a car. Then I can drop you off at the loading dock or something."

She gnawed at her lower lip. "How about you wait down the street? I'll walk from there."

The furious toe and finger tapping slowed to a moderate beat.

Suddenly, he lifted her, positioning her in his lap, settling her knees on either side of his powerful legs. "How much have you had to drink?"

There was the bottle at breakfast in the hotel and two bottles shared with Ben and Edna on the way to the courthouse. Maybe she'd had more than she thought. Certainly, her memory of the courthouse was fuzzed a little. Not that she couldn't remember the efficient ceremony or the clerk fangirling over Ash.

She wrapped her arms around his neck, loving how the conversation had changed between one beat and the next. The desire in his eyes heated the air between them. A breath escaped her, and she wiggled against his swelling cock. Perhaps she could act upon her fantasy.

He groaned. "You are playing with fire, babe."

Confidence and a sense of purpose swelled inside her chest. She tucked her lower lip between her teeth. *Would he stop her?* Her fingers smoothed down the cotton of his shirt as she traced the outlines of the muscles straining against the fabric.

"I want to do something."

He focused on her lips. "You've been drinking."

"Only a little." Her buzz had faded, and now, she was left with a strong desire to drive him wild.

"You had more than a little."

He tried to lift her off his lap, but she clung to his neck and buried her face next to his dragon tattoo.

"Let me do this."

Strong hands gripped her waist and lifted. "I don't want you to regret anything we do. I've done that too many times, and I don't want that with you."

Unwilling to fight him but not ready to give up, she let him move her off his lap. After he deposited her on the seat next to him, she crouched at his feet.

His eyes widened, but he showed no indication that he wanted to move her again.

She rested her hand on his thigh, brushing the side of the bulge behind his zipper. His cock hardened beneath her touch.

"I'll regret *not* doing this." She licked her lips. "I'm not ready to sleep with you—not yet, not..." She swallowed down the memories. "Not in the way you want, but I want to do this."

He put his hand on top of hers and stroked her pinkie finger. "I'm more than willing to wait." He leaned down and gripped the sides of her face. With a soft kiss, he lifted her off her knees, pulling her up and away from her goal.

She let him bring her halfway up, her lips following his mouth, but she broke off the kiss and pulled back. "I want this." This was about taking control, something she'd never done during sex.

She released the top button of his jeans and grabbed the zipper. His body stilled. But, once she released the zipper, the long, hard length of him surged forth.

She arched a brow. "You were supposed to buy underwear."

"Underwear is overrated," he said with his signature smirk.

"How convenient." She stroked the silky skin of his cock.

He hissed and grabbed her hand.

She brushed his hand away and took a firm grip.

As she stroked him, he threw back his head. "Fuck!"

"Sorry, you'll have to wait for that," she said with a snicker. "I have something else in mind. You're going to enjoy this."

A man like Ash must have had many lovers. *How would she compare when stacked up against them?*

Ash curled his fingers in her hair. "I should say no, but I don't have the strength to stop you."

"Then don't, but do you have protection?"

He lifted his hips, eager now, and fished out a foil pouch from his back pocket. "I always travel with one."

She'd been forced to perform this act many times, trained to please not only her foster father, but also a string of men willing to pay hundreds to rob her childhood of innocence. But, when Ash's emerald irises turned black with desire, she welcomed every step that had brought her to kneel before him. No matter how painful the past, she would not let it steal this moment. Forest always said the best way to conquer their demons was to take control and own the past.

Ash would enjoy her touch, and she desperately wanted to give him everything he desired. She ripped the foil and sheathed him. Then, she bowed her head and kissed the crown of his cock. His hips bucked as the tender touch of her lips enveloped and drew him into her mouth. She released him and licked the tip.

A strangled cry erupted from his throat. He gripped her hair. "I'm going to embarrass myself and come like a two-pump virgin."

"You're a rock star, Ash. You can handle this."

His brow lifted.

She ran her thumb up his shaft. "Sit back, relax, and let me do all the work. I've been waiting all day to make you squirm."

His eyes narrowed. "Rock stars don't squirm."

"We'll see about that."

She eased him into her mouth, and his palm slammed down on the seat, fingers curling and clawing at the leather. Her tongue swirled around his shaft, dancing down his length, as her cheeks increased the suction in coordinated pulses geared to drive him mad. But she wouldn't let him come too fast. She knew how to draw out his pleasure.

His hips rocked beneath her, grinding his pelvis into her face, but she had prepared for this reaction, and she rode his bucking jerks with quick sucks and flicks of her tongue.

"Holy fuck," he gasped as he palmed her head.

He twisted at the strands of her hair as she drove him ever higher in his need.

She swirled her tongue, tracing the path of veins from root to tip. He pulled her down on his cock, and his hips reared up as his ass clenched and quivered. Then, he relaxed and pulled out. She took in a breath before he jerked forward again and again, fucking her face with frenzied need.

Her palms pressed a steady pressure on his thighs, reminding him she was still there, while her mouth and throat opened for him, accepting each of his thrusts. As he drew out, her tongue caught the underside of his cock. The roughness of her tongue dragged against the sensitive tissue under the glans. She flicked when she could before he'd slam forward again with his hips.

Unintelligible sounds swelled up from between his vocal cords, primal animalistic grunts of energy and power, as he thrust. His fingers flexed, pulling and guiding her head.

Her tongue continued its assault, stroking with each of his thrusts. The warbling sounds turned to moans as his movements became less coordinated and more frenetic. When he lost his rhythm, she picked it up, using her lips, teeth, tongue, and her cheeks to combine suction and texture into a tactile sensation that changed every time he built up to a crescendo.

She knew how to read the response of his cock and balls, and when his orgasm approached, she held him on a plateau, refusing to let him come.

His fingernails dug into the flesh of her scalp as he desperately tried to take over the tempo and bring about his orgasm. Each time he drew close, she'd revert to her training, knowing his frustration would lead him to a much greater reward, but he wouldn't be able to hold out forever.

She listened for the change in pitch of his breathing, that reedy tone, signifying he was close. His breathing turned staccato. She cupped him and reached around to push on that special spot behind his balls to prolong his pleasure. His hips jerked in a final spasmodic wave, bucking and rocking against her face.

"Fucking yes!" he yelled in satiated bliss.

She clamped her lips around his cock and sucked him through the end of his last orgasmic wave. Then she kissed the crown and sat back.

He sat with his head lolling back. A surreal smile stretched across his features, and then his low throaty laughter filled the car.

He held out a hand and gestured for her to take it. She reached out, proud and satisfied with her efforts. He pulled her beside him, tucking her into the crook of his arm, and then kissed her brow.

She curled into his embrace. "I told you I'd make you squirm."

He tapped her nose with his finger. "If you ever tell anyone, I'll deny it. Rock stars don't squirm. You set the bar pretty high, and I can't wait to repay the favor."

Her heart skipped a beat. *Oh no, not that.*

Whole-body-shutdown events would come as she neared the crest of an orgasm, landing her in a state of cataplexy. That was why she'd avoid pleasure and one of the reasons Spencer thought she was frigid.

Shit. Shit. Shit!

She lifted a hand and cupped his cheek. Stubble rubbed against her palm. "I'm not ready for…that."

He squeezed her against his side. "I'm not rushing you," he said with a sigh. "I get that it's complicated."

She gave a nod. "More than you realize."

Chapter Fifteen

ASH SETTLED THE BILL WITH THE LIMO DRIVER, CONTINUING HIS cash-only trend, while Skye completed paperwork for the car rental. They'd made the decision not to approach the hotel in the limo and had the driver take them to a car rental agency. Ash had wanted something sporty, but she'd argued that they'd need something capable of handling the harsh conditions of the wintry roads.

When she reached for the keys, Ash snagged them out of her hand.

"Hey, I was going to drive," she said with a pout.

"Nope, you've been drinking. Besides, you're on a Secret Squirrel mission."

"Secret Squirrel what?"

"Your mission!" He forced the words out on a harsh exhale, a note of irritation threading through his voice. "Rescuing my baby?"

She stretched on her tiptoes to kiss him. "I'd never forget your guitar."

Damn, but he looked sexy as fuck, being protective of his treasured guitar. He hadn't yet shown that degree of possessiveness over her, but she could imagine the fire in his eyes once he finally captured a girl and made her his.

Unashamed to show his building desire, he rocked his hips against her body, pulling her flush against him. "God, you know how to drive a man crazy."

Ash had kept his word, regarding the no-sex clause. She'd cracked a barrier between them, blurring the lines when she'd given him that blow job. Now, every time he looked at her, a rising hunger would simmer in his gaze. And she loved his passion, raw and primal. Ash didn't frighten her like Spencer had.

Ash pulled her thoughts back to him with the firm pressure of his touch. His long fingers splayed against her back, kneading the muscles. He pressed against her, deepening their kiss, sweeping his tongue against the seam of her lips until she opened for him. Then, he delved inside, insistent and demanding but never taking more than she was willing to give.

She drowned in the taste of him. The man pursued his kiss with a vengeance, exploring the recesses of her mouth and claiming another piece of her soul. A moan escaped him as he ground his hips to show the full potency of his masculinity. Then, he growled, a sound growing deep within his throat, rumbling between them with determination and deepening desire. He kissed her and then moved his lips to trace the angle of her jaw until he settled on the hollow of her throat where he bit and sucked her into mindless oblivion.

Kissing and being kissed by Ash was not only sensual and decadent; he also made it fun. Everything he did had a hint of playfulness attached to it, and she reveled in how he lived such an unburdened life.

She felt brave, standing outside the car, and freed the button of his jeans to slip her thumb inside and tease the crown of his cock, flicking and stroking where she knew he was most sensitive. His cock twitched, coming alive under her touch.

"Ah, fuck, babe."

While he was mindless with his desire, she swiped the keys out of his hand. "My turn to drive."

His lust-hazed eyes blinked slowly. Before she knew what was happening, he spun her around and swatted her ass. When she yelped, he yanked the keys away and held them up, out of her reach.

"No drinking and driving." He kissed her and then opened the passenger door. "Climb inside."

She didn't have a choice, not with the way he buckled her into the car. With a wink and another stolen kiss, he walked to the driver's side, whistling the tune to "Insanity."

With a press of the ignition switch, the SUV roared to life. He eased them out of the parking lot and merged into the bustling afternoon traffic.

Feeling mischievous, she lowered the zipper of his jeans and freed his cock, stroking him from crown to root. "Ready for round two?"

Oral sex didn't activate her trigger the way regular sex did. Not that she couldn't handle traditional sex. She'd manage just fine as long as she focused on anything other than the sensations being pulled from her body and avoided the crest of an orgasm.

There was something different in giving pleasure to Ash. A genuine desire to please him wrapped around her heart and spread everywhere at once.

Ash gripped her hand and pulled it away. "I'll crash!"

"I'm pretty certain, you can handle yourself."

"We're making a pit stop." He shook his finger. "I need to buy condoms, and you need to sit up, face forward, and keep your hands to yourself. I'm not getting in a wreck because your fingers were wrapped around my dick."

She couldn't help the laughter spilling from her lips. "You're not carrying condoms? And, here I thought, men carried a stash at all times."

"Just the one." His expression darkened for half a beat before disappearing. "Back in my Jeep, I have a stash, but I left all that behind." His tone made her wonder if he was referring to something other than the condoms.

She tucked her hands under her legs and stared straight ahead. Ash couldn't have been clearer. They were going to have sex. *Would things be different this time?* She didn't think that was possible, but then again, with Ash...

Ash tapped the GPS to map out their route. "You okay?"

Startled, she glanced at him. "Yeah, why?"

"Got a weird vibe for a second."

Damn, he was perceptive. It wasn't fun to discuss her inadequacies. Better to hide them and hope for the best.

Ash pulled into a convenience store. Once inside, he made a beeline for the condoms while she picked out a scarf and a pair of tinted sunglasses. He paid, refusing to abide by her rule of splitting their purchases.

The Secret Squirrel mission consisted of disguising her face by wrapping her newly acquired scarf around her head. His plan was elegant in its simplicity and lacked any super Secret Squirrel activities. She was going to walk right up the front stairs of the hotel and out the back, carrying his baby.

How many Angel Fire fans lived in Niagara? Maybe Ash thought a little more of his fame than he should.

Three blocks from the hotel, Ash found a parking spot. He gave her a kiss before sending her on her mission. A block from the hotel, the low murmurs of voices filled the air. She stopped, gawking, at what looked like nearly a hundred eager Angel Fire fans crowded around the entrance. Several hotel employees lined the lower steps, holding the throng back.

Because of the freezing temperatures, everyone was bundled against the cold. She wasn't the only one hidden behind a hood, hat, or scarf.

She worked her way to the front of the crowd, dodging elbows and earning herself murderous stares, only to be confronted by the row of security guards.

"Sorry, ma'am." A large man wearing a hotel uniform held out his hand to stop her approach. "You need to stay behind the line."

The hotel had placed barricades along the front of the stairs. At the cordoned off area, Skye blinked—stunned not only by how many fans had gathered, but also at their expressions. Girls scanned the entrance as well as the road, a look of adoration filling their faces. Most held cell phones, ready to snap a shot of their favorite rock star. The boys and men in the crowd shifted with an amped up excitement. The crowd surged, creating a near frenzy, as people searched for the man they called Blaze.

Whispers of conversation floated to her while she struggled to find her hotel room key.

"Did you know Angel Fire was in Niagara?"

"I thought they were playing in DC?"

"No, just him." A girl to Skye's left tugged on her friend's jacket. "Blaze!"

A voice from behind belted out the latest gossip, "I heard he went to the courthouse."

"Why would he do that?"

"Did he get arrested again?"

"I hope he's not drinking."

"Or back on drugs."

"But what does that have to do with him being here?"

"Didn't you hear?"

"No. What?"

The guard stepped in front of Skye, putting up his hands to warn her back into the crowd. "Listen, lady, no card, no entry."

Now, where was that damn room key? After some digging, she found it hiding at the bottom of her bag. She held it up to the guard barring her path. "See? I'm a guest. I'm trying to get to my room."

The man blew out his breath. It coalesced in the chill air of the late afternoon, forming a white mist. He examined her key card with a careful eye.

She tried to tune out the crowd and focus on the guard. He was giving her key card more than a casual inspection, and she didn't know what she'd do if she didn't get inside.

"I'm telling you, I'm a guest!"

Another snippet of conversation drifted to her ears.

A group of teenage boys stood to her left. One punched his friend in the arm. "Can you believe he eloped?"

Those words had her shifting all her focus from the guard to the cluster of teens.

"Blaze got hitched?"

"That's what the post said. He married some chick no one's heard of."

"No way!"

Her heart skipped a beat. That wasn't the truth, but it made total sense how the rumor had taken root.

"Don't know why. Can you imagine what it must be like? To have chicks throw themselves at you?"

His friend grinned. "Yeah, I'd fuck all day long."

The hotel guard returned her key card. "Looks good."

He gestured her to the steps, and she stumbled, reeling with what she'd heard.

Her heart thumped all the way up the elevator to the penthouse suite. She texted Ash to tell him she'd made it, and then she packed the few belongings they had into their plastic shopping bags.

With her backpack full and Ash's guitar case in hand, her Secret Squirrel mission was complete. Now, she would have to make it out of the hotel without someone spotting her carrying a distinctive guitar case.

The plan was for her to leave through a side exit, but the crowd would spot her in a second. She called down to the front desk and explained her dilemma. A few minutes later, a hotel employee guided her to one of the loading docks.

She gripped the guitar case and hurried down the street, a sinking sensation settling in her stomach as the teens' conversations ran through her head. The problem with rumors was that they had a life of their own, spreading roots and taking hold where they shouldn't.

Other than the guitar being unwieldy, she made the three blocks to the waiting SUV without incident. No one noticed her or Ash's guitar, but she couldn't stop looking over her shoulder to make certain no one had followed.

When Ash saw her approach, he hopped out of the car and popped the hatch in the back.

"You'll never believe what I heard." She handed over his baby.

Ash took the case and kissed it. "It's good to see you."

Hands on her hips, Skye fixed him with a steely gaze. "You'd better not be talking to the guitar."

He didn't even have the decency to look sheepish as he gently placed his guitar in the back of the car. "Sorry, but my baby and I have been together for a very long time. Once you've been with me for fourteen years, we'll talk." He grabbed her backpack and set it next to the guitar. Only then did he give her a hug. "Thanks for rescuing her."

She drew him into a kiss but broke it off before it became too heated. They couldn't risk anyone spotting Blaze kissing a girl with a wedding rumor floating around.

"Hey, come back. I wasn't finished with that mouth." He leaned in for a deeper kiss.

She danced away, laughing at his playfulness. "Nope, I don't want to encourage you. Besides, we need to leave before someone figures out that Blaze is behind those god-awful sunglasses."

"Please don't call me that," he said.

"Why not?"

"It's my stage name." He rubbed at the stubble of his jaw. "My fans call me Blaze, and you're not a fan." His brows furrowed. "The other girls…"

Yes, she could complete that sentence. The other girls, the ones who took until he had nothing left to give, would scream his stage name. She loved that she had grown to know the man behind the name first. She liked Ash very much.

Once again, he fired up the car. Soon, they were back on the interstate and headed to Roanoke where he'd left his Jeep. He dialed in a hard-rock station, and they shared a comfortable silence, both blissfully satiated for different reasons.

A few hours later, they stopped for dinner, pulling into a fast-food burger joint. As she passed Ash his triple cheeseburger, he turned the channel to soft jazz.

"Ugh," she complained. "What happened to rock?"

"We've been blasting rock for the past three hours. I want something a bit more soothing. Lean back, and let it flow. Let it paint a picture in your mind."

She tried. The music swirled around her while she closed her eyes, waiting for a picture to unfold.

Ash poked her in the arm. "Hey, I asked you a question," he said.

She shook her head. "I'm sorry. What?"

"You said I'd never believe what they were saying. What did you mean?"

She shifted in her seat, stretching out the kinks in her muscles. He'd switched back to a rock station, and the heavy beat settled into her bones.

"It was stupid really. They were saying that you came to Niagara to elope."

Ash's hand twitched, and he pulled it away, firmly settling it on the steering wheel at the two o'clock position.

"Don't worry. It's just as stupid as the one who said you were arrested for drugs."

"Ah, shit." He grabbed her hand and lifted it to his lips, kissed her knuckles, and held them there. The heat of his breath pulsed against her skin. "Do you remember the forms we signed?"

"I signed where Marge told me to." She'd been pretty drunk, and she didn't remember much more than that.

"So did I." He tilted his head against the seat. "Shit, shit, shit."

"Ash…" She extricated her fingers from his death grip. Her stomach knotted with dread. "Please tell me you read those forms."

"I'm horrible with stuff like that. That's why I have a manager and a team of lawyers. They handle all that crap for me. I just sign on the dotted line. It didn't even occur to me to read it."

She sat back because she needed to hear the truth. "Did we...are we..." But she couldn't bring herself to say *married*.

"I don't know. Maybe?" Ash's sexy-as-shit voice cracked.

He was many things, but she'd never seen him unsure.

"What do you mean, *maybe?*" Skye's voice hitched. "There's no *maybe* in getting married."

He ran his fingers through his dark hair.

Forest was going to have a cow.

"We have to fix this," she said.

Skye's stomach churned with unsettled emotions. She lowered the window, letting the freezing air swirl into the car, stealing their heat but clearing her head. "This is the worst mistake ever."

Ash turned to her. "It's not like it would be the end of the world, Skye."

Whether they meshed or not didn't matter.

"We can't be married," she stated with conviction. "Besides, your fans might think we eloped, but when they find out it was all a big mistake, they'll be relieved. You and I can go back to our regular lives."

Why wasn't he freaked out? Did nothing rattle this man?

He amped up the music. "I don't care what the fans think. It's my fucking life. Roll up the window. It's cold outside." He jabbed at the temperature control, flooding the car with heat.

Tension filled the car with an oppressive weight.

She pulled out her cell phone and checked for messages from Forest. Desperate to reach out to the one source of stability in her life, she let her fingers fly over the keys.

She needed her anchor.

I messed up, Beanpole.

She brought Forest up to speed on the situation.

What's up, my summer Skye? Fair winds and following seas here.

He sent a naked picture of himself and another man taking a selfie off the bow of a yacht. Forest smiled as the man beside him kissed his cheek and cupped his balls. She rolled her eyes. Evidently no-porno shots meant something different to him than it did to her.

The man beside Forest looked to be a decade older than her brother. Blond and tan, he was well muscled and fit for his age. Thankfully, he wore a pair of Bermuda shorts although the erection he sported tented the fabric.

Naked and tanned, Forest seemed content. His grin was infectious, and she couldn't help but smile, seeing him happy. If only she shared that joy instead of this gut-wrenching fear…

Not that she wasn't happy or even content.

Ash made her feel alive, and she'd never felt so comfortable with a man. His fame hadn't changed his heart, and he didn't act like a pompous rock-star. They laughed easily and shared silences with grace—except for their current muteness, following the news of an unintended union.

They had a rhythm. It was insane, much like the song he'd written. But they did make sense.

His touch electrified her like no man she'd ever known, and as crazy as it sounded, he'd found the shattered pieces of her soul and put them back together. She couldn't describe it any other way, other than to say she'd been waiting for him her entire life.

It wouldn't be the worst mistake to be married, except they hadn't had a chance to really get to know each other. Marriage wasn't something she thought she'd ever rush into, especially as a mistake made by signing the wrong form.

The problem was, Ash had her acting out of character, and that, more than anything, made her doubts grow. Not to mention, how would she ever fit into his rock-star life?

She texted Forest back.

Check your inbox, Bean.

Her fingers tapped with impatience while Ash stared down the night road. His lips had tightened into a thin line. An Angel Fire song burst over the airwaves, one of her favorites, but he changed the station after the first few notes played.

"Hey, I like that song." She reached to turn the channel back.

He gave a shake of his head and restrained her hand. "I don't like listening to myself sing."

She jerked her hand away. "That's crazy. You have an amazing voice." She changed the station back as his voice belted out the haunting lyrics of "String Me Up."

Lips twisting with distaste, he turned the volume down, using the controls on the steering column.

"Why did you do that?"

"Don't you think we should talk about something other than my singing?"

"Not until we know for sure what happened."

"And you think being married is the worst thing imaginable? You really think this is a fling, that we're going to go back to our separate lives after this?"

The hurt in his voice swirled around her chest and then knifed deep in her heart. She turned to him, stunned. Surely, he saw this for the colossal mistake it was.

He cranked up the music, making further conversation impossible. Before she could defuse their conversation, her phone buzzed with Forest's response.

Married? WTF! U certain?

She typed her response.

No.

And then she waited, staring at Ash's shadowed profile, as they drove down the dark highway.

Finally, Forest texted back.

How can U not know?

I was drunk.

We need to talk.

Can't. He's with me.

WTF?

Forest's confusion rang in the brevity of his text.

Did you read my email?

She'd explained all about Ben and Edna and Marge with the papers, where one might or might not have been a marriage certificate. She should have read what she was signing. Ash should have read what he was signing. Ben and Edna should have noticed the mistake. This was a disaster.

What do you want me to do?

Forest was stuck in the middle of an ocean. There was nothing he could do, not that he'd let that stop him.

Nothing.

She'd have to sort things out in the morning, call and find out what had happened.

This is serious.

I know.

We'll see about an annulment. Don't do anything stupid.

Ash's scowl deepened, his fingers drumming in time to the beat of a Metallica song blaring out of the speakers, while his eyes focused intently forward.

Was this their first fight?

Her words had hurt him. What she didn't understand was why he wasn't as freaked out as she was. He had a lot to lose from an unwanted marriage.

Eyes closed, she blew out a breath. She reached out and touched his arm, shocked when he flinched. "I'm sorry."

For the first time, he ignored her soft words.

She turned the music down. "Ash, I said I was sorry." Her words bounced around the inside of the vehicle, sounding overly loud and overly empty.

His jaw clamped down, and his fingers gripped harder on the steering wheel. He signaled a lane change and moved the car into the passing lane, guiding them past a string of eighteen-wheelers, while keeping his silence.

She skimmed his bicep with a flutter of her fingers, a featherlight touch, but he gave no reaction.

He merged back into the right lane, and the lights from the semitruck behind them illuminated the interior of their car.

"I'm tired of driving," he announced. "There's an exit ten miles ahead. We can get a couple of rooms there."

A couple of rooms? What happened to sharing a bed? What happened to having sex?

They'd known each other barely three days, yet she could already read his tells. Seeing his lips pressed into a thin line told her everything about the direction of his thoughts.

This mess needed to be fixed, and she only knew one way to do that. She edged over in her seat and stretched to cup his groin.

He jumped, and the car swerved. "What the fuck?"

She stroked his cock and then squeezed him with her hand. He hardened under her touch.

"Fuck. You want to get in a wreck?"

"I'm apologizing."

"With your hand on my dick?" He tugged on her wrist, but she refused to move. "You don't have to apologize."

"You might want to keep both hands on the wheel," she said, unbuckling and stretching over the armrest.

Within moments, she liberated his swollen cock from the confines of his jeans. He groaned as she kissed the tip. The car swerved as she wrapped her lips around him, licking at the drop of pre-cum forming on his slit.

He tugged on her hair. "Apology accepted. Now, sit the fuck up before I wreck. As much as I like what you're doing—"

She silenced him with a lick from root to crown. He gasped and jerked his hips.

"Why two rooms?"

The car swerved as she seated him deep in her mouth.

"Stop that." The pressure on her head no longer pulled but pushed down as his hips thrust up.

She swirled her tongue around the tip of his cock, stopping to lick the underside where he was most sensitive. She cupped his balls and gave a gentle squeeze, pulling and tugging, almost to the point of pain.

"That's it," he said with a growl. The car jerked to the right, and he pressed on the brakes.

The uneven pavement of the shoulder made the car shudder as he slowed down from freeway speeds. Then, the car bounced as it transitioned from pavement to a rougher surface. *Dirt or turf?* With her head buried in his lap, she couldn't see.

Skye wasn't sure what Ash was up to, only that the suspension jostled her around. She bumped her head on the steering wheel as the car canted in every direction.

Were they crashing? She didn't think so because Ash was steering like he knew what he was doing.

"If you want to fuck, we're going to fuck, but we're doing it my way."

Chapter Sixteen

"If you want to fuck, we're going to fuck."

She froze at the passion laced in his words. *Why had he pulled off the freeway?*

"What do you mean, your way?" A stupid question. The moment she'd asked, she wanted to take the words back.

"Only that I don't like being teased."

His tone frightened her, but beneath her fear, an unbridled excitement stirred. He was the only man who'd ever come close to heating her body. *Would he be the one to push past her barriers? Or would her body collapse inward, growing cold and lifeless beneath his touch?*

He drove them into a farmer's field. Darkness enveloped them when he turned off the lights, but he kept the engine running, the car's heater warming them against the winter chill.

She needed to prepare him for an inevitable disappointment. "Ash," she began, "I don't think..."

He said nothing as he unbuckled and climbed out of the rental. A gust of cold air swirled inside, and she shivered against the chill.

She leaned forward and turned up the temperature. "What are you doing?" she asked as he walked around the car.

"Getting ready to fuck you."

For whatever reason, Ash's foul mouth had her wet and wanting. Before she knew what was happening, he had her door open and the seat belt unbuckled. He grabbed her and pulled her from the vehicle.

His eyes glinted with purpose. "I warned you." He pressed her against the side of the car, leaned forward, and kissed her with a rough and wild intensity.

Passion pulsed in the way he plundered her mouth, his tongue wrestling with hers in a quest for dominance. He cupped her face, and she found herself opening to him, unwilling to fight the inevitability of the moment. His licks turned to nips and then to teasing bites.

"Fuck," he said.

"Our three days aren't up."

He growled and restrained her hands. His breath came in heavy pants. "As I remember, we threw the no-sex clause out during our conversation in the plane. You've teased me all day with your fuckable mouth. I'm done waiting. I want you."

She gasped at the hard edge of his frustrated glare. Feral and determined, his lust could not be denied. His hot breath pulsed across her neck, raising the fine hairs at her nape, and the press of his cock between her legs shot electric pulsations straight to her core.

The cold barely registered. All she could feel was an escalating need as his touch engulfed her in flames.

"This is going to happen," he said, "unless you say *no* right now." He stared hard into her eyes.

Her skin prickled—not from the cold, but from desire and fear warring in her body. His touch drove her to consider the unthinkable. The hand gripping her wrists constricted and pinched her delicate skin, but she didn't care. She needed more.

Saying yes would grant her consent. No would take it away. She didn't have the strength to do either, hoping he would know when to stop because she sure as hell didn't know when that might be.

His lips, warm and smooth, covered her mouth while his tongue toyed with hers. Their breaths mingled until his exhalations became her inhales. A twisted smile of victory appeared on his face. He released her wrists and lifted her legs around his waist.

"You're mine." A deep hum began in the back of his throat, the melody to "Insanity."

He carried her to the back of the car, and opened the hatch. There, he put her down, and then slipped off her shoes and her clothing.

The light of the silvery moon peeked through scattered clouds, spilling through the windows and bathing them in an otherworldly glow. Her skin heated under his gaze. She scooted back while he kicked off his shoes and removed his pants, causing her heart to thunder in her chest.

He closed the back hatch, crawling over her, making her inch back. She was trying to get away, yet she was desperate for his touch.

"Condom," she said with a squeak.

In their hormone-fueled lust, getting knocked up would be the icing on the proverbial wedding cake.

"Fuck," Ash said with a growl. He fumbled and finally pulled one free. "You sure about this, babe?"

She ripped the pouch and slid the condom over his shaft, hoping that was enough of an answer because she didn't have the energy for words.

He kissed her neck and toyed with her nipples before heading to her pussy, but she wanted none of that, knowing what would happen if he stimulated her there.

"No," she said. "Please, just fuck me."

A look of surprise flashed in the shadows of his face, but he didn't argue. Instead, he positioned himself over her and lined the head of his cock against her pussy. Ever so slowly, he slid inside, burying himself deep, while her body came alive. The heat of his body blanketed her while he rocked a lazy but determined pace.

Despite his earlier urgency, Ash took his time. She crossed her ankles over his back, reveling in the sensations the glide of his cock elicited deep within her walls.

Before long, they were a melody of entwined limbs and desperate mouths, kissing and licking themselves into a frenzy.

He fucked gently but with purpose, and where she usually preferred Spencer to get in and out as quickly as possible, she enjoyed the erogenous slide of Ash's cock against her inner walls. And, each time he thrust forward, their connection would grow until even their breaths pulsed in concert with each other. His cock stretched her with a glorious fullness, and his fingers gripped her hips as he moved, each movement harder and faster than the last.

The sound of sex swallowed the silence of the night, and her soft moans joined him in a synchronous melody, their combined breaths fogging the windows. The flush of her skin and the warmth of his body heated the interior of the car. He pressed against her, superheating her body, as she dug her fingers into his hair. He guided every movement, and took his time, as if he were savoring the friction building between them.

He changed the angle of his thrusts, pulling a startled gasp from her lips. Again and again, he concentrated on that spot, turning her mindless with the need to combust.

Then, she felt it—that inevitable pressure building to a crescendo within. She closed her eyes, fighting the flood of sensation, but with the approach of her climax, oily images of her foster father crowded her mind.

His dirty body had writhed over her juvenile flesh as he'd spilled his foul seed deep within her body. He'd stolen not only her innocence but drawn pleasure from conquering her will. She hadn't had a choice; to refuse would mean more suffering.

Bile rose in her throat, and an icy tendril gripped her heart. From there, it spiraled outward.

The threat of pain—if not to her, then to Forest—had ensured she'd perform to the satisfaction of their foster father.

Memories resurfaced—the whippings, the electric shocks, and the icy submersions.

He'd forced her to choose—endure pleasure or see Forest punished for her failure.

The flood could not be stopped and had her panting between one breath and the next. But she wouldn't let her past ruin this moment...

Except her shoulders hunched on their own, pressing up to her ears, as she tried to drown out her foster father's voice. The memories wouldn't stop. They never would. Orgasms would forever be tied to great cruelty.

Despite her desire to experience this moment with Ash, muscle memory took over.

And, while Ash made love, oblivious to her sudden change, her moans of pleasure transformed to whimpers of fear. The fire in her belly dampened, extinguished by a past she couldn't escape, and tears streamed down her cheeks.

Ash's body stilled. "Skye? What's wrong? What happened? Open your eyes. Don't disappear." Desperation clung to his words, and his kisses fluttered over her eyelids.

He couldn't reach her because her mind had slipped to a dark place while her body endured. She refused to open her eyes, praying only for Ash to finish quickly and let it be done.

His fingers brushed her cheeks. "Skye? Shit. Shit. Shit!"

She'd hoped things would be different, but she was horribly wrong.

"No. Don't stop."

She wrapped her hands around his neck and tightened her legs around his hips, but he was already backing away.

"We're doing this together, babe, or not at all." He rolled to the side, pulling her tight against him. "What happened?"

What could she say?

"I want to understand what I did wrong."

His erection softened, drooping from his body, still heavy, if not nearly as engorged.

She ran a hand up and down her body, a vague gesture, and then did the same to his. "This...I can't do this. I thought I could, but I can't. When I get close...it gets complicated."

"You can't come?"

Oh, she could come. Under threat of bodily harm, hers and Forest's, she'd been trained to respond to the commands of a madman.

A smirk lifted the corner of his mouth. "I'm pretty sure I can get you to come."

"This isn't funny."

"I'm not laughing, Skye, but I think I know a thing or two about how to please a woman."

There was nothing remotely humorous about her messed up sexual history.

"But that's just it. Don't try. Don't make an issue of it. Just don't." She wanted to open up more, but to do so would invite the past into the present.

"Don't you see?" He drew a heart on the foggy window, spearing it with an arrow. "You've bruised my rock-star image by freezing up like that. I'm not walking away from this, from you." His words were meant as a joke but hurt nonetheless.

She tried pulling away, but he drew her back into his arms. "This is the most fucked up fuck in the book of fucks." Her tears flowed freely now.

He ran his hand from her shoulder to her hip, caressing her skin and raising fine goose bumps along the way. "Don't ever say that again, Skye. There's nothing fucked up about us. We don't have to rush this. I thought you wanted…I'll never push you like that again."

But that was the whole problem.

She'd never be ready—at least not for what Ash wanted. And he was a rock star with flocks of eager fans who could give him everything he desired.

She said nothing, letting her silence speak with thunderous intent.

"You're absolutely amazing." The timbre of his voice deepened as he pressed his lips to hers. "I don't know what happened, but I'm going to spend the rest of my life undoing whatever that bastard did, starting with tonight."

"But that's just it." She couldn't keep silent anymore. "Don't you understand? I don't want to be fixed." *And wasn't that the perfect lie?*

Unlike Spencer, who had taken what he wanted, Ash wasn't content to be a one-sided lover. He wouldn't stop until he figured out her broken body, but she didn't want Ash to see how damaged she was. She wanted the gentle rhythm they'd developed back in the cabin.

She'd rather keep her broken body locked down tight than relive her foster father's abuse. As long as Ash didn't force the issue, things would be fine. That strategy had worked well enough with Spencer.

"I don't know if I'll ever fix myself, and for the most part, I'm happy with who I am. I want to make you happy even if it doesn't work for me." She stroked his cock, glad to see him harden again.

He jerked at her touch. A low groan emanated from deep within his throat. "You want to fuck but don't want me to do anything for you?"

"Yes."

"That's not right. What if that's not what I want?"

She gripped the base of his shaft and stroked up toward the glans. "I can't give you what you want." She didn't know how. "But I can give you this."

His body shook as she moved her hand, pulling and twisting in a move she knew would drive him insane. His balls drew up into his body as she reached down to cup them.

A hiss escaped between his clenched teeth. "You're killing me here." He clamped his hand around her wrist. "I want to make this good for you, too."

"Then, I want you back inside me," she said. "You felt good, fucking me."

He reached down and rolled the condom off. "No. We're doing this together." His hand skimmed her belly and cupped her sex. "Or we're not doing it at all."

He didn't understand trauma. Some injuries took time to heal, and psychological scars sometimes never went away. If they were to have any sort of future together, he needed to accept her flaws.

She shook her head. "It's not that easy."

Despite what he'd said, this was *the most fucked up fuck* of them all. She shouldn't have relaxed the no-sex clause. They'd been having fun until sex entered the equation. But she'd thought…she'd hoped that this time would be different.

She was wrong.

Extracting herself from his embrace, she reached for her clothes. "Maybe we should go find that motel you were talking about and get some rest?"

He shook his head. "I'm not willing to give this up. Let me explore your body."

"I can't…"

"Relax, Skye. It's my wedding night. I plan on getting to know my bride."

"We're not married."

"You don't know that we're not."

"If we are, it's a mistake." One that Forest had sent their army of lawyers into fixing. He was a force to be reckoned with.

"Call it a fortunate misadventure instead of a mistake," Ash insisted. He pushed her hands aside, and he circled a finger around her nipple. "It's just you and me. Trust me not to hurt you, and when your mind starts heading in the wrong direction, I'll bring you back. No one is ever going to hurt you again."

He kissed her, tender and sweet, not demanding, not pushing. She took in a breath and opened herself to his touch. The rough callus of his finger dragged against her tender flesh. She gasped as he slipped his hand down, his finger slipping inside her folds. He stroked her from the inside out, but it was too much.

Her eyes closed while she accepted the inevitable. "You can't fix me," she said on a sigh. Carefully, she held his jaw and forced him to look at her. "I'm not broken, and I don't need to be fixed. Please accept this."

"I'm not trying to force anything."

She placed her finger over his lips. "This has nothing to do with you or your skill as a lover." She kissed him lightly on the lips. "Believe me, I wish I could give you that part of myself, and for the record, I've never gotten so close, but forcing me is only going to make it harder."

She gripped his cock, still hard and heavy with need. An involuntary shudder rippled through his body as she stroked him.

"But I can give you what you need."

He groaned as her fingers circled his glans. "Damn, don't hate me, but I don't want to say no."

"Then, say yes." She flicked under the head of his glans, eliciting another groan.

His cock jumped in her hands, stiffening even more.

She straddled him, determined to salvage the worst fuck of her life and probably his as well. "Do you mind if I take the top?"

He snapped his fingers. "Condom, please."

She handed him a condom from the pack.

He ripped the foil pouch and covered himself. His hooded eyes regarded her with serious intent. "This means more to me than you know. I just wish you would let me—"

She kissed the tip of his nose. "There's more to sex than an orgasm. I want to feel you inside me. I want you to take what you need." She smiled at him. "Fuck me, Ash. You can still make me yours."

He laughed and pulled her into position until her pussy hovered over his cock. "Someday, Skye Summers, you will be mine, all of you."

She laughed. "Someday…" *Probably never.* She lowered herself onto his shaft, enjoying the sensation of him filling her with each excruciating inch. "Fuck me like a rock star."

He kissed her and thrust upward. "With pleasure."

Chapter Seventeen

Skye woke to fogged windows and dawn breaking over a farmer's field, slowly giving way to a day bright with potential. Frost dusted the long grass and that chill invaded the interior of the car. The world looked crisp and ready to face whatever might come next. She wished she'd shared that sentiment. Instead, she wanted to crawl into a hole and forget all about the worst fucked up fuck of fucks.

Ash had stamina, more than she was used to with Spencer's one-minute blow-and-go. Ash had tried to reciprocate, but eventually, he'd accepted the truth. She'd given him an explosive orgasm, but her body had failed to relinquish years of conditioning.

Hopefully, he would accept that was the best she could give.

She nudged Ash. "Wake up, Rock star."

He moaned. "Shit, what time is it?"

"I have no idea, but it's light outside. We should get moving."

Draping an arm over his eyes, he curled his body around hers, pressing his hardness against her back.

She rolled over and found herself lost in his embrace. Kissing him on the lips, she gripped his shaft, stroking lightly, until his eyes closed, and he bit his lower lip.

"Do you want me to take care of this?"

His hips jerked. "Damn, I'll never get enough of you."

"I'll take that as a yes."

"Fuck," he said with a groan. "My fate is in your hands. Put me out of my misery."

She pulled out a condom and sheathed him, teasing him with a slow roll of the latex over the length of his cock.

His chin gave a sharp jerk, and his breath hissed when she straddled him. She leaned forward to kiss him, and then with a sinuous gyration of her hips, she slowly sank down. He groaned and thrust upward.

Being on top had always made her feel vulnerable and exposed, on display. Her hips moved in a rhythm that had been drilled into her from an age much too young. With Ash, however, she found joy in the subtle gyrations. What had once been a painful chore became beautiful with the expression of ecstasy etched on Ash's face.

As he climaxed, she collapsed over him—not with an orgasm of her own, but with warmth building in her heart and the joy that came from seeing him satisfied. She definitely could get used to this.

He lifted her off his hips. "That was so good. I almost passed out. I want to do that for you. I don't like taking from you like this." He removed the condom and added it to the bag of discarded latex. "My balls are officially empty."

"Trust me, you'll fill them up again. I'm a doctor; I know. And it's not about taking anything from me." She brushed her lips over his forehead. "I want to do this, and in my own way, it feels…good."

He hadn't tried to force the issue of her orgasm, but it bothered him. That worried her and cast doubt on their future.

He pulled on his jeans. "Get dressed, babe. We need to leave."

She shrugged on comfortable clothes, choosing sweats instead of the jeans she'd worn the night before. It would have to do until they could stop and buy something better.

Ash joined her up front and then started the car. A few moments later, he drove out of the field and back into the stream of interstate traffic. They drove to the next exit where he filled the car with fuel, and they used the restrooms.

She bought Ash a coffee at the Quick Mart and rose up on her tiptoes to kiss his cheek before handing over his cup. She paused at the pensive expression darkening his features.

"What's wrong?" She sipped hot cocoa, waiting for his response.

His fingers tapped the screen of his phone. His concern seemed to deepen with a twist of his lips and a furrowing of his brow. He tasted his coffee before answering, "It's my manager."

"And?"

"He's pissed."

"About what?" Silly question because there could be only one thing that would bother Angel Fire's manager.

Ash took another draw of coffee. "He's on damage control."

"Damage control?" She sucked in a breath, knowing well enough to be worried by that expression. "We'll be back at the airport to get your Jeep later tonight, and if we drive through the night, we can get to DC by morning. There's not much you can do about it now."

Ash tugged in a deep breath. "That's just it. He wants to take immediate action."

"Immediate action?" She waved at the sky. "Unless he can descend from the heavens, he's going to have to wait."

Ash pulled her close. "You're forgetting who I am."

"What does that mean?"

"He's on his way."

"On his way?"

"He took the jet…and we're meeting him at the next town."

She wasn't sure what to think about meeting Angel Fire's pissed off manager.

"And I should probably warn you, the whole band's tagging along. They want to know what the fuck I was thinking, getting married to a girl I'd just met."

She shrugged. "It was a silly mistake." And still not confirmed. "Tell them not to get their panties in a wad."

"Oh, that's priceless." He laughed. "I can't wait to see Spike's expression when I tell him that." Ash sobered. "The guys are cool, but they're protective. They believe I'm back on drugs or drinking again, and they think you tricked me. I'm afraid they're planning an intervention."

"An intervention?"

He nodded. "Just don't judge them. They can come off a little heavy-handed. Don't worry; I'll run interference."

"Oh." She didn't like the sound of him running interference. The last thing she wanted was to come between him and his band.

He fisted his free hand, turning his knuckles white. "What we have is meant to be. You get that, right?" He grabbed her, holding her tight against his chest, as if he were afraid to let her go.

"We'll just explain." She buried her head, enjoying the comfort of his arms. His rich smell enveloped her in a fog of everything right.

He kissed the top of her head. "Good. It took a lot for the guys to trust me after rehab. I've been clean and sober for too many years, and I don't want them thinking the wrong thing. It's not like I didn't…"

She returned his hug, trying to be supportive. Knowing how Forest struggled with his addiction, she understood how important it was to have his friends trust him.

"We'll get it annulled or something." She pulled back and searched his expression for a clue as to his thoughts.

His lips pressed into a thin line.

"Did I say something wrong?"

"No, babe." He finished filling the rental. "It'd be kind of a funny though, wouldn't it?" His eyes rounded with a hopeful expression.

"What would?"

"If we stayed married."

She got into the car and buckled in. "Who gets married after three days? That's insane."

He opened the driver's side door and climbed in. "You don't believe in love at first sight?"

She didn't. Instead of answering, she kicked off her shoes and pressed her feet against the dash.

"My dad claims he knew the moment he laid eyes on my mom. He married her three months later. My older brother, Seth, tied the knot six months after he'd met Sandie. Alec took longer. He and Gianna married two years after they'd started dating, but if you ask him, he'll tell you he knew the day he met her, too. The only reason they waited was because her father had insisted she finish college first. The men in my family just know."

Her stomach fluttered with the implication of his words. She deflected as best as she could. "I don't know about love at first sight or even true love. I thought I loved Spencer, but..." Bringing Spencer's name into this conversation might not have been the best choice, but the damage was done.

Ash turned on the radio and cranked the volume. Hard rock blared through the speakers, drowning out further conversation as he guided them back onto the road.

Her phone buzzed with an incoming text from Forest.

You want good news or bad?

Forest's words scrawled across her screen as a tease.

Bad news first, Beanpole.

Okay, my summer Skye…it's legal. You married a rock star.

Her heart skipped as her fingers clutched the phone.

Are you certain?

Of course Forest was certain. Their army of lawyers wouldn't get something like that wrong.

With her head slanted to the side, she regarded the man sitting beside her. Fingers tapping on the steering wheel, jaw clenched tight, Ash remained an intriguing mystery. He drew her in with an undeniable magnetism. *While she wouldn't call it love at first sight, would it be such a bad thing to spend more time with him?*

But she needed more time.

Ash had the volume turned up loud enough that it was clear he was done with talking. She turned back to her conversation with Forest.

What now?

You get it annulled. That's the good news.

She worried her lower lip with her teeth.

I think it's too late for that.

LOL! Thought you said you weren't sleeping with him.

We weren't.

Ah, past tense. So, is your rock star any good in bed?

Her fingers tapped the display.

How bad is it?

Considering there's no prenup, the ramifications are significant.

She didn't believe in prenups, but she also never thought she'd find herself accidentally married.

I'm in trouble, aren't I?

I'm sending a voice message.

She waited several moments, and then Forest's voice message came through. She dialed the volume down low and held the phone to her ear.

"Sleeping with him doesn't mean you can't get the marriage annulled. That's old-fashioned thinking. Canada is very clear on the rules regarding annulments. You can get one if one or both parties were unaware they were getting married. I'd say that one fits the bill. An annulment will take longer than a divorce though…if that's still what you want?"

She texted back.

How long?

Months.

Months!

She fisted her phone, deep in thought. Meanwhile, the first lyrics of an Angel Fire track blasted over the radio. She caught Ash staring.

"Shouldn't your eyes be on the road?"

"Who are you talking to?" A thread of jealousy weaved through his voice. He focused forward, but his eyes shifted to her phone, as if trying to scan the text.

She tilted the screen away from him. "Bean."

He pursed his lips. "What does your brother have to say? Did you tell him?"

"I did."

"And?"

"He thinks it's hilarious." That was partly true. Forest was eating the whole mess up.

"Really?" His mouth twisted into a wry grin. "I doubt that."

"Well, he has an odd sense of humor." No way was she going to tell him what Forest had really had to say. "Do you mind if I take a nap?"

She wasn't tired, but talking about their messed up situation made her head hurt. Avoidance never solved problems. Fortunately, she didn't care about resolving anything right now. What she couldn't figure out was why Ash wasn't upset by the whole mess.

Her phone beeped. Forest again.

U want me to come?

I thought you were in the middle of the ocean? How are you going to get here?

I'll have a helicopter pick me up. For you, I can be there, my summer Skye.

She shook her head, knowing he would move the world to be at her side.

No, Bean, I'm good. How far are you from landfall?

A few hundred miles out.

I didn't think helicopters had the range to fly that far off-shore.

There's one that does. It can scoop me up in a bucket and deliver me to you or to a jet that will take me to you.

Stay on your boat, Beanpole. I don't need rescuing. This is messed up, but Ash is good. I like him.

Like, like? Or like, love?

She hesitated and then typed her most honest response.

IDK.

She stared at Ash's profile. His fingers tapped out the beat to the song playing over the radio. His jaw worked in concert with the worry edging the corners of his eyes.

We'll sort this out. You hang on, my summer Skye.

Yes, Bean. XO!

Ditto.

Ash turned down the radio. "I thought you were going to take a nap?"

She turned off her phone. "Bean wasn't done scolding me."

Everything had changed between her and Ash with the mistake of two signatures.

She always knew their adventure would come with an expiration date.

Three days—that was the limit of their contract. She thought she wanted more, but not a till-death-do-you-part more. And his bandmates might not let her stick around.

Once the demands of regular life resumed and they descended from the dreamlike state of this vacation, they would face two very different lives.

She didn't fit in his, and he didn't fit in hers.

Chapter Eighteen

ASH AND SKYE DROVE TO THE NEXT TOWN WITH AN AIRPORT. AFTER dropping off the rental car, Skye headed for the shuttle that would take them to the passenger terminal. A whirlwind of possibilities swirled in the space separating her and Ash. Time slipped through their fingers as the inevitability of the real world approached.

Ash gripped his guitar. She held her backpack. They each clung to the pieces of their lives.

She followed the other travelers queuing up for the shuttle, but the weight of Ash's hand on her arm stopped her in her tracks.

"What's wrong?" she asked.

"We have a car coming."

She didn't even question the why or how. This was no longer Ash but Blaze, lead singer and front man of Angel Fire, whose manager chartered planes on a whim.

A black sedan pulled up outside the rental agency, and a large man climbed out the driver's side. He looked familiar until she realized he was one of the drivers of the Hummers the day she'd met Ash.

The man opened the passenger door. His appraising gaze settled on her, making her hands tremble.

"Mr. Dean"—then, he included her with a fractional nod—"Miss, the jet is waiting."

Ash hefted his guitar. "Hey, Sam."

Sam took her backpack from her tight grip while Ash loaded his guitar into the trunk.

Sam gestured to the car. "Have a seat, please. I'll take care of this." He lifted her tired backpack and gently laid it beside Ash's guitar.

Climbing into the car, she heaved a heavy sigh. Sam's appearance irrevocably erased the carefree world of a mountain cabin, hiking, and waterfall hunts. Ash's world of rock-star fame, fortune, glitz, and glamour barreled down on them. And she feared she was nothing more than an unwelcome interloper.

Once Ash joined her, she pressed her fingers against his arm, needing contact to galvanize herself against what would come next. "Who is he?"

Ash gave a strained smile. "Sam's a part of my security detail." He relaxed into the seat, kicking a heel over his knee and patting her hand. "Don't worry about him. He's cool."

With a sigh, she leaned against Ash, her stomach lurching with nerves. "Maybe I should drive home by myself and let you deal with your band."

Being thrust in the middle of whatever conversation Ash would have with his bandmates, plus an irate manager, didn't seem like a good idea.

"You're not leaving." He slung an arm over her shoulder, and she snuggled against the hard muscles of his chest.

Sam settled into the driver's seat and started the car.

"The guys can be a bit over the top," Ash said, "but don't let them scare you."

"I'm not scared." She resigned herself to the inevitable. "Just concerned." Like ripping off a Band-Aid, it would be best to get this over quickly.

Ash put a finger under her chin and turned her to face him. Sweeping forward, he brushed his lips over hers. At first soft and delicate, the press turned needful and raw, but she pushed him away, aware of the stern look Sam gave through the rearview mirror.

The sedan wove around the airport, leaving the passenger terminal behind.

"Where are we going?" She craned her neck, curious as to their destination.

"Relax." Ash's fingers sifted through her long curls, his eyes following every twist and turn of the strands.

"But look at my clothes!" She gestured to her baggy sweats. "I can't meet them like this."

"It's okay. They're cool," Ash said.

Easy for him to say. He wasn't the one facing down a group of strangers who believed she'd stolen their lead singer.

Butterflies danced in her belly, making her nauseous, but soon, the car pulled up to a smaller terminal, and she and Ash were climbing out.

He led her into a building where they passed through a security-screening checkpoint, and her backpack along with Ash's guitar were sent through an X-ray scanner. Sam then took the lead and ushered them out of the building and onto the tarmac where a full-sized commercial jet waited.

She pulled up short. "I was expecting something smaller."

When he'd said his manager was bringing the jet, she had imagined a Learjet, not a jumbo airliner. While she knew his band was popular, never had she imagined they had the resources to afford such extravagance.

Ash laughed. "Angel Fire doesn't do anything small."

A set of airstairs had been pulled up to the jetliner, and the hatch sat open. As she and Ash approached, a man called out from the open hatch. Moments later, men spilled out of the aircraft and bounded down the stairs.

She gripped Ash's hand...hard. Vaguely, she remembered the men from the coffee shop.

Ash squeezed her hand. "Bent is the one with the black hair. Noodles has the tribal tats. Spike is the one with the piercings. Not sure where Bash is."

One thing all the men shared, although distinctly different, was their devastatingly handsome looks. Forest would know their names and faces, but she struggled to get them right. Spike was easy. Metal pierced his flesh. Noodles, tall and somewhat lanky, didn't remind her of a noodle, but the tribal tattoos curved around his flesh, so she could remember the curves and angles and make a connection with a noodle. Bent was the hardest to find something easy to remember him by—until she took another look at the curled mop on top of his head. Curly hair meant bent hair. With her memory joggers firmly in place, she was fairly certain she wouldn't make a mistake in their names.

Another man stood at the top of the stairs. With broad shoulders and a bald head, he wore a T-shirt, black to match the color of his jeans, as he stared down at her with a fixed expression.

Ash pointed. "That's Bash. We went to high school together."

Even from a distance, Bash's eyes narrowed with suspicion. His mnemonic was easy. He was the one who wanted to bash in her head.

She grabbed Ash's arm. "I don't think Bash likes me."

"He doesn't know you." Ash disentangled her hand from his arm and brushed her knuckles with the sweetest kiss. "We're like family. Don't be surprised if they're a bit overprotective, but they're going to love you"

A cold wind blew across the asphalt, swirling around her legs and creeping down the back of her heavy coat. It sent a chill down her spine, prickling her skin and setting her teeth on edge. A general hum filled the air, but all the engines had been turned off, and there weren't any other jets at the private terminal. The air hung with an eerie silence. Odd in a place she'd expect to hear the drone of jet engines.

Ash's conviction was reassuring. She shivered and wrapped her arms around herself to hold in precious body heat.

A man in a suit joined Bash at the cabin door, the two of them leaning close and looking exactly like they were discussing her.

"That's our manager, Thomas Tuttle," Ash said.

And the only man not introduced by first name, like he wore his full name with the same hardness as the dark suit.

Ash pulled her close, wrapping an arm over her shoulder. The warmth of his body soaked into her but did nothing to dispel the chill emanating from the top of those stairs. She leaned in for support and for protection against the imposing group of men advancing upon them…upon her.

Thomas Tuttle's mouth settled into a scowl as he gazed down from the top of those stairs. She knew what he saw—a threat to his investment and a liability to his cash cow, the lead singer.

Spike reached them first. Her attention latched on to the three rings piercing his lower lip. *How did he ever kiss with all that hardware?*

"So, this is the chick?" Spike did a once-over, scanning her from head to toe and dismissing her just as quickly.

The man with the curly black hair stepped beside Spike. Bent's eyes narrowed with disdain. "What's the chick's name?" Bent's gruff tone made her feel inconsequential and unwanted.

Tension coiled in Ash's body as the glowing reactions she knew he had hoped for failed to materialize.

She sucked in a breath and thrust out her hand, hoping to salvage something of this meeting. Courtesy demanded they shake, and she hoped they would relax amid the common greeting. "Hi, I'm Skye."

Bent's eyes cut to her hand, but he didn't move to take it. His attention focused instead on Ash, something like a threat smoldering in his expression.

She refused to allow them to intimidate her. She'd seen far scarier in the back bay of her emergency department, strong men posturing who would crumble when she stitched up their wounds. She took a step forward, and purposefully reached down to clasp Bent's hand, forcing the issue.

With her best smile, she shook, using an exaggerated up and down motion. "You must be Bent?"

Spike's lower lip curved into a smile, lifting the three silver rings.

Bent's eyes rounded with surprise, but she released his limp hand before he could respond. She then extended her hand to Spike. "And you must be Spike."

Spike took her hand with a snicker to Bent. "I remember you now. You're the hellcat from that coffee shop."

"I wouldn't call myself a hellcat." She laughed. "Crazy maybe, depending on the day."

He smiled. "Well, that is to be determined. We didn't think much of it when Ash took off to return your bag. At least, not until he came back, all bloodied up. I'm thinking there's a story to be told."

She returned Spike's smile. "Maybe, maybe not."

"No maybe about it, considering you got him to marry you." Bent crossed his arms with accusation and stared down his nose, as if he'd solved some great mystery.

Noodles edged Bent out of the way. "No fucking way." His mouth gaped. "She's the one?" He slugged Ash in the arm. "What the hell, man?"

Ash's face darkened several shades of red, turning purple with anger. "Be careful what you say about my *wife*."

Wife? Seriously? It was nice for him to stick up for her, but it wasn't necessary. Not against these men.

"We're kind of still sorting that mess out," she offered.

Noodles held up his hands and backed away. "She's the one the song's about, isn't she? 'Insanity'? And what about 'Hunting Waterfalls'? That one about her, too? She's become your fucking muse?"

"I'm standing right here," she reminded him.

Ash gave a sharp jerk of his chin.

The one who seemed to want to bash her head in finally descended the air stairs and joined Ash's friends.

Bash's fingers curled, tightening into an aggressive display. "At least your songwriting hasn't suffered, fucktard."

She stepped to the side, worried about how things seemed to be escalating out of control.

"Shame you were thinking with your dick instead of your head." Bash shoved Ash. "What the fuck were you thinking, letting her trick you like that?" Another shove, and Ash was forced back a step.

Inserting herself between Ash and his friend didn't seem like the best idea, but doing nothing felt wrong, too. His other bandmates— Noodles, Bent, and Spike—stepped back.

"What the fuck?" The color of Bash's face matched the same purple hue of Ash's skin. "She got you smoking? Drinking? You shooting up again?"

Ash stumbled back. Storm clouds brewed in his expression, but he didn't defend himself against Bash although his fingers curled into fists. Then, they relaxed as he rubbed them against his jeans.

"Stop," he said. The single word reverberated in the hostile air, ringing like a bell and forcing Bash to silence. "You will not talk about my *wife* that way."

Again, the inflection he placed on that singular word had the fine hairs on her nape lifting.

Bash pointed. "No fucking way is that starstruck groupie legit. Tell me you were stoned, high, or drunk as a skunk when you signed on that dotted line. Because no way would you do that. She's nothing more than a cheap fuck. A mistake—"

Her head whipped at that comment, stunned he would say such a thing.

A throaty growl ripped from Ash's throat. "Fuck you."

"It's all over the papers."

Bash launched himself at Ash. The punch to Ash's face knocked him to the ground. Skye tried to run to Ash's side, but Noodles grabbed her and lifted her off her feet. She twisted, clawing at the tattooed arms of the man holding her.

"Goddamn it, woman," Noodles said. He dragged her back toward the plane and called out to Bent, "Help me out."

Bent cursed, "This is a fucking shitstorm. No groupies on the plane. That's the rule."

Noodles breathed down her neck as he dragged her back.

"Let me go!" she cried out.

Bash and Ash pummeled one another while Ash's bodyguard, Sam, made no move to intervene.

This was definitely not what Ash had been expecting, and it was time someone brought order to this mess.

She gritted her teeth, changing tactics. "Put me down, or I'll press charges. And, trust me, you don't want to mess with me." And she didn't care what Forest would say about keeping a low profile. She'd take these guys to the cleaners.

Noodles was smarter than he looked, or maybe there was just enough crazy in her voice to make him worry. He released her and took a step back, lifting his hands up and out. Even the imposing Bent didn't move as she rushed to the fighting men.

Her life wasn't in danger, but Bash was beating the crap out of Ash.

There was only one choice.

She jumped Bash, applying pressure to a nerve bundle in Bash's neck. Two seconds later, he was out cold.

Ash looked at her, his mouth gaping. "What did you do?"

She rolled Bash into a recovery position and aligned his airway. "Don't worry; he'll come around in a minute."

Sam, who hadn't moved while the men were fighting, rushed forward. She felt more than saw the large man barreling toward her and braced for impact.

Ash stepped between her and Sam, stopping his advance. "Skye's a doctor."

"She knocked him out!" Sam exclaimed.

Sure enough, Bash coughed with the urge to breathe. She lightly placed her fingers over his neck, feeling for his pulse. When his eyes popped open, she gave him one of her biggest smiles.

He blinked, dazed, as circulation returned to his brain.

She spoke slowly, making certain he understood every word, "I'm going to let you get up now, but if you even think of touching Ash, you and I are going to have another talk."

Bash started to move, but she pressed on his sternum, rubbing her knuckles against his chest. He gasped at the pain of sternal pressure, something she used in her job to determine the responsiveness of comatose patients.

She had his full attention now. "Do we understand each other?"

Bash coughed. "What the fuck did you do?"

"You're going to be a bit unsteady for the next couple of minutes. I suggest you take it easy. Don't be surprised if you need help walking."

She made a quick assessment of Ash's injuries, but other than a bloody nose, she didn't see any major damage. "You could pinch your nose," she said to Ash. "You know, to stop the bleeding?"

His gorgeous eyes regarded her with a mix of emotions—desire, affection, relief, plus something stronger that she wasn't willing to admit. He dutifully pinched the bridge of his nose to stem the flow of blood.

She needed to leave and let Ash deal with his band. The only problem was, she couldn't trust him *not* to chase her down.

She pointed an accusing finger at Ash's bodyguard, Sam. "Isn't it your job to protect them?"

"From fans, the press, and you, but not from each other. If they want to go at it like dogs, I'm paid *not* to intervene." He waved a hand. "And, here I thought, I was the only one who knew that trick. You've got my respect, Doc."

She ignored Sam and turned to Ash. "What does he mean, paid *not* to intervene?"

Ash extended a hand to Bash, who grudgingly accepted the help to stand.

Bash wobbled and fell against Ash but answered her question, "We get to beat each other up as much as we want. That's what it means." He gathered his balance. "Shit, what the fuck was that? Some juju move?"

"Its jujitsu," she said. "I thought you were going to kill him."

Bash put his hand to the back of his neck. "Just wanted to kick his ass. He went back on a promise."

Ash clapped Bash on the shoulder. "I've been sober the whole time."

"Then, how the fuck did you accidentally get married?"

Clutching at her chest, she took a step back. *How indeed?*

Ash's bandmates faced her down as a unit.

How was she going to defuse this tension?

Thomas Tuttle, with his stiff suit, finally found his way to the men of Angel Fire. "You certainly know how to create a shitstorm, Blaze," Tuttle said to Ash.

Ash's jaw clenched, and his lips thinned. He tugged her to his side, a place he seemed to like her best.

"There are implications we need to consider." Tuttle's cold, hard eyes swept down her body, his lips twisting as he took in her baggy attire.

His dismissive appraisal had her feeling like yesterday's trash. She hadn't endured this much scorn in a very long time. She hadn't liked it then, and she sure as hell didn't like it now. Tuttle could shove his implications and that fancy suit up his ass.

"I'm not something that needs to be taken care of," she said.

With a step to the side, she considered taking Tuttle out, but Ash pulled her back under his protective embrace.

"What are you suggesting?" Ash demanded.

Tuttle raised his hands in a gesture meant to soothe. "We must carefully evaluate what needs to happen next." No threat came from those hands, but his deep-set eyes latched on to her, ready to take her down—or at least pry her away from his star.

Only she didn't back down from the threat of men like him.

Not anymore.

"Like what?" Ash shifted his stance, tucking her behind him. He'd done the same thing with Spencer, shielding her from what he perceived to be a threat.

Tuttle continued his rasping words, "We'll discuss this on the plane. You've missed rehearsals, and we need to prep for this weekend's concert. I have an idea about what to do with…her."

His dismissive wave had her curling her fingers into the muscles of Ash's arm, digging in with her desire to rake Tuttle's eyes out of his sockets.

"We're not doing anything with Skye." Ash lowered his voice, making his wishes clear. "She's not a problem that needs handling."

Although Ash echoed her thoughts, the entire situation threatened to spiral out of hand if she didn't take charge.

Skye pressed her palm to Ash's shoulder and whispered, "Ash, maybe we should talk."

Ash pulled her some distance away, clutching her hand with a desperate hunger. "Don't listen to him. We might have rushed into this, but that's no reason to rush out of it."

"Listen, let's just cool it for a few days. Go talk to your bandmates and smooth things over. I don't think I should go with you." Her gaze darted back to the private terminal. She could catch a flight to Roanoke, retrieve her things from Bob's cabin, and still make it back to work on time.

He gave her a gentle shake. "Look me in the eyes and tell me you don't feel this."

The certainty in his gaze had her heart lurching.

Something existed all right—a nuclear explosive detonation.

She wanted more. Every moment with Ash had brought a profound sense of belonging. She didn't want to lose that feeling, except there was no way for it to last.

Her gaze cut to the plane and all the promises it held. If she set foot on that thing, entered his world, she'd lose a part of herself.

"We made a horrible mistake." She rested her hand on his arm. "This whole situation is making me uncomfortable. And I still need to get my stuff from the cabin. I think the best thing is a time-out. We can figure everything out later."

With Forest's help, she would fix this mess. Or Tuttle would. That man looked like he was used to fixing Angel Fire's messes. In the long run, it would be better to gain some perspective. Obviously, she couldn't trust herself to make rational decisions when Ash was around.

A swipe of the pen had landed them in this mess, and their scrawled signatures would deliver them from it.

"You're wrong, babe," Ash said, brushing wisps of hair from her face. "When I hold you, I know exactly where I belong. You're in my heart. In my soul. You're in the very air I breathe. Don't leave."

How could she respond to his poignant plea?

Time and distance. Time to sort things out, and distance to clear her head.

She'd narrowly missed an engagement to Spencer, and she wasn't ready to stay in a marriage with Ash.

Ash's passion and his desperation to hold on had her heart breaking. Splintering from the inside out, she craved every promise he'd uttered. For that reason, she had to free herself from the madness because it was foolish and irrational to continue. Like oil and water, his famous life and her quiet existence did not mix.

Tension tightened the creases at the corners of his beautiful eyes. *Or was it fear?* Perhaps he sensed her imminent flight. The cords of his muscles stood out on his neck, marring the perfection of his tattoo. The dragon's talons stretched on the bloody web, caught forever between flight and freedom. *Was that what the tattoo meant to him? Had she discovered its meaning on her own?*

No matter how much it hurt, it was time to end their adventure.

"Mr. Tuttle is right," she said with a sigh. "We need to think this through."

A desperate need for her brother's strength had her fighting back a flood of tears.

Ash did that thing with his lips. The thin line of determination challenged her with absolute assurance. His shoulders rolled back, and he stretched to his full height, staring down with his jaw clenched tight. His gaze lingered on her lips and then skittered away.

"You're wrong, babe. You know it, too. But I can't make you stay." He took a step back, releasing her from his grip. "I'm willing to give you space, but I won't give up on us. Someday, you'll realize how hard this was for me to do."

His fingers curled and then he shook them out. Despondency rolled off him in waves, leaving her reeling.

She rubbed at the ache flaring in her chest.

This was it—the end.

"At the very least, let me take you home." His hand opened and closed, grasping at the air and what was remaining of the shreds of time left to them.

But more time in his presence would open her up to changing her mind. Neither of them could afford that.

"I can take care of myself."

His eyes closed and then slowly opened. "I get that." He cleared his throat and took a step toward her, his hand stretching out, urging her to take it. "Don't let it end like this."

She didn't trust herself to speak.

Their eyes met, stretched over an impassable gulf even though only a few feet separated them. He held her in a moment of indecision.

Shaking her head, she pivoted and headed for the terminal.

A knife twisted in her chest. She lurched to a stop and turned, expecting him to follow. Instead, Ash's friends clustered around him, dragging him back toward the plane.

She ran for the sheltering warmth of the terminal. The automatic doors slid open and closed behind her with a hiss of finality. With a swipe to the corners of her eyes, she brushed away the stream of tears.

The employee who tended the hospitality desk looked up as she stumbled to a stop. "Ma'am?" He wiped down his counter. "Can I help you?"

She squared her shoulders. The thick lump in her throat disappeared after three strong swallows. "How do I get to the commercial passenger terminal?"

He picked up a phone and dialed. "Our concierge service will be here shortly. Is there anything else I can help you with?" His eyes darted to the door, to the jet she was not climbing aboard.

"Can you book a ticket?"

A blue glow lit his face as he woke up a sleeping computer screen hidden beneath the counter. "Yes, ma'am. Where would you like to go?"

"Washington National, please."

She splayed her fingers over the warm wood of the counter while the tapping of his fingers over the keys filled the uncomfortable silence.

"There's a flight leaving in two hours."

"Perfect."

More finger tapping. "Do you have a seat preference?"

"Window." She unslung her backpack and pulled out her wallet. "How much?"

"Angel Fire's account will cover the cost." A printer spit out paper, and he handed her the itinerary.

The door behind opened, bringing with it a gust of chilly air.

Her heart soared. *Could it be?*

With a smile tugging at the corners of her lips, she pivoted. Then, her heart came crashing back to earth. It was Sam, the bodyguard.

With a grimace, she turned back to the counter and glanced at the itinerary, noticing the first-class seat assignment.

Sam cleared his throat. "Miss, Mr. Dean asks that you join him on the plane."

"He sent you? Where is he?"

"On the plane, waiting."

A black sedan pulled up outside.

"You can tell Blaze that I'm not getting on that plane."

Slinging her backpack over her shoulder, she marched out, heading away from Ash and toward the sedan.

A few hours ago, Ash would have come for her himself. A few minutes surrounded by his band, and he'd become Blaze, the rock star who sent lackeys to do his work for him. She missed the man who shopped in secondhand stores.

Deep in her broken heart, she knew she'd made the right choice.

She slipped into the waiting car and shut the door.

The driver looked into the rearview mirror. "Which airline?"

"It doesn't matter." She wasn't getting on a plane—at least not one at this airport. She didn't want Ash to track her down because she sensed he might.

She thumbed on her phone and composed a simple text.

Forest! I need you!

She didn't need her little brother. She needed the man the scrawny boy had become.

His text came back.

Can you make it to LAX?

Yes!

On my way!

Somehow, someway, Forest would be there.

Chapter Nineteen

SIX HOURS LATER, SKYE'S PLANE LANDED AT LAX. THE FIRST-CLASS ticket to Washington National lay abandoned, and she'd bought a coach ticket headed west. Standing in the back aisle, waiting for the passengers ahead of her to deplane, she stretched out the kinks in her body.

To make matters worse, after her tears had dried, she'd turned her phone off Airplane Mode, only to find several emails and texts from Spencer. Her fingers trembled, and her stomach fluttered as she read his words.

Usually a man who got to the point, he'd flooded her inbox with chaotic ramblings. As she read through the emails, her stomach sank, and the first flicker of fear emerged. There were too many creepy photos of her with Ash—them leaving the coffee shop, climbing into the helicopter, even photos with Ben and Edna at the falls. *Had he sent someone to follow her?*

The last email had a picture of them leaving the courthouse with a demand to know why she'd married Ash. *How had he known when it had taken over a day for Forest to confirm that piece of news?*

The plane emptied slowly, but soon, she was moving toward the exit and one step closer to Forest. Like a child eager to see a long-lost relative, she wanted nothing more than to push past those ahead and run up the jetway. It had been ages since she and Forest had seen each other, almost two years, and if Forest had worked his magic, he would be waiting at the end of that ramp.

Her steps lightened as she approached the terminal. Forest was close. She could feel him, and he would take her pain away.

Walking up the exit ramp to the passenger terminal, she texted Forest.

Just landed. Meet U where?

A busy passenger terminal swirled with chaos all around her as she exited the gate. Children cried. Parents squawked commands that were more often ignored than obeyed. Bored businessmen clad in rumpled suits clutched briefcases and travel bags. Overhead announcements flowed in a ceaseless stream of noise and chatter.

Her phone buzzed, and she shrugged her backpack over her shoulder. She pulled her hair out from under the shoulder strap and nearly ran into the man walking on her left.

Look up, my summer Skye.

Her head snapped up. A formidable wall of muscle loomed in front of her and brought her to a halt. At six-foot-eight, Forest towered above even those who claimed to be tall. Her scrawny beanpole might have been small and spindly as a child, but he had sprouted into Viking glory with the onset of adult life. He stared at her with his Nordic eyes that were capable of terrorizing children while simultaneously making their mothers tremble with desire.

He'd grown a beard, making him look even more intimidating. The sun had bronzed him, and his normally pale blond hair had been bleached nearly white by the sun. He'd grown it out since she last saw him, and he had it tied back.

She gave her standard greeting, "Beanpole."

And he rewarded her with a flash of his immaculate smile.

She didn't embrace him. Touching brought uncomfortable memories if they were lucky and posttraumatic flashbacks and psychotic breaks if luck failed them.

His fingers clenched with the hug he would never give. "My summer Skye." His voice rumbled with his deep baritone, a sound as powerful as he was strong. He stepped close until mere inches separated them. He smelled of salt and sea.

He kissed the top of her head, gracing her with his fleeting touch. His lips rested for an eternity of microseconds as they reconnected through a fragile but indelible bond.

"I feel you, my summer Skye."

Her chest cracked from the pain. Her shoulders curved inward, and she desperately needed a hug, but she didn't dare move and breach his protective bubble.

Around them, the crowd flowed in a never-ending stream of busy travelers, but for Forest and Skye, the world had stopped.

Her bag slipped from her shoulder, and Forest caught it in his massive hand. Then, he did the unthinkable once again and curled his fingers in the strands of her hair—not quite a touch, but closer than he'd come in years.

Carefully, she leaned in. "I'm good, Bean."

But she wasn't, and he knew the truth.

She forced her hands to her sides. His trigger was her touch—a demon controlled but not yet conquered.

"Come." He released the few strands of her hair with a jerk, as if suddenly realizing how close he'd come. He swung her backpack onto his broad shoulder. "The jet is waiting."

"How did you get here?" She was dying to find out how he'd managed a pickup off a yacht in the middle of the Pacific.

"I knew you needed me. As soon as we sailed within range, I had a helicopter fly out."

"What about your great white whale?"

He huffed a laugh. "I gave him the best six weeks of his life. He has no complaints."

"That's a record. I'm sorry I ruined it for you."

In addition to his many quirks, Forest's hypersexual escapades were legendary.

"Ah, well, he might be worth keeping. We'll see…"

He gestured down the terminal, and she fell into step beside him.

Leaning close, he whispered, "And he sucks like a Hoover."

"Ugh." She scrunched her face and clasped her hands over her ears. She knew from personal experience exactly how hard that was to do. "I don't need the gory details."

"I've got pictures." His eyebrows lifted suggestively. The man loved to tease.

"Stop it."

"Maybe you could meet him?"

Meet one of his toys? She craned her neck upward. Maybe this wasn't a casual fling. "If you want me to."

"I left him a test. If he wants me, he'll figure it out." Her brother almost sounded hopeful.

She arched a brow, not sure what that meant.

While he never lacked for sexual partners—he was built like a house and hung like a horse—Forest lacked the most basic social skills that glued people together.

She had never been sure if it was the sexual trauma, if he was a high-functioning Asperger's individual, or if it was a combination of both. What she did understand was he orbited in a different sphere than the rest of humanity. For him, connecting on a personal level with anyone generally resulted in catastrophe for both parties and explained why his longest-lasting intimate relationship numbered in weeks.

They walked down the busy concourse, the crowds parting before them, people moving away from the force that was Forest Summers.

"How'd you get security to let you meet me at the gate?"

He wrinkled his nose. "You do remember, we recently acquired an airline?"

She shook her head. "No." She never kept up with his mergers and acquisitions. "When did that happen?"

He gave an exasperated moan. "I sent you a memo."

"You know I don't read half the crap you send me."

He flooded her inbox all day with their business affairs.

"Skye, you really need to pay attention. How long are you going to pretend—"

"Look, we had a deal. You handle the money, and I—"

He stopped and turned to face her. Icy blue eyes bored into her. "You can't ignore what we've built."

"I don't want anything to do with that money. It's tainted."

"Tainted, my ass." He cocked his head, and his voice rumbled. "We earned every fucking cent." He lifted his hand and pressed it to his head. "We're not arguing about this. If something were to happen to me—"

"Nothing is going to happen to you."

Others saw a fierce warrior when Forest Summers stared them down. He didn't care what anyone thought, which made him formidable in the boardroom, but all she saw was the scared, sodomized little boy curled in a ball on the basement floor. He knew this and allowed it but only because what he saw when he looked at her was much worse.

He leveled out his tone, smoothing out the rough edges. "If something ever happened to me, who would carry on our work? What would happen to the charities? What about the children? I know you're busy with your medicine, and I don't expect you to run the businesses, but you can't continue to be oblivious to what we've become."

"I don't need this right now." She shifted her focus, weighing his words, looking for hidden meaning.

Her stomach dropped as the doctor inside reared its head. *All those drugs, needles, and rampant sex?* He tried to be safe, but trying was lying in her book. Accidents happened, and viruses killed. She dealt with that every day.

"Is there something I need to know? Are you sick?"

"Damn it, Skye. Don't doctor me. I'm not sick."

"Are you sure?"

He tilted his head and stared at the ceiling tiles.

He breathed out slow and tucked his chin to his chest. His shoulders drooped. "I get tested every three months, like I promised. My last checkup was a month ago. I'm not dying. I don't have HIV or hepatitis or any other STD. Stop playing doctor, and be my fucking sister for once."

"Forest, what's going on?" When they got serious, nicknames disappeared.

"You got married. That's what's going on. The legal ramifications alone are staggering. He's entitled to half of what you own."

"I don't think he cares about money. Ash has plenty."

"Not compared to you. Does he even have a clue? Have you told him?"

She never talked money, and even though the hospital she worked in carried a piece of her name, no one had figured out the connection behind the endowment and the newest emergency doctor on staff. Her life remained compartmentalized on purpose.

She squinted. "You said I could get it annulled."

Forest started forward again. "The jet's waiting."

"You said we owned the damn jet. It'll leave when we get there."

With another frustrated shake of his head, Forest rocked back on his heels, releasing a pent-up sigh. "If I'd had them park at the private concourse, then yes, but we pay for every minute the jet sits at this one. You think I throw our money away, but that's not true."

No, he multiplied money without thinking. Forest had taken the cash their foster father had collected while stealing their innocence, and with a computer, the Internet, and a self-education in day trading, he'd doubled it, then doubled that, and done it several more times. It wasn't long before he'd added several zeros to their net worth.

While she had gone to college and earned her degree, Forest had turned thousands into millions. He'd invested in companies and soon added a ninth zero to their net worth.

"Says the man who bought an airline we don't need," she mumbled.

"I bought the corporation that owns the airline, not the airline. If you had bothered to read the memo, you'd know that. They have a charitable track record with battered and abused women and fund children's cancer research. I thought you'd be interested in that. Now, are you coming or not?"

She counted to three. He wasn't the only one who knew how to count. Well, one thing was certain. Within moments of being around Forest, she wasn't worried about Ash anymore.

Forest led her through the concourse until they came to their gate.

A young woman in her early twenties, dressed in a pencil skirt with a blue silk blouse, greeted them with a smile. "Mr. Summers, the pilots told me they're ready when you are."

Forest flashed a smile at the girl, and her cheeks turned a deep shade of pink. "Sara, let me introduce my sister, Skye Summers."

Sara thrust out her hand. "It's such a pleasure to meet you, Dr. Summers."

Skye tilted her head toward Forest, wondering why this woman looked familiar. Forest never did anything without purpose. "Nice to meet you."

Forest cleared his throat. "Sara is interning over winter break and next semester. She's a senior at Rice University, studying aeronautical engineering."

He guided Skye down the jetway, leaving Sara at the gate. When they were out of earshot, he lowered his rumbly voice. "You might not remember Sara, but we placed her with our first foster family. She was fourteen."

That made Sara's placement seven years ago. *She was their first?*

Skye turned around, widening her eyes. Her voice dropped to a whisper. "Her name wasn't Sara, Bean."

"No. She changed it. Like us."

"Does she remember me?"

He shook his head. "She doesn't remember much about that night. Only that the people who saved her were good. Jake and Allison Brenerkie adopted her after having her for a year in their foster care, and they rescued three more. She's had a good life. We did that."

Forest guided Skye onto the plane where an efficient staff seated them in two thick leather seats facing each other. As the crew prepared for takeoff, she settled in, pulling out her computer from her backpack.

Sara enplaned a few minutes later. She grinned at Forest and then went back to sit with the other staff for takeoff.

Skye laughed. "Sara has a crush on her boss."

Forest leaned back in his leather recliner. "She'll get over it."

As they were taking off, Forest's eyes narrowed. "So, you not only went off and married a rock star, but you had to pick Blaze? My fucking rock idol? Seriously, my summer Skye, that's wrong on so many levels. You're going to tell me everything."

The story of Ash began with Spencer, and she wasn't quite ready to broach that tangled web.

She crossed her arms. "I want to hear about you and your great white whale. How did you ever persuade anyone to get on a boat with you and travel across the Pacific?"

He huffed a laugh and kicked an ankle over his knee. "Now, *that* is an interesting story."

Forest's story took him on a two-hour tangent. He loved to tell a good story, but it came at a price. Never in her wildest imagination did she realize how creative two men could get on a boat.

After he showed her a particularly interesting photo, she leaned back. "I see you no longer have issues with rope."

He grinned. "Daniels has been helping me. I hope you get a chance to meet him."

She'd always imagined, if Forest ever delved back into the darker aspects of his sexuality, he would take the dominant role. It came as quite a surprise to see him submit. She flipped through that series of photos and tried to focus on the smiling pictures of the two men catching fish and collecting rainwater. Part of her hoped Daniels figured out whatever test Forest had left for him.

"What does Daniels do? You said it was his yacht…"

"He's in investment banking, properties and such. More old money than new, living off his inheritance, I think." He frowned at that comment. Forest hated wasting money.

"Does he know what you do?"

Forest pulled out the leather tie holding back his hair and finger-combed his shoulder-length locks. "He knows I have money but not who I am. I'm hoping he figures out my clues."

Sara hovered at the back of the plane. Forest waved her over and asked for water.

"Now, you've distracted me long enough." He took a water from Sara with a smile and leaned back. "First, you send this crazy prenup from that asshole boyfriend. Next, you text, saying you're taking a stranger with you on a trip. Then, you get hitched to none other than the lead singer of Angel Fire. What the hell are you doing?"

She didn't have a clue.

"Have you met the band, too?" He leaned forward, his eyes sparking with excitement.

She nodded. "It didn't go well."

He wanted to know all about Spike's piercings and if she'd noticed if they were gold or silver studs. He claimed they had some significance. He asked all kinds of questions about the drummer, but she didn't know which of the men played drums, and she didn't want to get into an Angel Fire one-oh-one with Forest.

They launched into a discussion about the tribal tattoos Noodles sported. Then, he asked about Bash, wanting to know if his eyes really were as electric blue in person as they were on the album covers.

"I have no idea, considering I had to take him out."

"You what?"

The explanation of subduing Bash led to another round of questions. She didn't mind the barrage; it kept her from discussing the one person who made her heart ache.

Forest leaned forward. "My summer Skye, why are you so sad?"

"I miss him."

She moved the conversation away from Ash to Spencer and how he'd trampled her heart. "I didn't have the strength to give him back his ring, and when Ash didn't show up, I figured it was better to have someone in my life rather than no one."

"I'm in your life."

She stretched out a hand and dared to touch his knee.

He flinched, and she withdrew her fingers.

"What matters is, I realized *why* I needed Spencer. Then, Ash walked into my life and turned it upside down. He believes it's fate."

"Those bitches suck."

That was their go-to line.

"Yeah, but Ash believes we were destined to meet. As crazy as it sounds, and I don't even know why I agreed, but he convinced me to let him join me on my trip." She breathed out a sigh and remembered the joy that was Ash. "I don't know if it was because I was so emotionally raw after catching Spencer with that woman or if I'm crazy, but taking a chance on Ash was the best decision I ever made."

"I'm not sure about the best decision. You wound up married without realizing it. And you claim I'm the one who needs a babysitter."

He was right on that point.

"It doesn't really matter. I ended it, and I have to work in the morning. I guess we'll meet with the lawyers after my shift to figure out the next step?"

Forest sipped on his water. "You're evading the question. I'm asking, what do you want to do about your *husband?*"

She scrunched her face. "You said I could get it annulled."

"You don't sound like someone who wants to end things."

She lifted her hands in the air, palms up. "I left him, Forest. I'm not sure I can be any clearer in what I want."

"I'll do whatever you want. I'm your shoulder to cry on. Just tell me what you need." He stared out the window at the sun setting over the clouds.

She needed a shoulder she could lean on and arms that would lock her in tight. She needed Ash. His intensity. His laughter. Ash's touch. Hell, something as simple as his smell would do.

She needed to know she'd made the right choice. *But, if she was leaving him, why did every thought begin and end with him?*

Unfortunately, her little beanpole couldn't give the physical comfort she needed. He would give everything else, but he couldn't give a basic hug.

She stared out into the sunset as the sky deepened toward night.

Chapter Twenty

FOREST HAD ARRANGED FOR A DRIVER TO MEET THEM AT THE airport, and they traveled to Skye's brownstone in a black limousine. She would have taken a cab, but Forest had refused. While he'd said he didn't like spending their hard-earned cash, he certainly had little difficulty with splurging on the finer things in life. Maybe she should have Forest take care of retrieving her stuff from Bob's cabin. Ash could take care of his Jeep.

As they rounded the block to her brownstone, a crowd overflowed the sidewalk in front of her home, spilling onto the street. Lights flashed as people lifted cameras over the crowd and snapped photos of the car.

"What the hell?" She leaned forward and peered out the window. Her heart caught in her throat.

"Get down, Skye," Forest said in a rumbly baritone. He yanked on her shoulder, trying to drag her away from the window. Then, he flinched when he realized what he'd done.

A man with a camera shoved a lens against the blacked-out window as the car rolled to a stop. The flash caught her in the eyes, blinding her. Her name was called out over and over again.

"Fuck," Forest said.

Flash after flash flickered as the crowd mobbed them.

"Don't worry; I can get you inside." Forest huffed a laugh, but his lower lip trembled. "Wrap your arm around me and stick to my side. I'll get a security team over here to help once we're inside."

She stared at her brother, stunned. *He wanted her to touch him?* From the car to the front door was well over twenty feet. *Would he last that long?*

"Bean, we don't have to stay. We can go to a hotel."

"It's late, and all your stuff for work is in there, right?"

She nodded.

"I'm a fucking giant. Who better to protect you?"

"But—"

"I've been facing a lot of my fears lately. Someday, I'd like to be able to give you a hug without breaking into a cold sweat or…you know. Let's start now."

It wasn't the cold sweats she was worried about. It was the meltdown that was sure to follow. This was a horrible idea.

"Okay, how do you want to do this?"

"I'll go first." His voice shook with rising anxiety, but he seemed determined to get her inside. "Hold on to my belt, and don't let go. They shouldn't touch you if they obey the law. I'll shove right on through those bastards. But have your keys ready."

She fished through her backpack and lifted her keys into the air. "Got them."

"Okay." He signaled to the driver. "Go."

As the driver opened the door, a cacophony of noise descended on them. Forest used his body to form a blockade while she got out of the car. She wrapped an arm around his waist, threading her fingers through his belt loop. As she pressed against him, his entire body stiffened, and his breathing hitched. Tremors vibrated through the fabric of his shirt as he struggled to control his breathing. Her physical closeness overwhelmed him, and she tried to pull away, but he clamped a hand over hers, pulling her forward.

A voice called out from behind them, "When's the baby due?"

Her head whipped up. "What?"

Forest growled, "Ignore them. Don't respond." With that, he tucked her under his arm, increasing their physical contact.

Cameras were thrust in her face, and light flashed in her eyes.

Voices called out random questions.

"Is Blaze with you?"

"Is this the end of the band?"

"Is it true that Blaze was high when you were married? Was this a drunken binge?"

"How long have you been seeing each other?"

The questions bombarded her, a wall of chaos she couldn't process. People pressed in close, screaming above their colleagues. Forest defended, pushing those too aggressive out of the way. He lifted and dragged her up the steps when she became overwhelmed.

Skye's heart hammered, her chest constricting with fear.

"Is it true you tricked Blaze into marrying you?"

"Is this a publicity stunt for the upcoming album release?"

"Did you marry him for his money?"

"Skye, where's the fucking key?" Forest shook her, his breathing little more than ragged gasps.

Her head spun from the endless questions.

Forest ripped the keys from her hand and fumbled at the lock. Moments later, the door creaked open, and he thrust her inside, pushing her away from him. She stumbled into the foyer as he slammed the door shut.

"Where's the fucking light?" His voice was hoarse and desperate.

"What?"

"The light!" he screamed. "Where's the fucking light?"

She found the light switch and flicked it on.

Forest scanned the narrow hallway. His entire body shook. His complexion was flushed, his pupils dilated. He struggled to take a breath, and then he staggered down the hall, yanking off his shirt and pulling at the catch of his jeans.

"Bean?"

He held a hand out. "Don't come near me. Don't you fucking come close."

He kicked off his shoes, but she saw the damage those few moments of physical contact had done.

Forest disappeared, desperate, responding to a stimulus conditioned into him by the demon of their combined past. A door slammed shut down the guest hallway, and an agonized moan followed.

She took in a shuddering breath. *How far back had those few minutes sent her brother on his road to recovery?*

There was a reason they didn't touch. She made a beeline for her liquor supply where she uncorked every bottle of wine and poured it down the drain. Once Forest achieved the physical release he needed, he would come looking for a chemical outlet for his pain.

There were no drugs in her home, and she would be damned if he started drinking again because of her. Not when he was so close to earning his sixty-day sobriety coin. Not when he'd come to help with her problems. His body couldn't avoid the conditioned response, and she knew his mind would struggle against the chains that bound him.

The next few days would test her brother's sobriety, and if he failed, it would be all her fault.

The cops came by twice to move people off the front steps of Skye's brownstone. The officers introduced themselves, expressed their sympathy for the disturbance, and gave Skye their assurances that they had the crowd controlled. After offering congratulations on her nuptials, they sheepishly asked for autographs from her husband.

She had saved one bottle of wine. Shielding Forest from the demon of his addiction had come at a hefty price—ten bottles down the drain. She poured a glass of chardonnay and stared at the shuttered windows.

Flashes of light flickered through the wood. Eager reporters would not give up on that one-in-a-million shot.

Already down one doctor due to maternity leave, Bob Manley couldn't afford to lose her as well. She had to work, but she couldn't leave her beanpole alone. Not in his fragile state. His compulsions and addictions were primed to explode with the emergence of a conditioned response that crippled him on many levels. It was another horrific reminder of the torture inflicted upon a poor frightened boy and a helpless girl.

In the meantime, Forest needed to be constantly watched.

Ten p.m. already, and one glass down.

She would have arranged for the protective detail herself, but the contact info was locked in Forest's phone. There was one other person she knew in town who traveled with a team of security experts, people trained in how to deal with the mob outside. The only question was whether Ash would accept her call.

Texting Ash instead of calling showed her weakness, but she didn't trust herself to speak. Her voice would crack and crumble as her heart fell to pieces. As succinctly as possible, she laid out her problem. There were paparazzi outside her house, and she asked if she could please borrow his bodyguard and one or two of his friends.

She hated asking for such a huge favor, but she needed someone large and strong enough to intimidate Forest—someone to babysit him and keep him from tumbling into a chemically induced fugue. Sam would lose in a fight against her brother, but all he had to do was keep Forest inside and away from any mind-altering substances during her day shift.

Her phone vibrated within seconds of sending the text.

Help is on the way.

His message told her nothing about Ash's state of mind. *What was he feeling? Did he miss her? Had she hurt him? Did he understand the reasons behind why she'd left?*

With a groan, she gave up on deciphering nonexistent clues in the simple text.

Her attention shifted to the hallway and the closed door of the guest room. Going to Forest would not ease his pain. Quite the opposite would happen, and she appreciated the sacrifice he'd made to keep her safe.

Her presence would exacerbate an already shitty situation. She'd give almost anything to sink into a simple brotherly hug and feel Forest's love surround her within the strength of his arms, but that was not how their relationship worked.

She had a few minutes before Ash's security team would arrive, so she went to her room and turned on the shower until the air thickened with billowy steam. She washed quickly, removing two days of grime, and then sat on the tiles where she hugged her knees tight to her chest, watching the steam swirl.

While she loved medicine with a passion born from a need to help others, Forest couldn't run their empire alone. She had obligations she could no longer ignore. *But was she ready to step into such a daunting role?*

The Elsbeth Beneficence Foundation funded several charitable organizations. The Brenerkie Foster Care Initiative was their first. A fourteen-year-old girl named Ivy was a victim who had been placed into their charter foster care system. The poised Rice University student Skye had met on the flight from LAX bore little resemblance to the young girl broken by abuse.

Maybe it was time for her to take a more active role in what Forest and she had created?

A pounding on the bathroom door startled her out of her reverie. She squinted through the fog. *How had Forest put himself back together so quickly?*

More pounding followed. A deep *thump, thump, thump* rattled the hinges.

Odd that Forest would bother to knock at all. Except for the no-touching thing, they had few boundaries. If she were taking a shower, soaking in a bath, or using the toilet, if he wanted to talk, he wouldn't have hesitated to barge in.

Had one of the reporters broken into her house?

Naked and sitting on the floor, she was completely exposed. A paparazzo could barge in, snap a photo, and run out before she could take the breath she would need to scream.

A now familiar rich voice called out from behind the closed door, "Skye, are you in there?"

She hadn't asked Ash to come, nor was she prepared to face him, not after walking away.

"Why isn't she answering?" That voice didn't belong to Ash although it seemed vaguely familiar.

"How the hell would I know?" Ash's desperation pulsed through the thin wooden barrier of the door. His voice caressed her skin, sending shivers down her spine.

She turned off the shower and dried as quickly as she could.

"Skye, can you hear me? I came as quickly as I could." A *thunk* sounded from the other side of the door, as if he'd dropped his head against the wood.

A gravelly deep voice roared out, catching her attention and making her jump, "Who the fuck are you? Get the fuck out of my sister's house, you fucking perverts, before I tear you apart."

Oh, shit. Forest.

"Sam?" The alarm in the second man's voice rose an octave and cracked.

Wrapped in nothing other than a towel, she yanked the door open, desperate to stop the cataclysm that Forest could become.

Ash stood by the door, braced and facing off against Forest. To his left, Sam held his hands out in a placating gesture. Beside him, Bash's eyes widened with fear.

Forest's icy-blue scrutiny darted between Ash, Sam, and Bash, but they weren't the only men in her bedroom. Two others stood between Ash, Bash, and her brother. They squared off against the six-foot-eight wild man intent on taking out two of Angel Fire's band members.

She lowered the register of her voice to a tone she hoped would calm Forest's aggression. "It's okay, Bean."

Forest shifted his attention between the five men, assessing the threat. Then, a transformation occurred, and she could guess what was going through his mind as he realized who stood before him. Ash and Bash were the front men of his favorite rock band, and he had them terrified.

Ash lifted a shaky finger. "That's your little brother?"

As the rush of male testosterone dissipated, she made introductions. "Ash, meet Bean. Bean, meet Ash."

"Hey, what about me?" Bash frowned at her. "What am I? Chopped liver?"

She pressed her lips together, remembering Bash's less than friendly reception. "Bean, meet Chopped Liver."

Bash sputtered at the insult, but she continued her introductions, enjoying the parade of shocked expressions rolling over Bash's face. "The big guy is Sam. He's a member of Angel Fire's security team." She turned to the other two men. "Sorry, I don't know you."

The man to her left lifted his hand. "Donald." He looked to be ex-Marine with close-cropped hair, a square chin, and a strong jaw, and he probably bench-pressed some ungodly weight for fun on his days off.

The other one gave a chin bump. "Reggie." He was a tall and handsome with ebony skin, six-foot-four or maybe taller, and probably used to being the largest man in the room. He eyed Forest with caution.

She guessed there weren't many men who out-massed Reggie. Sam impressed her and held his ground, his protective six-feet-plus stance shielding Ash and Bash, but he looked small with Forest so near.

And, as she stood in a roomful of men she barely knew, she realized she was wrapped in nothing more than a damp towel. "Um, now that everyone has been introduced, do you mind leaving my bedroom, so I can put on some clothes?"

"She didn't introduce me," Bash complained.

"Maybe it's because of your charm," Ash quipped. He tapped Sam on the shoulder. "It's okay. You can leave us alone."

Forest stepped clear of the doorway. "Everyone, out of my sister's room." He narrowed in on Ash. "Especially you."

Forest spun on his heel and took a step back down the hall. When no one followed, he turned back, using his growly voice to get everyone moving. "That was not a request."

Sam looked to Ash, who gave a nod of assurance, before he followed Forest to the living room. Reggie, Donald, and Bash trailed on his heels.

Ash grabbed the doorknob and started to shut the door.

Forest's voice carried from the living room. "That means you, too, Lover Boy. Don't you dare touch my sister when she's not wearing any clothes."

Ash shifted from foot to foot. "Is he for real?" He lowered his voice. "He does know we've had sex, right?"

Yes, if the most fucked up fuck of fucks could be called sex. She laughed at the memory of their first time because to acknowledge how bad it had truly been would mean facing a past still torturing her present.

"Unfortunately, yes," she said.

"And that we're married?"

"Right now, that's your biggest problem."

Ash ran his fingers through his hair, curling the dark strands around his knuckles. With a flex of his neck, the dragon sitting astride the web arched its wings. "Damn it, Skye, why did you leave?"

Before she could answer, Forest's bellow ripped through the air. "Get your fucking ass out here right now, Lover Boy. You do not want me to come get you."

She shook her head. "You should go."

"I'm not afraid of him."

"You should be," she warned. "Remember what I did to Bash at the airport?"

He gave an almost imperceptible nod and shifted toward the door.

"Who do you think taught me? Now, imagine an irate Bean doing that to you or Bash? Don't think for a minute that Sam, Reggie, or Donald would be able to stop him."

"He and I are going to have a problem if I can't touch you."

"Just go. Don't worry about Bean; you've got one up on him. You're the lead singer of his favorite band. He's more bluster than anything else. He's acting tough and trying not to be the starry-eyed fool. Use your rock-star charm and win him over. I'll be out in a minute."

Before Ash left, she tugged on his sleeve, pitching her voice low, careful so that it wouldn't carry to Forest in the living room. "Bean's a few days shy of earning his sixty-day abstinence coin. I emptied all the alcohol in the house, but I'm worried."

"Alcohol or drugs?" Ash asked.

"More drugs than alcohol, but the last couple of hours have been rough." Really, all it had taken were those few fleeting seconds of touch to send him over the edge. "I'm worried he'll relapse."

With Ash's history in rehab, he'd understand the pitfalls her brother faced.

"If you're not out in five minutes, I'm coming for you. I'll keep my hands off you for as long as I can, but I'm not making promises." Ash headed down the hall.

She shut the door and crumpled to the floor, her insides twisting in a sick knot. Ash hadn't kissed her. He'd barely touched her.

She dragged herself to her feet, dressed in sweats, and pulled on a loose-fitting shirt. All the while, she yawned, physically and mentally exhausted by the last twenty-four hours. And, while she'd expected a tense standoff between the men, when she emerged from her room, raucous male voices filled her living room with deep bass rumbles and guttural laughter.

The arrival of the sole female in the house silenced the men. They stared as she entered, making her feel self-conscious. Ash was the first to move. He jumped off the couch where he'd been sitting with Bash and strode toward her, wrapping her in a hug and finally giving her that kiss. The three bodyguards had seated themselves in her dining room chairs, having pulled them out in a staggered semicircle facing the living room.

Forest lounged in the leather recliner, kicking back, with ankles crossed and fingers steepled under his chin. His eyes narrowed, but he didn't move as Ash smothered her in one of his passionate kisses.

Her heart rate tripled with the heated press of Ash's lips against hers. Tentative to start, it didn't take long before he tugged her tight and displayed his possession with a bite to her lower lip.

Forest cleared his throat. "Do you mind? That's my sister you're manhandling."

Ash swept his tongue across her lips, teasing her with his tantalizing taste. He lifted his head, breaking the kiss. "Get used to it, dude."

"The name is Bean, not dude." Forest's glare knifed across the distance.

She gripped Ash's hand and gave it a squeeze. "Boys, let's not fight."

"Oh, we're going to have it out if he keeps that up," Forest said.

It hadn't escaped her notice though that Forest had yet to move a muscle. Her brother was testing Ash, measuring the mettle of the man she'd unwittingly tied herself to through the scratch of a pen.

"We're not having anything out, dude." Ash kissed her cheek and winked. "I think Skye gets to decide who does and doesn't touch her."

She held herself perfectly still, waiting for Forest's reaction. There was a time when she'd had no choice at all, when they'd both been coerced to perform unspeakable things, but Forest didn't flinch although a flash of anger flickered beneath his icy blues.

"Don't do this." She disentangled herself from Ash and went to sit on the armrest of the recliner, careful not to touch her brother. It was nearing midnight, and she needed to trust she could leave them alone while she slept. Although, if Ash stayed, she'd get very little rest.

"Look, I have work tomorrow." She returned to Ash, curling her fingers in his. "Thanks for coming. It means more to me than you can know, but it's time you leave."

His eyes widened. "I'm not leaving."

Bash jerked a thumb toward Forest. "Why are we here at all? You've got him to play bodyguard. He could just sweep you up and carry you past all those fucktards outside."

Forest's face paled at the mention of touching her again. If push came to shove, she'd call in sick and stay home, but she couldn't do that to Bob.

She spoke without thought, "It's complicated."

The moment she'd uttered the words, she wished to take them back. Ash was no fool. He understood the undercurrents swirling in that phrase.

His eyes darted to Forest and back to her with an unspoken question.

"How hard can it be?" Bash waved his hands in the air. "He's a fucking giant."

"Shut up, Bash." Ash fixed Skye with a stare, demanding an answer. "You really want me to leave?"

No, she didn't, but if he stayed, he would want to sleep with her, and she wasn't ready to deal with the difficulties of another disastrous attempt at intimacy.

With her heart hammering, she gave a nod.

Ash's gaze slid to Forest and then back to her. His jaw tensed. "Sam and the guys will take care of the crowd outside and make sure you get to and from work safely."

Forest cleared his throat. "Never mind. I—"

"Thank you, Ash," she interrupted. "I really appreciate the help. I didn't know what to do."

Ash cleared his throat. "Bean, have you ever seen a stage crew set up before?"

She wanted to kiss him in that moment. Toss everyone out of the house and reward Ash for being so fucking perceptive. Sam and his crew had an excuse to escort her to work, but she needed someone to watch over Forest. He didn't have a sponsor in town, not that he wouldn't be able to find a meeting, but this was good. Ash couldn't have offered a better bribe.

No way would her brother refuse an opportunity to hang with his favorite metal band. She could work in peace, knowing someone was watching over him.

"That's a wonderful idea." She spun to face the trio occupying her dining room chairs. "When they take me to work, you can come with us and then go watch the band set up." She looked over her shoulder and locked eyes with Ash. She mouthed, *Thank you.*

Ash smiled, but it looked forced.

"Great. It's settled then." She pressed her fingertips to her temples. The beginnings of a headache threatened, and she needed sleep. She gestured to Ash to follow her to the front door.

She leaned in and gave him a hug. "Keep him safe. Don't leave him alone."

"I want to stay, Skye. You're killing me."

Pressing a finger against his lips, she shook her head. "I know, and I'd love it if you did, but I have a long shift tomorrow. I'm exhausted, and I owe it to my patients to be well rested. We'll figure everything out."

"Skye…"

The desperation in his voice had her heart breaking, but she needed to do the right thing. The only problem was, she didn't know what that might be.

Turbulent eyes stared her down. "I feel you slipping away, but I'm warning you, I'm not losing you."

Her fingers brushed against his chest. The solid beat of his heart thumped beneath her palm, the steady rhythm centering her, while his message filled her with the promise of something she desperately desired.

"I'm here, but I need space."

He pressed her fingertips against his lips. "I've had women throwing themselves at my feet for years. I've gorged myself until I'm sick of it. You can't even imagine how many…" He hugged her tight. "You're the first who's seen the real me. I know none of this has gone the way you'd like, but that doesn't mean it's not exactly the way it is meant to be."

"Ash—"

"Let me finish." His voice cut through her hesitation. "My father said I would know. I never really understood, and I certainly didn't believe, not until I met you. Don't run. I'll give you all the space you need, but I'm coming for you, and I have every intention of making you mine."

He released her and walked back to the others, grabbing Sam aside for a quick conversation. Reggie and Donald escorted Ash and Bash outside to a waiting car and then returned. A barrage of flashing lights and a stream of questions spilled through the open door. Sam took the men to the dining room while she lowered herself onto the couch to ponder Ash's promise.

Forest extricated himself from the chair, stretching to his full height. "I'm beat."

"Good." She led him down the hall, stopping at the hall closet to pull out pillows, blankets, and towels for her unexpected guests. She barred the entrance to the guest room, pointing back to the living room. "You're sleeping on the couch, Bean."

"What?" Forest shifted to move around her, but she stepped in his path, taking advantage of his inability to touch her without consequence.

With a grin, she thrust the linens toward him. "The couch."

"What the fuck?"

"One of them will keep watch, and two will sleep in the guest room. You're on the couch."

His eyes narrowed. "I'll be fine, my summer Skye. Besides, you emptied all the booze."

That meant he'd already checked. One more reason for Ash's security men to watch over him while he slept. She couldn't chance Forest slipping out the back window and seeking chemical relief.

"It's really not for you. I'll sleep better, knowing you're on the couch while one of them watches you snore."

"And to think I came here to save you."

She reached out to grab his hand, such a natural gesture, but she jerked back, curling her fingers into her palms.

His eyes narrowed. Slowly, he stretched out his index finger and stroked the sleeve of her baggy shirt. "Sorry, I thought I would be strong enough."

"You will…one day. And you did save me. You've always been there when I needed you."

"We're pretty messed up, aren't we?"

"We're healing every day."

"Do you think we'll ever be normal?"

She gave a small laugh. "Normal by whose standards, Bean?"

"Yeah, well…" He shifted the topic of conversation, his eyes lighting up. "I can't believe I hung out with the lead singer and drummer of Angel Fire."

"And, tomorrow, you'll meet the rest of the band."

"I can't believe you went and married Blaze."

"His name is Ash."

"Whatever. Blaze is a better rocker name. Your husband and I are going to have a talk."

"Be nice…"

"I'm always nice," he said with an evil grin.

"Right." She eyed him from head to toe. "All of you."

He spread his hands out wide. "Not my fault I sprouted. I'm not your little Beanpole anymore."

"You'll always be my Beanpole."

"Have you thought about what happened in Niagara?"

"No."

Forest leaned in close. "He wasn't drinking, Skye."

"No."

"I mean, he wasn't drunk. Not like you."

"Yeah, so?"

"And you want me to believe he didn't know what he was signing? I find that hard to swallow."

Ash had mentioned he relied upon his lawyers to do the reading for him. *But what was Forest trying to say? Ash knew?*

"Don't you think he deserves to know who he married?"

"He knows who I am, and he's not really my husband."

"Legally, he is," Forest warned. "And, from what little I've seen, he wants to keep it that way. Makes me wonder what he knows."

"He doesn't know anything about it."

Forest tilted his head. "Give him the annulment papers, and we'll see."

"Can we discuss this later?"

"Go to bed, my summer Skye." He jerked a thumb at the trio methodically checking her door and window locks. "I get that you asked them to babysit me, but are you sure they aren't babysitting you as well?"

If Ash was afraid she'd run off again, what better way to make sure she stuck around than to keep her surrounded by his security detail?

THE NEXT MORNING, SAM AND REGGIE ESCORTED HER TO WORK while Donald remained behind with Forest. They sandwiched her between them and ran the gauntlet. The cameras mauled her like they wanted to devour her.

Oddly, the only thing going through her mind was how she was going to get her hot cocoa, but Ash had taken care of that. Her order had been called ahead, and Reggie leaped out of the car to claim her beverage. With the morning ritual intact, they pulled outside the emergency department and rolled to a stop.

"Wait here," Sam said.

"Why?" She peeked outside the car window. Nothing seemed out of place.

Reggie laughed. "Standard procedure, Mrs. Dean."

Mrs. Dean? But she didn't have time to correct him because Sam returned and helped her out of the car.

"We're good," he said. "Hospital security has pushed back the camera freaks. Ready for work?"

She sipped the hot cocoa and slung her bag over her shoulder. "I get off at eight. Will I see you then?"

Sam crossed his arms. "You'll see me all day. I'm not going anywhere."

She shook her head. "You can't come with me." She lifted her badge. "Hospital policy. No badge, no access. I'll be fine. Unless one of those camera-toting zealots is an actual patient, they can't get back to where I work."

Sam's jaw worked back and forth, and he rubbed his neck. "I don't know. Mr. Dean won't be happy about that."

She took another sip of the warm drink, savoring the full-bodied flavor of the chocolate. "It's not up to him." She put a hand on Sam's arm. "Seriously, I'll be fine. Besides, I work in a secure zone. We have metal detectors at the entrance." She stared at all six-foot-plus of him from her more diminutive height.

Sam didn't look pleased, but she reassured him that everything would be all right.

"I'll call when I'm done and meet you right here."

His eyes narrowed as he slid into the vehicle. "Promise?"

"I promise."

"You'd better. I don't think I can handle it if you disappear again."

She took a step back and tucked in her chin. "What do you mean?"

"Let's just say, Mr. Dean was beside himself when he couldn't find you. We went to every terminal and checked every airline." He reached for the door but paused before closing it. "Where did you go?"

She shrugged. "I'm not giving up all my secrets."

And then she smiled. Ash had come after her.

She remembered the last time she'd been at work and her first kiss with Ash.

Chapter Twenty-One

SKYE'S SHIFT THREE DAYS AGO HAD KEPT HER RUNNING FROM ONE catastrophe to the next. She hoped for another equally busy day—not for trauma or emergencies because those came at the expense of pain and suffering, but for easy, fixable things. Something that would keep her day jumping and her mind focused. Thinking about Ash and her future with him consumed too much emotional energy.

She walked to the nurses' counter, spotting her mentor, Bob. He appeared less tired, standing tall, and his hair wasn't a mess of combed-through worry. Nancy stood across from him, her head nodding in response to whatever he was telling her.

When Skye tapped Bob on the shoulder, he turned and lifted a single eyebrow. "Seems like you've had an eventful three days, Dr. Summers. Or should I say Dr. Dean?"

All conversation stopped. Silence rarely happened in the middle of an emergency department.

The sudden weight of it smothered her, leaving her breathless, but she composed herself and dropped her bag behind the counter. "I have no idea what you're talking about."

"Oh, come on!" Sally, one of the respiratory therapists, looked at Skye's finger. "Where's the ring?"

Nancy came flying around the corner, screeching, "Dr. Summers, you married a rock star. Spill the beans!"

Her coworkers crowded around, offering congratulations and surprise at the sudden change in her relationship status. A few asked for autographs or even tickets to the upcoming concerts where Angel Fire would be playing on Friday and Saturday nights.

She grinned, remembering how Ash had told her he needed to be back in town by Friday because he had a *thing*. That'd evidently meant putting on a show in front of tens of thousands of screaming fans.

Bob hung back, crossing his arms, an unreadable but concerned look etched on his face.

After a few minutes, she waved everyone away. "Enough already. I need to get Dr. Manley out of here."

She extricated herself from her coworkers. "You ready to sign out your patients?"

He gave a curt nod. "Are you okay?"

"I'm good for my shift, but we probably need to talk."

"Yes. It seems things have changed for you."

He walked over to the patient status board, which listed all the critical patients and the state of their current medical workups. Exam status, labs, and X-ray studies were marked with red boxes or checkmarks, denoting their to-do or done status. As always, the board was full.

She couldn't help but smile at his stern but fatherly expression. "Tell me about the patients, Bob."

Most looked stable, but a full day of work stretched out in front of her, perfect for a troubled mind. There wouldn't be any time to worry about the problem named Ash.

Bob signed out all the patients, focusing on those who were critical. Before he left, he hesitated, seeming to struggle with what he wanted to say. "Looks like your nobody became a somebody."

"I guess he did."

"And Spencer? How did he take the news?"

She had yet to deal with that string of emails and texts. Spencer remained a problem. He was still out of the country. By Tuesday, he would return, and then she'd give back his ring.

"Still working on that."

"He'd have to be living under a rock not to have heard, considering it's all over the news. You sure you want him to find out via the tabloids that his fiancée married another guy?"

"I'll take care of it, Bob."

"I hope Mr. Somebody works out for you." Bob placed a hand on her upper arm. "And, if Spencer lays a finger on you, let me know." He picked up his things and left without another word.

She dived right into patient care, checking on the critical patients first and making certain their evaluations were complete before moving them to intensive care. Then, she waded her way through the less urgent stream of patients, and the hours whittled away.

Taking care of others always brought fulfillment to her life. If she couldn't fix herself, at least she could stitch other people's lacerations, splint their fractures, and treat their diseases. She couldn't imagine doing anything else, and she wondered about the wisdom of stepping away from medicine to run the foundation with Forest. Perhaps she needed to rethink that choice.

Before she knew it, the shift wound down to a close, and Bob returned. They repeated the patient sign-out process, this time with her signing out patients to him.

Her original plan to ask for Friday off vanished under the realization of how happy she felt surrounded by her coworkers and by the gratefulness of the patients she touched.

The black sedan waited outside along with Reggie and Sam, who held back the few bold photographers who'd managed to track her down. Sam escorted her to the car and slid in beside her while Reggie blocked a particularly aggressive cameraman who had tried to get in her face.

"How was your day?" Sam asked.

Sam was a cutie, but she wasn't interested in getting chummy with Ash's security team. "Busy." Hopefully, he'd get the message with her one-word reply. She leaned against the window and stared out the glass. "Can you stop at the coffee shop on the way home?" She had a craving for cocoa.

"Uh…" Sam shifted on the seat beside her. "We're supposed to take you to the Verizon Center."

"Verizon Center? I'm not going there. I have work in the morning. I want my cocoa and one of the sandwiches they make, a hot shower and my bed."

Reggie huffed a laugh. "Told you so. Pay up."

She didn't see anything funny about that bet.

Sam pulled out his cell phone. "He's not going to like this."

"I don't care." She laid her head against the seat. "He doesn't work twelve-hour shifts in an emergency department."

Besides, whatever Ash had planned didn't fit within a doctor's busy schedule. If he thought he could snap his fingers and have her come running, that wasn't going to happen. He needed to put his rock-star ego in check.

Stifling a yawn, she closed her eyes. "Just take me to the coffee shop."

After a quick stop, they pulled up to her brownstone, only to find the crowd outside had grown.

"Stay here, Mrs. Dean," Reggie said.

She didn't correct him even though that was the second time he'd called her Mrs. Dean.

Reggie hopped out and jogged to the door, carrying her backpack, cocoa, and sandwich. He returned a few minutes later, using his bulk to push back the crowd.

"Get ready," Sam said. "Just like this morning, we'll escort you inside."

They clearly had plenty of practice with this type of thing and impressed her with their skill. Sam climbed out and used his body as a shield while Reggie blocked the crowd. Cameras lifted over his shoulder, shooting blindly. When Sam closed the door to the car, Reggie moved beside her, bracketing her between him and Sam. Together, they hustled her up the short walk and got her inside.

She gave a deep sigh when the door closed out the noise. "Is my brother home?"

The house creaked with silence.

"He's at the Verizon Center for the sound check. Donald's with him."

A soft grin ghosted across her face as she knew how excited Forest must be while surrounded by his idols. She sat at her dining room table and pulled out her meager dinner. The decadent aroma of cocoa wafted up and filled her nostrils with its incredible scent. She inhaled deeply, and a day's worth of tension disappeared.

"Um, you don't have to stay."

"We don't mind," Sam said.

"I'm not that interesting. I'm going to eat, read a little, and go to bed. I'm sure Ash needs you more than I do."

Sam agreed with a nod. "We'll just check the locks."

"Have at it." She waved at the door.

They made quick work of their security sweep.

"We'll be back in the morning to escort you to work. Make sure you lock the door behind us."

Reggie refused to leave until she assured him that she would do exactly as instructed.

A few moments after she shut the door, he tested the lock, making certain she'd followed his instructions.

Ensconced in her home, alone, silence descended like a welcoming blanket of comfort and relief. She hadn't been alone in the past four days and relished the solitude. She finished her dinner and drained the last of the cocoa. Too early for bed, she headed to take a long soak in her tub.

A couple of hours later, a heavy banging sounded on the door to her bathroom. Only Forest could beat on a door like that. Before she could tell him to come in, Forest had the door swinging inward.

"Hey, my summer Skye, how was your shift?" He had a lightness to his step and a grin on his face. He sat on the lid of the toilet.

The man couldn't touch her over layers of clothing without a meltdown, but seeing her naked did nothing. His triggers made little sense, but then neither did hers. She grabbed a washcloth and covered her lady parts. He might not care, but she did.

"Steady, busy."

"Anyone die?"

Inappropriate as always. He had a morbid fascination with death.

"No. How was your day?"

She curled her legs up, bringing her knees to her chest, trying to find a more modest position. Not that his eyes focused on anything other than her face. Visually, she was as appetizing as chopped liver to him.

"Pretty cool. Got to meet the whole band, and watched their sound check. They played a few sets. Amazing to see it all come together. I think I want to start a production crew. Can you imagine?"

In fact, she could.

"Bash is an amazing drummer."

Bash? Which one was he? She fell back on her mnemonic. He was the one who'd beaten up Ash. And he'd accompanied Ash to her house last night. She added to her memory jogger. *Bash banged on drums.*

"I thought the bigger guy was the drummer, the one with the curly hair?" She struggled to remember the name of the curly-haired guy. "Bent?"

"Yeah, but Bent plays bass. Bash is the drummer. Spike plays guitar, and Noodles is on keyboard. Don't you pay attention to anything I tell you?"

Not when it came to his music obsession, and she had nothing to help keep their instruments straight.

"Not really."

"Ugh, you're horrible. Okay, here's your Angel Fire one-oh-one. Blaze and Bash have known each other since high school, but they had a major falling-out a few years ago over Blaze's drug use. It practically broke up the band. Bent and Noodles forced Blaze into rehab and kept Bash from leaving Angel Fire. Blaze went into rehab, and the entire band took a sobriety pledge when he got out—well, no drugs; they all drink. Except Blaze. He doesn't touch anything. He's been clean for a few years now. We spent a lot of time talking about addiction."

That was a good sign. If Ash and Forest were trading addiction stories, maybe it would help Forest stay clean.

"My day was amazing. Blaze was pissed, by the way, when you didn't show up."

She shrugged. "I have to work, and his name is Ash."

"Probably best you didn't show up actually."

"Why?"

"Those guys have groupies coming out of their ears. I've never seen so much loose female flesh. Made me want to gag. And, for whatever reason, the girls kept throwing themselves at me." He barked a laugh. "I was peeling half-naked women off me all night long."

"Oh my!"

"I guess my proximity to the band gave me some sort of celebrity status."

"I doubt that."

Forest was painfully handsome to men and women even though he didn't realize it.

"Have you looked in a mirror lately? Women drool over you and then cry their eyes out when they realize you're not interested in playing for their team."

He surprised her when a flush colored his cheeks. "That's not true."

"Ah, my poor Beanpole." She snickered at his discomfort. "To have been surrounded by all that wanton female flesh…"

He pressed his hands on his thighs and stood. "That's why it's good you're not there. They were all over your husband, but don't worry. Blaz—Ash pushed them away." A hint of respect ghosted across his face. "Actually, he kept sending them to me!"

She laughed at that. "And you turned them all down. Poor things."

He released the leather thong holding back his hair and shook out his pale blond strands. He stuck his tongue out and pulled a face. "Why would I want tits and pussy when I can have shaft, balls, and ass? Besides, I have someone waiting in the wings." The corners of his mouth turned up, and his eyes brightened.

She suspected there was more to his fling than he was ready to admit. "Is he still floating around somewhere in the Pacific?"

"He made landfall yesterday, but I doubt he's figured out my riddle. We'll see if he earns the right to be a part of my life."

"Maybe you shouldn't test people like that." *What was happening to her brother?* He never kept people around. He was a use-them-and-lose-them kind of lover. *Who was this Daniels he kept going on and on about?*

He gave her a look. "Yeah, maybe I should take things slow, like you. Speaking of which, or whom, your hubby was dead set on coming over here tonight. I told him, no way in hell."

"Bean!"

He shushed with an upraised hand. "Hey, we had a long talk about what might or might not have happened in Niagara."

"You didn't!"

"I voiced concerns."

"Shit, Forest."

A single eyebrow lifted at her use of his given name, usually reserved for the most serious conversations.

"It's my duty to look after you."

"I'm the big sister here. Don't forget it." Technically, she was a few weeks younger than him, but when it had mattered most, she'd been the one who held him together.

All color drained from his face. "You stopped being my big sister the day—"

"Stop. What's done is done."

They needed to move past what had happened. It was time to heal.

"Don't let *him* define who we are now."

His Adam's apple bobbed.

"You and I are family. Brother and sister, nothing more, no matter the past." She grabbed a towel and wrapped it around her body. She would not subject him to the burden of her naked flesh. "Put your arms around me, Bean. Hug me. I need it."

"I can't." His body shook, and he backed away toward the door.

"You have to."

"But the things I did—"

"Were never your fault." She prayed this wasn't a horrible mistake.

He'd violated her in every way imaginable, forced by an even greater threat, as their foster father watched them play out his fantasies for his perverse pleasure. She hadn't been the only one to endure forced orgasms.

Their bond had been born out of that abuse. It had tried to destroy them, but together, they'd found the strength they needed to be free.

"You can't fix me."

"Why not?" But she knew he was right. She'd said those same words to Ash.

Ice-blue eyes stared down at her. "Go to bed, my summer Skye. We're watching your hubby play tomorrow night. He's expecting you at the show. The annulment papers are ready, but I think Lover Boy is determined to keep you."

Chapter Twenty-Two

FRIDAY PASSED IN A BLUR. HER TWELVE HOURS EXTENDED TO A fourteen-hour catastrophe as a multicar pileup had stressed the services of the emergency department. Like Bob had done many times for her in the past, she stayed to manage a trauma code while Bob tried to save another life.

Her cell phone buzzed nonstop during the chaos—Sam wondering where she was, Forest checking in, Ash asking if she was coming to the concert, and Reggie demanding to know how much longer until she was finished.

Finally, she had one of the nurses take the cell phone. It was too big of a distraction. Her hands were busy with more important things, like inserting a chest tube into a patient's chest. Air escaped with a whoosh, and her patient's blood pressure rose while his heart rate stabilized.

She snapped off her gloves and tossed them in the trash. "Give him another unit of blood, and get him to the OR."

Bob wandered in, peeling off blue paper scrubs. "You doing okay?"

"Yeah, my last patient is on the way to the operating room. You?"

"Good. He was the last critical one. I really appreciate you staying to help." He placed a hand on her shoulder. "I've got it from here."

"You sure?"

Several other patients from the multivehicle pileup had yet to be seen.

"I'm good. Besides, don't you have plans?"

She never should have told him about the concert or what had happened at Niagara. He'd been fathering her since she mentioned it, asking about Ash, his intentions, and if he treated her well.

Meanwhile, Reggie waited. She collected her cell phone. Reggie had left half a dozen messages in the past hour alone. His uneasiness wasn't difficult to understand. He had one task for the evening—get her to the concert and, by extension, to Blaze.

She missed the easygoing Ash with the beat-up Jeep who shopped in secondhand stores and chased waterfalls on a whim. The man who wore pajamas and strummed a simple guitar had disappeared with the revelation of his superstar status, becoming Blaze, who commanded the adoration of millions.

Forest had mentioned a sea of groupies. The idea of entering that chaotic world set Skye's teeth on edge. She had already formulated and rejected too many excuses as to why she couldn't attend. In the end, there wasn't a single valid reason she couldn't go. Her exhaustion might get her out of the evening, but she'd never lie to Ash.

Or Forest.

Her brother was beside himself with his all-access backstage pass. Tonight, he would see one of his dreams fulfilled, and she wanted to be there to share in the excitement.

Bob patted her on the back. "I love your dedication to this place. You work too hard. Seriously, I've got this. Enjoy the rest of your night. You're not working this weekend, right?"

"I'm not."

"I'm surprised you haven't asked for any time off."

She gave a hard swallow. Bob the Boss was much easier to handle than Bob the Paternal Figure. "We're already short-staffed…"

His gaze softened. "We can always make allowances for family. I reworked the schedule. Take the next two weeks off."

Her eyes widened in shock. "How'd you do that?"

"We have some ancillary staff with ED privileges looking to pull extra shifts."

"You didn't need to do that."

"I know, and I knew you'd never ask. Consider it a wedding gift. Take time to get to know your new husband."

"Bob—"

"Go. Get out of here. I don't want to see you around this place until after you've had a proper honeymoon." He lightly pushed her on the small of her back. "Enjoy your rock star—doctor's orders," he said with a laugh.

If only she could.

An hour later, Reggie escorted her out of the black sedan and through a rear entrance to the Verizon Center. The press of thousands pulsed around her, and an unrelenting beat thumped in her bones as the deep bass of Angel Fire's music settled in her jawbone. Reggie's gentle hand guided her up a set of stairs, through an industrial pair of doors, and down a concrete hallway. He shielded her with his body, blocking the crowd ahead and forging a path forward.

Men in jeans and black shirts with *Crew* stamped on the fronts and backs filled the halls. Most had earbuds lodged in their ears and black boxes attached to their waistbands. She shifted her backpack on her shoulder and slogged along, tired and weary after such a long day.

People stared, perhaps recognizing Reggie. A few of those looks were more pointed than others. Maybe her picture was in the news already. She had no idea how fast these things worked.

As they wove their way deeper into the bowels of the venue, the crowd thickened. Fewer crew members filled the halls as more and more groupies stretched out against the walls. Tall, lanky females with micro miniskirts and macro boobs advertised their various assets to any who cared. There were plenty of men who took advantage of the display and the blatant jockeying for social position.

She received odd stares. Not only did she look like crap, but fatigue also pulled at her, sapping her energy. Without the demands of the emergency department to concentrate her focus, all she could think about was sleep.

Although never one to attend concerts, let alone rise to the ranks of those allowed backstage, she could guess how things worked. The most beautiful would advance to the inner sanctum. Impress the right people, and they'd have a shot at meeting the band. *Wasn't that the ultimate prize? How many of these had overcome those hurdles in the past and scored the prize of her husband?*

Her eyes narrowed as she passed buxom blondes and leggy brunettes, their tight dresses barely covering their asses and their five-inch fuck-me heels accentuating long legs. Flawless makeup and perfectly styled hair contrasted sharply against her messy bun and her work-worn mascara-less face.

What the hell had she been thinking, coming straight from the hospital? The further they traveled, the more the bimbos were draped over men, moving ever closer to their final goal. *Surely, the inner sanctum had to be close?*

A heavy beat thumped through the walls. A steady wave of sound pounded in her chest, felt more than heard and pulsing with a demanding rhythm. The beginnings of a headache settled behind her eyes as the roar of the crowd cascaded through the halls.

Almost ten p.m., so the concert had to be coming to an end.

Reggie ushered her through a phalanx of burly men in black pants and shirts stamped now with *Security* instead of *Crew*. Beyond them, the throng thinned, but the quality of the bimbos jumped from overly pretty to straight-out gorgeous.

Reggie finally led her to a door labeled with a single star. "In here, Mrs. Dean."

She placed a hand on his arm. "Please stop calling me that. It's Skye or, if you must, Dr. Summers."

His frown radiated his displeasure, but he refrained from saying anything more. "You can leave your bag here. It'll be safe." He held out a hand to take her bag.

Without protest, she handed him her backpack.

"I'll put this in a locker and then take you backstage where you can watch the rest of the show."

Ash's music was beyond incredible, and to see it performed live would be amazing.

Reggie kept her moving, and before she knew it, he had her climbing a short flight of metal stairs. A wave of sound crashed into her, pressing against her chest, and it made it difficult to breathe. Her ears protested the chanting of tens of thousands mixed with the heavy beat that was Angel Fire's unique rock sound. Carrying pure emotive brilliance, Ash's voice poured into her soul, drenching her in a wash of angst and a primal need so fierce that she wanted to scream and shout with the rest of the masses.

Her heart thumped in synchrony to Bash's drumming. Reggie cupped her elbow and led her into the wings where she had an unobstructed view of Angel Fire onstage.

Nothing could have prepared her for the magic of the five men bonded together by music. Noodles's fingers flew over the keyboard while Ash and Spike thrashed their guitars, leaning back-to-back, as they picked out a particularly complex riff. Bent stood left of center, feet spread wide, head hung low, his arm strumming out the reverberations of his bass guitar. Ash's deep voice filled the concert with his tonal melody while Spike backed him up on vocals.

"Wow!" She raised her voice to be heard above the thundering noise.

"Fuck yeah." Reggie leaned close to yell into her ear, "Your brother's over there!"

Forest stood at the edge of the stage, a shit-eating grin plastered on his face. His hair hung loose down his back, a white cloud of frenetic energy, as he banged his head to the beat. His entire body pulsed from the excitement of watching his favorite band, up close and personal.

She hurried to him. "Bean!"

His arctic gaze turned to her. "You're late." His rumbly voice carried easily, despite the noise.

Lifting up on her tiptoes, she raised her voice. "My shift ran long. How's the concert going?"

His teeth flashed white with his grin. "Fucking awesome. It's almost over though. You missed the whole show."

She could lecture him on the relative importance of saving lives compared to watching a concert, but that would be wasted breath. She focused instead on the guitar-wielding rock god belting out the chorus to one of Angel Fire's original hits. The audience roared and joined Ash as he sang the chorus.

Spike rocked the guitar, lending vocal support, as Ash grabbed the microphone. The phrase *sex on a stick* came to her mind as he played to the crowd.

Her attention shifted across the stage and landed on those hidden out of sight, like herself. Stagehands and security lined the edges, an ever-present dark sea of support. Interspersed among them were the women who screamed and gyrated with the beat of the music, hoping to garner the attention of the men onstage.

A look at her crumpled scrubs had her spirits deflating. This was not her world. Everyone around her was partying, amped on adrenaline, where all she wanted was a bed. Hell, she'd settle for a couch, something she could collapse into and forget the day.

The pounding music increased the throbbing in her head.

Onstage, a spotlight illuminated Ash, and he tilted his head back, that beautiful voice hammering out lyrics to the frenzy of Bash's beat. The band was on fire, and the crowd amplified the energy the band poured out, feeding it back to them. She'd never experienced anything like it, and while everyone around her fed off the combined energy, each pulse drained her last reserves.

Just as she was about to ask Reggie to take her back, Ash turned, picking her out of the dimness. His face lit up with joy, and he gave Spike a fist-bump.

As Spike, Bent, Noodles, and Bash carried the music, Ash swung his guitar to his back and ran to swoop her into a hug.

He spun her, laughing. "You made it."

Sweat saturated his T-shirt, but she didn't care. The strength of his arms settled her mind, and the pulsating headache eased. A woodsy spice and musk filled her nostrils. She breathed in the aroma of coming home as he kissed her. The contact was too brief, and she wanted more, but he put her down and backed away.

"Don't you dare move." He raced back onstage, moving seamlessly back into the music. He rejoined Spike, jamming on the guitar, and finished out the rest of the song.

Roaring filled the arena as exuberant fans expressed their adulation. Ash pulled the microphone from the stand. He walked back to the drum set and said something to Bash. His friend gave a nod. Ash jerked his chin to Spike and Bent, who joined him, as he walked to the keyboards where he said something to Noodles.

Bash held his drumsticks over his head and clicked them together, establishing the beat for the next song. Spike and Bent moved to the center of the stage with Ash, the three of them holding still with their guitars at the ready. Bash began a slow steady beat on the drums, a hypnotic rhythm that tunneled into her gut.

Ash took the mic. "This is new. Something we've never played before a live crowd." He chuckled and flashed a rock-star grin as he blinked into the lights. "Don't get pissed if we fuck it up."

The crowd screamed.

Noodles played a key on the keyboard. A single resounding note filled the arena. He followed it with a second warbling chord as Bent's bass added to the soulful sound. Bash doubled up the beat, layering in complexity, as Noodles began a melody she'd heard once before on an acoustic guitar in a cabin in the woods.

Spike lay down the intro to Angel Fire's newest song. Ash cupped the mic in his hands, closed his eyes, and pulled in a deep breath. Then, he belted out the opening lyrics of "Insanity."

Beside her, Forest jumped. "Holy hellfire. A new fucking song."

Forest bounced as Ash huffed out words to a song she'd watched him create. It sounded much different with the power of the band behind it, richer and full-bodied.

Spike's harmonizing blended with Ash's voice. The audience screamed as the band moved into the chorus. The energy of the arena escalated. Ash opened his eyes as the audience exploded. He turned to her, and the crowd melted away. They were the only people in the arena as he sang about insanity.

It was true. Whatever this thing was between them, it was crazy. She had no idea what the hell they were thinking. No possible way this could ever work, but she knew, in her heart, that Ash would find a way.

A tear trickled down her cheek, and she let it fall.

The wild energy of the crowd proclaimed "Insanity" as Angel Fire's next mega hit.

Applause descended in a deafening tsunami of sound as the sea of ecstatic fans erupted with their screams and adulation. Skye cupped her hands over her cheeks, using the motion to wipe at the tears before anyone could notice.

Ash spoke to the crowd, thanking them for the evening, and then launched into an encore set.

She stepped close to Forest to yell into his ear, "I'm tired, Bean. I'm going to wait in the dressing room."

He gave her two thumbs-ups. "See you."

A quick search, and she found Reggie. "Can you take me back?"

"Don't want to wait for the end?" he asked.

"No." She gave a shake of her head. "I'm exhausted, and my head is pounding. I think I need some water and something for my head. Do you mind?"

He took ahold of her upper arm in a gentle grip. "No problem. Stay close."

The farther they moved from the stage, the worse her head ached. This thing between them was crazy. It would never work, as much as Ash would try to find a way. She had to find a way to say good-bye.

Chapter Twenty-Three

REGGIE LED SKYE BACK TO THE BAND'S DRESSING ROOM. THE ROAR of the fans followed them and then disappeared with the closing door. She hadn't paid much attention when Reggie first brought her here, but now, she took a moment to appreciate her surroundings. She spun around, amazed and then was thankful for the sanctuary of silence.

He moved past an outer grouping of tables toward the furthest and most private of three seating areas. To her left, a galley kitchen held a refrigerator and what appeared to be a fully stocked bar. He took her to the smallest seating area, but there was nothing simple or plain about the opulent leather of the sofa and matching chair. A mahogany coffee table had been buffed to such a deep shine that her reflection stared back from the surface, looking every bit as exhausted as she felt.

"The band usually hangs out after the show, greeting fans and dealing with the local press. Considering the latest news, Mr. Dean will probably be tied up with more than his fair share of interviews." He headed back to the door. "I have to be at the meet-and-greet, but if you need me, just call."

They'd traded contact information during the drive over, and she had not only his cell number, but Sam's and Donald's as well. She sank onto the couch, reveling in the buttery texture of the expensive white leather.

"Thank you, Reggie."

After he departed, she stretched out and covered her eyes. Her ears rang from the sudden silence, and a dull ache settled behind her eyes. A few minutes later, the outer door opened and brought a discordant rush of too many voices layered over Angel Fire's pounding rhythms.

"Uh, sorry to disturb you," Reggie said.

She sat up, rubbing her eyes, and winced at the pain seated deep behind them. Her headache didn't seem to be going away.

He walked over and held out a stage pass hooked to a lanyard. "Here, put this on. If you leave, you'll need it to get back in here."

"Thank you." She slipped the lanyard around her neck and settled it over the one she used at work.

He jerked a finger toward the door. "You think you'll be okay?"

She nodded. "I'm just going to lie down for a bit. I'm good."

He left her again, and she lay out on the couch, allowing her eyes to drift closed. Images of Ash onstage dominated her thoughts.

A potent, almost painful sexuality had rolled off him as he brought his music into being. His guitar playing and the magnetism of his voice had created a raw synergy that obliterated rational thought. Despite her indecision about their future, an insistent voice told her not to worry. Instead of the hundreds of overly eager groupies, he had chosen her. And, with that, fatigue pulled her into a state halfway between wakefulness and sleep where she contemplated the implications of the past three days.

A door slammed open, and jubilant shouts and people spilled through the outer doorway. The loud raucous laughter of deep male voices had her jolting to a sitting position and blinking the sleep from her eyes.

Spike bounced into the room first. His multiple piercings flashed in the light. A leggy brunette had herself draped over his arm, pressing her boobs against his chest.

Bent shoved past them, using his linebacker physique to shoulder Spike and his female appendage to the side. Bent had three girls in tow, all of them squealing as he pulled them to the nearest set of couches. Noodles followed next with a woman clutching each tattooed arm. The women clung to the keyboardist as he led them toward one of the seating areas.

Bash followed with Ash, their heads pressed together, deep in conversation. Bash had a redhead tucked against his side. Bash thumped Ash on the shoulder and gave a chin bump toward Skye.

Ash captured Skye's gaze across the length of the room, and he blew her a kiss.

The band's security team entered next—Sam, Reggie, Donald, and a few others she didn't recognize. Forest was with them. He was easy to spot with his shock of white hair, and he was head and shoulders over Angel Fire's security team. The last one closed the door and sealed off the din emanating from beyond. The men seated themselves among the tables, leaving the band members to occupy the couches. Forest waved to her but joined the security detail.

Spike, Bent, and Noodles arranged their collection of women in the largest grouping of couches. Noodles extricated himself and staggered to the bar where he grabbed an armload of beer. Spike and Bent disappeared under a flurry of female flesh as the women divested themselves of skimpy miniskirts and barely there tops.

This was the life of a rock star? Her imagination had fallen far short of reality.

"Don't hold my past against me," he'd said.

Well, she wouldn't, but would he have the strength to do the same when her time came?

Ash lowered himself beside her and nuzzled her neck with a kiss. "Hey."

Bash settled his redhead on the couch across from them. "Be back in a sec, Kit."

Ash looked around the room. "God, what I wouldn't give for that cabin in the woods." His words wrapped around her, expressing her nearly identical thoughts. "Feels like we didn't get to spend any time there." His finger drew a heart over her thigh.

"We didn't," she said with a wistful sigh.

She lifted a hand to his neck and stroked the outstretched wings of the dragon.

He shivered at her touch. "We need to fix that. I believe I owe you a honeymoon."

"Ash…" She pressed against his chest.

The cotton clung to his skin, dampened by the exertions brought on by a multi-hour stage event. Even his sweat had her heart racing. Warmth moved through her palm, up the length of her arm, and settled right in the base of her heart.

Things were getting out of hand on the set of couches one seating area over. She avoided looking that way, knowing what she would find. She shook her head, realizing the direction of her thoughts. She couldn't judge Ash's friends without judging him as well.

Ash leaned over and pressed his lips to her mouth. Hot and heavy, his kiss swept through her, demanding and insistent. Her lips parted for him while her thoughts spun in a furious maelstrom. It'd been less than a day and a half since she left him at the airport, yet it seemed like ages since they'd been alone. Within that small span of time, so much had changed.

Escalating cries of rising passion emanated from the other corner of the room. She broke off the kiss and turned to look. She'd never experienced such an openly consensual display. Naked females fawned over Bent, Spike, and Noodles—kissing, licking, stroking, and gyrating themselves toward a frenzied completion.

Ash gave a chuckle as he watched her staring at his friends. "Sorry, backstage tradition."

Her lips tingled, as did the tips of her fingers, and a roaring rushed past her ears, muffling all other sounds. Shadows pressed in from the periphery, rushing to sink her into the blackness of memory.

"Skye? Skye! What's wrong?" Ash patted her cheek with his hand, not quite a slap, but the sting caught her attention.

"What?"

"You zoned out on me." His eyes drilled into her, concern etched in the furrow of his brow.

Zoned out? It was much worse than that. She'd been on the verge of an all-out panic attack. She needed to breathe.

"I'm okay. Maybe more tired than I thought." While not technically a lie, she hated being evasive.

The sound of sloppy sex escalated and could no longer be ignored. She struggled to hold herself together. Bent, in particular, enjoyed his women. They squealed as he moved from one to the next, and as he did, a shiver of revulsion inched its way down her spine.

Ash put a finger on her chin and turned her head back to him. "I'm right here, babe."

"I'm sorry."

A lopsided grin filled his face. "The guys get crazy after a show. We like to burn off a little steam before heading back to the hotel. Knock one out, as it were."

"I see." She also heard the pronoun he'd used. Not *they* liked to burn off steam, but *we*. *Was he expecting her to have sex with him here? In front of his band? With his security detail watching? With Forest?* Now, *that* would add fuel to an epic meltdown event. That couldn't happen.

The slapping of flesh on flesh sounded to their right. In front of them, Kit slid off the couch and went to her knees in front of Bash. He unzipped his jeans and pulled out his cock.

She needed to get out of there. *Would Ash ask that of her?* She bit her lower lip, praying he wouldn't, just as one of the girls gave a warbling long orgasmic wail. Another panted with escalating cries.

Spike grunted, "Fuck yeah, I win."

"Damn," Noodles said. "I always lose this bet."

"I've got magic fingers," Spike proclaimed.

Bent cursed, "Shit, girl. Give it up all ready. I'm losing the game."

Bash laughed as he flexed his hips and threw his head back. "I'm not playing, Bent, and I don't think Ash is either. You lose." He gripped Kit's ginger curls and fucked her willing face. "Ah, fuck, your lips are amazing. Faster, babe. I'm almost there."

Skye's breathing accelerated. Similar scenes from her past pushed against the locks of the memory vault. Breathing deep only made things worse as the scent of sex settled deep in her nasal passages. Purposeful male grunts told her that, now that the women had been satisfied, Noodles and Spike were focusing on their needs.

Dread uncoiled from her gut and stretched caustic fingers along her nerves. Her skin drew taut against the pressure, growing cold from the outside in.

Ash pulled her to him. "What's wrong?"

Someone big sat down. "Hey, Lover Boy, I'm not cool with this scene. It's time to take my summer Skye home."

"For the love of God," Ash cursed. "Back off. She's my wife, asshole. I've got this."

"*My sister* is losing her shit, and you haven't a fucking clue." Forest pointed to Bash getting his blow job and to the other members of the band fucking the groupies a few feet over. "And, as much as I like your music, I don't know fuck about you. I'm getting her out of here." He stood and towered over Ash. "I'm sure we understand each other."

Forest extended a hand he knew she would never take. "Come, my summer Skye. I've got you." His hardened ice-blue eyes dragged her back from the blackness creeping in. He gave a nod, understanding exactly where her mind had landed. He knew this memory well, because he shared it.

With a shaky voice, she moved on autopilot, latching on to the deep baritone of Forest's voice instead of taking his proffered hand. "Thanks, Bean."

"You're not taking her away." Ash leaped to his feet. "She's with me now."

Noodles swaggered toward the bar as he zipped his jeans. "What's wrong, Ash? Old ball and chain won't wet your willy? Figured you'd have her blowing you or riding you hard by now. What's up? Married life got you down already?"

Ash's face turned red moments before he launched at Noodles. He dived and dragged Noodles to the ground, punching as they fell.

Ash flipped Noodles over onto his back and clocked him in the jaw. "Don't you ever disrespect Skye again, you fucking bastard."

"What the fuck happened to you, you pussy-whipped wimp? You used to bring three or four girls back after a concert and fuck them all. Win the game every time. You haven't even gotten her shirt off."

Noodles swung at Ash, but Ash blocked.

His voice came out in a menacing growl. "That's my wife!"

"Yeah. Got that. Why aren't you fucking your wife?" Noodles lay flat on the floor, not moving a muscle. "You think this one is going to last? She's a doctor, for fuck's sake. Way out of your league. I give you two weeks."

Ash knocked Noodles out cold. "Bastard."

Not a single member of the security team intervened.

Ash turned to her, agony scrawled deep into his features. "I'm so sorry."

The redhead hadn't stopped her oral ministrations during the fight.

Bash pulled her off his dick. "Ah, fuck, we're leaving? I'm not done." Frustration edged his words.

Ash shook his head. "No. You stay." He took in the naked women and his bandmates, and then he turned to Skye. "This isn't what I want anymore." He walked to Forest and didn't back down when Forest puffed out his chest. "I don't care what you say. She belongs with me. You get what I'm saying?"

"So long as you understand what happens if you hurt her," Forest said. "And as long as you stop acting like an ass."

"If I ever hurt her, there's nothing you can do that'd be worse than what I'd do to myself."

Ash took her hand. "I'm sorry. I wasn't thinking." He turned to the security team sitting at the tables. "Get ready. We're going to the hotel."

"I want to go home." She squeezed Ash's hand and lowered her voice to a whisper. "I won't come between you and your band."

Noodles moaned on the floor, waking up. He rolled over and pushed up on his hands. Then, he collapsed back down. "You fucking punched me."

"You deserved it," Ash said with a grunt.

"Shit. That's not right." Noodles rolled to a sitting position. He stared at Skye, a look of awe in his expression. "What have you done to him?"

"Don't answer." Ash pulled her toward the door. "If we go back to your place, your brother will make me sleep on the couch. I need to feel you, Skye. You're slipping away."

"Isn't anyone going to help Noodles?" she asked.

The rest of the band was busy getting off. Even Bash had gone back to enjoying his redhead. All the security folks sat at the tables, playing cards or surfing their cell phones, with the exception of Ash's personal trio. Reggie had disappeared out the door while Sam grabbed her bag from the locker where Reggie had it stored.

Noodles raised a hand. "You hit me over a girl. First, Bash, and now, me? What is it about this one that's so special?"

Ash gave Noodles a hand up. "She's the one." He spun Noodles toward the bar. "Don't fuck with her."

"Shit, man, you *are* insane."

For whatever reason, Skye had the impression that Noodles wasn't as upset by that.

Reggie waited by the door, speaking into a headset microphone. "Donald says the car is pulling around, sir. You ready?"

Ash gave her hand a squeeze. "Stay by my side, babe. This is going to get intense."

Despite all her doubts, being tucked under his arm made her feel safe. The warm scent of him flowed around her, intensified by the deep musk of his sweat.

"You need a shower," she said. "You smell rank."

"So do you. That's the first thing we're taking care of when we get to the hotel." He kissed the top of her head and looked to Reggie.

"We're ready."

Were they?

Chapter Twenty-Four

REGGIE PULLED OPEN THE DOOR LEADING OUT TO THE HALL, AND A flood of sound and light barreled toward Skye, making her wobble against Ash. A line of security held back the crowd, and Reggie led her and Ash forward with Sam following with Forest.

Skye blinked and covered her ears. *How did Ash live with all this attention?* But he ate it up. Even with his hand holding hers, he raised his other arm, waving to the fans and giving his rock-star smile.

Forest stepped around their small group and pushed Reggie out of the way. "Here, let me lead. I have a way with crowds."

As always, a bubble of space formed in front of Forest, the crowd making room for the implacable force that was her brother. While he cleared a path, Ash followed in his shadow, drawing her along beside him. Sam and Reggie moved into position, flanking them, while simultaneously protecting their rear. Forest seemed to know exactly where to go, surprising her, until she remembered that he'd spent the day helping with the sound check.

Her grip on Ash tightened as he sheltered her from the crowd.

"I have you, Skye. I'm never letting you go."

She breathed out a deep sigh.

Women cried out their undying love while reporters hammered Ash —Blaze—with a rapid-fire stream of questions he couldn't possibly answer.

Sam and Reggie hustled them to a waiting town car. Forest held the door open while Ash helped her inside. After everyone was seated, Forest slammed the door shut. Automatic door locks engaged, and a blessed empty silence fell upon them.

When they arrived at the hotel, Sam and Reggie held the lobby crowds back while Forest used his impressive presence to once again clear the way. A short elevator ride saw them delivered to an impressive penthouse suite. Six bedrooms led off a main living space, and Ash led her through the living area, not stopping, to head down the left hallway.

He clasped her hand with a possessive resolve, refusing to let go. "You're mine for the rest of the night," he proclaimed.

Forest arched a brow, questioning if she truly was okay. Other than a bone-deep weariness, she had no problem with spending the night with Ash. It was the rest of her life that concerned her, but despite that nagging doubt, for right now, being with Ash felt right.

He pulled her into his room and released her hand. She wandered, ignoring the king-size bed and everything it promised, to stand before a wall of floor-to-ceiling plate-glass windows. The city buzzed with activity, buildings glowing with the light of those inside and cars swerving through traffic. The pulse of the city spoke to her, all those people living different lives.

Did any of them have as messed up of a life as she led? Probably. Hell, who was she kidding? She took care of the sickest of the sick.

Fatigue—that was the root of her depressed mood.

Behind her, Ash twisted the lock to the door, and the snick sounded too loud in her ears, defining their seclusion from the rest of the world. *Would the Ash who'd hunted waterfalls return, or was the rock star, Blaze, still with her?*

"When the guys get here later," Ash explained, "it can get even weirder than what you saw after the show. I don't want any of that spilling in here. I know you must be tired, and we haven't had a moment alone since…"

She'd left him at the airport.

"We party hard," he continued, "and I'm not going to lie about it, but I won't apologize either. I never hid my past, but it's just you and me from now on."

He'd been up-front to a fault about his past and even more forthright about his desire for the future. She hadn't hidden her past exactly, explaining only those few details necessary, but she certainly hadn't shared the full extent of it. He never asked for more, and she wasn't yet willing to divulge her secrets. He would run far and fast once that happened.

He claimed he was tired of gorging himself on sex. She hoped that was true. If her experience with Spencer had taught her anything, something other than sex would have to interest a man if she was going to keep him.

And, now, they were painfully alone, locked behind a hotel room door. Alone meant she would have to face, if not their future, then at least their very potent present.

And Ash took no time in proclaiming his intent. He devoured the distance between them. His purposeful long strides brought him to her before she could take a second breath. He stole all the air around her, making it impossible for her to think.

She took a step back, turning toward the bathroom. It was an evasive move but all she had. "Well, I'm tired, and you stink. Any chance we could take that shower?"

There, she could give him a hand job or a blow job and move his mind through and past sex. She'd be able to hide her issues behind the steam. It had worked with Spencer often enough, and she prayed it'd work now.

A victorious expression brightened his face. "A shower sounds awesome."

He peeled his shirt off and tossed it to the floor. He kicked off his sneakers and tugged at the fly of his jeans.

She smiled as she walked to the bathroom, analyzing what was to come with clinical efficiency. *Ugh, she was such a mess.*

"This is going to be so much better than the back of a car," he said.

Yes, their epic fuck. At least things could only get better after that fiasco.

The long, hard length of his cock bobbed as he joined her. Steam billowed out of the shower and folded around her in a warm blanket of mist.

She stepped into the spacious two-person shower enclosure and pointed to the door. "Close that, please. I like my showers steamy."

All she really craved was sleep. If she had been at home, she wouldn't have bothered and would've fallen into bed, fully clothed. With Ash, in his post-performance afterglow and rank sweat stench, there was no way to avoid the shower.

His presence enveloped her, wrapping her with a potency of male desire and need. She wanted nothing other than to tap into his sensual energy. To come alive at the touch of a man was her hidden dream, and she held out the smallest hope that she could do that with him. To not cringe or flinch or hope for his quick completion— those were her prayers, but worry was the enemy, too, because it smothered all the joy in being with him.

Ash wrapped his arms around her waist and dropped his forehead to rest against hers. A long moment passed with his steady exhalations, pulsing between them, while the weight of their circumstance settled into the silence.

Husband and wife. They were lovers as well as strangers.

His fingers combed through her hair, straightening the mess of curls. He massaged her neck and her shoulders, and then he dug into the knots of her back. Then, he found her hands and entwined their fingers, sinking his brow against hers, intensifying their connection.

She followed his gaze down to where he clasped her hands. His calloused fingers traced hers, lacing them together. And, beneath their hands, his cock jutted, engorged with his arousal and full of his need.

Her chest filled with a warm glow beneath all the worry.

She could do this. With him. If she tried really, really hard.

He stepped back, taking his warmth with him. Chilly air filled the empty space between them. His expression had her heart clenching, desire etched into the strong features of his amazing face, tension clenching at his jaw, and indecision swirling within the depths of his eyes.

A miserable knot tightened in her belly. She had seeded his doubts, and the weight of them would suffocate him. How to fix things remained a daunting task.

Without asking, Ash spun her around, facing her away from him. Then, his hands touched her nape, sweeping from her neck to her shoulders. His fingers dug deep into the knots of her muscles.

With a groan, she breathed slowly while his fingers forced the tight muscles to surrender to his will. Rough calluses dragged against her skin, sending tiny shivers shooting down her spine and up her nape. She luxuriated in his touch as he pressed and kneaded with expert precision.

Her muscles fought his onslaught, but they were no match for the insistence of his touch. Soon, her muscles relented, all tension easing under the heat of the water pouring over her skin and the fire stoked by his touch. He began to hum, and the beauty of the thick, low timbre vibrated over her skin, caressing her nerve-endings and soothing the swirling chaos of her thoughts.

"You carry a lot of stress, babe," he said.

A shiver of hopeful excitement tingled through her, unbidden, as he moved down her spine. No other man had ever made her tremble with anticipation. Ash knew something about back massaging, too. He pressed at the pressure points beneath her scapula, making her hiss when he found a particularly sensitive spot.

"Too hard?" He eased up.

Yes, but it felt so good. "No. Keep pressing."

He leaned into the troubled spot, causing her to cry out.

"You sure?"

"Yes."

He increased the pressure, and she breathed against the pain. Moments later, the muscle beneath his finger fatigued and released.

"I don't want to hurt you," he said, concern lacing his voice.

"You won't." She'd endured worse. "It feels amazing."

The press of his fingers hurt but with a good kind of pain.

His hands continued their magical dance as they traced their way down her spine, moving one vertebra at a time. Her breaths quickened as she braced against pain, and they hitched with another sensation, lifting the tiny hairs on her arms.

"Well, it's supposed to feel good, not hurt. Let me know if it's too much." He kissed her shoulder, the sweep of his lips blazing a fiery trail along her skin. He collected her hair and straightened it down her back. "I love your hair." His fingers returned to her shoulders and pressed, causing her to gasp as he hit on a sore spot. "Stop?"

"Mmm...no." She loved how he checked in while continuing to work the muscles.

"How about we wash out this hair?" He guided her under the shower through the fog of steam billowing out.

She pinched her eyes shut, knowing it would soon be time to take care of him. He positioned her under the stream of water, wetting her hair, and when she stepped away to lather in shampoo, he gave a jerk of his head. He squeezed out shampoo into the palm of his hand.

"You're going to need a lot more than that," she said with a soft laugh.

"Don't worry; I'll take care of you."

Of course, he meant something other than simply washing her hair. That promise still hung between them.

He had the most divine hands ever created on earth, and she loved that he had yet to go after her breasts or pussy. He seemed to truly care about making her feel comfortable. She tilted back and let him pamper her with the best scalp massage she'd ever experienced.

"Time to wash the rest of you." His gentle words brought all of her fears crashing back to the surface.

Before she could say a word, he leaned the length of his body against hers and wrapped his arms around her waist. A low moan issued from his throat.

"Don't disappear on me, babe. Close your eyes and feel me. Just relax and enjoy the moment."

He traced a finger up her arm, tickling the roughened skin of her elbow and massaging her forearm. Electricity sparked between them, and her body thawed under his touch. He continued his exploration, slow and determined, and he seemed intent to let this moment stretch between them forever.

His fingers drifted over the backs of her hands, stroking lightly. There was no hesitancy to his touch, but neither did he seem hurried. It was as if they were trapped in time, stuck within a moment of sensual bliss. And where his touch was sure and exact, she found herself trembling.

Their fingers interlocked, and he raised their clasped hands to nestle beneath her breasts. His embrace encased her within the cage of his strength, and as he pressed his entire body against hers, she felt cocooned by his protection and supported by his strength.

Safe wasn't a word she regularly used, but Ash had broken through her barriers. He'd never hurt her; only her hesitancy would hinder them.

A future with Ash is what she wanted, and that realization had her heart hammering out a pounding rhythm. *But would he grow tired, the way Spencer had?*

Suds covered them, trailing off her hair and running down her back. Their skin slid against each other, slippery with the shampoo and heating with desire.

"You doing okay?" his husky voice whispered in her ear. "Any triggers?"

She bit her lower lip, not trusting herself to speak, and she nodded.

"Yes, you're okay? Or, yes, this is tripping memories?"

And what if it were?

If she wanted him in her life, she would have to force herself past her issues because no man wanted a broken woman in his bed.

"I'm okay." She would tell him the truth—up until the moment she had to lie.

"If I do anything that bothers you, promise you'll let me know?"

He surprised her at every turn.

What would he do? While her reaction was predictable, it tended to happen at the worst possible moment. *Could she trust him?*

She practiced her avoidance again. "Um, I have to use conditioner on my hair. If I don't, I can't get the tangles out."

He laughed, but the tone of his voice told her she hadn't succeeded in distracting him. "Okay."

She tilted her head back and reached around to take his cock into her hand.

He shifted away. "No."

"Don't you want me to—"

"Not until you're comfortable with me touching you. I'm not in a hurry, Skye." He nuzzled the soft hollow of her neck. "We have all the time in the world."

And damn if she didn't wish to give him what he wanted.

She turned around and laced her fingers around his neck. "I appreciate what you're trying to do. I really do. But don't try to fix me."

His stare caught her off guard because she saw a hunger there that matched her deepest desire. Face-to-face with him, she couldn't look away. He wanted more than sex. He wanted her happiness. She didn't doubt his desire to fix her, but that was not what she saw reflected in the intensity of his gaze. His passion terrified her because it freed her from her burdens and made her feel blissfully alive. She was only just realizing what that might mean.

His body molded against hers, merging them together into one person. He kissed her, shoving his hands in her hair, gripping and pulling, until she groaned with the possession. She wrapped her arms around his back while he coaxed a deeper kiss. She couldn't help but flex her hips, rocking against the hard press of his cock. And, as she did, her pulse thrummed past her ears, racing with a gathering heat. She reached between them, eliciting a hiss, followed by a deep moan, as she stroked his shaft.

He placed his hand over hers, stilling her motion. "Stop."

"But…"

It wouldn't take long for her to bring his climax toward an inevitable conclusion, but he refused to let her, gripping her wrist and holding it still.

His eyes latched on to hers, a darkness brewing in their depths. "We give, and we take, babe. I won't take without giving something back. I need to touch you, too."

"You can take me any way you want." Fucking had never been a problem. He could bury himself inside her, and she would be content for him to take everything he needed.

"That's not what I meant, and you know it."

Defeated, she released her hand from his pulsing cock. "You want me to come, and I told you, I can't."

Not without images of her foster father filling her head, ripping her tender flesh apart with his prick, as his slimy flesh slapped against her bruises. Or, the worst memory of all, the violation forced upon Forest to compel her orgasmic release or face something much worse.

Ash shook his head. "All I'm asking is for you to trust me. I want you to feel as good as you make me feel."

Men always thought they could fix things.

As steam billowed all around them, his stare hardened, as did her resolve.

Men were so fucking obstinate.

His insistence, while gallant, prolonged the shower and kept her from her bed. Fatigue pulled at her muscles and fogged her brain. Her seduction, grabbing his dick and tugging on it, crass as it was, seemed to be failing.

The corners of his mouth twitched as he tried to resist the sensations she pulled from his body. With a flick of her finger under the head of his cock, he sucked in air as her grip tightened around his shaft. She stroked him from root to crown and arched a brow as she stared him down.

"You got me by the balls here," he said.

She winked. "I know."

"I'll never give up, you know."

She lowered to her knees. "Accept me for who I am. Accept what I can give." *Please don't judge me by my past. I can't change any of it.*

Steam heated her cheeks. She could smell him. The perfume from the shampoo lathered his skin, but the musky aroma of his arousal had her nostrils flaring.

She blinked, and as she opened her mouth to take him in, a harsh emotion emerged. Simmering anger rose from her gut.

This was what her foster father had stolen. Intimacy remained an impossible dream.

She pushed her anger aside and kissed the tip of Ash's cock. Wrapping her lips around him, she explored his velvety length. Hard as steel, his cock jerked and swelled. Eagerly, she licked, swirling her tongue around the tip.

His guttural low groan encouraged her exploration, and when his legs began to shake, she knew he was getting close. He grew harder and hotter in her mouth. She licked and sucked, letting his moans guide her next step. She cupped his sack, caressing his heavy balls, careful not to rake the tender skin with her nails.

Ash's moans intensified as she swallowed his full length, overcoming her gag instinct to take him fully. She sucked and then pulled out, slow, dragging her tongue along his length. His body shook, hips thrusting forward, trying to take over and fuck her face. She loved the effect she had on him, how he would come undone under her touch. She loved every moment and allowed him the freedom he needed. And, as he fucked her mouth, his sharp, uneven exhalations filled the shower with the urgency of his need.

"Holy fuck!" He grasped the wet length of her hair, pulling and guiding her head as he desired.

He was close, and she coaxed his climax to completion with measured long pulls of her mouth. And then, finally, his body went rigid. He wrapped her hair around his wrist, holding her face against his groin, as the aftershocks of his orgasm shot through him.

She licked and sucked, swallowing every last drop, until his cock slipped from her lips. She watched him struggle to regain the smoothness of his breath.

"Goddamn, I've never..." He released her hair, letting it fall against her back.

Yeah, she knew the rest of that line.

Lead singer, rock-star extraordinaire, used to bringing groupies in by the dozen, he'd probably been sucked off by more women than he could remember, and none could hold a candle to her skills. Those bimbos hadn't been trained from the age of twelve or been forced to practice day and night to perfect their skills.

Her cheeks turned hot and not from the steam. As she was camouflaged by the water, Ash had no idea she was in the midst of breaking down. She might have overcome adversity and risen to a profession of respect, but she had not outgrown the ghosts of her past.

The fates had to be laughing now. She was married by mistake to a rock star who'd fucked scores, if not hundreds of groupies. *Wasn't it ironic that he'd married a true whore, and how would she explain that to the in-laws? A minister and his grade-school teacher wife?*

Her cheeks blazed with shame.

"Skye?" Ash lowered to his knees and clasped her within his embrace.

She let her hair hang forward, desperate to hide her emotion. "Yes?"

"Why won't you let me do that for you?"

"I told you why." *Hadn't he been listening?*

"You told me you were forced to…to do things, but I want to make new memories to replace the bad ones. Don't you think we should at least try?"

Best to lay it right out here. He obviously didn't understand.

"There was more to it than simple abuse." So much more.

She took in a deep breath, but he cut her off.

He leaned his forehead against hers. "I love you."

She melted into his embrace. His touch did that to her, encapsulated her in a shroud of protection where she could envision herself safe. But her mind remembered, even as her heart struggled to love.

Ash came from a family who believed in true love. He was a man running from fame and the cheap groupie hook-ups that came with it. As much as he rebelled against his stereotypical roots, he craved to return to them. A woman with her past didn't fit into a minister's family full of picket fences, picnics, and never-ending hugs.

"I don't need to be saved," she said.

He cupped her chin and forced her to look at him. "I'm not here to save you, but I will. I love you, and that's something you can't run away from." His eyes pinched, as if trying to convey something he thought she wouldn't understand.

And the irony was, he was probably right. She didn't understand him at all.

"Then, what does it matter?" She pulled his hand away from her chin. "I like making you feel good. Why can't that be enough?"

He rocked her under the flow of water streaming over their bodies.

"Someday, I'm going to show you why it isn't enough." He kissed the top of her head. "For now, I won't push, but I need you to allow me to touch you."

She cringed. *How had they circled back around to that?* "Ash…"

"We'll start slow, like the massage. I'll stop when you tell me to."

So much hope was held in his voice; she didn't want to crush him out of hand.

"You're not going to give up, are you?"

He shook his head. "Never."

"What if I don't agree?"

"Then, you leave me no choice."

"No choice?" This was it then.

"You'll force me to take a vow of chastity."

Her eyes widened. "You'd give up sex?"

He brushed the backs of his fingers against her lips. "I won't have you serving me. I told you, I'm in this for the bigger prize. That means all of you, not just pieces of you."

"But…"

"I don't know anything about abuse or how to help you, but I'll learn. We'll learn together and find help if we need it because I'm in this with you, for better or for worse. We never exchanged vows, but I believe them in my heart."

She reached out and traced the curve of his bicep. "About that, I wish we'd taken the time to get to know each other better."

He tilted his head back and opened his mouth, letting water pour in. He spit across the opposite shower wall. "You would've run for the hills once you found out who I was."

"Technically, I knew who you were before we got married."

And he still didn't have a clue as to who she was, both past and present.

"Well, you're mine now, Skye Summers Dean. You belong to me."

She belonged to him only until he learned the truth. After that, he wouldn't be able to sign the annulment papers fast enough.

Chapter Twenty-Five

THE NEXT MORNING, SKYE SLIPPED OUT OF ASH'S BEDROOM SUITE and went to find Forest. The only clothes she had were the scrubs she'd worn from the day before—comfortable but dirty.

A cascade of bodies filled the main living area. Crew members and groupies in various stages of undress were draped over one another in their post-coital haze. Empty alcohol bottles lay strewed about the place, but there was no evidence of powder lines, bongs, or needles.

A quick search failed to reveal her brother. She nibbled at her lower lip, wondering how Forest had fared against the temptation of alcohol. Ash had promised he'd have someone watching out for him. *But had Forest caved to the temptations of his demons?*

Her need to find Forest overrode the social conventions of not peeking in private bedrooms. There were six in the penthouse suite —one for each of the band and one for their manager, Thomas Tuttle. She tiptoed among the sleeping guests and pushed open the doors.

Bash, Bent, Spike, and Noodles each slept soundly in their own beds with at least one naked girl in bed with them. Only Thomas Tuttle's room was empty although the bed had certainly seen action the night before. More importantly, Forest was nowhere to be found. *Why was he not in the penthouse?* Ash had mentioned Forest had to bunk with security. *Where did they sleep?*

She walked back to Ash's room and fished her cell phone out of her backpack.

Where are you, Beanpole?

A quick search revealed her sneakers, and she slipped those on while waiting for his reply.

Downstairs.

She released her breath.

You with anyone?

My babysitter.

Another relieved breath escaped her lips.

Still sober, my summer Skye. Relax.

Can we talk?

Always.

Her heart skipped, and she wondered about the annulment papers their lawyers had prepared. She'd done some serious thinking after Ash had fallen asleep. Their worlds didn't make sense together, but they did.

He texted.

I'm eating breakfast. Want to join me?

Okay.

Lover Boy coming?

He's asleep.

A few minutes later, she found Forest in the hotel restaurant with Reggie. A half-demolished stack of pancakes sat in front of Forest alongside a plate of eggs and bacon.

Reggie waved her over when he saw her enter. "Good morning, Dr. Summers."

"Please, call me Skye." She smiled at him.

"Good morning, Skye. If you don't mind"—he pushed back from the table—"I'll go check on everyone upstairs."

"Thank you for staying with Forest."

Reggie shrugged. "After-concert parties can get kind of tiring when you've been around as long as I have. To tell you the truth, it was kind of refreshing to be apart from it all. Your brother is an interesting guy."

"What did you do all night?"

Reggie put his hand to the back of his neck and stretched. "He straightened out my finances."

Of course.

"Can't believe I've been making so many mistakes." He stood and shook Forest's hand. "Thanks, pal."

"No problem," Forest said. "Just call, anytime."

As Reggie left, she gave Forest a look. "Did you really spend all night discussing finances?"

He nodded. "Yeah, and I set him up with an investment account."

"Your favorite band was upstairs, partying, and you were talking investments with one of their security guys?"

"Well, my favorite band drinks and fucks chicks. The only one who doesn't drink was holed up with my sister. That kind of leaves me out on pretty much every level."

"I'm not really into the rock-star lifestyle either," she said.

Forest's voice softened. "Funny, because it doesn't look like you want to end things."

But she should. "He deserves someone who isn't broken."

"You're not broken."

She returned a flat stare, unwilling to argue the truth. "Okay, how about this? He comes from a religious home. What are his parents going to say when they learn their son's wife was once a whore?"

Forest's eyes narrowed. "You were never a whore."

But men had paid money to have sex with her. She would've done anything to keep her little Beanpole safe.

"Get your food, and we'll figure this out." He directed her to the buffet line.

When she returned, his pancakes were gone. The waiter stopped by and put a hot cocoa in front of her place.

"Thank you." As she set down her plate, her hand shook so hard that she nearly dumped everything onto the table.

Forest gripped her wrist, holding it steady, without flinching.

She stared, stunned by his touch and the ease with which he continued to hold her hand.

"I refuse to let *him* rule my life anymore," Forest said. But sweat broke out on his brow. "You shouldn't either. When I touch you, I remember how he made me enjoy it. I still *feel* it. And it makes my insides twist. But it wasn't my choice. I've decided that I let him control me for far too long. It's time for you to do the same."

"Forest…" She pulled away, seeing the strain in his face.

He grabbed her hand, a determined expression on his face. "I need to be the kind of man who can protect my sister. I hate what happened the other night. I hate what those few moments did, and I haven't stopped thinking about it since. It's never really been an issue, me not touching you, but only because it was too easy to keep my distance. I never realized how handicapped that made me until I could barely protect you. If I can't protect my summer Skye, what kind of man does that make me?"

He released her then and took a sip from his coffee. His hand shook with fine tremors. "It's time to overcome this, to kill this demon. And, like drugs, I'm going to win this war. I'm not Pavlov's dog even though he conditioned me to be. Neither are you. It's time to stop." He rolled her hand over in his and gave it a squeeze. "Beginning with a simple touch."

"I don't know how to do that."

A presence clotted the air behind her. Forest glanced over her shoulder.

"Good morning." The cultured deep voice had the hairs at her nape standing on end.

Thomas Tuttle balanced a plateful of scrambled eggs and sausage links in one hand and a plate of pastries in the other. Despite the early hour, he was dressed in a suit, and his short brown hair was slicked back with gel.

"Do you mind if I join you?" He sat before either of them could answer, placing his dishes on the table. He flagged down a waiter and ordered water and coffee.

"I'm surprised to see you down here. I would have thought you'd still be upstairs. The guys don't usually start moving until noon, especially Blaze." He shoveled eggs into his mouth.

Where she slept was no business of his, and Ash had been up at the crack of dawn every day he'd been with her. *How well did this man know her husband?*

"I was looking for my brother."

Tuttle put down the fork and extended his hand. "I don't think we've formally met although I've heard a lot about Dr. Summers's brother. Thomas Tuttle, Angel Fire's manager."

Forest shook hands. "Nice to meet you." He didn't give his name, but Forest liked to play with others and see how many buttons he could push.

After an awkward silence, Tuttle cleared his throat. "What did you think of the show last night?"

"Pretty cool," Forest said.

Tuttle looked to her. He spoke, his mouth full of pancake, "Not many people get to see the show close-up. Tonight's should be just as good. Maybe you'll get to see the whole thing this time. I heard you only got to watch the last few songs."

Why was he keeping tabs?

"I had to work late."

He nodded. "How exactly is that going to work out with Blaze?"

"Excuse me?"

"Well, I was wondering about the logistics. Are you going to give up your practice to follow him around the country? Or will you be moving to LA where the band is based? How are you planning on working out this marriage, if it is indeed a real marriage?"

If she had hackles, they'd be bristling by now. She was two seconds away from gouging his eyes out.

Forest twirled his knife over his knuckles. "Why do you care?" He pitched his gravelly voice lower. Only a fool would ignore the implied threat.

Tuttle leaned across the table and captured her in a stare. "It's my job to watch out for the band. I manage their problems. This marriage, for example—"

"What are you trying to say?" She hadn't liked him when they first met, and she liked him even less now. "I'm not a problem."

He gave a slow blink and licked the cream off a puff pastry. "Let's say, I find it interesting for anyone to meet and marry in three days.

When that's combined with marrying one of the richest rock stars in the country, I find it concerning."

"I don't like your tone," Forest growled, "or what you're implying."

"I'm not really sure about what you stand to gain from this situation," Tuttle said to Forest.

Forest leaned forward, his hands fisting, but Skye hovered her hand over her brother's, not touching but close enough to force him back into his seat.

Tuttle pulled out a stack of papers from his pocket. "Look, there's no reason for this to get ugly. We're prepared to make this easy on all involved."

"We?" *What the hell was he talking about?*

"We're prepared to offer a generous settlement."

"Settlement?" She couldn't believe her ears.

"Yes, provided you sign a nondisclosure agreement. Everyone walks away, as if this whole mess never happened. You go back to your job, and Blaze continues with his. A nice clean break."

Forest ripped the papers from Tuttle's hand. He scanned the ink. "A hundred thousand dollars? What the fuck? You want to buy her off? Does Blaze even know?"

Tuttle pushed away from the table and wiped crumbs from his chin. "That figure is more than fair compensation for a week of your time, Ms. Summers."

Her eyes narrowed. "It's Dr. Summers."

"Well, I'm sure it will go a long way to paying off any student debt you might have acquired. Let me know, but this is a time-limited offer."

"You didn't answer Forest's question," she said. "Does Ash know about this?"

"Look, Dr. Summers, this isn't the first time we've had to settle with some starstruck groupie who thought she'd get a piece of Blaze. This is his way of asking nicely." He pointed to the documents. "Take the settlement, and walk away."

"Or what?" She leaned back and crossed her arms, certain Ash would never have agreed to this but equally terrified he might have.

"The press isn't kind. They have a knack for digging up things we all wish to keep buried."

Forest pounded his fist on the table and rose to his feet, but Tuttle didn't flinch under Forest's intense stare. "You need to leave."

"I've known Blaze a long time, and he can be impetuous, leaping before he thinks. He seldom stays with one woman for long. You're little more than the flavor of the week." He straightened to his full height, and the hardness of his gaze softened. "I don't mean to be cruel when I say that, but I believe it's best for all involved if I'm brutally honest. I'd hate to see you get hurt." He pushed the papers closer. "Take the offer. You have a job, your life, and your reputation. Don't throw that away on a fling."

Forest shifted his gaze to the papers. He seemed to be giving Tuttle's offer consideration. Either that, or he was warning her away. Sometimes, he was impossible to read. Her insides tumbled about, a seething mass of doubt and worry.

Tuttle was a bastard, but a vein of truth rang through his words. And the last thing she needed was a bunch of curious reporters digging into her past. Forest had concealed much of it, but secrets had a way of seeking the light.

"I want to speak with Ash about this." She didn't believe Tuttle, but she couldn't help the doubt creeping into her mind. What Tuttle said could be true.

"There's no need. He's already signed."

A chill settled in her chest, and the bottom dropped out of her world.

Ash hadn't read what he'd signed. That was what had gotten the two of them into this mess to begin with, leaving the question hanging as to what Tuttle gained by breaking them apart.

There was irony in that. A random signature had joined them, and another would free her from that bond.

She pulled the papers close. "We'll get back to you, Mr. Tuttle."

"I'm sure you will, but the settlement is fixed. There's no room for negotiation." He excused himself, leaving her and Forest alone.

She grabbed the papers. "I want to go home, Beanpole."

"You and me both, my summer Skye." Forest's gravelly voice wrapped her in comfort.

She might lose Ash, but she'd always have Forest.

"I'll leave a message, telling him I went home. He has his concert tonight, and I don't want to wake him. Give me ten minutes."

"Okay." Forest pointed to the Belgian waffle station. "Those waffles are calling my name. I'll meet you by the front desk, but we're coming back for the concert."

"If you insist."

In all honesty, there was no way she would miss a chance to watch Ash gyrating onstage even if it turned out to be the last Angel Fire concert she ever saw.

Chapter Twenty-Six

THE ELEVATOR DOORS PARTED. SKYE STEPPED INSIDE AND SWIPED HER room key for the penthouse level. She stepped to the back to lean against the paneled wood when a hand thrust between the sliding doors. Clad in an expensive wool suit, Spencer's sudden appearance had her tucking into the corner. His signature scent, Versace, flooded her nostrils and sickened her stomach.

"Spencer." His name sputtered from her lips. *How had he found her?*

He rushed toward her and gripped her arm in a punishing vise. He punched the button for the mezzanine level, and although she wanted to scream, she found herself mute.

"You've been ignoring my texts. And then I had to hear about this crap in the news? Is it true?" He shook her, his fingers digging into her skin. "Did you marry that guitar-hero punk?"

"You're hurting me."

She tried to free herself, but he clamped down even harder.

The elevator stopped at the mezzanine. When the doors opened, he yanked her out, scanning left and then right. Pulling her with him, he headed down the empty corridor.

"Where are you taking me?"

"Somewhere we can talk."

"There's nothing to talk about."

"Oh, we have a lot to discuss." A muscle jumped in his clenched jaw.

"I told you, I wasn't going to marry you, not after what I saw."

His scowl deepened.

"I'm with Ash now," she said with a pathetic squeak.

"Not for long." He barked a harsh laugh. "Your rock star has quite the reputation. This isn't the first time he's had to buy off an overly zealous fan."

"How would you know?"

He gave a derisive snort. "Angel Fire is a client of my firm."

Spencer's firm handled many celebrity clients, but he didn't work in that division. *What favors had Spencer called in to examine the Angel Fire accounts?*

"Mr. Tuttle gave you the settlement agreement. You'll sign it, if you know what's good for you." He headed down the hall, angling toward an exit, indicating access to the parking garage. He yanked her inside the stairwell.

"You can't force me to sign anything, and I'm not coming with you." She should resist, but old habits had her shaking, terrified of what he might do in anger.

"I can, and I will. And, as soon as your divorce is official, you'll marry me, like you're supposed to. I've invested too much time, Skye Summers. You belong to me."

He was officially out of his mind.

"Let me go." Surely, there were security cameras recording. *But where was help when she needed it?*

For years, she'd blindly accepted Spencer's controlling manner, allowing him to push her into an abusive relationship. She'd only ever experienced affection under the guise of abuse.

Until Ash.

Now, she knew love didn't have to come at the end of a stick, a belt, or a string of harsh words. Everything she'd thought she understood about love had turned sideways. It wasn't her job to please a man. All she had to do was accept what was freely given. Ash's love came without demands. He gave without taking. He didn't hurt or yell or make her feel like she had to step carefully with her actions or words.

Spencer showed no signs of letting go, but she wasn't helpless. She closed the distance, giving Spencer what he wanted, but she only gave the illusion that she was submitting to his will. He never suspected anything until her fingers wrapped around his neck. She applied pressure to his carotid artery, using the same maneuver she'd used on Bash at the airfield.

In less than two seconds, Spencer stumbled on the landing, collapsing on the floor. When he passed out, his chest didn't move with the rhythm of breath. The danger of that technique settled like a weight on her shoulders. It could kill. She crouched beside him and felt for a pulse. A thready beat fluttered beneath her fingers.

A few moments later, Spencer came around, groaning and struggling to form words. "Elsbeth!" he growled. "You're going to pay for that."

That name stopped her in her tracks. "What did you call me?"

"That is your real name, isn't it?"

No one should know that name. She and Forest had buried it a decade ago.

He rolled to his side and held his head. "What the fuck did you do?"

She'd almost killed him, and she would have, if she'd pressed a little longer. Now that she knew he knew her name, she almost wished she had.

Spencer swallowed, and his Adam's apple bobbed. He pushed himself up to a sitting position, reeling as blood rushed back to his head. He'd be a bit disoriented for the next few minutes.

She needed to leave.

Now.

The red glow of the exit sign beckoned, but he'd used a name he had no right knowing. And that terrified her.

He put his head between his knees. "What the fuck is going on?" He brushed off his suit and then stood on shaky legs, putting a hand flat to the wall to support himself. "Once your divorce is final, we'll get married, and if you're really good, we might put all this behind us."

"Married?"

He cocked his head. "Don't test me on this."

"Or what?"

He shifted his position, moving too close.

She backed away.

"Do as I say, or I'm going to make a very public disclosure of exactly who Angel Fire's lead singer married."

Her entire body went still.

"Imagine what will happen," he continued, "when the world finds out that Dr. Skye Summers got away with the murder of Clark Preston. Or when Blaze finds out how intimately you and Bean truly know each other?" He gave a harsh laugh. "Or that you're no angel. I know you were once a whore."

Forest's words returned to her, and she clung to them with a desperate conviction, hoping they were true.

"You were never a whore."

And Forest was right. She hadn't sold her body to her foster father's clients. Her foster father had done so.

Spencer was recovering quickly, becoming more dangerous as his strength returned. "I'm assuming he doesn't know?"

She'd lost her chance to run, and somehow, Spencer knew her deepest secrets. Her silence gave Spencer exactly what he needed. She'd validated the truth of his words, but she had a gut feeling there was more.

"Won't your little guitar hero love finding out that little secret? Incest, a whore, and a murderer."

Blood roared in her ears, thundering so loud that she barely made sense of his words.

Incest?

Never.

Murderer?

The courts had decided otherwise.

She and Forest weren't related by birth, only bonded by circumstance and tragedy. Those records had been officially sealed. Forest's army of lawyers had erased all evidence of their childhood as well as the ensuing trial.

A Cheshire grin spread across Spencer's face. "My father worked on that case, and he kept copies of the more interesting videos."

Her gut tightened into a hard knot, and she fought the bile rising in her throat.

His father?

No!

Forest had performed a background check. Spencer's father had had nothing to do with their case.

"You're lying."

The prosecuting attorney had been Ryan McDonald, a name she would never forget. Spencer's last name was McAdams.

How had she and Forest missed this?

Feral and raw, Spencer's slimy smile stretched across his face. "I know what you did for your foster father, and I saw how much you liked it. What I don't know is why you never liked doing it with me?"

"I've met your father."

He laughed. "You met the man my mother married."

No, Forest had checked. Renault McAdams was the name listed on Spencer's birth certificate. They'd missed some connection.

Spencer had seen the videos. He'd witnessed the forced orgasms. That meant he also knew what she'd been made to do to Forest and the things Forest had been forced to do to her.

Spencer's eyes narrowed. "And, all this time, I thought you were a frigid bitch. Now, I know what you like."

"Don't ever call me that word again." She slapped his cheek.

She didn't even see the blow coming. Her cheek stung, and her eye teared. She gulped air, stumbling back, while the tang of copper hit her throat. The bastard had split her lip.

"I suggest you never even think of striking me again." Spencer advanced, and she cowered from his overwhelming presence. "You won't like what comes next." His grin widened. "Or maybe you would?"

She'd run from abuse and refused to consign herself to a life with someone like Spencer. Never again. Edging toward the exit sign, she placed distance between them.

"I find it interesting," he said, "how all details of the case disappeared. I can only presume Bean had something to do with that. Or should I call him Forest now? I always knew there was something not quite right with how close the two of you were. Honestly, it's perverse."

It was perverse, and if they'd been biological siblings, it would have been worse. The saddest part was, it wouldn't have stopped their foster father. Who knew how many children he'd sexually traumatized before she ended his life?

Not that any of that mattered anymore. What mattered was the truth. And she couldn't let that loose on the world.

"Spencer, you can't go public with this." She'd do anything to keep that secret locked in the deepest, darkest place.

"Why would I drag the name of my future wife through the mud?" His eyes narrowed. "What would become of your charitable giving? Your foundations would crumble. Imagine my surprise when I found out that you're not the struggling doctor you led me to believe. You and Forest have been busy little bees."

Spencer knew everything.

She gripped her stomach, battling revulsion and fear.

"Now, gather up those papers, dear. You have a wedding to plan."

Unless she agreed to marry him, Spencer would expose her secrets. It didn't matter if she had been found innocent. Fallout from the press would be intense. Their foundations might not weather the storm. *And what would become of their foster home project? And her career?*

Thirty floors above, Ash slumbered. He'd written about insanity, not knowing the full depth of her complicated life. She didn't want to lose him, but neither could she destroy everything he had built.

"Don't hold my past against me, Skye."

Her past was much worse.

But could she return to Spencer and live a life of fear?

She'd endured it once, and she couldn't fathom living the rest of her life controlled by another. There would be consequences. She might lose everything. But she wanted to live free even if it didn't include Ash.

Ash had opened a new world, a way of living in the moment instead of being trapped behind rigid rules meant to structure and protect her. She wanted freedom, and for the first time, she believed she deserved a good life.

She spoke in a steady tone, accepting the consequences of her decision and sealing her future, "Tell the press. Tell them about the beast who beat me, raped me, and whored me out when I was a child. You can't hurt me any more than he did."

And, if Spencer had read the sealed court records, he knew exactly what she'd done to her foster father.

Spencer's mouth opened, his jaw working.

She silenced him with an icy tone. "I don't care what you do, but I will never be yours."

He might still come at her. She half-hoped he would.

Backing away, she took two steps down the flight of stairs, heading to the door below. Spencer didn't move, caught short by her declaration.

She made it down to the landing. Still nothing from her ex-boyfriend, ex-fiancé, ex-whatever. It didn't matter what Spencer was, only that he wasn't in her life anymore.

But Spencer was a vindictive bastard, and he would follow through on those threats. She and Forest would face them together, head-on, like they had with their foster father. Together, they would get through whatever Spencer threw at them.

Spencer's voice stretched out, damning her future. "He's going to leave you, Skye. He signed the papers once, and when he finds out you're a murderer, too, he'll sign them again."

His words cut like a whip because they were true. She had killed even if the courts had decided otherwise.

She took a step and then another until her momentum carried her through the doorway and away from the toxic morass that was Spencer McAdams.

Spencer would cost her Ash. He'd make certain that Ash knew every sordid detail. But Ash would always be a part of her life even if he wasn't in it. He'd taught her about the power of love and that love could exist without pain.

She wanted more of that.

She fumbled in her pocket, looking for her cell phone. Her fingers stabbed at buttons, selecting Forest's name for a text. She pressed the tiny microphone icon, not trusting her fingers to type. She could barely hold the phone as it was.

"Ran into Spencer. He's going to the press. He mentioned Clark Preston. He knows I killed him." The phone converted her words into text, and she hit Send.

It was time to say good-bye to Ash.

Her phone beeped.

Ash responded to her text.

Who's Clark Preston?

Chapter Twenty-Seven

Skye stared at Ash's text. Her stomach sank with horror as she realized she had sent the text to the wrong person.

Who's Clark Preston?

His words held a question she wasn't prepared to answer.

Clark Preston's name brought shudders so strong that her body wanted to curl inward into a tight ball. It was why she and Forest never mentioned his name, relegating the monster forever simply as *foster father*. His name gave power, even in death. It had taken years to erase all mention of him from their lives. And, for the better part of a decade, his vileness had remained nameless.

But, now, Spencer had brought her foster father's taint back into her life. Spencer had seen the depravity she'd been subjected to, watched the videos, and probably combed through transcripts of the trial. *What else did Spencer know?*

She brought her fist to her mouth, choking back a strangled sob.

Ash now knew that name, too. He would look. He would dig. He'd set his team up to investigate.

She eased out a breath and pushed away from the wall.

Spencer was a problem for later. Right now, she had a bigger issue with Ash. He'd responded and asked a question while glossing over the most damaging part of that text. She'd admitted to killing her foster father, a secret meant for her and Forest alone to take to the grave.

As she stumbled forward, the lobby beckoned with the promise of escape.

The only person she could depend on waited for her there. Forest would know what to do about Spencer and how to best protect everything they had built. They would deal with Ash...later, and she would need to decide what to do about her career.

At least Forest was an easy man to find. Unmistakably towering above the crowd, his white-blond hair acted like a beacon and drew her toward him. She made a beeline for the man who was much more than a brother. He was her other half.

She hooked a finger through Forest's belt loop and gave a tug. He seemed to know it was her, and she drew him forward, barely losing her momentum.

But some of that might have had to do with the shock spread across her face and the urgency of her words. "We need to leave. Now."

Forest allowed her to guide him out of the crowded lobby. Fear dictated her actions, and she knew, without a doubt, that he knew something horrible had happened. They could read each other so well.

When they exited the hotel, he hailed a cab. He opened the car door and slid in beside her, all without saying a word.

"Where to?" The cabbie looked into his rearview mirror.

Forest rattled off her home address.

"No," she said. "Not there."

Forest gave a sharp inhale. "Okay. Take us to the National Mall."

"Mall's pretty big," the driver said. "Any particular place?"

Forest shrugged. "We're tourists. Surprise us."

Silence descended between them as the cab driver maneuvered through lanes of flowing traffic. Forest tapped his fingers on his thigh while she stared out the window, unwilling to speak with a stranger so close. Her phone buzzed with texts from Ash.

Half an hour later, they found themselves at the base of the Washington Monument. Forest stood beside her, his hand a hairbreadth from hers, close but not touching.

"You going to tell me what's up?" He didn't look at her, continuing to admire the stone monument.

She shivered against the chilly air. "Spencer knows our foster father's name." She turned to him. "And mine. He knows my name."

No reaction came from Forest. Instead, he breathed out a single word. "How?"

"He said his father prosecuted our case."

"How did we miss this?"

How indeed?

Cool wind numbed her cheeks as it buffeted them. They were the only ones not rushing. Tourists and workers hustled down the Mall, jackets wrapped tight. Overhead, a brilliant blue filled the sky. It was such a gorgeous day, and she wished her mood matched the beauty surrounding them instead of the cloying fear wedged in her gut.

Forest pulled the hair from his face and secured it with a leather thong. "I made sure those files disappeared. I broke so many laws…"

"Evidently, his father made copies. Spencer found them."

"I vetted Spencer. His father is a lobbyist."

"We missed something."

Ash's text tone kept her phone buzzing.

"You going to answer that?" Forest pointed to the phone clutched in her hand.

She wasn't. Ash's texts had become increasingly frantic, repeating similar versions of the same panicky phrases. There were over fifty of them now.

Where are you?

What's going on?

Who is Clark Preston?

What do you mean, you killed him?

He'd finally broached the most damaging comment in her hurried text.

Answer me.

Are you in trouble?

Come to me, Skye.

Don't run.

And the most often repeated, the one that shattered her heart, was the simplest of them all.

I love you.

He wouldn't love her once her murderous past came out or when he found out about her and Forest.

She gripped the plastic casing of her phone as it warbled yet again.

Come back.

"You know, those things come with a mute button," Forest quipped.

"I know." But she didn't want to turn off the sound.

"You can't hide this from him," Forest said.

"I know."

"The courts found you innocent."

Another stated fact. Surely, he had some piece of wisdom to share in her time of need.

Instead, Forest's hard eyes stared down with the same resolute determination as the night when everything had changed. It was the one secret they'd agreed to carry to the grave, and she had unwittingly spilled it.

Two truths had come out of that night. They were innocent. And their foster father had deserved to die.

She gritted her teeth and ground out her words, "Damn it, I know!" She ran her fingers through her hair. "Spencer's going to break the news to the media."

Forest's deep bass rumbled beside her. "Is that how you want Ash to find out?" He shifted beside her, leaning fractionally closer without actually touching. "Think about it. How would you want to find out?"

She shrugged.

Forest blew out a breath. "He deserves the truth, my summer Skye, before that asshole blows it up on the front page of the tabloids."

"Ash is going to hate me."

"Maybe." Forest took a step forward and gestured for her to follow. "But don't you think you should let him decide for himself?" His voice dropped an octave. "Especially if you decide to keep him."

A deep pull of cold air surged into her lungs. "I can't keep him." *Not after this.*

Forest angled his chin down. "Seriously? After that song he sang onstage last night…" His left eyebrow arched, "'Insanity'? That man isn't letting you go."

"But he signed those papers——"

"I have a feeling his manager had a part in that. Poor boy probably had no idea. I see it in your eyes, my summer Skye. In your heart, you know it, too."

Forest pointed down the Mall. "Let's walk. I'm freezing my ass off." He pulled out his cell phone, and his fingers danced over the screen.

"What are you doing?"

"Strategizing," he said with a grin. "It's a beautiful day. Let's play tourist a bit while you sort out your thoughts. Then, we'll head back to your place and grab a hot shower and a change of clothes. And, please, answer that damn phone."

Her fingers flexed, and she twisted her wrist to scan the string of texts sent over the past five minutes.

Where are you?

Don't run from me.

You belong with me.

You're my light, my life.

Was he writing another song? His words looked like lyrics, sounds that carved a hole in her heart.

Her finger hovered over the screen. A second later, she began to type.

Ahead of her, Forest held his phone to his ear. He turned when she stopped walking to put distance between them. He had an instinctual understanding of what she needed, and walked in a wide circle, far enough away where she couldn't hear his conversation, so she had the illusion of privacy to compose her text.

Spencer showed up at the hotel.

Ash replied.

Are you okay?

Yes.

Did he hurt you?

No. Did you know his firm represents your band?

A moment's delay occurred before Ash responded.

No. Where are you?

I'm with Bean.

Good, but, goddamn, where are you?

Your manager gave me the papers you signed.

What papers?

He didn't know? Her heart warmed. She'd known deep in her bones that he would never have signed those papers if he'd known what they were, but faced with his scrawled signature, she'd had doubts. They'd discuss that later.

Spencer gave an ultimatum.

???

She caught Forest's guarded expression. The bright sunlight glinted off his hair, making it gleam in the late morning sun. What a man Forest had become. Only she remembered the broken boy weeping on the concrete floor.

Forest spoke into his phone as he continued his circuit around her position. He gave a slow nod, letting her know she was not alone. It was the strength she needed to tell Ash the truth.

Clark Preston was my foster father. He raped me the first night I entered his home. Bean arrived a few months later. He abused Bean, too. Then, it got worse.

Her phone beeped.

Oh, Skye...

She continued. *He trained me, and eventually, he sold me to those who would pay.*

How old?

She was twelve at the time, but she wasn't willing to discuss that yet.

You asked me not to hold your past against you. I'm asking the same of you.

I'd never do that.

If he only knew...

Ash continued. *I love you.*

His message couldn't be clearer.

Spencer's going to the press. That text was meant for Bean. I was trying to warn him.

What happened to Clark Preston?

I killed him, but there was no way she would send that in another text.

Forest's circling stopped. His brows knit together as he whispered urgently into his phone. Likely, he was deep in conversation with their army of lawyers, lining up a strategy to deal with Spencer's attack. She didn't envy Forest's task of dealing with the media circus.

He shielded his eyes from the overhead sun and took up his pacing once more. Her heart was breaking, but at least Ash was still texting.

Tell me.

I pleaded self-defense and changed my name.

What does Spencer hope to gain?

I haven't told you everything.

I don't understand.

Spencer wants my money.

Ash's response bleeped. *I don't understand.*

Ash had millions, but she and Forest had a hundred times more.

I need to tell you something about Bean. He's a savant when it comes to numbers. He feels their rhythms. It makes him an unstoppable force in the investment world.

I already know that.

Not everything.

She had yet to tell him the one secret that would end things between them. There were many things in her life she could live without, but there was one person she would never give up. No matter how much she loved Ash, she would never walk away from Forest.

Once Ash learned what she and Forest had been forced to endure, he would leave in disgust. Spencer had called it incest, and while not technically correct, they shared a familial bond. There was no way she could keep both men in her life, not with that history. *What man could stomach the closeness she and Forest shared, knowing they'd once been intimate?*

Her chest heaved with the pain of the confession. Shoulders curling inward, she wrapped her arms around herself, desperate for a hug. She collapsed to her knees as a sob tore from her throat, and her phone scattered to the ground. Her cheeks froze as the brisk wind chilled her tears.

Heavy footsteps pounded from behind, Forest moving faster than she'd ever heard, but his massive bulk sounded lighter and swifter than she remembered. Stomping toward her were black combat boots and tree-trunk legs that supported a mountain of a man.

"My summer Skye, do not cry."

"Forest?"

If he was standing in front of her, then who was running up from behind? She twisted and gasped at Ash sprinting toward her.

Ash slid to his knees, out of breath, with his luminous eyes blazing in the light of the sun. Green dragon scales shimmered in the reflected light, the exact shade of his eyes.

"I'm already desperately and forever yours, Skye Summers." Ash wrapped her in his arms.

Words choked in her throat, but she managed to spit them out, "How did you get here?"

"You have a very persistent brother."

Persistent? "You need to know—"

"I already know. And it doesn't change a thing. I love you."

How could he? She reared back to stare into his eyes.

Behind him, Forest circled. He lifted his phone. "I've been chatting with Lover Boy, my summer Skye. I told him everything while you were fat-finger texting him."

Everything?

Ash nodded, and through the pain in his gaze, she knew Forest had disclosed their second darkest secret.

Forest grinned. "The two of you totally suck at communication. So, let me sum it up for you. Yes, Lover Boy signed the divorce papers, but the dumbass hadn't read them. I already chewed his ass off and told him what I'd do if he ever did that again. I also told him you had annulment papers drawn up, but that you aren't going to sign them. The two of you are a piece of work."

"Bean—"

He raised a finger. "Be quiet." He pocketed his phone. "Ash knows about the trial and acquittal…on account of self-defense."

Ah, at least one of their secrets remained theirs to keep. While she had acted in self-defense, what had happened had been premeditated.

Forest continued, "I told him the rest of it—or at least the CliffsNotes version."

She tried to speak, but Forest silenced her with a shake of his head.

"I told Lover Boy that, if he wanted you, he needed to come, and he came, my summer Skye." Forest then pointed to Ash. "Now, don't fuck this up."

Ash's smile beamed. "Never."

"Good. Now, you rushed into this marriage, which was totally fucked up, but no way in hell will you rush out of it. No divorces. No annulments. No separations. No nothing. You're stuck with each other for…I don't know…let's set a date. Six months?"

He seemed pleased with himself and nodded before continuing. "In six months, if you decide you really made a mistake, we'll draw up papers and make your separation official. But I'm betting that won't be necessary." He shook his head. "Man, this love crap is exhausting."

Forest scratched the side of his head. "You know, it's cold as shit out here. Do you mind if we head home? I hear there's this mediocre band playing a half-decent show in town tonight."

"Half-decent?" Ash laughed. "Thought you were a fan?"

"Meh." Forest waved. "A real fan would have had an autograph or two by now…" He headed to the curb where a black town car was pulling up.

"When did you arrange for that?" She stared at the car as the driver got out and opened the door.

"Multitasking, my summer Skye. Now, get in."

Ash pulled her to her feet and gave her a kiss on the lips. "You think you can do it?"

"Do what?"

"Give me six months? I warned you, I'm in this for the bigger prize."

"And it doesn't bother you that Bean and I—"

"Our pasts belong in the past. I want your future. Do I get six months to prove we belong to each other?"

She bit her lower lip.

"I only have one rule," he said.

"What's that?"

"Easy," he said with his signature smirk. "I want to touch you."

She pulled back, but he held her fast.

"I won't push your triggers," he said, "but I damn well intend on making new memories."

"I don't know if I can make that promise."

"All you have to do is try. We'll get help."

"I don't need professional help, Ash. I'm fine."

"I don't know anything about what you went through. How to help you? How to step back? How will I know if I'm pushing too hard or not hard enough?"

Hearing his words forced a truth to settle around her heart. He loved her, and she could no longer deny his conviction. Her heart bloomed with a radiance she had never felt before.

Tuttle's words—*"flavor of the week"*—returned to her, bringing back all her doubt.

"Why me?" She sought an answer she could hold on to. "When you can have anyone you want, why me when I'm so broken?"

He pulled her close. "You see me. From the first moment we met, you've seen me. I never knew how powerful that could be. Until you came into my life, I didn't know I could be free."

Her fears refused to subside. "What about your family? Your band? What will they think when Spencer—"

"Mom will deal. Dad is all about the Lord's forgiveness. And the guys are already scared to death of you and your juju moves. Now, you have even more street cred with them. Don't worry. Fate brought us together for a reason." He thumped his heart. "Try to believe because life isn't worth living alone."

She wished she'd had his confidence. "I don't believe in fate."

But, staring at him, she could no longer deny the truth. Ash Dean had mended the cracks in her heart.

He winked. "That's a shame because fate has bound our lives together. I'm not stopping at six months." Ash's smile flashed in the light. "I intend to spend the rest of my life uncomplicating yours. Skye Summers Dean, will you be my wife?"

"I like the sound of that."

Forest called out, impatience showing in his voice, "You two going to stand there, talking all day, or are you going to get the hell inside?"

Ash gave her the oddest look. "I want to go to Niagara in fifty years. We'll find some young couple foolishly in love and have them help us renew our vows. How does that sound?"

A single tear slid down her cheek. She didn't need six months or even fifty years.

"It sounds really good."

"Then Skye Summers," he looked at her with an expression full of love and conviction for the future, "will you be my wife?"

Theirs was a story of insanity, but fate had woven their separate strands together. Insane? Absolutely. But she wouldn't have it any other way.

Her decision was made.

"Yes."

~

Dear Reader,

As a token of my deepest gratitude for joining the unforgettable journey of Heart's Insanity, I have a special treat just for you—a FREE bonus scene that will take your heart on a wild ride!

Rejoin Ash and Skye, our beloved protagonists, six months down the road. Witness their love blossom and grow, like a melody that lingers long after the final chord. This exclusive bonus scene unveils intimate moments, whispered promises, heartfelt healing, and the electrifying connection that will leave you breathless.

Grab your virtual backstage pass and download the free bonus scene today, and allow yourself to be transported back into the enticing realm of Heart's Insanity.

Thank you for being a cherished part of the Heart's Insanity family. Your passion for these characters and their story fuels my own creative fire. So, embrace the opportunity to witness Ash and Skye's journey beyond the final page, and let their love story resonate within your soul.

Download the FREE bonus scene now, and let the rhythm of their love echo in your heart once more.

With heartfelt appreciation,

Ellie Masters

~

Needing more of the Angel Fire Gang?

Join the men of Angel Fire as they tour with the USO tour in support of the troops overseas.

Hearts Desire is the next installment in the Angel Fire Rock Romance Series.

READ HEART'S DESIRE TODAY.

It's HOT in the desert as TSgt Ryker Lyons and Major Tia Meyers, members of the Air Force Special Ops Surgical Team, struggle to save lives. When the mega band Angel Fire comes on tour, TSgt Ryker Lyons is presented with the opportunity of a lifetime. He'll get to play alongside his rock idols. But when things heat up, will he be forced to make a choice between the music running in his veins and the woman he loves?

⭐⭐⭐⭐⭐

"When you mix Hot Rockers with Military Special Ops You get the Whole Package! Heart's Desire has it all: Alpha Men, Steamy Scenes, & Heart Pounding Romance."
~Amazon Reviewer

GET YOUR COPY OF HEART'S DESIRE NOW.

Are you interested in Skye and Forest's Story? Keep turning the pages to read about their indelible bond, why Forest calls Skye his Summer Sky, and how you can get their story, ASHES TO NEW, for FREE.

THE END...FOR NOW!

TWENTY-EIGHT

Sample Chapter: HEART'S DESIRE

BOOK TWO IN THE ANGEL FIRE ROCK ROMANCE SERIES

You can get your copy of Heart's Desire here.

WITH MUCH GRUMBLING, SMILEY BROUGHT OVER A BASS GUITAR AND thrust it at Ryker. "You play?"

"From time to time."

Ryker took the guitar by the neck. He checked it out, expecting to ask for a plug-in, but Smiley had brought him the guitar ready to go. As Ryker fluttered his fingers across the strings, he allowed his eyes to close and breathed in the rich vibrations of the instrument in his hands.

"I've got an electronic tuner around here somewhere," Smiley offered.

"No need," Ryker said. He fingered a string, listened, then twisted the corresponding tuner, and adjusted the pitch. Testing again, he was satisfied with the tone. He thumbed through the next three strings, making minor adjustments until he was satisfied the entire instrument was in tune.

"You've got a good ear," Smiley said with surprise. "Not many can tune a guitar that fast, let alone using just their ears."

"I've always had a good sense with sound," he said, not bragging, but stating a fact.

"Rhythm?" Smiley's question came with a direct challenge.

"I'll let you be the judge." He glanced up at T and fixed her in his stare as he coaxed out the beginning bass beat to Deep Purple's "Smoke on the Water."

All work halted in the hangar as airmen stopped to listen to the impromptu jam session.

It took a moment to settle in, but he loved music, and his muscle memory rushed back. "Smoke on the Water" was an iconic piece of rock history and one of the first great riffs every boy who picked up a guitar learned. He'd been no exception, but he felt a bit rusty and ran through only the first few stanzas before switching to a few of his favorites.

A bass riff wasn't the first thing most people thought of when asked about their favorite songs. The majority of rock music centered on the lead guitar, not the bass, but there were a few bass riffs that served as the driving force of a song. He loved those the most.

It didn't escape his notice that these first few moments were his unofficial audition.

He switched from Deep Purple and rolled right into one of his favorites from Rush. Geddy Lee wasn't only the lead singer for Rush; he also played bass while singing and even hit the keys from time to time. Geddy had come up with a few intricate bass lines over the years. Ryker's favorite was "YYZ."

He slid into the first few riffs, losing himself to the deep reverberations of the music. Again, he didn't play the entire song but transitioned into one of Metallica's classics—"Orion." Cliff Burton, Metallica's bassist, had done for bass guitar what Jimi Hendrix had done with the electric guitar—leading innovations from one song to the next. Ryker laid down the instrumental from "Master of Puppets." This riff took bass playing and stood it on its head, turning the underlying supporting role of the bassist to leading the melody line. "Orion" might be one of his all-time favorites because it was one of the few songs a bassist could play and carry the entire song.

T stared at him—not him really, but at his fingers gripping the neck and fingering the strings. Her exotic eyes went wide, and her mouth formed a tiny O of surprise. He let the music fill the hangar and watched with fascination as the sound captivated and enraptured her soul. Slowly, she clasped her hands, closed her eyes, and swayed on her feet. The movements of her body followed those of his music. He loved being the driving force behind even this small moment of happiness in her life.

Forest folded his arms across his chest, tucking his chin down, as his gaze settled over Ryker and the guitar slowly coming to life in his hands. Ryker continued to play, not yet scratching the surface of what he could do.

Red Hot Chili Peppers' bassist, Flea, had a knack for melodic bass lines and a gift for adding his funky flare. Ryker ran through several lines of "Give It Away" and "Suck My Kiss" before laying into "Californication." The distorted bass was true genius, hitting the listener with a punch to the gut. It was a fun track to play, and he went through several verses. It was better with the overlying vocal melody, but each time the riff came around, it altered with subtle changes, making it more interesting to the ear and just plain fun to play.

"Shit," Smiley said, "I don't know if you're playing the guitar or the guitar is playing you, but I can say for certain, you play like you're fucking it. Raw. Powerful. Damn, what the hell are you doing in butt-fuck nowhere and not onstage?"

Ryker glanced up, happy to see the respect building in the crew boss's eyes. "Wasn't in the cards for me," he said. "How about a little Who?"

Smiley jumped off the stage and leaned against it. "There's nothing little about The Who. Lay it on me."

John Entwistle, known as Thunderfingers from The Who, had treated the bass as if it were the lead instrument. Playing any of their songs was a blast. Ryker launched into the bass solo from "My Generation," a standard for bass playing that all up-and-coming bass players aspired to play with any skill.

"Fuck yeah!" Smiley's eyes twinkled, and he lay down an accompanying beat with his hands, palming the hard floor of the stage. "You've got this!"

"The man can play." Forest's deep growl rumbled through the hangar, bringing the airmen at work closer to the stage.

Ryker glanced at the growing crowd. "How about a true classic?"

"Whatcha have in mind?" Forest asked.

He was going to have fun with this one. The intro and verses of the iconic classic rock band The Beatles were legendary. He hit the first few notes of "Come Together." Forest gave a nod of appreciation, and Smiley's grin nearly split his face in two. T's eyes shimmered. As long as she was enjoying his playing, he would continue. Smiley kept up his beat on his makeshift drum, and they played that one together all the way through. As he wound that down, he glanced at T. A smile lit her face and brought an answering grin to his.

"Toss me out a song, T," he called. "Give me one of your favorites."

Her eyes widened, nearly popping with her surprise. "Oh, I don't know. I barely know the songs I like, let alone their names."

Forest's eyes narrowed, and he piped up, "How about Floyd? Can you play 'Money'?"

Could he? It'd taken some time to learn, and it was a brilliant piece of music. Roger Waters had created gold when he matched the bass riff with the coins and cash register sounds in the beginning of the song.

"I fucking love that song," he said.

A difficult bass line, it was written in 7/4 time, but he'd conquered that challenge years ago.

He and Smiley ran through the gamut of the great rock songs, playing "Sweet Emotion" by Aerosmith and even hitting on Hendrix's "Fire." The airmen tasked with setting up the hangar grabbed seats and formed a loose semicircle around the front of the stage. Ryker's playing brought grins, smiles, laughs, hoots, and a generalized pump of energy to those gathered. All they were missing was a lead guitar, a keyboard, and a real set of drums. For himself, the music carried him away, taking his worries and concerns and pushing them to the fringes of his thoughts for a sliver of time. It was him, the music, and memories of an elusive dream he'd long since given up.

Feeling emboldened, he launched into one of Angel Fire's top hits. The bass riffs of "Heart's Insanity" vibrated through the hangar. A few seconds later, a haunting guitar melody picked up mid-verse, coming in with perfect timing. Ryker glanced up, his brows drawing together, but he couldn't see where the music was coming from.

And then it began; the beat dropped on the drums. Not Smiley's palms thudding on the stage floor, but the deep, throbbing power of the drum kit. He turned toward the stage, his mouth agape, as Angel Fire's lead vocalist sauntered to the edge of the stage, guitar slung over his neck, fingers picking out the notes. With a cocky grin, Blaze joined Ryker in the song. Blazing green eyes gave a wink while the song came to life. Dressed in worn-out jeans and a simple black T-shirt, Blaze stood over Ryker while his gaze cut out over the small crowd.

Ryker held down the bass riff while Blaze took over the lead of the song and circled them back to the beginning. He let the intro play out and then belted out the beginning lyrics of Angel Fire's hit song.

Ryker's fingers never once stopped or faltered even though he'd been stunned into speechless awe. The part came for harmonizing, and Blaze arched a brow, silently asking Ryker if he was brave enough to jump in with vocals. He needed no encouragement, took in a breath, and belted out the lines, melding his voice with a rock legend.

The moment demanded no hesitation, and he was going to live every second as if it were his last.

Ryker could hardly believe he was not only jamming with the band of Angel Fire, but also adding his vocals to their latest hit. He wanted to pinch himself, thinking it had to be a dream. At least, until he glanced at T.

Her attention had been fixed on him while he played, but with the arrival of the band, her eyes strayed to the men onstage.

Ryker turned—in part to continue his jam with Blaze, but also to take in the band members. He knew them all by heart. Hidden behind the drums, all he could see of Bash was the energy of his arms banging out the beat. Big and brawny with dark, curly hair, the bassist, Bent, gave a nod to Ryker's playing. Noodles, tall and lanky with dirty-blond surfer hair and his array of tribal tattoos curving around his arms, stepped up to the keyboard. His fingers pressed on the keys, but no sound came out. The roadies hadn't yet connected his instrument. Spike, with his multiple piercings, stood left of stage center. Like Blaze, he'd picked up his electric guitar and slung it around his neck. Without missing a beat, he joined in, layering more complexity on top of the growing music. Bent clasped his hands behind his back. He was the only one of the band who hadn't checked out his equipment, but then Ryker was playing Bent's instrument.

A feeling of unease came over Ryker, unsure of what the man would think of having someone else play his part, but Bent merely stretched out his neck and opened his mouth. Liquid silk flowed out from his vocal cords, harmonizing with Blaze. Ryker fell silent, stopped his singing, and soaked in the magic of the moment.

Blaze continued until the last of the lyrics and the song ended with the resonating chords that never failed to bring a chill to Ryker's spine. He pressed his palm over the strings, quieting their deep notes. Blaze lifted his guitar over his head and gently placed it down. Then, he vaulted off the stage.

"Holy fuck, but you've got some skills." He thrust out his hand. "Nice to meet you."

Ryker started to put the bass guitar down, but Smiley took it, freeing him to return Blaze's greeting. "Blaze! Wow, it's an honor."

Bash extricated himself from the drums. Spike and Bent came to the front of the stage, both hopping down to the hangar floor. Noodles remained onstage, fiddling with the keyboard.

"Call me Ash," Blaze said. "That's what my friends call me." He hooked his thumbs in the front pockets of his faded denim jeans and glanced at Forest. "Hey, bro."

"Where's my sis?" Forest demanded with a deep rumble.

"Cool your heels. She'll be here soon." Ash's eyes cut to T, and Ryker knew exactly what was going through his head.

"She'd better be," Forest asserted. He walked over and clapped Ryker on the back. "This is Tech Sergeant Ryker Lyons. You said you wanted to do something special. Well, I found something pretty special."

The other members of the band introduced themselves.

Bent was the last to greet him. "You've got some skills with the bass and not a bad set of pipes."

"Thanks. I'm kind of in awe right now." The smile on his face had to be huge because his cheeks hurt from his grin. "Just feeling humbled."

Ash rocked back on his heels. "I think we should have a bass-off. Pit you and Bent up against each other, like a battle of the bands but a battle of the bassists."

Ryker took a step back and raised both hands. "Oh, hell no. I know my limits."

Bent squinted and considered the idea. "Now, that could work. It would be a shit-ton of fun."

"Wait. What?" Ryker looked between Bent and Blaze—Ash— wondering what they were thinking.

"That was my thought," Forest said, "and in this case, the dude has real talent. You wouldn't have to carry him. Not to mention, it would be great PR. Get him onstage with the band, and put him in a head-to-head with Bent. The troops would go crazy."

Ash rubbed at his neck, drawing Ryker's attention to the intricate spiderweb and dragon tattoo. Unlike most active duty, Ryker was one of the few who remained tattoo free. A result of his upbringing, he'd never been rebellious enough to go against the strict teachings of his minister father. However, if he ever inked a tattoo, it would be something like the one Ash had. The dragon perched in the middle of the web had been drawn in three-dimensional relief. The black bird it gripped in its claw was so intricate, the feathers shimmered in the light. And he loved the blood dripping from the strands. Yeah, when he got inked, it would have to be something like that. Except he couldn't think of any one thing he wanted permanently placed on his body. Until he decided, he'd stay in the minority—a tat-free freak.

"I love it. I really love it," Ash said. "Did you speak to the USO about our other idea?"

"We've tossed it about." Forest swept his arm out and walked over to T. "Actually, this little lady might have a solution to several problems."

Problems? What problems? Ryker was eager to ask, not really clear on how T fit into Angel Fire's tour plans.

Whatever Forest was about to say was cut off by a high-pitched female squeal shooting through the hangar. "Tia!"

T turned toward the sound, and her hands flew to her cheeks. "Skye? Oh my God, you did come." T's comment placed a frown on Forest's face, confusing Ryker.

T met the lithe beauty, who separated from an escort consisting of the medical group commander and chief. Angel Fire was a band who came with more than a little bit of clout, it seemed. All the base commanders had come out to support them.

He felt more than a little overwhelmed, surrounded not only by his favorite band, but also the big brass of the medical operations command. He grew silent as the brunette jogged up to greet T. The women hugged and squealed and jumped up and down. It was the first time he'd seen T act in such a feminine manner. The women looked like sorority girls reuniting and were completely oblivious to the score of men who watched in enraptured silence.

"You," Forest said with a huff, "were supposed to be a surprise for Tia."

"I," Skye said firmly, "know how much Tia hates surprises." She shook her head and rolled her eyes. "Did you really think I wouldn't email her?"

Forest turned the gravity of his gaze on T. "You knew?"

She flapped a hand at him. "Of course I did, but you were having too much fun, thinking you had something on me."

T pulled Skye to the side, and the rest of their conversation was lost to Ryker and the others. The women put their heads together and caught up on each other's lives. After a moment, Skye pulled T over to the medical group commander where she made introductions.

Ryker turned his attention back to Ash, whose brows pinched together, a brooding expression filling his face.

Forest jabbed Ash in the ribs. "If you think you can stop her, go ahead and try, but with Tia doing what she does, you're going to be hard-pressed to say no to Skye."

Ash frowned. "Saying no to Skye is impossible. Once she has it in her mind to do something, she's unstoppable. I just wish you didn't encourage her."

"Lover boy," Forest said, "I am well aware of what Skye is capable of. She needs no encouragement. You forget, I grew up with her."

"I know." With a deep sigh, Ash turned his attention back to Ryker. "So, you up for playing with us?"

"I am," Ryker said, surprised he sounded so calm. Thank fuck he hadn't stammered like a damn fool.

Like Ash, his attention followed the path of the women. T's hungry perusal of the band members hadn't escaped his attention. She was smart, and as stupid as her getting-laid plan was, he realized she'd already thought and decided on a path that would limit her risk.

There was no way he would let her sleep with any of the airmen on base. Add Angel Fire into the mix, and he was in full-on protect mode. She'd regret that decision for the rest of her life, and sleeping with a man she didn't care about wasn't going to ease the heartache of her breakup with douche-bag Scott.

He'd protected her from bullets and sheltered her with his body. This would be no different.

Ash rocked back on his heels. "We'd love to have you play with us."

He glanced at Bent. "Thanks. I'd be honored to stand with you for even one song."

Bent gave a shake of his head. "Hey, dude, you don't get it. It's our honor to share the stage with you." When Ryker arched a brow, Bent asserted his statement. "I'm living my dream, but it's because of people like you that I get that chance at all. Now, what do you say we take some guitars and jam for a bit?"

"I don't have a guitar of my own."

Forest laughed loud and hard. "Seriously, lover boy? We travel with extras. As hard as Bent is with his gear, I've got twenty bass guitars sitting in crates."

"I'm not that hard on them," Bent said with a growl.

"You don't see the receipts," Forest countered.

"I don't have to see the receipts," Bent said. "That's why we have you."

Ash rubbed his neck, his hand gliding over the spiderweb tattoo with the dragon clutching a black bird. "Hey, guys, I'll catch you later." He took off after T and Skye, jogging to catch up, as the girls exited the hangar with the medical group commander.

You can get your copy of Heart's Desire here.

TWENTY-NINE

Get a FREE Copy of Ashes to New, Prequel to the Angel Fire Series

I HOPE YOU ENJOYED HEART'S INSANITY AND WOULD LOVE TO OFFER you a special **GIFT**. As my reader, you can get a **FREE** copy of **Ashes to New**, the prequel of Heart's Insanity.

Get my Copy!

Ashes to New is **NOT** a romance. It's something else entirely. It's a story about the fiercest kind of love; about enduring, surviving, and never giving up. This is a story of Forest and Skye, before they became Forest and Skye. It gives the backstory of how they became who they are.

"You're beautifully broken... my summer sky, my light in the darkness."
~Bean

Trigger Warning

Trapped within an abusive foster home, Elsbeth and Forest find there is light in the darkest places. With hope is as limitless as the summer sky, all they need is the love of one another to survive.

Sexually abused and tortured, they cling to each another as their only constant in a roiling sea of agony. Through it all, Elsbeth holds on to a single ray of hope. At eighteen, both she and Forest will no longer be victims of the foster care system. But time is not on their side. Master John has come for a visit. Escape is no longer an option, not if they plan to survive. Faced with a future of degradation and abuse there is but one choice left...

This book is graphic with triggers; it's not for the faint of heart

What reviewers are saying...

"A TRAGIC, GUT-WRENCHING, HEARTBREAKING TALE OF SURVIVAL"~ **Cynthia**

"Stunned."~ Robin

"Ellie Masters blew me away with this book. Ellie takes us back to Skye's childhood. We learn of the abuse she suffered. We also learn just why she wanted to become a Doctor. I cried with these characters and rejoiced in their bravery. Even if one has never suffered abuse this story is one everyone should read. It will help you see why a person may have PTSD from abuse."~ Crystal

Get my Copy!

First Chapters: ASHES TO NEW

PREQUEL TO THE ANGEL FIRE ROCK ROMANCE
SERIES. THIS STORY IS NOT A ROMANCE. IT'S A TALE
OF SURVIVAL AND HAS ABUSE TRIGGERS.

THE HALLS OF CARL SANDBURG HIGH SCHOOL FILLED WITH
jubilant shouts, raucous cheers, and a generalized mayhem
celebrating the end of another year of school. Students emptied
lockers of books, folders, and laptops. Old spiral-bound notebooks,
filled trashcans lining the halls along with mounds of papers no one
cared about anymore. And while Elsbeth's classmates rushed to say
their goodbyes, she walked in a cocoon of silence, gripping the
contents of her locker tight to her chest and keeping her gaze set
three feet forward avoiding any and all eye contact with her peers.

But she couldn't avoid all attention.

Mr. Peterson leaned against the doorframe leading into his
chemistry lab. He was talking with Scott Masterson, a junior like
Elsbeth. Scott was wildly popular, a jock with a brain, straight A's,
and working toward a football scholarship and a ticket to his future.
She envied him the freedom to pursue his goals.

"You'd better behave this summer." Mr. Peterson's voice was stern
but caring. "We need our star player if we're going to make State
next year."

"Yes, sir," Scott said, combing his fingers through the mop of bangs covering his forehead. He noticed her then. "Hey Ellz," he called out. "Got plans for tonight? Marvel is playing and a bunch of us are going. You want to come?"

Scott had been trying to get her on a date for the better half of last semester. She'd always been too busy. Not a complete lie, but other things filled her evenings and weekends. It simply wasn't cheering, or band, being a member of the volleyball team, or dating.

With a shake of her head, she declined…again. "Sorry, but I've got plans, and my foster father isn't keen on the whole dating scene."

"Ah, it doesn't have to be a date, just a bunch of us kicking it around."

Hugging her books, she stamped down the wave of anxiety building in her chest. "I'm sorry. I'd love too, but…" But she simply couldn't.

The hopefulness of his expression fell. "Maybe another time?"

She gave a fractional nod. "Sounds good." Moving to the center of the crowded hall, she made a move to escape the awkward exchange, but Mr. Peterson stopped her in her tracks.

"Elsbeth." His words hit her in the chest and stopped the trudge of her feet.

"Yes, Mr. Peterson?" The softness of his gaze tunneled straight to her heart, destabilizing her shields.

"You weren't going to leave without saying goodbye to your favorite chemistry teacher, were you?" Mr. Peterson spread his arms out wide, welcoming her into his personal space.

Elsbeth curled her lower lip inward, biting hard. While she adored Mr. Peterson, and he was without a doubt her favorite teacher, to be that close to a man had her insides churning. But with his arms outstretched, she couldn't refuse, not without raising eyebrows, or worse.

"Be safe this summer." He folded her into the briefest, and most platonic, of hugs. "Do you have anything special planned? Did you enroll in that summer program at the University I mentioned?"

The observership? No. Definitely not on the allowed list of summer activities.

She loved how he encouraged her, and adored him even more for slipping the lists of colleges with undergraduate pre-med programs inside her lab notebook. He'd been the one who'd told her about the highly competitive, six-year medical school programs as well.

"Goodbye, Mr. Peterson," she said, and he finally released her. Perfect timing too, already her breathing accelerated.

A glance at the clock hanging over the doors leading outside counted down her fate. Less than an hour remained. She should stay and linger within the halls to memorize every detail. Those images would serve her well in the months to come, but staying meant risking unwanted conversation. And while she remained a frustrating mystery to her peers, she didn't care. A pretty girl who was too school for cool, Elsbeth's brain would determine her future, not her standing within the social hierarchy of a mid-rate high school. She brushed off the advances of boys, and kept those rare girls interested in befriending the geek-girl an arm's breath away. Friends were liabilities.

With a heavy sigh, she followed her fellow students out and into the embrace of summer. To them it represented freedom, but for Elsbeth the endless days would be nothing but a stretch of time to endure.

∼

HOME.

The word conjured many images. A home should be a place of light. A place of love. A place of sanctuary and hope. Home was where weary souls rested their heads as day deepened to night and slumber brought peaceful dreams. Home was a place to recharge and recuperate from the toils of a difficult day. Elsbeth's home was located at a crossroads where reason fled and insanity took root.

The Tudor monstrosity which the state foster care system assigned as her 'place of residence' dominated the middle of a three-lot spread at the end of a long cul-de-sac. The owner had purchased the lots to either side for the privilege of setting his home apart. Not that Clark Preston needed more space. It was the status which came with the message.

Despite everything the house embodied, Elsbeth looked forward to coming home if for only one reason. Her foster brother, Forest, bounced a soccer ball from knee to knee, his tall, lanky form a mess of spindly limbs too long for his growing frame. She called him her little beanpole for good reason, but this last year he'd started to sprout into the nickname. An odd bird, his quirky personality hid a brilliant mind. He wasn't the only one with too few friends.

He glanced up, his shock of blond hair glowing in the afternoon sun. Forest let the ball drop where he kicked it back and forth in a blinding array of footwork. "Hey Ellz." He stopped kicking. The ball rolled a few short feet away until it came to a stop against the azaleas. He turned his gaze upon her, an old soul looking out from behind the palest blue she'd ever seen. "Guess it's officially summertime."

With a deep breath, she clutched her school books against her chest. Yes, summer, but she had the classics to keep her company. Moby, Shakespeare, and Jane Austin would smooth out the dark times ahead.

"What are you doing outside?"

Forest was more of a computer geek than a jock. He was happiest with the glow of a retina display lighting his room and stimulating his mind. Her foster brother didn't play video games. He made them. Self taught in the language of code, Forest tinkered and created his escape, while she read herself into one.

Forest jerked a thumb toward the house. "He called the maids," he said with a grimace. "We're having company."

Her stomach turned in knots. "Tonight?"

"Yeah, told me to let the maids in, and then said to stay out of their way."

"Did he say *who* was coming?" Please don't let it be the fat, slobbery judge.

With a shake of his head, Forest retrieved the ball, and then drew her into a hug. He was tall enough for her to rest her head against his bony chest. When Forest had first entered her life five years ago, he'd been shorter than her, small and fragile. She leaned into his embrace, shaking.

He kissed the top of her head. "Ellz, we'll get through it. We always do."

A tear leaked from the corner of her eye. She brushed it away. "But, you know what he's like with company." She was supposed to be strong for Forest, but the mention of visitors on the first night of summer had her trembling.

Pressing his lips against her forehead, he tugged her in tight. "It's a moment in time, my sweet Ellz, but only a moment, and like everything else, it will pass."

Clark Preston was a demon she understood. She'd learned how to survive his trials and tests, but when he invited others to share in his appetites, her coping skills struggled to keep up. And while it would be easiest to lose herself within the insanity, she had Forest to protect, and one other. Still naive, he believed in the possibility of a brighter future. Forest would be eighteen soon, and she would follow a few months later. Freedom beckoned, but first there was senior year to endure. She worried what would happen when faced with the possibility of graduation and a man who would refuse to let them go.

An accident had stolen her parents and separated her from a baby brother. Forest had lost his family to something much worse, and yet somewhere within that tragedy, they had found each other. Forest's resilience astounded her, because he believed they would be delivered from the evil which filled their lives. Even when she'd held him on that very first night, when he'd been broken, battered, and left bleeding on the basement floor, Forest had believed. She hadn't had the heart to tell him the truth.

Neither of them were escaping this hell.

The front door opened and two cleaning ladies exited. The older one walked over, her black and white maid's uniform impressively immaculate after her labors. "We're all done," she said. "We couldn't get into the basement to clean. If your father wants us to clean down there next time, he'll need to remove the lock."

"Yes ma'am," Forest said with a gulp, his grip around her shoulders tightened. "I'll be sure to tell him."

The women secured their gear in the cleaning van and pulled out of the driveway, waving as they drove off.

With a sigh, Elsbeth walled off her mind from what her body would soon endure. "Come on, Beanpole." It was half-past four. Clark Preston would be home within the hour. "We have to prepare."

Please consider leaving a review

I hope you enjoyed this book as much as I enjoyed writing it. If you enjoyed reading this story, please consider leaving a review on Amazon and Goodreads, and please let other people know. A sentence is all it takes, but a book lives or dies based upon its reviews. Thank you in advance!

Goodreads: https://elliemasters.com/HeartsInsanityGR
Amazon: https://elliemasters.com/HeartsInsanity

ELLZ BELLZ

ELLIE'S FACEBOOK READER GROUP

If you are interested in joining the ELLZ BELLZ, Ellie's Facebook reader group, we'd love to have you.

Join Ellie's ELLZ BELLZ.
The ELLZ BELLZ Facebook Reader Group

Sign up for Ellie's Newsletter.
Elliemasters.com/newslettersignup

Also by Ellie Masters

The LIGHTER SIDE

Ellie Masters is the lighter side of the Jet & Ellie Masters writing duo! You will find Contemporary Romance, Military Romance, Romantic Suspense, Billionaire Romance, and Rock Star Romance in Ellie's Works.

YOU CAN FIND ELLIE'S BOOKS HERE:

ELLIEMASTERS.COM/BOOKS

Military Romance

Guardian Hostage Rescue Specialists

Rescuing Melissa

(Get a FREE copy of Rescuing Melissa

when you join Ellie's Newsletter)

Alpha Team

Rescuing Zoe

Rescuing Moira

Rescuing Eve

Rescuing Lily

Rescuing Jinx

Rescuing Maria

Bravo Team

Rescuing Angie

Rescuing Isabelle

Rescuing Carmen

Rescuing Rosalie

Rescuing Kaye

Cara's Protector

Rescuing Barbi

Military Romance

Guardian Personal Protection Specialists

Sybil's Protector

Lyra's Protector

The One I Want Series

(Small Town, Military Heroes)

By Jet & Ellie Masters

EACH BOOK IN THIS SERIES CAN BE READ AS A STANDALONE AND IS ABOUT A DIFFERENT COUPLE WITH AN HEA.

Saving Abby

Saving Ariel

Saving Brie

Saving Cate

Saving Dani

Saving Jen

Rockstar Romance

The Angel Fire Rock Romance Series

EACH BOOK IN THIS SERIES CAN BE READ AS A STANDALONE AND IS ABOUT A DIFFERENT COUPLE WITH AN HEA. IT IS RECOMMENDED THEY ARE READ IN ORDER.

Ashes to New (prequel)

Heart's Insanity (book 1)

Heart's Desire (book 2)

Heart's Collide (book 3)

Hearts Divided (book 4)

Hearts Entwined (book5)

Forest's FALL (book 6)

Hearts The Last Beat (book7)

Contemporary Romance

Firestorm

(Kristy Bromberg's Everyday Heroes World)

Billionaire Romance

Billionaire Boys Club

Hawke

Richard

Brody

Contemporary Romance

Cocky Captain

(Vi Keeland & Penelope Ward's Cocky Hero World)

Romantic Suspense

each book is a standalone novel.

The Starling

~AND~

Science Fiction

Ellie Masters writing as L.A. Warren

Vendel Rising: a Science Fiction Serialized Novel

Books by Jet Masters

If you enjoyed this book by Ellie Masters, the LIGHTER SIDE of the Jet & Ellie writing duo, and aren't afraid of edgier writing, you might enjoy reading BDSM themed books written by Jet, the DARKER SIDE of the Masters' Writing Team.

The DARKER SIDE
Jet Masters is the darker side of the Jet & Ellie writing duo!

Romantic Suspense
Changing Roles Series:
THIS SERIES MUST BE READ IN ORDER.
Book 1: Command Me
Book 2: Control Me
Book 3: Collar Me
Book 4: Embracing FATE
Book 5: Seizing FATE
Book 6: Accepting FATE

HOT READS
A STANDALONE NOVEL.

Down the Rabbit Hole

Light BDSM Romance
The Ties that Bind

EACH BOOK IN THIS SERIES CAN BE READ AS A STANDALONE AND IS ABOUT A DIFFERENT COUPLE WITH AN HEA.

Alexa

Penny

Michelle

Ivy

HOT READS
Becoming His Series

THIS SERIES MUST BE READ IN ORDER.

Book 1: The Ballet

Book 2: Learning to Breathe

Book 3: Becoming His

Dark Captive Romance

A STANDALONE NOVEL.

She's MINE

About the Author

Ellie Masters is a USA Today Bestselling author and Amazon Top 15 Author who writes Angsty, Steamy, Heart-Stopping, Pulse-Pounding, Can't-Stop-Reading Romantic Suspense. In addition, she's a wife, military mom, doctor, and retired Colonel. She writes romantic suspense filled with all your sexy, swoon-worthy alpha men. Her writing will tug at your heartstrings and leave your heart racing.

Born in the South, raised under the Hawaiian sun, Ellie has traveled the globe while in service to her country. The love of her life, her amazing husband, is her number one fan and biggest supporter. And yes! He's read every word she's written.

She has lived all over the United States—east, west, north, south and central—but grew up under the Hawaiian sun. She's also been privileged to have lived overseas, experiencing other cultures and making lifelong friends. Now, Ellie is proud to call herself a Southern transplant, learning to say y'all and "bless her heart" with the best of them. She lives with her beloved husband, two children who refuse to flee the nest, and four fur-babies; three cats who rule the household, and a dog who wants nothing other than for the cats to be his best friends. The cats have a different opinion regarding this matter.

Ellie's favorite way to spend an evening is curled up on a couch, laptop in place, watching a fire, drinking a good wine, and bringing forth all the characters from her mind to the page and hopefully into the hearts of her readers.

Connect with Ellie Masters

Website:
elliemasters.com
Amazon Author Page:
elliemasters.com/amazon
Facebook:
elliemasters.com/Facebook
Goodreads:
elliemasters.com/Goodreads
Instagram:
elliemasters.com/Instagram

Final Thoughts

I hope you enjoyed this book as much as I enjoyed writing it. If you enjoyed reading this story, please consider leaving a review on Amazon and Goodreads, and please let other people know. A sentence is all it takes. Friend recommendations are the strongest catalyst for readers' purchase decisions! And I'd love to be able to continue bringing the characters and stories from My-Mind-to-the-Page.

Second, call or e-mail a friend and tell them about this book. If you really want them to read it, gift it to them. If you prefer digital friends, please use the "Recommend" feature of Goodreads to spread the word.

Or visit my blog https://elliemasters.com, where you can find out more about my writing process and personal life.

Come visit The EDGE: Dark Discussions where we'll have a chance to talk about my works, their creation, and maybe what the future has in store for my writing.

Facebook Reader Group: Ellz Bellz

Thank you so much for your support!

Love,

Ellie

Dedication

This book is dedicated to you, my reader. Thank you for spending a few hours of your time with me. I wouldn't be able to write without you to cheer me on. Your wonderful words, your support, and your willingness to join me on this journey is a gift beyond measure.

Whether this is the first book of mine you've read, or if you've been with me since the very beginning, thank you for believing in me as I bring these characters 'from my mind to the page and into your hearts.'

Love,

Ellie

THE END

Made in the USA
Monee, IL
03 July 2024

61161578R00213